the
FLIPSIDE
of
PERFECT

Books by Liz Reinhardt available from Inkyard Press

Rebels Like Us
The Flipside of Perfect

the FLIPSIDE of PERFECT

Liz Reinhardt

11/21

Recycling programs
for this product may
not exist in your area.

ISBN-13: 978-1-335-47044-7

The Flipside of Perfect

This edition published by arrangement with Harlequin Books S.A.

For questions and comments about the quality of this book, please contact us at
CustomerService@Harlequin.com.

Inkyard Press
22 Adelaide St. West, 40th Floor
Toronto, Ontario M5H 4E3, Canada
www.InkyardPress.com

Printed in U.S.A.

"Be nice to your siblings. They're your best link to your past and the people most likely to stick with you in the future."
—Mary Schmich, *Chicago Tribune*

To my amazing siblings:
Katie, Zachary, Jack, Megan, Jessica, Jillian, Jamie.

It's a fantastic honor to be your big sister,
even when you're annoying. Love you guys.

1

Freshman Year

*Last Day in Florida Keys/First Day back in Michigan after
Summer*
Two Weeks before the First Day of School

FLORIDA

When I was a little kid, I always thought I was double lucky
for having two of everything—two families to love, two
houses to grow up in, two sets of siblings, two times the gifts
and attention and laughs. But this summer—the summer I
was fourteen—I start to see the flaws in that logic.

"Della! You really smell-a! I just have to tell ya! 'Cause I'm
a nice *fella*!"

My brother, Duke, stands in my doorway, drumming the
wall next to my bed with his palms, singing the ridiculous
song he just made up to get me out of bed.

Any other summer morning, I would have launched assorted stuffed animals and pillows at his head and laugh-
screamed for our sister Dani—Duke's twin, older than him
by seven minutes—to save me, and she would have flown
down the hallway to my rescue. But this summer has been
so different.

After weeks of trying to talk to Dani, make her laugh,

or help her forget her sadness, I learn a very hard lesson: the worst thing you can go through is watching someone you love suffer without being able to do anything to help them.

"C'mon, bugbite. Pancake time!" Duke scoops me out of bed and throws me over his shoulder. Or tries, anyway. "Oof. You're, like, twelve feet tall all of a sudden, Jolly Green Giant."

Having to walk down the hall to our sunny kitchen instead of being bounced on Duke's shoulder definitely takes some of the fun out of our morning rumbles.

As we head toward the smell of breakfast pancakes sizzling on the frying pan, I ask Duke the same question I've already asked a million times this summer.

"Is Dani okay?"

Duke pushes his thick hair off his forehead and blows out a long breath. "You know how tight she and Nan Sunny were. We're all really sad. Like…this has been the hardest year of my life, and I miss my grandma every day. But I think it's the worst for Dani."

When Nan Sunny had a heart attack and died suddenly this past winter, Dad called Michigan to let me know, but part of me hadn't totally believed it was true. I still come around corners and expect to see her all over our cozy cottage. I'll find little things—her tortoiseshell hair combs in the bathroom cabinet, her thin-framed embroidery glasses on the TV stand, her tulip-patterned shower cap tucked into a pile of towels in the laundry room—and I'll immediately feel sucker punched.

"I miss her so much, too." I let Duke pull me into a bear hug.

My brother always smells like freshly turned dirt—probably because he's always digging around in it. With Dani locked away in her room so much this summer, Duke and I have been going "treasure hunting"—he'll lug his metal detector to a random patch of yard or beach, swing it around in slow arcs, get a ping, and then we'll take bets on whether it's going to be total garbage or the find of a lifetime.

It's almost always garbage, but that's okay. I miss hanging out with Dani, but I love spending time with my big brother, even if we're mostly just digging holes.

"You know she would have told you, you need to eat." I point to his chair and do my best impression. *"Eat, eat! You're too skinny! Look at your bones! Eat!"* Nan Sunny lived in Italy until she was fifteen, and she still had this great accent, especially when she was talking about her two passions—food and family.

Dad laughs. "Feels like she's standing in the kitchen with me. Mornin,' sunshine. I'm sure gonna miss seeing this little face every day." Dad squeezes my cheeks, making my lips puff out, and kisses my forehead. "You all packed up? Ready to get back to it?"

"Mmm-hmm," I murmur. I don't want to admit that I'm packed, but I'm not remotely ready to go back. Usually by the time summer ends, I'm eager to see my sisters and Mom and my stepdad again. And I've always been so excited for the first day of school, because I am—as Duke so charmingly describes me—"a bona fide Grade A nerd." But this fall is the first fall since preschool that I won't be going to Trinity Lutheran, the K–8 private school Marnie, Lilli, and I have all attended since we graduated from Good Shepherd Pre-K.

I'll be a high-school freshman at St. Matthew's. It's weird to think Marnie and Lilli will put on their green-and-yellow-plaid jumpers, and I'll wear a navy-and-white kilt; Mom will drive them to the school of our childhood, and Peter will drop me off at my brand-new high school, alone.

My stomach rolls over every time I think about it.

"Are *you* excited to go back to school?" I ask Duke as Dad loads a heaping pile of banana and chocolate chip pancakes with whipped cream on my plate. Nan Sunny would have made the whipped cream in her mixer, but we just use the canned stuff now.

"Not even a little bit. Dad, hit me!" Duke holds up his plate, and Dad's smile is full of mischief. My brother and my father don't always see eye to eye, but they can both be super goofy. Dad settles a pancake on the spatula, tests its weight, and slings it. Duke catches it half on his plate, half with his hand, and whoops before sitting down at the table with me. He shakes the whipped cream container and tilts his head back, filling his mouth with the fluffy stuff.

"Aren't you, like, even a little bit excited for senior year?" I prod. "You're, like, *such* a good student."

"Meh." Duke shrugs. "I make good grades. That's not really the same thing as being a good student. Most of the time I'm pretty bored at school, but this year the local community college is doing a program with the seniors, and I got in at the last second. So, maybe this year will be cool?" He stuffs a huge bite of pancake in his mouth and seems to swallow without chewing. "I'm not betting on it, though."

"I think you're finally going to find your place in college." Dad plunks down next to me, his calloused hand cupping a mug of steaming coffee, and eyes Dani's door nervously. "A smart guy like you needs to be challenged, and Coral High was never gonna do that."

Duke gives Dad a curious look, but a creak from Dani's door focuses our attention in her direction. She comes out in a loose maxi dress, hair fixed, makeup on, and we don't even try to hide our excitement.

"Hey! Good morning! Come eat!" we all cheer in a chorus of voices.

"Good morning, everyone," Dani says softly. Her smile is the best thing I've seen in days.

"Can I get you some coffee?" Dad jumps up and heads to the pot.

"Ye—um, no. No thank you. Just milk, I think."

"Sure. Milk it is," Dad says. "And pancakes?"

"Okay. They look great." Dani is saying all the right words, but her voice sounds flat and dull. We all pretend not to notice.

"Can *I* have coffee?" I ask. Dad closes the milk carton and squints at me.

"I dunno, sweetie. I don't want to stunt your growth."

"Dad, she's, like, a sasquatch already. Let her have a cup of joe." Duke ruffles my hair and winks at me.

"How would you like it fixed?" Dad grins when I hesitate. "Tell you what, I'm going to make it light and sweet for now. You let me know if you want it different next time."

"Sounds good." When Dad puts the coffee in front of me, my hands shake, I'm so excited.

The first bitter sip is kind of a letdown.

Dani reaches out and gives me a soft shoulder squeeze. "It's an acquired taste, Dell. You'll learn to like it."

"Or you'll always hate it," Duke cuts in. "Like I do."

"You must be excited to see Marnie and Lilli and your mom and Peter today," Dani says as Dad puts her pancake in front of her.

"I do miss them." I clear my throat and drop my voice to a whisper. "But I'm scared to start high school. Now that I'm headed back to Michigan, it finally feels, like, *real*."

"Oh, Dell!" Dani scoots her chair closer and hugs me. I hug her back, tight enough to make up for all our lost hugs this long, dreary summer. "I wish I could be there on your first day! Don't worry. I know you're going to do amazing." She fingers the silver bracelet with the dangling heart clasped around my wrist. It was a graduation gift from her, Duke, and Dad.

Dad had it sent to my school on graduation day, so I got to open it—along with a bouquet of sunflowers and a teddy bear wearing a graduation cap—in front of all my classmates. Getting those gifts should have made me so happy, but all I wanted was my family there with me—my *whole* family. I'd felt pangs of the same loneliness on birthdays and holidays, but I'd always had Lilli and Marnie there to distract me from how much I was missing the other half of my family. I graduated from middle school, and half the people I loved most in the world weren't there to see me walk across the stage. That sucked.

"I haven't had a first day of school without Lilli and Marnie since I was just a little kid," I tell Dani. "I know it's weird, but it's almost like, because I have to act brave when they're around, I kind of convince myself to be brave by default."

I'm horrified to realize my words make my beautiful sister cry again.

"Not weird at all! That's just you being an awesome sister." She hugs me tight again, her shoulders shaking. "I'll be thinking about you on your first day, okay? I know we can't really call or text while you're at school, but I'm going to go to chapel before classes and light a votive for you, just like Nan Sunny used to do for all of us on the first day, for good luck."

I bury my face in Dani's shoulder, and I cry a little with her because it's so unfair and sad that Dani's had to be mom and grandma and sister to me this summer. I promise myself that this is going to be the year I start to act a little more grown-up, start to be a little braver. By next summer, maybe Dani won't feel like she always has to worry and take care of me—maybe she and I can just be sisters...and friends.

We get ready to head to the airport, and for the first time, everything feels unsettled and gross. I've been dividing my time between two places I love for all these years with only small dips of sadness, but now I'm drowning in regret. Instead of feeling double lucky—two houses, two families, more love and happiness for me—I feel torn in two.

When we get to the airport, Dad engulfs me in a long hug. "I'll sure miss you. Ask your mama to call me when you land."

Duke's hug comes with a noogie at the end. "Keep drinking coffee, bugbite. I don't need my baby sister towering over me before she's in tenth grade."

Dani smooths down my hair. "I know this summer was a bummer. You just wait until next summer. I *promise*, it will be the best summer of your life. Knock 'em dead, Dell."

Saying good-bye to my family in Florida reduces me to a

sobbing puddle, and despite the flight attendants' kindness and extra cookies, I'm wrung out and exhausted when I finally touch down in Michigan.

MICHIGAN

Mom hugs me, long and tight, as soon as I'm off the plane. "Why are your eyes so red?" she asks. "Did you use the rosewater spritz I packed for you? Sweetie, you *know* how dry the cabin of a plane can be. Let's get you home so we can try on your uniforms."

Peter gives me a warm hug, gathers my bags, and leads us all to the car. Marnie and Lilli link their arms through mine, and we amble through the parking lot like a tiny, awkward flock of long-legged birds.

"—and so we totally thought, because I'm so tall, I should play *basketball*, but it winds up I'm really not that good." Marnie has been rambling nonstop since I stepped off the plane, and she keeps tugging down, hard, on my arm, making my shoulder sore. I almost snap at her because I'm so stressed from this morning, but I stop myself and remember that she's just excited. I wish I could share that excitement, but the only thing I feel is exhaustion. "But they had *volleyball* games, and, like, I'm really good. I mean, *really* good. Do you want to play when we get home? *AJ?* Do you want to play? Dad got me a net and everything."

"I'm so glad you found out you're good at volleyball," I say dully, my brain clouded. "I'm not feeling up to playing anything today, though. Maybe tomorrow?"

Lilli isn't talking my ear off, but she *is* singing both parts of the call-and-repeat camp song "Little Red Wagon," which is so grating, even her angelic voice can't make it tolerable.

Mom and Peter herd us into the car, and we head home, Marnie still talking a mile a minute, and Lilli still singing about the little red wagon's broken front seat and dragging axle as I gaze out the window. It's so weird how this morning I watched the sandy beaches of Key West fly by, and now I'm looking at the emerald green fields of summertime Michigan.

Which makes me think about how I've never seen a winter in the Keys. I've never celebrated a Fourth of July in Michigan. Dani and Duke have never gone ice-skating in the little birch wood behind my grandparents' lake house. Marnie and Lilli have never eaten crabs, fresh out of the trap, after a long day on the boat.

The more I think about it, the more I feel like my sadness is radioactive, like it's burning through me and poisoning everything.

When we pull into the driveway, I announce that I have to use the bathroom and race upstairs, where I head to my bedroom instead and shut the door quietly, so no one will come looking for me right away. My mom has redecorated my room while I was gone—it's all done in soft blues and yellows, very elegant and way more grown-up than my lilac room was, but it doesn't feel like *my* room. Tears course down my face as I try to figure out why I suddenly hate everything about the life I used to feel so lucky to have.

A soft knock on the door has me wiping away my tears. "Come in!"

Mom pads into my room and gives me a small smile. "AJ? What's wrong, sweetie?" She sits on the bed and puts her arm around me while I hiccup and cry through a ragged explanation of all the ways this summer sucked.

"Shh," she soothes, pushing my sticky hair off my face. "I'm not going to sugarcoat it for you. It's tough. Losing Nan Sunny must hurt so much. And being fourteen is awful. Having to split the year up like this is hard.

"Listen, I know it feels like it's always going to be this stressful, but it *will* get better. I promise." She kisses my forehead and pulls a tissue out of the box on my bedside table. "Now stop crying. Here, blow your nose and wipe your face."

I do as I'm told, and my mother goes to my closet and pulls out my uniforms. "Can I try them on later?" I ask pitifully.

"Sorry, sweetie. We have to get them altered, and we're already behind the eight ball." She gestures for me to stand, and I take the uniforms and go behind my dressing screen, which Mom had reupholstered with delicate birds and flowering vines. When I come from behind the screen, she has her sewing kit laid out on the bed and starts to pin the uniform. "You know, Duke and Dani are graduating high school next summer. They'll probably start spending more time on their own when they get jobs and go off to college. It's okay if you decide you don't want to go to Florida for the whole summer." Mom keeps her voice as smooth as the silver pins sliding into the creased fabric.

"I *want* to go," I rush to say. "I know I'm a little down, but it's probably just, like, from the flight and everything."

"You'll be in high school this year, too. You may want to do something more constructive with your summers. Look how excited Marnie was about camp this year. She found a whole new sport she loves. I know you enjoy seeing your dad and the twins, but…just think about it." She turns me by the hip and finishes pinning my sleeves. "You're growing up. Things change when you grow up, and it hurts. It sucks, but it's true."

I turn to look at Mom, and a pin stabs the sensitive skin under my arm. I bite back against the pain. "You're probably right, Mom," I say, knowing that if I keep arguing, she'll dig in and try harder to convince me that her way is the best way—my mother can't help it. When she thinks she has the answer to your problems, she doesn't stop until she gets you to agree with her.

"Trust me, sweetie, I understand this isn't easy. But you know you can always come to me if you need help. Your dad and I will do anything to make sure you girls are happy and successful." She turns me around, backs up to look me over one more time, and nods. "You're perfect."

"Thank you, Mom."

I realize that, if I want to keep going to Florida, I'll have to give up on trying to figure out how to fit my two lives together. It isn't going to work, and I'll just wind up giving Mom more ammunition for her *constructive summers* argument. I have to pull back and let her focus on other things. When I'm in Michigan, I'll be AJ, big sister, good student, obedient daughter, all-around overachiever. When I'm in Florida, I'll be Della, baby of the family, funny and fun, a jokester, and general happy-go-lucky sweetheart.

I don't love this compromise, but it is what it is. I'll keep my life divided and learn to deal with the fact that my heart is going to feel permanently torn in two—which is a better option than being forced to choose just one life and letting the other fade away.

★ ★ ★

The summer I turned fourteen, I learned that I've never had doubles of anything—I've had halves. If I'm not careful, I risk losing even more.

And so I begin to purposefully bisect my life, keeping each beloved part separate and protected. As the years go by and the lines between my two lives grow more rigid, I realize there isn't a single person in my life who knows both AJ and Della.

Maybe not even *me*.

2

Oldest Sister

Three Years Later
Last Day of St. Matthew's, Junior Year
Pool Party at Lex's House

MICHIGAN

Harper Johannsen's Last 4 Phone Code: 2269

2-Number of doting/smothering parents in the USA

2-Number of unknown parents in China

6-How old we were when we became BFFs

9-The grade we were in when we met our third BFF (Tessa Whitman)

Tessa Whitman's Last 4 Phone Code: 1574

1-Tessa's one brother, Logan, is a freaking hottie, but Harper and I admire him from afar because she'd be furious if we ever admitted we crush on him in secret

5-The number of states Tessa's lived in: Connecticut, Georgia, California, New York, and Michigan

7-Her birthday month

4-The number of people in her perfect family

Lex Henson's Last 4 Phone Code: 8686

8-Birth month—Lex pretends astrology is horseshit, but he's super into the fact that he's a Leo and reads his horoscope every day

6-The grade we were in when he held my hand on the bus ride to
the University of Michigan Museum

8-The grade we were in when he kissed me on the last day of school,
behind the lockers in the eighth-grade hall

6-The number of letters in his middle name—Melker—which he
hates with a passion and keeps a secret from everyone

When my phone rings, no cute emojis or pictures pop up to
instantly identify the caller. Just ten good old-fashioned digits marching in a neat row.

I love the anonymous secrecy of my system. I like assign-
ing details to these numbers, making them fit random scraps
of information about the people I love, and it makes my brain
buzz when my phone rings—it's a little puzzle to figure out
who's on the other end. It's wild how many of my shared contacts wouldn't recognize each other's numbers by digits alone.

"Who's texting?" Marnie stretches the seat belt until it
jerks her back to the seat, trying to look at my phone on the
center console.

I'm at a red, which is the only reason I glance over. I don't
play with texting and driving after a junior girl from St. Matt's
and her younger cousin died in a crash last summer—they
found her phone with the *LO* of the *LOL* she was typing still
pending in her messages.

"Harper and Tessa." I flip the phone over and focus on the
road instead of Marnie's pleading expression. "Rising Seniors
only, Marnie. You know that."

Lilli sits forward in her seat and taps Marnie's shoulder. "My
youth group is going to Boyne Mountain for the weekend.
Come with us, Marnie."

"Ugh, that's, like, *four hours* away." Marnie's whine has the exact pitch of a mosquito's scream. "And I get carsick anytime I'm in that creepy church molester van."

"It's not a molester van." Lilli chuckles when she says it. Unlike me, Lilli finds Marnie's mood swings and petulant pity parties endearing. Maybe because Lilli was born with superhuman levels of patience. "And that's not even that long. We're doing Vanpool Karaoke. C'mon, we always need an alto, and Langley Mendoza *is not an alto*."

Marnie and I glance at each other, then back at Lilli, whose face is dark for a few long beats.

Marnie shudders. "I'm scared to sing with you. You're too intense about music."

Lilli's face clears like the clouds after a flash summer storm, and she pastes on the angelic smile she's been practicing since her early child-performer rehearsal days. Is her smile real or just super convincing? Hard to tell.

"I'm just *joking*," she insists. "Anyway, you have nothing to worry about because you have the most beautiful contralto in the world, and, honestly, I'm kind of jealous, Marnie. This would be the perfect time for us to do the duet I've been begging you to do, like, *forever*. C'mon, we're barely going to see each other. I have to go to Nashville in, like, nine days, and AJ's leaving even sooner." Lilli looks at me from under her perfectly curled lashes. "AJ, maybe you could catch a later plane? Just this one time?" Lilli pleads.

I shake my head and give her a bland "No." I've mastered Vanessa Jepsen's *No, and don't ask again* tone, and when she hears it, Lilli clamps her mouth shut and moves on to wheedle Marnie.

"You'll be gone longer than any of us, Marnie. I know volleyball is, like, really important to you, but you play so much during the year." When Marnie and I both look back at her in surprise for a second time in ten minutes, she shrugs again. "I know, it's super normal for us to be so busy. And I get I'm sometimes the busi*est*, but I guess I wish we could do something together during the summer sometime."

Lilli presents her request so wistfully, it tugs at my heartstrings in a way that Marnie's demanding whines never do. Of course I feel pressure to let my sisters come to the pool party, but this moment between us won't last if I pull up at Lex's house with them. The rules for the Rising Seniors Pool Party are pretty much etched in stone, and following the tradition is kind of the whole point. My kid sisters won't be welcome *on premise*. This is a ritual specifically reserved for Rising Seniors—I remember spying on Tessa's brother's party and being so jealous (also Harper and I enjoyed drooling over his abs while we fumed, even if we never told Tessa *that* part), but the longing has always been part of the deal— you don't get the payoff without the anticipation.

"I promise we'll do something before I leave." I have no clue *when* we'll be able to squeeze anything in, but I'm going to try to figure it out, make it right, the way I always do. "But this is a rite of passage. You can't just barge in."

"I know." Lilli nods her agreement without hesitation, then turns to Marnie. "That's why I think Marnie should come to Boyne Mountain. At least she and I could get some time together. Two sisters are better than nothing, right?"

"Maybe AJ should ditch her stupid friends and this stupid tradition and come with us," Marnie challenges. She narrows her eyes at me. "Do you even really *want* to go, or are you just doing it because everyone expects you to?"

Do I want to go?

I love my friends and Lex, but hanging out with them—especially together—is draining. On the other hand, I'm about to leave for an entire summer in Florida with my other family—the one my friends don't even know exists—so I'm pretty sure I can make it through this one night with my besties and boyfriend.

I *love* my little sisters, but—

"I think it's stupid. Like, okay, so you're doing it because it's tradition, but *why*? Can you even explain why?" Marnie's bottom lip is bulging out, and while that gimmick might work on Peter, I'm immune...and annoyed.

"This isn't a debate, Marnie. And it's not like you'd win, if it even *was* one, with that weak argument. You know what? I don't need a reason." I pull into our circular drive and park. "Out," I order.

Lilli hops out and comes to the driver's side window. "I love you, AJ! Have a good time." She pecks my cheek and whispers, "Also, can I borrow your new tortoiseshell Ray-Bans, *please*? They're so *classic*."

"Yes, punk." I ruffle her hair. "Don't lose them. Have fun. Drink a virgin daiquiri for me on the lazy river, all right?"

She throws up a peace sign, makes a kissy face, and runs in the house with a shrill "Thank you!" thrown over her shoulder, blond ponytail sparkling like a sunbeam.

Marnie simpers in the passenger seat, arms crossed. Marnie and Lilli are what our grandmother calls *Irish twins*, which means they were born less than a year apart. Peter always jokes that finding out Mom was pregnant with Lilli when Marnie was only three months old played a direct role in his hasty vasectomy later that same month. Whenever Marnie acts like a brat or pouts, Mom chalks it up to all the time she wasn't able to be the baby long enough before Lilli was born. You'd think fifteen years would be ample time to grow the hell up.

"Can I come? *Please.*" She bites out the polite part of her request like an afterthought, and that makes me bristle again.

"Look, Marnie, I know things have been weird with Jaylen and everyone else—"

"She didn't even want to talk to me at the Spring Fling. Like, she actually turned around and walked the other way when I asked her if she wanted to borrow my ChapStick, like I'm some kind of *disease* she's going to catch. I felt like such an idiot. And she only came to our house so she could leech off your popularity like a…social vampire. Basically it was the same thing she did at Winter Formal. It's so gross, like, how she's just *using* me, and I have no choice but to shut up and take it." She curls her lip, but her anger deflates a second later and fat tears roll down her cheeks. "I have, like, *no one*, AJ. I'm worse off than Hester Prynn. At least she had her baby to hang out with."

"Marnie, I get it, and it sucks. I *know* it sucks. But this pool party isn't going to be fun for you if you come. Everyone will just be annoyed you're there, no offense. Underclassmen aren't allowed, and if I bend the rules for you, it will just irritate everyone." I clutch the steering wheel, trying to balance giving my sister comfort and booting her out before I have to deal with another emotional meltdown from her. "Plus, you *do* have me. You have Lilli. If you don't want to go with her—

which I really think you should, honestly—Dad is home this weekend. He'd be down for a *Mario Kart* marathon with you. You know that. School's over. Jepsen House Rule 3 isn't in effect anymore."

"Mom will probably say my summer reading *is* homework and make me do it before I play." Marnie sighs and wipes the tears away with her knuckles as she draws in a shuddery breath. "Lilli's youth group is *full* of the most annoying people on Earth, AJ. Don't look at me like that. You hate them all, too."

"I do *not* hate them." I pause. "I mean, okay, they're a little…obnoxious," I admit. Now that I think about it, I'd rather take another grueling hot-yoga class with Mom than listen to those little Broadway hopefuls (more like doubtfuls) tune up dramatically and harmonize along to never-ending clean versions of pop songs. "So stay home with Dad."

"No way. I heard Mom say they're renting some old movies—like that one where Maya Hawke's dad and Joyce Byers are kind of dating, and he's *so* whiny, but she's also kind of dating Zoolander, but he's really preppy. Plus they're making that weird seafood stew that takes all day to cook and stinks up the whole house."

"Ah, it's the paella and *Reality Bites* date weekend." I absentmindedly flip to my mother's blog on my phone and see the links to some Lisa Loeb song and a picture of our gleaming countertop laid out with jumbo shrimp and chorizo and saffron and all the other trappings of paella with blinking animated hearts on the picture. It always weirds me out a little to see the stat counters—like it's bizarre to know that 12,386 people and counting have had an inside look at everything from our bathroom renovation to my and my sisters' school dances, but I know that Mom's blogs have helped other moms who aren't as confident about the whole motherhood thing. Sometimes she'll show us emails and DMs she gets from moms on the brink, thanking her for being open and sharing, and I get why her honesty is important…even if it sometimes feels incredibly invasive.

"Look, hang alone for a while, and I'll swing by and bring you to Harper's to sleep over, okay?" I suggest in compromise.

Harper and Tessa will *not* be happy, but oh well. I can't please everyone.

"I don't want Harper to tell me how big my pores are and try to make me do some stupid mud mask." Marnie shakes her head. "And Tessa never laughs at my jokes. Does she laugh at *anyone's* jokes?"

"Tessa's just kind of intense." Tessa is smart and witty and has a biting sense of sarcasm, but her threshold for silliness is incredibly low. "I don't know what to tell you, Marnie. That's my best offer. Take it or leave it."

"If you let me come now, I won't eavesdrop or annoy you guys or anything." Marnie claps her palms together in front of her body, prayer-style. "I just really, really want to *swim*. You won't even see me or hear from me. Only maybe if I cannonball, that's it." She raises her blond eyebrows and widens her eyes hopefully. I hate shooting her down, but I also imagine lounging in the pool, sipping on an ice-cold pop… then getting splashed by Marnie's relentless cannonballing.

Hard. No.

"Sorry. Text me if you change your mind about tonight." I steel my resolve and just keep telling her to get out, gently, then more firmly, until I basically push her out of the car and drive off while she's still sitting on our driveway's paving stones, head buried in her crossed arms. I don't check my rearview.

Yes, I feel terrible and shitty.

Yes, I feel relieved and free.

Yes, the war between those feelings burns like acid in my gut as I'm changing into my yellow gingham ruffle bandeau-top bikini in one of Lex's five guest bathrooms. The suit isn't really my style, but Mom was the deciding vote when Tessa and Harper were trying to help me pick one for today's party, and it *is* super cute. The yellow brings out the glow of my early summer tan and the golden highlights in my dark hair, and the color is also a nice contrast for my blue eyes. So it technically works, even if it isn't my favorite. It's just not super *me*. I think about the neon-orange flower-print string bikini tucked in my dresser at Dad's in Florida. It's my favorite bathing suit ever, the one my big sister, Dani, is always asking to borrow, but I can clearly envision the triple faces of horror Mom, Tessa, and Harper would wear if I tried it on for them.

Tessa looks sexy in her olive crochet-overlay suit, and Harper looks sweet in her high-waisted navy-and-white-striped bikini.

"Oh my God, I wish I could pull off a bandeau," Tessa whines, cupping her generous breasts. "You look so freaking cute. I'd be scared of the girls making a surprise appearance."

"I look like I'm in middle school, and you two look like you're about to crush your college study abroad in Mykonos." I reach for Harper's enormous old-glam movie-star sunglasses and slip them on my face with a sigh. "If you didn't have such crap eyesight, I'd totally try to steal these. Your prescription makes my head spin."

Harper cackles, and Tessa motions for her to scoot closer to me so she can snap a picture of us together with the camera her brother, Logan, bought her for her birthday. She placed third in our school district's photography competition, and her brother was crazy proud. He saved all his summer life-guarding money to get her a top-of-the-line camera.

"You guys can't really *understand* what it's like to have a big brother," she humble-bragged when she got the camera. "I mean, Logan's so annoying sometimes, and he acts like he's twenty years older than I am instead of two, but I know he always has my back. The bond we have is just *different* than the bond between sisters."

I rolled my eyes and muttered, "You don't even *have* sisters, so how would you know?" and had to bite my tongue when she said, "And *you* don't have a brother, so maybe let's just drop it?"

Duke would have been *highly* offended if he knew his years of big-brother teasing, supporting, and taking care of me were going unrecognized. But I couldn't tell Tessa that I have excellent sportsmanship because Duke watched, unmoved, while I cried and screamed any time I lost at Monopoly. He never turned me down if I asked him to play a game, but he refused to let me win. I couldn't explain that Duke taught me the best way to use a metal detector to find treasure—or *a lot* of bobby pins—at the beach, which led to my first newspaper feature when I found the mayor's wife's lost heirloom wedding band buried in the sand under the pier. I still have the cutout of the article, complete with a picture of the two of us, me with a gap-toothed smile, Duke lanky, hair shaggy and sun-streaked. My eyes look to the side, where Duke stands, arm around my shoulders, grinning down at me with total pride.

I wish I could tell Tessa and Harper about Duke and Dani and my dad, but it's too complicated at this point. I'd never be able to do justice to my family and our incredible life in Florida, and I don't want to attempt to talk about them and wind up leaving Harper and Tessa with the wrong impression.

I get totally *gleeful* when Tessa pulls her superior shit with people we mutually hate; when she directs it at me, it fries my patience. Especially when I want to throw in her face just how incredibly wrong she is.

"No duck faces. Candid," she commands, and I check my instinct to explain what *candid* means before I fake-laugh at a joke Harper fake-makes.

"I'm going to record for a second." Tessa tucks the camera aside and takes out her phone. Her face knots into a serious artist's scowl, which seems a little much for someone trying to manipulate angles on an iPhone to get the best Boomerang, but whatever.

She flips the screen and shows us the short, loopy video of our fake fun, which, once we stop posing, becomes real fun. We fall over each other giggling and whispering evilly about the latest hot rumor—that our class president, Calla Tommison, gave St. Matthew's resident bad boy, Hector Tonning, a blow job on the civics trip while the docent was droning on about some rotunda at the Kelsey Museum of Archaeology.

"I don't think it's true. I mean, Hector's kind of a man-whore, but he's not, like, *desperate*." Harper's mouth twists into a bratty scowl, the one she makes when she doesn't instantly get what she wants.

"Calla is smart and hot." My internal feminist rages up to defend Calla, even though it's obvious Harper's shitty attitude actually has nothing to do with Calla and everything to do with a serious bout of unrequited love. Harper flirted with Hector at Homecoming, but he made it clear he wasn't interested in being some rich girl's boy toy. "And no sex shaming. It's not feminist."

Tessa, who was busy playing in the marching band that night and missed Harper's minitantrum over being turned down, adds fuel to the fire by showing us a picture that just got posted of Calla's and Hector's hands interlocked, sunlight dappling their skin. It's on *his* account.

"Well, that went from blow jobs to romantic-couple pics quickly. I guess it was love at first swallow," she says, snickering.

Harper makes a gagging noise, and I shake my head at Tessa's crass joke, wondering what kind of gossip people spread about Lex and me. We're notoriously private about our relationship. I honestly don't even talk to Tessa and Harper about him much (especially since they hate him). But I don't think it's about protection and boundaries, like it is when I keep quiet about my family. With Lex it's more like even *I'm* not sure what exactly we are to each other, so I never feel comfortable gushing about him. How embarrassing would it be to post a picture of the two of us holding hands only to have him tease me about it later…or show it to his summertime flavor of the week?

"The contrast of light and shadow *is* really good in this

picture, though," Tessa muses, still overanalyzing the shot of Hector and Calla.

"Hey, Annie Leibovitz, give it here." Lex strides into the foyer in coral trunks that complement the sweet tan he gets from using his mother's private tanning bed year-round—he was *furious* when his mom had a little too much sauvignon blanc and let *that* tidbit slip while I was over for a New Year's Eve party. He's holding a basket—his mom also told me *every* basket in their house is from this specialty basket company called Longaberger that went out of business, so I happen to know the teeny-tiny basket Lex is holding right now goes for a grand on eBay. He shakes the unbelievably expensive basket, gesturing for Tessa to drop her phone in.

She rolls her eyes. "My God, you're not, like, *a celebrity*. Why do you care if we have our phones? Afraid we're going to post unflattering pictures of you all over social media?"

"There's no such thing as an unflattering picture of a person as naturally photogenic as I am. I'm taking your phones because I didn't go to all this trouble to host a party so you could waste hours making boring-ass Boomerangs no one—*literally no one*—wants to see. You can participate in actual social life like it's the early 2000s, or you can leave." He shakes the basket harder, and I wince when I hear the handle crack a little.

Tessa clutches her phone to her chest. "I want to take pictures."

"My dad hired a professional to do candids, plus there's a photo booth. No one needs your grainy, experimental crap. Give it up." Lex and Tessa square off and glare at each other. I push between them and drop my phone in the basket.

"Tess, it's actually a good idea. We're always bitching about how we need to be more present. Remember how you made me listen to that Buddhist monk's podcast last month?" I nudge her and she sighs, double-checks her lock screen, and places the phone in the basket with a hot scowl just for Lex.

Harper pecks out a text before she drops her phone in. "Just letting Mommy know I'm going all Amish tonight." She smirks at Lex. "If you're going to be a bossy dick, your party *better* be worth it. We could have had this at my place… I don't have all these draconian technology rules."

"But you have Mama Bear Johannsen, and it's impossible to have fun when she's hovering," Lex points out.

We all love and fear Mama Johannsen, but no one—not even Harper—argues with Lex's point. My best friends saunter through the cavernous living room to the back deck, which is covered with tons of navy-and-silver beach balls emblazoned with the St. Matthew's lion mascot. The patio has been divided into seating/lounging areas, a slushy bar, a photo-booth area with a mound of props, and a DJ booth.

"A DJ?" I raise my eyebrows. "Um, you already have, like, state-of-the-art surround sound out here. Isn't a DJ a little over the top, even for the Hensons?"

Lex puts his arm around me and gives me an approving once-over. "That suit is your color. Look at me and smile." I do as I'm told, holding a sweet smile in place as I catch a glimpse of the beautiful, artsy-chic photographer who snaps a picture of us and gives a quick thumbs-up. Lex brushes his lips over mine. "Of course it's over the top. Buuut, Papa Henson thinks I'm taking that internship with the law firm he set up for me, so this party is my reward." His smile is little-boy mischievous. "Turns out money *can* buy him love." Lex waves his arm over his head, and I follow his line of sight to his father, who's manning their colossal stainless-steel grill. Mr. Henson gives Lex a thumbs-up and lifts his Samuel Adams in a toast.

"Lex, he's going to freak out when he realizes you're actually going to that rock camp. When do you plan to break it to him?"

"Not *now*, obviously." Lex draws the tip of his index finger down my nose. "Look, I know you think I'm spoiled, but this is how he raised me to be. If I just rolled over and went to the internship, my old man would drop dead from shock. We push each other. It's what we do, how we work. Secretly he loves it." He pulls his finger away and kisses the tip of my nose.

I shake my head at Lex. I'm not looking forward to what will happen when Mr. Henson catches wind that Lex has lied to him—contrary to Lex's insistence, I don't think he secretly loves Lex always sneaking around behind his back. Lex kisses my nose again, then one more time, until I can't hide my smile. Just when I let my guard down and enjoy this sweet moment, I notice the photographer padding around behind us and wonder how much of Lex's sweetness was for the shot.

"I think you should tell him. It's gross not to."

"Telling him is a total AJ move," Lex snorts, pausing to wave and greet the entire lacrosse team, who wave back and beeline to the grill in a carnivorous herd. "Anyway, don't think he's just some *really nice* dad trying to help his son become a defender of the environment or immigrants—he's trying to send me to one of the most morally bankrupt litigators' offices in Michigan. We learned about some local cases they handled in civics, and Petrolloni could barely give the lesson without popping a blood vessel. I'm doing a *good* thing by going to rock camp. This world doesn't need me adding my shameless brilliance to the wrong side of the legal system."

"But you think the world needs you to be a rock star?"

"I can't play anything," he says with a shrug. "And my voice is only okay. So I guess I *need to go to this camp to unlock my hidden potential.*" He croons the sentence, then wraps an arm around my waist and blows wet raspberries on my neck until I'm screaming with laughter and begging him to stop.

He does stop, but only long enough to scoop me into his arms and toss me into the pool. By the time I sputter to the surface, laughing and wiping my hair back, Lex has caught the DJ's attention, and the hits of our junior year shake the speakers.

I forget about Marnie, sitting in the driveway pouting. I forget to constantly check to see if Lex is posing with me or just enjoying my company. Harper, wearing a giant inflatable cowboy hat, has captained a team of girls on swan floaties against the boys on pizza slices in what looks like a cross between chicken and water polo. I bask in the warmish Michigan sun, head tilted back, soaking in the sound of splashes and laughter.

When the sun sinks low, we all climb out of the pool and sprawl on the velvety grass, stuffing our faces with barbecue Mr. Henson dishes out like a grill king, and slurping down slushies that turn our lips neon blue, red, and purple. Tessa lies on her back, fanning herself with black-and-white photo-booth strips that feature us posing like it's our job, wearing stick-on mustaches, feather boas, and giant sunglasses.

"I almost don't want to leave for camp. Wouldn't it be cool

if *this* was summer? Our whole summer. Like, pool parties and hanging out together every day?" Tessa rolls over and cups her chin in her hands. She's echoing what Lilli said in the car earlier, but I don't think that's too weird. It's the time of year for everyone to be nostalgic and a little burned-out. "I mean, I *love* camp, but… I guess it's just been getting old the last year or two. Maybe *I'm* just getting too old for the whole camp scene."

Harper twirls her sunglasses and props herself up on her side, a lopsided mermaid crown from the photo booth still netted in her hair. "I hear you. Like, I love my family, I re-ally, really do, but my mom hyperschedules our vacations, and it's like, can we just *chill*? Yes, *of course* I'm happy I saw New Zealand last summer, but it's more like I took some guided academic tour of New Zealand. My mom got this list of thirty-six must-see things, and we did *all thirty-six*! We didn't have a single unstructured day."

Lex stops gnawing on a rib bone and says, "You know what I dream about?"

We whip our heads around to gawk at him.

"Do sociopaths dream?" Tess asks, and Lex tosses a beach ball in a perfect arc that bounces off her forehead.

"Yes, princess, even those of us with reduced emotional receptors have dreams."

I wiggle closer to him, intrigued. "I feel like I should have at least a basic idea of what you're about to say, but I have *no clue*. Does that make me the world's worst girlfriend?"

"Maybe." He leans over to kiss me, a quick peck that's definitely done for dramatic flair. "Prepare to get a rare look at the inner workings of Lex Henson's brain." He sweeps his arms wide, like he's setting the stage. "In my dream world, I roll out of bed at noon, head to the kitchen, stuff my face with whatever Lita stocks the fridge with in the summer. I head out back and float in the pool, where I work on my tan and listen to my playlist loud enough to have the neighbors call in a noise complaint. I get out and shower around four or five, then head over to the burger joint or dive restaurant where I do some kind of menial labor for hours on end. Then I end the night dirty as fuck, stinking like the fryer, and head out for some late-night partying with the rest of the crew wherever we can find a deserted field to drink in until we pass out. *Fin*."

"Isn't that, like, the plot of five different teen movies?" Tessa asks, eyebrow popped. "'Cause it sounds like *Fast Times at Ridgemont High* meets *Pretty in Pink* with a twist of *Say Anything*."

"I've seen exactly zero of those movies, but it *does* sound familiar," Harper says with a frown. She holds up a finger. "Wait a second! Wait… I know where I've heard that *exact* description." She narrows her eyes at Lex, and I feel his entire body tense next to me.

He looks spooked. What could possibly be making the unshakable Lex Henson look like all the blood's been drained from his body?

Harper jabs her finger at him, a smug smile curling on her lips. "The story Hector Tonning told in civics, when Petrolloni was saying that we're all a bunch of pampered babies who don't know the meaning of hard work… Your big dream is the exact story Hector told about his summer working at that Mexican restaurant on East Main! Plagiarist."

Lex's blanched look is replaced by two red flags of hot shame unfurling up his neck and splotching over his cheeks. "I don't remember that."

It's creepy how measured his voice is. If I wasn't looking at his face—clearly stamped with guilt—I'd buy his lie. But I can tell Harper has hit a nerve, and it strikes me as weird that Lex—Lex with the perfect, pampered life—would dream about having the life of a totally average working teenager.

"Bullshit," Harper sneers. "Everyone was talking about how cool it was that Hector blew up Petrolloni's spot, and I remember you telling him how badass it was. Admit that you have a bro boner for Hector and his tough-guy lifestyle."

"*I* have a boner?" Lex's color evens out, and Harper's triumphant look falters when she realizes she pushed him too far. "Look, maybe I was half listening to Tonning's bragfest about his super macho, blue-collar life, but there was only one person hot and bothered that day, and it sure as shit wasn't me, *Harper*." He feigns shock when she blows air through her nostrils hard and fast, daring herself not to cry. "Oh, shit, did you think your little crush was a big secret? Look, sorry, Harpo, but your Greaser hero obviously loves to tell a tall tale, and the whole The Stuck-up Rich Girl Has a Thing for Me story made for some pretty hilarious locker-room talk."

"Stop it, Lex," I warn. I reach for Harper's hand, but she snatches it away. I ignore how badly that stings because I know she's about two seconds away from straight bawling, and my show of sympathy won't help her bottle those tears up.

"What, she can dish, but she can't take it?" Lex flops back on the grass and flings one perfectly sculpted arm over his eyes. "Typical."

Harper gathers up her humiliation and channels it into rage. "You're such a fucking phony, it makes me sick, Lex. Like, just embrace that you're Daddy's little sociopath. You think it's some big joke that *I'm* apparently a princess? Um, talk about irony? Look at this stupid, overdone party. You're trying *way* too hard to prove you're not this pampered prince, but face it… You are what you are, and it's *not* the blue-collar hero of your pathetic dreams."

Oof.

I realize I'm sitting up, completely tense and in full peace-maker mode, ready to break up this fight before it tumbles past the point of no return.

"Hey, c'mon, stop it right now." I use the loud, no-nonsense voice my sisters call The Headmistress.

"So, it's cool if your boyfriend just, like, insults me to my face?" Harper demands.

Tessa holds her hands up, surrender-style, and Lex smirks, happy to fan the flames. "Well, if the truth just happens to be an insult…" he begins.

I don't let his insinuation sit long enough to boil over again.

"Enough!" I yell, pointing a warning finger at Lex. Harper opens her mouth to say something else, but I shoot her one of my *Don't you even think about it* looks, and she closes her trap faster than Marnie when she's in deep shit, waiting on me to shovel her out. "I'm so sick of listening to you two squabble. You know what? The truth is…we're *all* phonies. Every one of us."

Tessa balks. "I am *not* a phony."

"Really?" I'm not looking to make this whole situation

explode, but I'm not a big enough person to let Tessa's comment slide. "So, you've always *loved* horror flicks?"

She presses her lips together and studies her perfectly maintained cuticles. "I mean, they're important to watch. For cultural reasons. I mean, you can't just, like, *ignore* an entire genre of cinema," she mumbles.

"You almost threw up during *The Babadook*. I watched you keep your eyes closed through most of *Midsommar*." Just hearing the title is enough to make her grimace. I get it… Even bringing that movie up gives me the chills, and I've been watching Jason movies with Duke and Dani since I was in kindergarten. "You did it because you didn't want Logan to think you were a wimp, and that's *fine*."

"That's called *exposing yourself to new things*. It's completely different," Tessa protests. "That's *not* being a phony!"

"It is if you pretend that you like the thing you actually hate just so you can impress someone you look up to." I make sure my voice is gentle enough not to start a nasty brawl but firm enough to get my point across.

I'd expect Lex to be on my side about this, but, as usual, he's as loyal as a double agent.

"So, are you the phoniest one of all of us, AJ?" He laughs when he says it, and once I go from being the enforcer to the butt of the joke, everyone relaxes a little. Even Harper smiles.

"Why do you say that?" I wonder if he knows me better than he lets on or if he's just that good at bluffing.

"What do you even *like*, AJ?" He grabs my ankle and drags me closer to him. With my foot between his hands, he starts a massage I don't ask for or want. There's a particular rage I feel when I'm simultaneously irritated with him and turned to putty in his hands, and that rage burns white-hot through me right now. "School? Nope, I don't think you like school. You just like getting good grades, making the teachers and your parents happy. Do you actually *like* any of your twenty thousand after-school activities? Nah. You just like the shiny trophies and all those bullet points on your college résumé." He slides his thumb up the center of my foot and presses hard along the arch. My toes crack, and the flash of discomfort is countered by the incredible release of tension. "I don't even think you like *me*." His eyes glisten the way they always do when he feels challenged. He drops his voice to a purr, like some jungle cat. "I don't think you even like *them*. You just like being in charge of everyone."

"I *definitely* don't like you right now." I try to kick at him, but his fingers close around my other ankle with a tight bite. He has me shackled. "Let me go."

"Tell me something you like." He stares at me, his fingers tight on my skin. My friends have gone quiet, waiting.

I look up at the purpling evening sky and think about the sun setting over the ocean, like a perfect ball of orange cantaloupe melting into the water.

I think about Duke taking me for long walks on the beach with our metal detectors, how we'd fall to our knees and dig like puppies when we heard the telltale beeps, never knowing if it was a bottle cap or a diamond ring we were about to unearth. I think about dancing on the wide back porch of my dad's old house, my feet on the tops of his mud-encrusted boots; I think about making up synchronized-swimming dances full of flips and underwater handstands with Dani, while her favorite station blared on the crackly outdoor speakers for hours; and then, as my brain flips through Florida memories, I think about Jude Zeigler, my childhood nemesis and full-time sparring partner at my dad's shop in Florida.

I try to imagine Jude here, at this party, scowling at everyone, his dark eyebrows low and *judgy* like they always are. Jude has a code of behavior that's ironclad, and deviations don't sit well. He would have confronted Lex about how ridiculously romanticized he made working a menial-labor job sound—because that's Jude's authentic life. He's worked as hard as an adult since we were in middle school.

Jude Zeigler can be irritating as hell, but he is who he is, completely, and there's something super attractive about that. Especially when I compare that to Lex's mind games and drama.

"You know what I like? I like guys who respect boundaries." I pull up and shove at Lex's chest, knocking him back on the grass. He grins, totally in his element when the drama is dialed all the way up. "And I like leaving a party before it totally sucks…which means I should have walked out of this one about an hour ago." I stand up, and Lex slow-claps as I stalk back to the house, shivering in the cool Michigan dusk.

"Hey, AJ!" Harper chases behind me, Tessa at her heels. "That got weird quick, huh?" She beams as if she bothered to defend me or defuse things when I came to her defense against Lex, and for a long second, I honestly don't know if I even want to respond to her.

I finally decide not to start some big drama before we all leave for the whole summer. It sucks that I can't always be honest with my best friends, but this is the way it's always been. When we disagree, it can get ugly fast—but I know they'll always be here for me as much as they can be. I some-times wish I could include them in every aspect of my life, but I just can't. It's fine. No friendship is perfect.

"It's always weird with Lex."

"Sociopath," Tessa huffs. "AJ, you could do so much bet-ter. Are you guys taking a break again this summer?"

We grab our phones from the basket in the foyer and head to the guest room where we left our bags. I beeline to the bathroom to change. "Yeah," I say through the door. I keep my voice cheerful, but I let a few tears wobble down my cheeks. "You know, it's easier that way. I mean, it's not like it's all Lex's idea. I want to have fun over the summer, too."

That's partially a lie. I've tried the whole fling thing, and it doesn't work for me. I think what I'd really like is to date a guy who wants to commit to me, but that's not who Lex is. I don't try to force him to be someone he's not, and there's no one else I want to be with.

"Lucky!" Harper yells.

I take a soft cotton ball from the crystal jar on the vanity and wipe away my mascara streaks. Today was supposed to be pure summer fun, but I'm just as exhausted as I would be after a long day of school and extracurriculars. I consider fak-ing a stomach bug and heading home, but I check my phone and see I've missed thirty-eight texts from Marnie chroni-cling how unfair her life is and whining about our parents' PDA. I know if I go home, she'll direct all of her energy at me, and I definitely can't handle that now.

I step out of the bathroom and smile at my best friends. I'll go to Harper's, carb out, watch movies, maybe steal a glass or two of Mrs. Johannsen's boxed wine… It will be fine.

"How do you deal with going to a camp that's all girls, Tessa? Don't you miss being around guys?" Harper asks. Harper's been chasing boys around the playground since kindergarten, so the idea of a no-boy summer is her literal definition of hell.

"There's a boys' camp across the lake," Tessa blurts out, then blushes a little. She hesitates before the next sentence. "And there's a guy who goes there. We've been meeting up every summer for the last three years, so...yeah. There's that."

"What?" Harper squeals, bouncing on the neatly made bed so hard, she sends a dozen velvety throw pillows flying. "You've had a secret boyfriend for *three years*?"

"Not everyone overshares every detail of their lives."

"Is he a troll? Are you *embarrassed* about him?" Harper demands. Tessa bites her lip hard, and I wonder if she regrets opening up. "You are, aren't you? What's wrong with him? Is he ugly? Is he in 4-H?"

"Shut up, Harper." I lock eyes with Tessa and nod toward the bathroom. She flies in and slams the door behind her. "What's wrong with you?" I hiss. "You're making Tessa upset. Just because you have diarrhea of the mouth when it comes to your crushes, doesn't mean everyone does."

"C'mon, you're seriously blaming *me*, here? Tessa has kept her summer boyfriend a secret for *three years*." Harper rolls her eyes. "That's practically catfishing."

"That's definitely not catfishing."

Harper ticks off on her fingers all the ways Tessa's deception is unacceptable, and I half listen, wondering what she'd think if she found out about my secret family and life in Florida.

"Also, maybe he's, like, trashy? Although, I guess if he can afford to go to a camp like Tessa's, he's probably not a total delinquent."

"Do you mean *trashy* or just *poor*?" I narrow my eyes at her, but she refuses to feel ashamed of how gross she's being.

"Is there really a difference? *Really?*" She pops her Lilly Pulitzer dress over her suit and pulls her top off through the armhole, like we're in a middle-school locker room. "Don't get all holier than thou. I just have the guts to say what everyone else is thinking."

Before I can argue with her, Tessa comes out, and I can tell she used the cotton balls to sop up some tears, too.

"Don't say a word to me, Harper," Tessa growls, then holds up her phone. "Here. Robbie. Band geek, hippie, poet, dork, and maybe…no, *definitely* the guy I…love."

Even Harper isn't cruel enough to say anything stupid in response to that declaration. We all gather around and look at a gangly, long-haired, hippie-looking guy with a huge, goofy grin and eyes for Tessa and Tessa alone.

"Why didn't you tell us?" Harper asks as she squints at the picture.

"Because… I'm not embarrassed. He's just…he wouldn't fit in here. I didn't know what you guys would think of him or say about him. So I didn't give you the chance to."

"He'd be ten times cuter if he cut off that gross hair," Harper sniffs, but when Tessa looks like she might lunge for her throat, she quickly adds, "But he's definitely super cute. Good job, Tess."

For a second it feels like the time might be right for me to share, too—

"Are you going to read us his love poems?" Harper cackles, and Tessa's face falls.

"Forget it. I knew I shouldn't have said anything," she mutters. "Let's bounce. I need some Advil and an *Office* marathon. Your place?"

I watch Tessa try hard to keep the upper hand, but it's obvious from the way her shoulders slump that her feelings are hurt. In our crew, hurt feelings are something you rebound from, and you do it quickly. I squeeze her shoulder, and she gives me a half smile.

"I'm calling in an order to that Thai place you love. What do you want?" Harper asks Tessa, her olive branch too little too late.

Tessa accepts anyway.

"Larb. And lots of mango sticky rice for dessert." Tessa and Harper head to Harper's car, heads bent together over the menu on Harper's phone, but I hang back when I hear Lex call for me.

"Hey, I've been waiting for you to come back out. We cool?" He ducks in for a kiss, but I pull back.

"We're fine. I'm headed to Harper's. Thanks for the party."

"Stay." He takes my hand and holds tighter when I try to pull back.

"No."

"There will be fireworks," he singsongs.

"I've had all the excitement I can take for one night." I pull away. "Let go. Tessa and Harper are waiting on me."

"Hey…" He rakes his fingers through his hair and blows out a long breath that echoes through the marble foyer.

"Sometimes… I can be a real dick. Beyond my usual levels. Tonight, I was a big-time dick."

I wait for him to say more, but apparently that's it. He skids just short of an apology, and I just barely forgive him.

"I know." I reach up to kiss his cheek, pat it, and head back to my friends. "Have a nice summer, Lex."

"See you around, AJ."

I slow down, wondering if he'll come to me again, try to bridge the weird gap we always have between us, but when I look over my shoulder he's gone. When I get to the door, Harper is already backing into the driveway.

"Sorry, AJ! We didn't realize you hadn't left yet. Good thing we saw your car at the last second."

I laugh it off, but part of me—the part that's itching to get home to Florida—wishes they hadn't.

Can my summer in Michigan be over? I'm ready for my time in Florida to begin.

3

Airport Transformations

*Detroit, Michigan (DTW) to Atlanta, Georgia (ATL) to Key
West, Florida (EYW)
8:55 a.m. to 3:42 p.m., 6 hours 47 minutes*

MICHIGAN

AJ's Travel Ensemble:
- dark-wash, skinny travel jeans
- cute leather travel loafers
- sleeveless cream silk blouse
- stylish navy blazer, sleeves cuffed crisply to show off the seersucker lining
- tasteful gold bangle set (gift from Mom and Peter for my induction into the National Honor Society)
- hair in a neat bun

Della's Travel Ensemble:
- buttery soft leggings, "lunar explosion" print
- sparkly flip-flops
- two neon tank tops (layered)
- neon sports bra (straps exposed)
- ornate, rose-gold cross necklace (gift from Grandma Beloise for my First Holy Communion)
- hair in a crazy cascade down my back

I started doing an entire fashion/hair change in the airport bathroom before my flight from Michigan to Florida when I was right around eight. I can still remember the outfit Mom picked for me to travel in: a pair of crisp khaki capris and a pale peony polo with white Keds and a big bow in my French-braided hair. I peered in the mirror before we left and thought about how babyish I'd look next to Dani (who was already practically a teenager), but I didn't want to risk an argument with my mother. So I rolled a pair of rainbow short shorts, a white tank with my name airbrushed on it, and a pair of flip-flops (all relics of my Florida life that I'd kept in a suitcase under my bed) into my carry-on. I arrived in Florida looking—in my mind, anyway—*so cool*. Ten years later the tradition continues; I leave Michigan as prim and proper AJ and arrive in Florida as free and wild Della.

I'm just topping my AJ Jepsen outfit off with two swipes of MAC lipstick in demure Melbourne that will be wiped away in a few hours, when I hear more noise than usual downstairs. I grab my Kate Spade clutch and head to the sunny dining room to see—

"Wow...*everyone* is here." I check my tone so I don't sound as frustrated as I feel. "Um, what's up, guys?"

"Surprise!" Lilli practically vibrates in her chair. "We thought you might want company on your ride to the airport, so we're driving you!"

"Driving me? To the airport?" I look from my baby sister's beaming face to Peter's peaceful smile and then Mom's annoyed pucker—it's like Mom senses my annoyance, so she automatically sets *her* annoyance dial three times higher on principle.

"It's your lucky day, kiddo." Peter points to the center of the gigantic farm table, which is piled high with crispy bacon and golden-brown waffles—gluten-free but delicious, because Mom is an amazing cook. "A big, hot breakfast and your favorite household chauffeur to take you to the airport."

I sit down and pile my plate under Mom's watchful eye, smiling automatically for the picture she snaps, which might very well end up on her blog. Since we never know what Mom will use, we always have to be photo-ready, and now it's practically a reflex to pose for a minute or two for documentation before we dive into real life. Even though I'm not remotely hungry, turning down Mom's big surprise breakfast would hurt her feelings and put her in a shitty mood. I'd like to avoid that at all costs, so I will force down the waffles and manage to look appreciative while I do it.

"So, you're telling me that instead of getting privately chauffeured to Detroit Metro by your company, I have to sit through Lilli's enforced sing-alongs?" I try to make it a joke, but it definitely comes out more like a gripe.

Lilli's face falls, just for a split second. "It's totally okay if you'd rather not!" She's good at pretending to be cheerful even when her feelings have been eviscerated; she's had years of practice from bitterly venomous small-town talent-show judges. "I know I can be annoying with my singing sometimes."

A twinge of self-loathing stabs me through the heart, and I'm about to apologize for being such a jerk when our mother jumps in.

"AJ, you don't have to take your crappy mood out on Lilli. She thought it would be nice to go together—"

"I just, like, thought we could talk and stuff. Because we never really got to hang out after the last day of school like we said we would." She shrugs her bony shoulders like it's no big deal that I dropped the ball and left her hanging, and I officially crown myself the world's Assholest Big Sister.

"Hey, it's a great idea, seriously." I rub her arm gently like I used to when she was a baby nodding off in her car seat next to me on a long drive. Her whole face lights up—having kid sisters is like constantly walking by a box of stray puppies that are begging you to adopt them. "I'm always nervous about flying, so I was feeling snappy. I shouldn't have taken it out on you. I'm sorry, Lil."

It's a lie. I *love* flying, but I need an out, and Lilli actually *does* hate to fly, so it's an angle that hits her right in her empathetic heart.

"No problem at all!" My little sister's energy level instantly charges back to full force, and I remind myself how much power what I say and do has over her. I want to use that for good, not to tear her down. She blithely swipes a piece of bacon through a pool of maple syrup and chirps, "And, like, seriously, no singing, I promise. I'm going to have to sing every single day this whole entire summer, and even though I *love it*…I need a break sometimes!" She eats the sticky bacon and gulps down some orange juice while Peter clears his throat and turns his attention to me.

"I know you've got a lot on your plate today, but have you given the internship any thought?" He leans forward on his elbows, trying not to look too eager. I know for sure he's attempting to play it cool when he takes off his glasses and cleans them with the corner of his polo—it's his tell. "I know how important your time in Florida is, but no one will begrudge you taking a stab at something that could open so many doors. These opportunities don't come around every day."

"I do want to. Seriously, I do. But this summer is really important…" I eye Lilli, who, I notice, has stopped chewing her crunchy bacon so she can hear better. "This might be the last summer…you know…"

I'm not sure how much to safely say in front of Lilli. My sisters know I have a different bio father, and they know I have another set of older siblings, but we generally keep the details scarce. I don't know if it's because of our Midwestern reluctance to expose any complicated feelings or because we're such a tight unit—the congregation at our church and our teachers nicknamed us Triple Threat Jepsens—but we don't acknowledge that our perfect, quirky little family is actually a lot more complicated than it seems.

Mom eyes me and heaves a sigh. "You're being so melodramatic," she says, without a trace of irony.

Keep your mouth shut, keep your mouth shut, I lecture myself, knowing full well the cost of calling my mother out, especially when she's in one of her edgy moods.

"Vanessa, it's not melodrama," Peter says, and I feel a warm rush of affection for my calm, logical stepdad—though, the term *step* is verboten in our house. As is *half*, which is why my sisters and I never, ever refer to each other as *half siblings*. "AJ's summertime with her family is incredibly important. But as a father…" He pauses, like he knows how complicated it is, how knotted all our ties are. Lilli stares at him, eager to hear more, and Mom makes a short hiss of warning. Peter plows on anyway, bless. "As a father, I know *any* dad would be happy for his kid to go ahead and do this, even if it meant losing some time together. Okay, I said my piece. Vanessa? You look like you want to jump in."

Peter is an incredibly skilled diplomat—which I guess he'd have to be to navigate the big personalities of the four Jepsen women on a daily basis.

"Just do whatever you want, AJ." Mom starts clearing the table with a dangerous amount of force. Peter winces as two handmade Italian serving bowls clank together sharply. "I have more than enough on my plate figuring out what I should do with Marnie this summer. Or are we just letting everyone do whatever they feel like doing, Peter?"

Peter puts a hand on Mom's wrist, and she stops, closes her eyes, and takes a deep breath. He pulls the bowls out of her hands and places them on the table, then tugs her onto his lap. "Hey, hey, listen to me. I know you're stressed," he says, rubbing her back in slow circles. Mom seems to melt against him. "You're our glue, honey, and that's not an easy position to be in. What can we do to help?"

She nestles her face into his neck, and he runs a hand over her red hair, the same color as Marnie's. "You're our rock. What would I do without you?" She adjusts the glasses she knocked crooked on his face. "Thank you. I'm just feeling really overwhelmed. This summer is going to be so complicated, and you know I don't do well when I can't make a plan."

I nod to Lilli, and she and I start to—*very quietly*—clear the table. We tiptoe into the kitchen to do the dishes and let our parents finish talking in peace.

"Where *is* Marnie?" I ask, my voice low enough that it can't be heard over the running water.

Lilli grabs a plate from my outstretched hand and rubs it dry with a linen dish towel. "She got into another *huge* fight with Mom about volleyball camp when you were at Lex's saying good-bye last night. She slammed her door and everything. And then she listened to, like, *every* Lana Del Rey album super loud on repeat, and Mom said she had to go meditate with her noise-canceling headphones on or she'd break the door down and smash Marnie's speakers with a sledgehammer."

"Jesus Christ." Jepsen House Rule 12 *forbids* door-slamming, and House Rule 15 says music must be played at a respectful level. "So, that's why Mom's in such a bad mood?"

Lilli keeps rubbing the plate, even though it's clearly dry.

I take it out of her hands. "Lil?"

She looks up at me. "You won't tell anyone if I tell you something, right?"

For a second I panic, thinking about the secrets I already keep for Marnie—secrets that I constantly wonder if I should have let an adult know about a long time ago. But this is Lilli; my youngest sister is as sweet and sunshiny as Marnie is impetuous and mercurial.

"You can tell me anything. You know that."

She nestles closer to me, tucks a piece of hair behind her ear, her thin fingers shaking so hard the glitter polish throws sparkles around the room, and whispers, "One of my You-Tube followers is the daughter of a big, *big* record-label CEO, and Ronnie heard this rumor that she played my Advent song for her mother, and they've been, like, playing it non-stop at the offices and talking about it and about maybe setting up a meeting with me. I guess they're, like, worried I'm so young and all, but they really, *really* like my music. That's the rumor, anyway." Her mouth pulls into a tiny bud, and her eyes bug out wide.

"Ronnie told you that?" Lilli's agent is a very businesslike, serious woman who shoots straight from the hip. She would never give Lilli false hope. If she told her about a supposed rumor, it's likely way more than unsubstantiated whispers.

"Mmm-hmm. So Mom is, like, *freaking out* because if this works out—" Lilli cuts that thought off before she can formulate anything concrete. "And it's, like, so weird. I don't know what to do. I don't know if I should post a new song? Should I do a vlog? Should I just, like, chill out? Mom and I have been talking about it, and there's no way to know what to do."

"What do you *want* to do, Lilli?" I ask, but I know the answer is never simple, at least not for the Jepsen girls. When you have the weight of so many opportunities and expectations pressing on you all the time, everything is complicated.

"I think I know what I *don't* want. I don't want to get pressured to make music that I think sucks or that I'll be embarrassed about. And I don't want to do a whole, like, makeover of who I am, you know? I talked to Pastor Kitty for, like, two hours after youth group last week, and we talked about what makes a truly good life versus what makes a life everyone envies from the outside, and it's just really hard to know how to do what I want without losing my way." Lilli presses her fingers to her throat, the home of her mermaid-gorgeous voice, and her delicate little face crumples with worry.

I turn off the water and wrap my arms around her. "You are so talented and so smart, Lil. Sometimes I feel like you have things figured out better than I ever will. I know you're thinking about things and praying about them, and I think that's maybe half the solution to your problems right there. As long as you keep reflecting on things, I think it's all going to be great. And you know I'm always here for you. We all are."

She rubs her face on my shoulder and breathes out a little sigh. "I wish you could come with me and Mom. You and Marnie. I always feel better when you guys are with me." She pulls away and looks up at me, her golden hair fuzzed around her head like a halo. Her eyes narrow with mischief, and she gives me a wicked, teasing grin. "Too bad you guys have voices like bullfrogs or we could have been, like, the Beach Boys or Heart or something."

I gasp in mock shock. "I do *not* sound like a bullfrog, you little ass." I tickle her under the armpits until she's screaming with laughter and gasping for breath. "Take it back, brat!"

Lilli is squealing for mercy when Marnie walks into the kitchen, hair a lopsided mess, scowl dragging her face down. "What are you doing in here? Your laugh sounds like a hyena on crack, Lilli. You guys woke me up."

"Good morning, sunshine." I head back to the sink and Lilli trots over to help me again. "Everyone—*except you*—was up bright and early because we're going to the airport. As a family."

"You guys ate breakfast without me?" Marnie glares at the scraps I just finished scraping into the garbage.

"Mom didn't call you?" I turn my eyes to the sink as I sponge the plates off with such force, soap bubbles splatter everywhere. When I look closer at Marnie, I see the dark circles that ring her puffy eyes. She was definitely up all night crying.

"No." Marnie crosses her arms tight across her chest.

"Mom's pissed at me." She marches to the cabinet, grabs a box of cereal, gets the milk out of the refrigerator, and bangs a bowl Lilli and I just washed and put away onto the counter. Marnie fixes her breakfast and shovels a huge spoonful of cereal into her mouth. "Why would we drive to the airport?" she asks with her mouth full. "Why doesn't Dad's company just send the car like always?"

Lilli chews on her bottom lip, and I give her a quick squeeze of reassurance. "Stop whining. It's sister time."

"Stupid," Marnie declares, letting milk dribble down her chin on purpose. "We were supposed to, like, *actually* hang out. This is a super pathetic consolation prize."

"We get to hang out," Lilli protests feebly as Marnie sneers at us both. "And there's that slider place we can go to by the airport that has the truffle fries."

"It would have been cool if we went to Green Dot Stables for sliders as an *actual* day hanging out, not just a stop on the way to drop AJ at the airport. *That* would have been cool. This just sucks." Marnie practically tosses her bowl into the sink.

"Hey, watch it!" I snap at her retreating back. "You know, if you don't want to help, you could at least not screw everything up!"

Marnie flies across the room and sticks her finger in my face. "I'm sorry I can't just shut up and never, *ever* say what I'm thinking like you!"

"Guys, please stop fighting," Lilli begs, eyeing the dining room nervously. If Mom hears, she'll come out and yell at us…or, worse, try to mediate and get us to make peace using all of the tricks she picked up listening to her favorite parenting podcasts.

"I'll say what I'm thinking right now—you messed up, Marnie, *big-time*, and you almost dragged us all down with your stupid decisions. Mom and Dad think they're doing something *nice* by sending you to this *super expensive* volleyball camp, and I don't get why you can't just suck it the hell up and *go*! You live for volleyball, you have nothing else to do this summer—"

"So, I should just let myself get shipped off and do something I don't feel like doing because—according to you—*I have nothing else to do*?" she demands. "You wouldn't understand. You don't have anyone telling you what to do every summer… You just get to leave everything!"

"You don't know what you're talking about, as usual," I say, dropping my voice.

Lilli is making little whimpering sounds in the back of her throat.

"You're right. I *don't* know." Marnie gets right up in my face, so close I can see her oversize pupils, black as ink. "Why don't I know? I'm your sister. What's the big secret, AJ? Why does our family *never* talk about anything?"

"Um…" Lilli tries to warn us, but it's too late.

Mom marches into the kitchen and points to Marnie. "Get upstairs and get presentable. I expect you down here in exactly fifteen minutes. We're getting in the car, we're going to take AJ to the airport, and there will be *absolutely no bickering*. Do I make myself clear?"

Marnie's chin wobbles as she looks from one of us to the

other. She gives a sharp salute. "I'll be ready to pretend every-thing is just fine in exactly fifteen minutes. Aye aye, Captain."

Peter puts an arm around Mom's shoulders before she can scream at Marnie for her disrespect. "It's a phase, Vanessa. Let her express how she's feeling."

Mom rubs her temples. "I feel a migraine coming on."

"Are you okay, Mom? Do you want me to make you a pine-apple and ginger smoothie?" Lilli asks, nuzzling close to Mom.

"That would be amazing, sweetie. AJ, could you get the prescription migraine medicine that's in my bathroom vanity?"

"Sure."

I'm surprised when, a minute later, prescription bottle in hand, I find Mom standing in the doorway of the bathroom.

"AJ, did Lilli get a chance to talk to you?" Mom sits on the marble vanity top and twists her hair into a lazy bun, letting it fall back down in shiny strands over and over. My mom looks like she could be another Jepsen sister.

"She mentioned that Ronnie said there might be a record label that's interested." I hand Mom the pill bottle and watch as she uncaps it and throws two back.

"I've been praying about it, talking to your father about it, reading every article and blog I can find about getting into a singing career too young, and I don't have any idea what to do." My mom searches my face, and I realize she's asking for my input.

"I think Lilli has all of us, and she's an old soul. No one ever guesses she's only fourteen. I mean, she has a good head on her shoulders." I absently twist the tops of Mom's perfume bottles so the labels all face out—Chanel Beauty, Marc Jacobs Decadence, Benefit Maybe Baby.

"It could dramatically change things for us. As a family." She sighs. "I'm not worried about you and Lilli. You girls are tough, you can adapt. It's Marnie who worries me. I've tried so hard to help her get her footing this year, but it feels like she's spiraling. I thought she'd be so excited about this volleyball camp, but nothing makes her happy lately."

I'm not sure how to tell my mother that what Marnie wants more than anything is some space to breathe, some time away from everything everyone expects her to do, because Mom might have follow-up questions I'm not ready to answer...so I chicken out yet again and don't say anything at all.

"Sweetie, I want you to enjoy your time with your father and Dani and Duke this summer, but...I want you to think about what Peter suggested. You'd only need to leave a few weeks early, and it might be a really good thing for you. I know you haven't been able to do anything you really care about during the summer because you're always at your father's."

"I love going to Florida," I say, my gut twisting. Every other year, I've been able to just hop into the cool interior of the company car and get whisked to the airport without having all of this drama to deal with. I'm so ready to shed the complications that come with being the eldest Jepsen daughter in Michigan and embrace the simplicity of my life as the baby of the Beloise family in Florida. "Going to see Dad and Dani and Duke is exactly what I want to do."

"AJ," Mom says, drawing my name out. "Seriously? C'mon, sweetie. In another lifetime, I lived in that poky little backwater town. It's a dead end. There's nothing for a bright, intelligent young person there. Don't get me wrong—it's great to visit with family, but you're only young once." She slides off the vanity and stands in front of me, smelling light and flowery with an undernote of vanilla. "You don't need to waste your entire summer working in a bait shop and drinking cheap beer on the beach with a bunch of local kids who will never leave that one-horse town." She smooths the collar of my blazer. "You're destined for bigger and better, sweetie. Don't let anything stop you from going after what you want. I almost let that happen once. It's easy to lose sight of who you are when you're always busy dealing with other people's problems."

My mom kisses my cheek. I hug her, annoyance and affection making me hold on extra tight.

"I know, Mom," I say with a sigh. I'm sure she'd be shocked to realize I actually *do* agree with her advice one hundred percent—which is why I have to leave Michigan to head to Florida every summer, for the entire summer.

We head back downstairs. Peter already has the car started, and Lilli hands Mom a travel mug with her smoothie in it. Marnie slumps into the back seat, a pair of dark sunglasses shading her face. Despite Lilli's adamant promise, we wind up singing along to an old station Mom picks with lots of Gwen Stefani and Sheryl Crow. It's totally fun, even if I do sound like a bullfrog. Even Marnie joins in with her rich contralto when "All I Wanna Do" comes on, which was one of her favorite songs when she was a kid. I watch the flat, cool, green suburban yards give way to alternatingly beautiful and ugly stretches of Detroit cityscape. We stop for sliders at the old horse-stable restaurant, and, before I know it, we're at the airport, I've checked in, and I'm ready to go through security.

"Well, this is it." I hate having to say big, emotional good-byes at airports, but it looks like I don't have much of a choice. I hug Peter first.

"Think about the internship, okay?" He leans in a little closer and drops his voice to a whisper. "Talk to your dad about it. Trust me, he'll understand." He gives me a wink. "I love you, and I miss you already, kiddo." His voice goes thick, and I soak in his reassuring, solid hug for an extra few seconds.

Mom is next. "I left the ticket open-ended. If you decide to head back earlier, say the word, and we'll get you wherever you want to go. I still think the internship is the best idea, but there are always last-minute camp or travel opportunities. I hate to see you waste a high-school summer. You don't get many, and they go by so fast. Trust me, you'll look back and regret it." I kiss her soft cheek and move away quickly, before she can lecture me any more.

"Thank you for talking to me about things this morning," Lilli says quietly, rubbing her golden head on my shoulder and sniffing so deeply, I wonder if she's smelling my perfume for comfort, the way I still sniff Mom's. She turns to me with a huge smile, and my heart flip-flops with love for my little rising star of a sister. "You seriously made me feel a million times better. Also I never gave you back your sunglasses, but is it okay if I wear them this summer?" I roll my eyes and tell sweet, conniving Lilli that of course she can snag my favorite sunglasses, hug her tight, and wish her luck. I take a long look at her face, still round-cheeked and starry-eyed, and I hope that, no matter what comes at her this summer, I still see that sparkle next time we're together.

Marnie is last. "I should have packed myself into one of your suitcases," she gripes.

"You'd hate it in Florida. Way too hot and humid," I assure her. I hug her, feeling super guilty for our fight when she grips onto me like she's drowning. "Hey, volleyball camp will be awesome. I promise."

"You hate volleyball," she says into my hair.

"But *you* love it. And you'll meet cool people. You'll play all day long. It will be amazing. And I'll see you in a few weeks. Okay?" I pull back and watch her face twist. Of course nothing with Marnie can ever be easy.

"Actually, it's not really okay, but what choice do I have?" She crosses her arms. "I guess I'll endure it."

"Grow up, Marnie," I hiss.

That's the last thing I say directly to my sister before Peter gently reminds me of the time and my family waves as one bunch, three teary, smiling faces and Marnie's stubborn frown.

I don't look back as I wait my turn. I picture my family already piled in the car, jamming to some sweet tunes as they drive back to our house, and I hope that's exactly what they're doing.

"Adelaide," the TSA attendant says. It's a little weird hearing my full name. "That was my grandmother's name!"

I smile. I'm polite. I'm polished. For a few more minutes, I hover closer to the AJ end of my spectrum, but a quick trip to the nearest bathroom changes that. I choose a stall and carefully tug off my binding, sophisticated outfit. The soft leggings hug my thighs, the sports bra and tank tops let my shoulders relax, and I shake out my hair and head to the mirror to do my full face of makeup.

Cat eyes, deep lipstick, false lashes, contouring, bronz-ing—it takes twenty-five minutes and makes me look older, sharper, and more than a little intimidating. An older woman huffs when she has to choose a sink farther from the paper towels because I have my things spread all over the counter. AJ would have apologized and shifted for her. Della gives her the stink eye and continues to get a little brasher and a little less serious with every stroke of the makeup brushes.

By the time I'm done, I barely recognize myself, and I love it. I love these moments in the in-between, where I'm not quite AJ and not exactly Della. When I don't have to lie to anyone.

Right now I'm like a giant, molting dragon, and my mood feels exactly like what I imagine a beast shedding its too-tight skin would feel. I pointedly ignore the overeager lady seated next to me who's trying to lure me into checking out her cat's Instagram account; I switch off my phone after scanning the first few mopey texts from Marnie, knowing full well they won't stop for the duration of the flight; and I sit still and focus on becoming a bigger, bolder version of myself.

4

Mid-June
Key West

FLORIDA

When the plane finally touches down in Florida, I text my family in Michigan to let them know I've arrived safely, then elbow my way to the front, unconcerned with the grumbles from the other passengers I barge past. My sparkly flip-flops smack in rhythm as I head to baggage, where I see Dani, Duke, and Dad standing with a huge glittery sign that says, "Welcome home, Della!" My heart breaststrokes into the same spot in my throat where it was when I said good-bye to my family in Michigan.

In one day I left home and came home, and my happiness and melancholy twist together in an uneasy wrestling match that's one of my most familiar feelings.

"Dad! Dani! Duke!" I bellow, sprinting to them as quickly as my impractical footwear allows. I hurl myself into Dad's arms, squealing as he swings me around like I'm seven instead of seventeen. Duke and Dani crowd on either side of me, sandwiching me in a tight hug.

"Look at your hair," my sister gushes, holding out a long, dark strand. "Please tell me you want to leave it long this summer? It's *so* beautiful!"

I pop my bottom lip out. "I thought the best stylist in the Keys could hook me up with an inverted bob and some hot pink in the back?"

Dani closes her eyes and takes a deep breath. "How about a cute lob and some deep purple?"

"Oh my God, can we please talk about *anything* else?" Duke moans.

I reach out and press down on his crazy curls. "Um, are haircuts a hot-button issue right now?"

"Wouldn't he look so handsome with a nice undercut?" I can practically see Dani's hands itching to take a razor to our brother's hair. She sighs. "He says he doesn't have time. The university is around the corner from my salon!" Dani squeezes Duke's cheeks in her hand so his lips pucker out. "With my help, you'd need a bat to keep the girls away."

"I don't hab a probwem wit da girls. 'Cept maybe dat dere's too many chasing me," he says through his squashed lips, and we all laugh.

"We gotta drive by the salon. You'll be blown away, Dell," Dad declares, kissing my temple, then Dani's. He looks at her with total pride in his eyes. "Can't even believe this one owns her own damn salon at twenty-one." He lets out a low whistle, and Dani blushes.

"Dad, seriously, you act like I pulled myself up by my bootstraps and did it all alone, when that's so far from the truth. I couldn't have done it without a million different people helping me." Dani raises her eyebrows as our dad shakes his head.

"Dad, c'mon." She ticks off her fingers. "You cosigned my loan. Ms. Laverne passed me an enormous client base when she retired, after she taught me basically every trade secret in the book. And Nan Sunny left me the seed money—" My sister's voice catches, and Duke and I both move closer to her, like we're trying to protect her.

Dani is the AJ of the Beloise sibling group, but just because she calls the shots doesn't mean Duke and I aren't there to back her up anytime she needs us.

I take her hand. "I'm sorry, Dani. I know how much you still miss her."

Her hand flies up, and she closes a fist around the locket she's worn since Nan Sunny died. I still miss the sweet, funny woman who treated me like her own grandchild and helped Dani and Duke after their bio mother, Allie, passed. It's weird to realize that I was just about Lilli's age when she died. Looking back, that Key West summer felt gloomier than a Michigan February.

Dani was especially brokenhearted—I remember trying so hard to make her laugh and take her mind off things, but it was like she was totally checked out. We were all super relieved when she threw herself into cosmetology school and dual-enrolled at the local university like Duke did; even if she was keeping ultrabusy just to avoid the pain of her grandmother's passing. But it all worked out perfectly. She wound up with so many credits, she graduated early and went straight to work doing what she loved. Her mentor took her under her wing and transferred forty years' of Key West's most loyal salon patrons to Dani when she retired.

Dani is my idol. She basically epitomizes *hustle*, and she's done it all her own way. I only hope I'll be half as cool as she is one day.

"I'm dying to see Dani's salon. Hey, there's my suitcase now! I'll grab it, and we can go," I say, but Duke grabs my bag off the carousel and throws it on his shoulder as Dad leads us to his old, banged up CJ-7 Jeep. I pat the dented metal of my dad's ancient, cool ride and jump in the back, where there is a Dr Pepper Cherry and a bag of tropical Skittles waiting for me—the same snack I've had on my way home from the airport since I was sitting in a booster seat between Duke and Dani.

We fly along the highway with the top down, our hair wild in our eyes, Creedence Clearwater Revival blasting on Dad's crackly speakers, the Florida sky bright as a scoop of rainbow sherbet. I stretch my lungs with long breaths of salty air and smile at Dani, who gives me a nearly identical smile back. When I hit my sixteen-year-old growth spurt, Dani and I started getting asked regularly if we were twins. I lean my head on her shoulder and breathe deep, the way Lilli did to me at the airport. My sister's sun-kissed skin smells like jasmine with a tangy hint of sea salt… I wonder how I smelled to Lilli.

"I'm sorry we missed your big end-of-the-year debate." Dani strokes my hair, working the tangles out without even realizing she's doing it. I close my eyes and let my big sister take care of me. "I know we're far away, but we're always rooting for you. You know that, right?" Her voice is quiet enough that the guys don't even hear us from their seats up front.

"Of course I know that. And, trust me, you didn't miss anything. I haven't thought about the debate once since the last day. I lost my prime position to some brownnosing trans-fer from St. Genevieve's, so I was basically a benchwarmer. Honestly, I just needed to stick with it for the season so I could slap it on my résumé. No big deal."

I spent so much time at debate club, so many hours wrapped up in something I couldn't care less about. I lost my spot to a transfer because the coach could tell my heart wasn't into it. Why did I devote so much time to something that I knew I had no interest in? Lex's words from the big end-of-the-year bash echo through my brain: *Do you actually like any of your twenty thousand after-school activities? Nah. You just like the shiny trophies and all those bullet points on your college résumé.*

"It really *is* a big deal." Dani, the perpetual sunshine-bringer of our family, sounds defeated. "I mean, you're nearly out of high school. So much is happening for you…and I feel like I miss most of it." It feels like every knot she undoes on my head transfers straight to my stomach. At moments like this, I realize exactly how much my dual life sucks. "You're so smart, and I know your mom is a great support, but when I was your age, I would have loved to have an older sister to lean on… Maybe I wouldn't have made so many mistakes."

"Mistakes?" I slide my arm around my sister, shocked when I see her brush tears away with trembling fingers. "Dani, you're, like, *perfect*. Like, you make me feel like I'm doing a shitty job as a big sister to my little sisters because I could *never* live up to you. You're always there for me. You have more drive than anyone I know. You're smart and talented and con-fident. I mean, look at everything you've achieved." For some reason, everything I'm saying to reassure her just makes her cry harder. Desperate to stop her tears, I joke, "You know,

Dad sent me the copy of *Key West's Entrepreneurs*. You were number one in the 'Thirty under Thirty,' *and* you looked like a total hottie on the cover."

She chokes out a tear-clogged laugh. "*Why* does he insist on showing that article to everyone? Ugh…look." She points to an over-the-seat pocket that holds multiple copies of the magazine with Dani's gorgeous face smiling on the cover, and we both howl with laughter. "I'm glad Dad's proud," Dani says, this time wiping tears of hilarity from her eyes, "but couldn't he be…more reserved about it?"

That makes us howl louder. Stephen Duke Beloise is many things, but reserved is definitely *not* one of them.

"What are you chuckleheads laughing about?" Dad asks when we pull in. He's smiling so wide, it's got to hurt his cheeks.

"Sister stuff, top secret," Dani says, then hugs me hard and whispers "I love you *so much*" into my ear.

We get out and straight gawk at the beautiful storefront with delicate scrollwork lettering and gorgeous lighting that makes the whole place feel warm and sparkly. Dani's place is called Time after Time Salon, which the *Key West's Entrepreneurs'* article informed me is a tribute to the song her mom and Dad danced to at their senior prom, the night Dad proposed. Dad and Allie—Dani and Duke's mother—were high-school sweethearts who got married really young. I know from the way Dad's face tightens when he talks about her that her death still hurts him badly. She got cancer when Duke and Dani were still really little, which is when Nan Sunny came in to help out, just before my mom and I burst in for a quick year or so, then disappeared. Or, at least Mom did.

I keep coming back every summer, trying to soak up all the love they pour on me.

Dani unlocks the doors and bustles in, flipping on more lights and holding her arms out as I look around. "So? What do you think?"

"The pictures did *not* do this place justice." I tilt my head back and twirl around, looking at the gorgeous ceiling tiles and glistening chandeliers. "We don't have anything like this in my hometown in Michigan. I haven't even seen anything this fancy in Grosse Pointe."

"Maybe I should open a salon there," Dani muses.

Dad fake shivers. "Baby, you've never felt a windchill of negative twenty before. You don't have a flamingo's chance in the Arctic of adjusting to that kind of weather."

"Twenty below? Below *zero*?" Duke pushes the hair out of his eyes to squint at me. "Is it really *that* cold where you live in Michigan?"

"They don't even close school unless it's twenty-*five* below in my district," I brag.

Duke's eyebrows shoot so high, they're completely hidden by his mass of curls. "I can't imagine you anywhere other than the beach."

"Our baby sister is made of tougher stuff than you think," Dani says. "For example, she's willing to cut off several inches of gorgeous hair; meanwhile, you're crying over two inches of that wild-beast mane."

"Fine. If Dell can deal with twenty-below-zero temperatures, I guess I can deal with looking like a hipster asshole." Duke plops in a chair, and Dani runs to snap a cape around his neck.

While the buzzers whir, I walk over to the wall behind the gleaming cherrywood reception desk. There are pictures— me and Dani on the beach in matching polka-dot bikinis; Bennie, her long-term sweetheart, and Dad out on a boat reeling in a giant swordfish; Duke, hair overlong, smiling from the hammock by the pool behind the house; a beautiful black-and-white shot of Nan Sunny when she was a high-school senior, next to a soft-color photo of Dani's mom from her senior year; and several of friends I don't recognize from the church we attend every Sunday, including a few with a cute little curly-haired boy. Dani nannied for a little while in high school. I bet this is the family she nannied for. Or maybe he's one of the many distant cousins I've heard about but can never put a name to at our big family reunions at the end of the summer.

"Are you sure you don't want to have your welcome-back party right away?" Dad hunkers down to look at the pictures, drawing the scratchy pads of his fingers over them softly.

"I want Gram and Pop to be there." My paternal grandma and stepgrandpa are on a cruise in Norway or something, but they'll be back in two weeks.

"They already said they don't mind," Dad wheedles.

I drape an arm around his waist and bury my head in the sleeve of his Belo's Bait and Tackle T-shirt, the cotton worn so soft, it feels like silk. "That's because you're a bully. You bullied them."

"Never," he insists, eyes crinkling at the edges from his smile.

"You just want an excuse for a party." I cross my arms, and Dad quirks an eyebrow.

"Are you accusing me of using my baby girl's homecoming as an excuse to drink gallons of sweet tea and eat fresh shrimp and dance all night with all our friends and family?" When I glare at him, he tilts his head back and bellows out a clear, loud laugh. "Guilty!"

Sometimes I wonder how my mother ever left my funny, charismatic, action-hero-handsome father for Peter. Not that Peter isn't fantastic, in his own nerdy way. He's just so quiet and brainy and…calm. Peter is definitely *not* the spontaneous life of the party my father is. Mom is also so outgoing and high-energy, it just seems like she and Dad should have worked. But maybe the old saying about opposites attracting is true after all.

"Dad, you really wear me out, but I love you anyway." I'm hoping to get a smile when I quote a line from one of my favorite childhood books, *Olivia*, which I used to make him read to me over and over again when he put me to sleep at night. Instead, his eyes well up and glisten. "Oh, Dad…"

He pulls me into a tight hug and says, "All kidding aside, you're growin' up so damn fast, Dell, and it's harder to deal with when we skip months between visits. One year I'm reading you that book about the funny pig every single night, and the next it's that spunky little Junie B., then Baby-Sitters Club graphic novels, then *actual literature* I never even bothered to read—all in a blink." He pulls back and pets my hair down. "I know I'm probably being sentimental, but this year feels big, ya know? You'll be off doing amazing things soon. Hell, next year you won't come down here at all. You'll be too busy packing on up for college."

If there's one thing that can throw me into an instant panic attack, it's thoughts of college. I can't wrap my head around a version of my life different from the exact way it's been these last seventeen years—school year in Michigan, summers in Florida. What will happen when I have summer jobs and internships I actually want? I can't give up my family in Florida, and my family in Michigan will expect so much from me… I have no clue how I'm going to keep the perfect balance, and the stress of it makes my stomach churn.

"Ahem." Dani interrupts Dad's melancholy and my full-blown panic attack, gesturing to the cape she's holding in front of Duke's face. When she whisks it away, we gasp.

"Hell, you're actually a good-lookin' dude under all that shaggy fur, son," Dad says around a laugh.

Duke rubs the bare back of his neck and shakes his head from side to side like he's testing the new, lighter weight. It's amazing what a good haircut can do. My older brother went from harried nerd to polished and confident adult in fifteen minutes. He cleans his glasses and shrugs at his reflection, but there's no way he's not happy with what's staring back. Even my clueless brother has to realize what a vast improvement Dani has made.

"I guess Dani's not a total hack," he says begrudgingly, yelping when she tosses the broom at him, hard.

"You are *literally* an artist." I run to get the spray cleaner and help Duke. "Duke looks like one of those guys who tries to lure you into buying lotion at the mall."

"That is *not* a compliment, Dell." Duke runs a hand over his short hair. "They are the most annoying people in the world. Worse than door-to-door knife salesmen. Worse than CrossFit fanatics…no, *vegan* CrossFit fanatics."

"Maybe, but they have great hair." I head to the chair when Dani intercepts.

"No, ma'am." Dani takes the bottle of cleaner out of my hand. "Duke is *happy* to clean up *by himself* while I cut your hair." Duke rolls his eyes as he sweeps his own shorn curls into a pile, and Dani gives him an approving nod, then turns her attention to our father. "Dad, don't you need to head to the shop?"

"Yeah, I probably better." Dad rubs a hand down his face. "I don't even want to look at the inventory sets, but I need to just swallow that damn frog."

"I'm sure Jude won't mind helping." Dani clips a cape around my neck with sure fingers, but I don't miss the worried frown reflected in the mirror, no matter how hard she tries to hide it from Dad. "And I'm more than happy to take a look at the books."

"Absolutely not." Dad's usually mellow voice is a little sharp, but my sister doesn't flinch. "You've got enough on your plate running your own business and keeping your own house. You don't need to be worrying about your old man, sweetie. I can handle it."

"Okay." Dani doesn't press, but she gives Dad a long stare. "But the offer stands. You need me, say the word, and I'm there."

Dad kisses her, then me, then claps Duke on the shoulder. "Mind helping your old man get some boxes unpacked when you're through here? This year's summer help has been real disappointing. I've never had so many kids quit with no explanation."

"They probably don't want to work under Commandant Zeigler," Duke breathes, and I snicker.

"Hey, now, c'mon. I know Jude can be a little intense, but he's been a real help around the place," Dad says.

"He's definitely worse than any vegan CrossFit fanatic. Oh my God, he probably *is* a vegan CrossFit fanatic. Even if he isn't, he's still *the worst*." My declaration is ruined when I accidentally suck in a strand of stray hair Dani's combed forward and have to gag it back out. "He acts like he's eighteen going on eighty. He's super condescending, thinks he knows everything… Last summer he told me that he *loves Excel*. Who in their right mind *loves Excel*?"

"He's told me the same thing. Damn, he's such a nerd… and that's a real burn coming from a nerd like me," Duke chimes in.

Dad looks at Duke the way he often does—like Duke is a foreign movie without subtitles he's trying his best to understand. Though Duke and my father could be clones looks-wise, they're about as different as two blood-related people can be in every other respect. It's like Duke is Sid Vicious's version of "My Way" and Dad is Frank Sinatra's… Same song, totally different vibe.

"You know, Dell, I think Jude rubs you raw because you kinda like him." Dad winks at my gasp of disgust. "He's a good-lookin' kid, good head on his shoulders. And I've seen him make eyes at you for the last two summers you've been down, at least. I think he just might have a thing for you."

"No! Ew. Absolutely not." As soon as I say it, I realize I *doth protest too much*. "I mean, Jude is *okay*. I don't hate him, obviously. How can you hate the human equivalent of a warm egg-salad sandwich?" Duke snickers at my Jepsen-girls inside joke, and I love the tiny way my two lives connect in that second. "But he definitely does not and never will have *a thing* for me. Unless bossing around the boss's daughter is his *thing*. Then, yes, he has a serious *thing* for me, and his *thing* caused me many, many hours of recounts on stock last summer. My nightmares are still filled with tiny rubber squids."

"Didn't you two do those restocks *together*? *Alone*?" Dani asks in a traitorously suggestive tone.

"Are you seriously siding with Dad on this?" I yelp, but Dani just paints the bleach on my hair, not bothering to hide her smile.

"Call me when you need a pickup." Duke puts his hands in front of his chest, prayer-style, and mouths *Save me, please*.

"We'll probably be about two hours." Dani waves them out with her hand. "Shoo. You boys have work to do, and Dell and I want to gab. Bye!"

"Jude has no interest in me that way." I wait until I hear Dad's Jeep start up to announce this, but I want to set the record straight as quickly as possible.

"You are *very* wrong," Dani says breezily as she mixes the dye and sits on the granite counter with that dopey grin on her face. "He's had a crush on you for *a while*."

It sucks that I'm trapped in this chair with product on my head, staring at my own face blushing in the mirror. "Jude is into work. *Work* is his crush."

"Jude is into Belo's because, yes, he has a good work ethic, which is admirable—but he also loves Dad. And he definitely amps up his hours when you're around." Dani raises her eyebrows suggestively.

"Dani, he amps up his hours because it's summer, so he has no school, *and* it's our busy season." I glare at her, but her smile only widens. "It has *nothing* to do with me at all. Plus, I have a boyfriend. Kind of."

At the mention of Lex, her smile flips upside down. "Luke?"

"Lex."

"I thought you two were on a break last summer."

"We were. We kind of do that…in the summer." The blush that just faded off my face is now trailing over my neck, rising up my cheeks, and singeing my ears.

"Hmm." Dani checks the timer and swallows back whatever she was about to say.

"What?"

"Nothing."

"I know you want to say something."

I wish I could get out of this chair and keep myself busy during this awkward-as-hell nonconversation, like Dani is doing right now. She straightens the receipts, wipes down every gleaming surface, and sweeps up nonexistent hair before she says, "I wish I could meet him, just to see if maybe there's something I'm missing. But I don't think I'm missing anything." She pins me with a long look. "Am I?"

"Lex is super smart. He's really funny. He's athletic. His parents and my parents have been friends for a really long time. We've been dating for a while now. Off and on." I pause. If I was in a technical debate, I'd lose against a slug in a coma with that halfhearted defense.

Dani supports herself with the broom, leaning to the side, her eyes dreamy. "Bennie lost a spelling bee on purpose in fifth grade so he could sit next to this girl in our class who was crying her eyes out after she got eliminated. Spoiler alert: that girl was me." Dani's smile is soft and sweet as newly spun taffy. "He dressed as the Beast this Halloween so he could escort his little cousin, who went as Belle. He comes in every single weekend to help Dad, and he refuses to take a single cent of pay. I've known him since grammar school, and even though he was always popular—captain of the baseball team, student-council president, prom king—the thing I love best about him is that he's so kind. His heart?" She curls her fingers into a heart shape and then pulls them super wide. "It's ridiculous how big his heart is. And *that* is why I am head over heels, crazy in love with Bennie Ortiz. I literally thank God every day that we went from friends to boyfriend and girlfriend two years ago. Now, tell me again…what am I missing about Lex?"

I open my mouth, then snap it shut. It's not fair to Lex that I don't have more to say. He is an amazing guy, a guy worth telling stories about. He's just not…he just doesn't feel like he's *mine*. Dani doesn't press for more details as she rinses the bleach out of my hair and puts on the pink dye. I'm grateful that she jumps to other topics.

"How is Marnie doing with volleyball? How is Lilli's singing going? How is your mother's blog? Peter's work?"

I answer each of her questions, and there's a tug in me because 1) I miss my family in Michigan and 2) I wish there was some way to bridge my two lives that wouldn't throw my entire world off-kilter. But the reality is that I can't be who I am here if I bring in too much of my life there, and vice versa. There's no single version of me that works in both places. Maybe that's fine, because there's no way my two families could really merge into one, no matter how much I wish that could happen.

Just when I'm reaching peak nostalgia about Mom, Peter, and my little sisters, I check my notifications, and that brings me right back down to Earth. I see that Marnie has posted another passive-aggressive, melancholy video to social media, whining about how sorry she feels for herself this summer and hinting that the blame lies with her cruel family. While I understand she's bummed, I have no patience for her whole woe-is-me shtick. Lilli put up a black-and-white shot of her bed, liner notes spread everywhere, her guitar in her lap with the caption Feeling kinda cute, might share a new song...<3. There are already thousands of likes and comments begging her to share, and though it really has nothing to do with me directly, panic floods through me on Lilli's behalf. I can't imagine how overwhelming it would feel to have that much attention—even positive attention—focused on my every move. Mom posted a link to a blog article she wrote titled "Preparing for the Empty Nest: Pitfalls to Avoid as the First Bird Spreads Their Wings." I guess I'm the *first bird*? Jesus, she's not wasting any time booting me out of the proverbial nest. I do a quick scan of the article and feel the usual jumble of emotions: pride over how awesome her writing is, the cringiness that always comes from reading about myself from her blogworthy peppy-mom perspective, and, mostly, a deep longing for her to take all these feelings she has about me and this transitional time and actually talk to me about them. Not in some sanitized, repostable way; just with the kind of honesty—and conflict—that Dani and I share during our talks. But that's just not how things work between me and my mother, and I imagine we'll only get more distant when I go wherever I'm headed for college. Peter is a social media black hole, and he's proud of it. But there *is* a text message from him with a link to the registration page for the internship he wants me to sign up for.

Sigh.

"Why the long face?" Dani asks as she rinses my hair.

"Do you ever feel totally overwhelmed by family stuff?" I ask, oldest sister to oldest sister.

She leads me back to the chair and starts making confident, dramatic cuts. I watch hunks of dark hair plop to the floor. "Yes and no. I've been the pain in the ass everyone is worried about before, and our family has given me a lot of grace, so I try to be patient when Dad and Duke frustrate me. For example, Dad is proud of being independent, sometimes to a fault. He needs to tell me *before* shit hits the fan, but he doesn't always do that because he's so sure he can figure everything out on his own."

"What's going on with Belo's?" I'm almost afraid to ask.

For a second Dani's frenzied pace slows down, and my hair stops flurrying all around me. "I'm not going to lie to you, Dell. Things are pretty bad. There are some huge online retailers who have really cut into our profits, plus a sporting chain store just opened fifteen minutes away. People from out of town don't even realize Belo's is here." She steadies herself and goes back to her lightning-fast cutting. "But Dad's getting help. He's working on a few angles. There are options, for sure."

"I can help," I offer.

"Of course you'll help," Dani says, squeezing my shoulder.

"But you're also here to enjoy your summer. Trust me, the time you have to be young and carefree goes by like this." She snaps the fingers on her free hand, and there's a sad knowing in her eyes. "Before you know it, the decisions you have to make are bigger than you're ready for, and they don't really seem to stop. I'm not complaining," she adds quickly. "I'm happy to have everything I have. Just...enjoy the time you have to be carefree."

It's an echo of what Mom said before I got on the plane, and I wonder what about Dani's life fills her with so much regret. Does she wish she'd gotten a degree somewhere other than the small local college ten minutes from the house we grew up in? Does she wish she hadn't started working so early or taken on so much business responsibility so soon? Is it Bennie? Great as he is, does she wish she'd dated more? I want to ask, but Dani's flipped on the hair dryer and is paying close attention to making my hair smooth and perfect. Between the blare of the dryer and her extreme concentration, I decide keeping my mouth shut is the best option.

"Ta-da!" Dani finally says, spinning me to face the mirror. "Okay, I'm glad you talked me into the bob. Look at those cheekbones."

She rests her chin on the top of my head, and we look so similar, especially since I did my makeup the way she taught me, that we could be mistaken for twins. My love for her presses my heart tight against my rib cage and makes me gasp for my next breath.

Dani's eyebrows furrow. "Do you hate it? I can totally do something diff—"

I hop off the chair so fast I leave it spinning and hug her

tight to me. "I love it. I love *you*. Thank you so much." When she wraps her arms around me, I feel sure everything will be okay. My shoulders relax, and my breathing slows—Dani is better for my mental health than the daily meditation app my mother made me download.

"I'm so, so glad you're here," she whispers.

Just then we hear a car door slam.

"That must be Duke." I grab the broom, but Dani, phone in her hand, smiles and grabs it back from me.

"Duke is still helping Dad with something and couldn't get away. Go ahead and open the door for me, will you?"

I don't trust my big sister's *look*—it's the look of someone *definitely* up to no good—and the second I see the rusty Jeep Comanche parked out front, the puzzle pieces lock into place. "Nope, I'll sweep."

I reach for the broom again, and Dani whips it around and swats me on the butt with the bristles. "Get! He came to pick us up because he heard you were here."

"I didn't ask for that!" I hiss, but I head to the door and swing it open. "Hey, Jude." I force a smile. "You really didn't have to come out. We could have waited."

"I'm happy to help."

My childhood archnemesis's voice is deeper than I remember. The scraggly mustache he tried too hard to pull off last summer has been replaced by a very attractive five-o'clock shadow that dots his wide jaw and killer cheekbones. He's buzzed his dark hair close, and it gives him an edgy look that's at odds with his brown, thick-lashed doe eyes. He wears his usual uniform—a faded Belo's T-shirt and tattered cargo shorts, threadbare Chuck Taylors, and a silver St. Christopher medallion that I've never seen him without.

Jude Zeigler leapfrogged from decent-looking to straight hottie over the course of a single year, which is yet another thing I hate about my life divide. If I'd been able to watch his slow metamorphosis from boy to man, I would have been able to build up a resistance. As it is, the mix of shock and my purely chemical reaction to the *serious* pheromones he's putting off means I'm thinking very anti-archnemesis things about Jude Zeigler and how he might look with his shirt off.

"Isn't there a lot to do at Belo's?" I ask because work is and always has been our default common ground.

He sticks his hands in his pockets, and I notice the bulge of his forearms—have I ever noticed anyone's forearms before? "My shift was actually over a few hours ago. I hung around because I knew Belo was picking you up from the airport today, and I didn't want him to have to shut down the store. He's been excited about you coming home for weeks." There's a long, slightly awkward pause. "So…how was your flight?"

"Uneventful, thank you."

He nods. "Uneventful is good when it comes to plane flights. Did you get those cookies? The ones in the red package? I can't remember which airline gives them out, but I think they're the best part about flying."

I hold up a finger and grab my purse from the hook near the door, rifle around, and pull out a pack of Biscoff cookies. "These?"

"Hey, that's them." He puts one hand out like he's going to take them, then seems to second-guess if I'm offering and gives me an awkward thumbs-up instead.

I roll my eyes. "Take them. The flight attendant gave me an extra packet."

He looks at his thumb like it's an alien digit, then takes the cookies, staring at the wrapper like the ingredients are the most fascinating thing he's ever read in his life. Maybe they are. This *is* Jude we're talking about. Hot or not, he's kind of a snooze.

"Thanks a lot." He tucks the cookies in his pocket and nods over his shoulder. "Is Dani ready? Should we head out?"

"Let me check." I'm so relieved to break through the awkward tension in the lobby, I practically sprint to the back. "Dani, Jude's ready to take us home."

"Oooh." Dani's eyes are innocent, but I can see the sly smile curling on her lips. "Change of plans. I forgot it's Bennie's sister's birthday. We're going to swing by to have cake, but I'll be at the house later, of course. You should go ahead, get settled."

"I don't believe you." I cross my arms, and she holds her phone up—not *too* close but close enough that I can see Bennie's text, which says *Can't wait 2 c u!* "That's not evidence, Dani. He could have sent that for a million different reasons. You're trying to play matchmaker, aren't you?"

Dani presses a hand to her heart. "*Me?* Never." She winks. "Get going. You wouldn't want to be driving down the highway in the moonlight on a warm summer night... You might fall in love with Jude Zeigler."

I snort. "That's like falling in love with a really attractive algebra book. Not gonna happen. Jude is definitely a Grade A hottie, but... What?" I register Dani's widened eyes and my stomach plummets. I don't have to turn around to know he's standing there. "Hey, Jude. Um, ready to go?" I turn very slowly, expecting him to be annoyed, but he actually looks amused.

"Sure. Let me just get my exponents and radicals in order, and we can jet."

"About that… I actually really love algebra, so…" I turn and level my evilest glare at Dani, who looks like butter wouldn't melt in her traitor mouth. "I'm sorry. That was… I was just being an asshole. Sorry."

He shrugs. "No worries. I love algebra, too." He pauses, and I'm sure he's going to rag on me about the *Grade A hottie* thing, but Jude has always had really good manners (like a proper gentleman), and he just tells Dani good-bye and lets us know he's going to wait in his truck.

"Look what you did!" I growl, but Dani obviously doesn't feel an ounce of remorse. In fact, she's cracking up at my distress.

"You two would be so cute together. But if you don't feel it, just accept the ride and let it lie. Jude is way too much of a good guy to bring up what he overheard." Dani waves her hand. "Shoo, gorgeous."

I give her a reluctant good-bye hug and wonder if I can just call a Lyft and text Jude that I'm fine to get home on my own. But I decide making a perfectly nice—if boring—guy come all this way for nothing would be ridiculous. Sure, it's a little awkward—thanks to my big mouth—but I've dealt with more embarrassing things before. I can handle this.

5

June

FLORIDA

The interior of Jude's ancient truck smells like sunblock with an undertone of fish. We buckle up, and Jude gestures to the radio.

"Lady's pick," he says with this old-time gallantry that's surprisingly charming.

I turn the dial to a local station that plays classic rock, figuring that's a safe bet for Jude. I always listen to it with Dad when we go on long drives to find secret fishing holes. The first song is "Free Fallin'" by Tom Petty and the Heartbreakers.

"This is a great song," Jude says, and, with zero hesitation, he busts out singing as we pull onto the highway.

At first I'm so stunned by Jude's total lack of embarrassment about going all karaoke-superstar in front of me, I stare, slack-jawed. But "Free Fallin'" is a really awesome song to sing along to when you're driving, and even though I'd never belt a song out in front of Lex (Lilli is right—my voice is pretty bullfroggish, and Lex would definitely beg me to stop if I

THE FLIPSIDE OF PERFECT • 87

sang along to the radio), I join in with Jude, who gives me an encouraging nod at my first croak. "That's it! Sing it, Dell!"

Soon we're both howling along, windows down, wind whipping through the cab of the truck, perfect Florida summer air flooding in around us, and it feels unexpectedly excellent.

I don't know all the words to the next song, but we're on a roll now, so I sing the chorus and backup vocals and dance along in my seat when I'm not sure about the lyrics. Jude's voice is a rich, deep baritone that Lilli would approve of, and I find myself just a little bit swoony over it. Our carpool karaoke goes on for four more songs, until we finally pull up at my Florida house.

He cuts the engine just as John Mellencamp finishes singing about Jack and Diane, and we both sit in silence, looking at the house where Mom and Dad brought me home from Lower Keys Medical Center when I was a newborn and where I spent every subsequent night until I was around one. What would it have been like to grow up with both of my biological parents, Dani, and Duke in this pale green bungalow, with the enormous windows, right by the ocean? What would life have been like to have only been the baby of the Beloise family—or, weirder yet, the middle child of the Beloise family?

"Belo said he and Duke were going to be back by eight," Jude announces. The cracked clock on his dashboard reads seven thirty.

"I have a key, of course. I'm fine. Thank you for the ride." I should get out. This is my house; it's not like I'm creeped out or nervous. But the house isn't really home without my father standing in the kitchen, making me welcome-home pancakes while Duke and Dani shuffle the monster stack of Uno cards at the granite counter.

"Do you mind if I wait until they get here?" Jude turns his soft, dark gaze on me, and I feel a twisting creep in the pit of my stomach, like a vine is taking root and unfurling all through my chest. "I know you can take care of yourself, but Belo thought you and Dani were both coming home. I think it would bum him out if he knew I dropped you off at an empty house your first day back, you know?"

Jude's being diplomatic. Like Peter. The vine blossoms, and I hear myself saying, "Sure. Do you want to wait on the porch? If we go around the side, we can catch the sunset."

"That'd be cool."

As soon as we're sitting on the porch swing, so close I can smell the clean, salty scent of his skin, I wish I'd suggested we stay in the truck and turn the radio back on, keep singing along to old songs. Now we have to fill the quiet with inane small talk that will most likely turn to bickering. Sure, Jude is hotter than I remember and maybe even nicer—but he and I are very different and have never gotten along. It's only a matter of time before one of us says something that rubs the other one the wrong way.

"Did you have a good flight?" he asks.

"You already asked me that." I don't mean the words to hit as bluntly as they do.

"Oh, yeah, the cookies." He pulls the packet out of his pocket and opens them, offering me one. "Sorry. It's been a long day. Want to share?"

I don't want to eat a dry cookie without a drink, so I get up and head into the kitchen, breathing the perfect, familiar scent—lemon and sunshine and heady jasmine that grows under the windows—and grab two glasses of sweet tea from the pitcher that's always full in the fridge.

When I come back, Jude looks surprised to see me, like maybe he thought I ditched him. I hand him a glass, and after he thanks me, we chew on the spicy-sweet cookies and drink the ice-cold sweet tea as the sun glides lower and glows brighter, like it wants to show off in these last few minutes before it's replaced by the moon. There's no reason to fill the easy quiet with small talk, and we probably could have sat in companionable silence until my dad and siblings came home, except...

"Jude, you'd be brutally honest with me if I asked you something, right?"

He puts down his glass and turns to look me dead in the eye. "Yes."

I take a deep breath and hold it for a few long seconds, then exhale and ask in a rush, "What's happening at Belo's?"

Jude's eyes flick to the side, but he forces himself to look back at me. "Honestly? I don't know all the behind-the-scenes details, but from what I can tell? Things aren't great."

"Why not?"

"Inventory's been sitting on the shelf for so long, I've had to make major adjustments to the ordering schedules, especially for live bait. We don't have enough work for the number of part-timers we usually hire, which is actually kind of a relief because we also don't have the payroll to keep them on. The last two summers were pretty bad, but ever since they opened that sporting goods store in Marathon, it's gotten even worse." Jude reaches out and pats my hand, which, I realize, is shaking.

"My great-grandfather opened that bait shop." I put my clammy fingers to my forehead to steady the spin in my brain. "My family has owned Belo's for generations. There has to be something we can do. I can't even imagine my family without Belo's."

He's still patting my free hand gently like a little nervous grandpa. "Maybe I'm just being a pessimist. Dani gave Belo the number for some financial guys. He's thinking about re-branding, maybe getting more active on social media? I don't know if that will help—"

"Of course it will help!" I don't mean to snap, but I know my dad, and urgency isn't his thing. Dani would have bull-dozed through to help him more, but he's clearly not telling her the whole story, plus she has her salon to worry about. Duke has always been perfectly clear about the fact that he does *not* want to join the family business and would, instead, like to dig up boring historical stuff and spend all day cata-loging it in some dusty office at an ancient university.

But *I'm* here now. And I'm in full-debate mode, laying out my argument and formulating a plan like AJ would. I'm swinging my arms around. I'm banging my fist against my palm like it's a gavel. I'm on fire to fix things in the one place where I've never had to fix anything before.

"People want authenticity. They want to shop local, they want the little guy to survive. We just need to spread the word, get customers in and talking about Belo's. We need to make sure we don't go down without a fight." I'm pacing fast, expecting Jude to toss around some ideas or maybe just hype me up the way Lex would, but he watches, wide-eyed, and listens. This is atypical Della behavior. The Della Jude knows loves lounging on the roof during lunch breaks, flirting with cute customers, and going on long runs to pick up coffee or lunch for everyone. That Della is a blast, but she's useless right now. "There's a way through this. I can help get Dad back on track. We need to start with a plan... Promotions and giveaways, a hashtag, a redesign of the logo—we'll go back to the original, like they did on *Parks and Rec*. Vintage is where it's at."

I glance at Jude, waiting for him to chime in or at least agree. Belo's means a lot to him, too. My dad took Jude under his wing years ago, and he's been essential to Belo's since. Jude and my father are similar in so many ways—their stubbornness, their drive, their love of the outdoors and salt life—but they're different enough that they balance each other out. Jude is introspective and contemplative where my dad is extroverted and action-oriented, which makes them a good team when it comes to running the store.

"I think it's so great you have all this...passion. It's amazing. I'm kind of surprised, just because you didn't seem that interested before," Jude begins carefully, and my hackles are already up. "Just...turning things around at Belo's may not be a quick fix, you know?"

"I'm sorry, did you forget I'm Belo's *daughter*? I'm in this for the long haul, whether I like it or not." Out of the corner of my eye, I see the sun splashing around its gaudiest golds and creamy oranges, but neither of us pays the spectacle any attention. "Do you think I just pop in every summer to play

Malibu Barbie, then skip back to Michigan and forget all about this place?"

"Not at all," Jude answers, his voice quiet. "I just know… Belo said you might have things going on this summer, and next summer you'll go to college, so he didn't want you to get caught up in all of it."

The fact that my dad talked to Jude about me but left me out of the loop about Belo's really stings. In Michigan everyone takes me so seriously, and there's so much expected of me, it's overwhelming; here I'm completely expendable, as fleeting as a summer tourist, and no one seems to think I can handle anything more serious than a new haircut and a neighborhood block party.

"Does my dad think I'm just—what?—going to evaporate once I start college?"

"I think he's trying to be realistic about how much you'll be around."

"I'm not just going to abandon everyone here!" I protest.

"No one thinks that." He squints at me. "But you'll be gone for college. Taking classes, traveling, meeting people. Do you really think you're going to want to keep coming here all summer, every summer?"

"This isn't just some fun vacation spot for me." I close my eyes tight as Mom's and Dani's warnings mingle in my head, twisted together. "This is my *home*. I'd always choose to come here. It's not a waste of my time."

"I know this is your home, and I know you like coming here." He cocks one eyebrow, and his look is pure condescension. "But there's no denying it's kind of a waste of your time."

"What's that supposed to mean?"

"Belo said your mom called him about this once-in-a-lifetime internship. She told him they had, like, thousands of applicants, but your proposal was chosen."

"My mom called Dad?" I'm embarrassed when Jude looks at me curiously, like it never occurred to him that my parents' talking would be such a surprise to me. I bet Jude's parents are straight out of some 1950s family sitcom, with Jude lapping up their attention, a perfect little worker-bee son. "I wish she'd stop butting in."

"You're lucky to have parents who care enough to butt in."

"I don't need another lecture from you on how ungrateful I am, okay?" I snap. "This isn't work. You're not in charge of me here. Actually, you have no idea what you're talking about right now, so maybe *you* should butt out."

"Fair enough." He clears his throat. "But if you want an outside opinion, you should think about taking the internship or traveling or whatever. We've got it handled here, and it's not something you need to waste your summer worrying about."

He's exceptionally handsome. It's a shame he's also such an ass.

"Jude, if my father needs help, he can count on me. No matter how much you think you get it, there's no way a seasonal, hourly worker can really understand what it means to be part of a family business that spans four generations." My word daggers hit their mark. Jude rubs his breastplate like my digs were slingshot rocks aimed at his heart, and I steel myself against the jabs of guilt I already feel. "Please do *not* assume you know what is and isn't a waste of my time." I hear the crunch of Dad's tires on the driveway, and relief floods through me. "Thanks for the ride and for hanging here with me, but my family's here now. I'm sure you need to get home."

I stare him down. He opens his mouth like he wants to say something else. Then he shuts it again, nods, and says, "I'm really sorry if I overstepped, Dell. I just… I don't want you to think I'd leave your dad high and dry. I've got his back, always. I love your family."

His words are a thousand times kinder than mine, but I feel just as miserable as he looks.

Instead of walking around the porch and using the steps, Jude leaps over the railing and lands easily in the sandy soil below. I hear him greet my dad and Duke, then the headlights of his Comanche cut across the yard for a split second, and he's gone.

"Hell, will you look at that sunset." Dad takes a seat next to me, and I cuddle against his side, loving the feel of his arm draped over my shoulders. "Too bad Jude didn't accept my offer of pancakes."

Of course he didn't. Jude wouldn't try to insert himself where he wasn't wanted. I feel another pinch of guilt, but I force it back down. Jude's a local. He has tons of friends and family to go see. Having to drive out here and babysit me was probably the last thing he wanted to do tonight. I didn't push him away—I gave him a good excuse to run far from my family's drama for the night.

At least, I tell myself all of that is the truth.

"Come on in, bugbite, let's shuffle the Uno cards before Dani gets here," Duke says, calling me by his old nickname for me like he always does. It's an annoying little-sister nickname, not a nickname for an older sister who gets shit done. Marnie calls me General Buzzkill when she's pissed that I'm ragging on her, and Lilli started calling me the BBS, Big Bossy Sister, after her Roald Dahl phase. Sure, they're negative nicknames, but they command a certain amount of grudging respect.

I've always appreciated how little responsibility I had as Della, but now I realize it's always been a double-edged sword. No one will take me seriously here unless I pull an AJ.

I just wish forcing my two worlds to collide didn't fill me with so much anxiety.

6

Perfect Opportunity

Last Autumn
BioLive Technology Laboratory
Chief Adviser: Peter Jepsen, PhD

MICHIGAN

If there's some kind of formula for the perfect day, it would definitely include the crisp gold and crimson of autumn leaves, a piping-hot latte sweetened with loads of sugar and topped with extra foam, and a field trip—the quintessential educational excuse to skip another grueling day of school.

"I'm definitely not looking forward to Huang's bullshit-project assignment." Lex hands me the latte he stopped to grab me before we get on the bus and head to the STEM center at Peter's job site. He slips an arm around my waist, letting his hand drop to cup my ass after a few seconds. "But this? A little jailbreak with the most gorgeous girl at St. Matthew's? *This* is nice."

I pivot away from him and shake my head. "You know Huang will take away points if he witnesses any PDA. And don't think for a second I'm sneaking off to fool around with you just because you called me *gorgeous*." I make sure to add an extra blade's edge of disdain to the last word.

"What?" He stretches out his arms, mock-innocently, and throws back a gulp of scorching hot black coffee as he eyes me over the lip of the cup. "What's wrong with *gorgeous*? Is this some kind of feminist thing?"

"You told that guy walking his boxer that his dog was *gorgeous* this weekend. I'm not some moronic freshman hanging on your every word like Julia Tran. If you want to impress me, you need to increase your vocabulary or use the limited words you know more carefully."

Lex isn't remotely offended. In fact, when I act like an ass-hole, it seems to turn him on. He tugs me to the side, behind a tree, and kisses along my neck under my cashmere scarf while Huang starts herding students onto the bus. Lex's lips feel good skimming my sensitive skin. I lean back against the tree as half the class stampedes to get choice seats.

"C'mon, let's go. Unlike you, I don't get my rocks off making Huang's blood pressure rise." I take his hand, and, though I try to drag him as fast as I can, we're still the last two on the bus. He immediately goes in for another nuzzle, and I push him away. "No."

"Did I do something to piss you off?" he asks with the kind of confidence in his own charm that only a guy as handsome and effortlessly magnetic as my sometimes-boyfriend can afford to be. "I'm sure I can make it better." He goes in for another kiss, and I practically shove him off the vinyl bus seat.

"I know this will probably blow your mind, but sometimes I just don't want you pawing at me. *Full stop.*"

"My pea brain probably won't be able to grasp it, but try—for my sake—to explain what exactly is making me so ig-norable today."

"Other than your out-of-control ego and your rank coffee breath?" There are times when I feel like our banter verges on verbal abuse. I'd never admit it to him, but sometimes it makes me sad how Lex and I bring out the absolute worst in each other.

His laugh draws the instant attention of half the bus. "My God, it's *crazy* how sexy you are when you're ruthless. Seriously, though." He switches gears like a very experienced actor who was joking with the crew right up until the moment when the director yells *Action!* "What's bugging you?" The way his eyebrows crush down and his lips pull in a concerned frown are so convincingly sweet, I *almost* buy it. Almost.

Lex Henson is a master charlatan.

"It's the internship," I whisper. I shouldn't need to whisper, since we're on a noisy bus, sitting practically on each other's laps, and speaking low; but I don't trust any of these nerds as far as I could throw their puny asses.

"The internship?" He looks as bored as I'd expected him to be. If Lex decided he wanted this internship, he'd have it with a single bat of his overlong lashes. Lex is the kind of guy who effortlessly gets everything he wants, and I long ago gave up being frustrated by his never-ending streak of good fortune. Maybe that's why it's such a thrill to constantly shoot him down.

"Peter wants me to take it." I can't keep the misery out of my voice. "It's a few weeks this summer of lab work, tests, and fieldwork, working one-on-one with some of the best scientists in the field… It's an amazing opportunity."

"Sounds like it's probably up your egghead alley. Take it."

"I don't think I actually *want* it."

"Jesus. Then don't take it, AJ." Lex closes his eyes and leans his head back on the seat. His short, glossy brown hair rubs against the pleather and makes a subtle swishing noise.

"But I feel like I *should*. I had a really good idea, and I'd learn so much. Plus Peter will be disappointed if I turn this down. And if my mom gets involved, it's going to be a fight."

"You know that's normal, right?" Lex lives for fights with his parents. If he could record them for Pay-per-view, he would in a second.

"Maybe for you."

"For teenagers everywhere. AJ, you make me feel like a failure. What a waste of all the hours I've put into trying to corrupt you."

"Peter will be there today, ready to show me around." I wring my hands and feel a cold sweat break out on the back of my neck. "It's too much pressure. I feel like I'm going to puke."

"Here, puke in this if you have to." Lex hands me the paper bag from the coffee shop. "Why do you get yourself so worked up? You know you don't have to do this. There are options."

"What options do I have? We're on the bus, on the way to the lab." I open the paper bag and breathe into it slowly and steadily. It's a routine I've fallen back on dozens of times before, and the crinkle and whoosh of the expanding and contracting paper is strangely comforting. Mom has lectured me about how it's been scientifically proven that using a paper bag is ineffective and simple breathing exercises are a better coping mechanism, but I prefer to stick with what works for me. I also just get a thrill from ignoring her advice sometimes. "Be a total asshole," Lex suggests. "Or ditch. We'll smoke and drink and take the car out without permission. We can have some sex, listen to some rock and roll. It'll be a banner day of *not* doing exactly what's expected of you for once. C'mon, it'll be fun."

"Peter would be so disappointed."

"You're always worried about who's mad at you or disappointed in you—"

"Except you. I don't care if you're mad at me," I interrupt, leaning my head on his shoulder.

Lex kisses my ear. "Even that. I think you're a jerk to me because you know how much I love it. I don't want to admit it, but I think you might actually be...*nice*." He fake shudders. "Face it. You're a people pleaser, and that means you sometimes wind up doing crap you don't want to do when you should learn the most important word in all of feminism."

"What word is that?" I ask, wondering if I can guess.

I can.

"It's *no*," Lex says with a naivety that's so cute, I'd pinch his cheek if he had a quarter ounce of body fat anywhere on him.

"So easy for you to say," I groan. "I've told you *no* literally a dozen times today, and you haven't listened once."

Lex rolls his gorgeous eyes. "Well, whatever you decide, you'd better do it fast. We're here."

The bus screeches to a halt, and I see Peter in front of the building, trying his best to look nonchalant, but his eyes are zeroing in on the bus windows, searching for me.

Lex keeps his hand at the small of my back as we shuffle off the bus. "Stand your ground," he whispers. "Think about what *you* want for once."

"Hey, ace!" Peter waves me down and gestures for me to come over. I try to drag Lex with me, but he chuckles.

"Hard pass. I'm going to find a couch in one of the lobbies to take a nap on. Huang can't keep track of all of us." Lex squeezes my hip and walks in the opposite direction with the kind of confidence that stops anyone from approaching and asking him where he's going.

"Hey, Dad." I smile politely at his coworkers, who all look a little overeager to meet me. I shake hands and laugh obligingly at the *She'll be our boss soon* jokes. I introduce Mr. Huang to Dad, and my knowing such impressive (to nerds) people actually gets Huang to crack a very stiff smile and insist I should tour with my dad and meet up with the rest of the group for lunch.

Peter puts an arm around me and leads me to the labs where I've popped in with Mom, Lilli, and Marnie once in a while before we get lunch together or if we need to drop something off. I've never been here as a candidate for an internship, though.

"Let me show you around." Peter and I are both into science, so he's definitely pinned it on me to carry on his legacy. BioLive is a huge think tank/lab and Peter basically runs the place, so it's only natural he'd want me to take one of the prestigious internship positions.

We're looking at an amazing water-purifying system that uses hydraulic soil and shoreline plant-root systems, and Peter is gleefully telling his coworkers that my saltwater version is going to work even better once we work out any kinks in the prototype. Their reaction is genuinely positive, and it's that sense of excitement that makes me want to work with these brilliant, bold people. If I didn't have to choose losing out on seeing my family in Florida to do it, I wouldn't hesitate to take this internship.

I hold on to that thought, and it helps me gather the courage to air some of my objections to Peter once his coworkers disperse. "Dad, I love BioLive. They do amazing stuff. But I'm your kid. Don't you think it will look fishy if I get one of the spots?"

Peter gestures for me to sit on one of the curved metal stools by a stainless-steel counter. He takes off his glasses and rubs each lens carefully. "The committee that considers internship applications has nothing to do with me or my department. Every application comes to them coded anonymously, and the best ideas are actually discussed via teleconference with representatives at our other branches around the country. Even if I did something underhanded to move your idea to the top of the pile—which I didn't—it had to be strong enough to go through multiple rounds of committee deliberations." He puts his glasses on and beams at me, shaking me back and forth by my shoulder. "Your prototype for the organic mobile ocean-filtration systems really intrigued the teams. They loved how you incorporated the mussels and oysters with the sea-sponge and algae growth."

"I'm not sure it will work." I love that Peter has so much faith in me, but my idea is just that—an idea based on a lot of periodical-based research hinged on something my dad always joked about. *Shouldn't like oysters as much as I do. They're the garbage disposals of the ocean. Actually feel pretty guilty eating these little guys after they worked so hard keeping the water so nice and clean.*

My design idea also grew from my dad's annoyance with a few local sport-fishing companies that were fattening up farmed fish and releasing them for unsuspecting tourists so they had better chances of ostensibly catching a big one in the wild. Dad said they might as well have underwater cages full of fish and just spring them when a guy wanted a big trophy to brag about—and that made my imagination go wild.

"That's the beauty of a prototype! You come here, and a bunch of other scientists will test possible designs until the whole thing is bulletproof. Honestly? I made it a point not to peek at what you were submitting, and I didn't ask the committee while they were processing. When Kalpana came and told me you'd won a spot, I had her show me your submission. It's brilliant."

"Thanks, Dad. And I get why it's such an incredible opportunity. It's just, the timing…" I trail off, unsure how Peter will respond to this particular issue since we never bring it up in our house.

He claps his hand on my shoulder. "Hey, I get it. You don't get much time with your family in Florida. It must be really frustrating. I'm so happy you've had these summers to visit. And I understand if you're not ready to give that up yet. But you're a junior in high school. Next summer you'll be packing up to go to college, and, after that, you won't see any of us as much anymore. This might be a good way to test the waters."

My mouth is dry, and my palms are clammy. Peter is right, and what he's saying is obvious. I've just been blocking it out of my mind for so long, hearing it spoken out loud like it's no big deal throws me off-kilter. I'm *not* ready. I'm not ready to give up my summers with Dad, Dani, and Duke. I'm not ready to give up seeing the ocean every day, playing cards with my older siblings, and watching the sunset on a boat with my dad while he tells me funny stories about people he's met and adventures he's had in the wild. I savor every second with them, and the summer always slips by like the sand in a timer during a game of charades. Now I have to face that, after this summer, that's it. When will I ever get to see them? Not knowing the answer to that question floods me with immediate panic.

Will I ever be able to celebrate my achievements with my *whole* family? I want them *all* there for my high-school and college graduations. What about if I get engaged, married, have kids? It's almost unthinkable that I've managed so many years without my two worlds colliding, but what's the answer now, moving forward?

All I know is, as amazing as BioLive is, I don't want to give up a single day with my family in Florida. Maybe it's childish of me to refuse to face the future, but it's what I want, at least for this summer.

Think about what you want for once.

Lex's words echo in my ears.

I look at Peter.

I just need to tell him.

No big deal.

Just say it.

Say, *I appreciate the opportunity, but I can't accept it right now.*

Say, *This entire project was dreamed up because I was still so homesick for Florida weeks after I got off the plane in Detroit.*

Say, *If I'm going to test this out, I want to talk to the people who love and live with those waters every day of their lives, not some sci-*

entists in a lab who have probably never seen a body of water bigger than Lake Superior.

I open my mouth and say, "I'll think about it."

I tell Peter I'm going to rejoin the tour after lunch, give him a hug, and stalk off to find Lex. He is, as he promised he'd be, napping on a couch in a quiet lobby area.

"Lex?" I shake his shoulder, and he wakes up with a start, his bed head so attractive it looks like he did his hair that way on purpose.

"Hey. So, are you officially future Little Miss Science Geek, or did you tell those nerds you weren't interested?" He rubs his eyes and wipes the drool off the side of his face without any embarrassment. Lex is well aware that he always looks amazing, even drooly.

"I didn't completely chicken out." I hang my head, and Lex stands and puts his arm around my shoulders.

"The old *I'll think about it*?" He chuckles when I grimace at how easily he called my bluff. "Look, you know your problem now is that you've got to dodge the conversation every time he brings it up…and your dad geeks out about science stuff as hard as you do, so that's gonna be a lot. My advice?"

He waits, and I finally sigh. "I can't believe I'm taking advice from someone with such a faulty moral compass."

"Which is a great lead-in for my advice, thank you very much. Pick a reason you're saying no… Maybe you'd miss your usual nerd camp too much this summer, maybe you want to try a camp with poor supervision and loose structure like I'm going to—"

"You'd want me to go to camp with you?" I'm honestly

just joking with him, but when I see the appalled look in his eyes, I wish I'd kept my mouth shut. "I'm *kidding*, Lex."

His relief is so intense, it's insulting. "I mean, you know you're the best. But, c'mon, seriously? You and I have a pretty different idea of what constitutes fun. So, like I was saying, say all your friends are expecting you at nerd camp or whatever…"

Lex keeps going, telling me to just hammer out one excuse over and over, never deviating or adding anything in. The weird thing is, he keeps talking about me going to camp like he's sure that's what I do every summer, even though he's never explicitly asked, and I've never told him any details about what I do every year. I kind of just let him and my friends assume I'm doing something academic and résumé-enhancing. It's not at all hard to believe. That would be classic AJ.

"The bottom line is, you've got to do what you want to do, you know? You can't let everyone else make the big decisions for you. That's a recipe for misery. You're smart." He pauses. "What was your winning proposal, anyway?"

I explain about the mobile cages equipped with ocean life and vegetation that can aggressively filter an area, then be moved to do the work again somewhere else.

"Damn. That's a really good idea. Would it work?" he asks.

"The internship was supposed to help me figure that out. Do you get why I'm conflicted? This could be incredible. What if I don't do it, and I lose out on helping, like, take this huge step forward for ecology?"

He kisses me softly, laughing at me right against my own face. "I know this probably never occurred to you, but no one's actually expecting you to single-handedly solve the world's environmental crisis before you graduate high school. I know you're an overachiever, but damn, this is intense even for you."

"What if I don't take this internship, and this idea goes nowhere? That's some heavy guilt to have on my shoulders." Guilt that, I'm fairly sure, will fade when I get to Florida and relax into a life that's so much less intense and driven than my life here.

"Remember when we had to watch that documentary in Rahn's class last year about the electric car and how Big Oil basically killed it before it could go into production?" I nod, and he says, "Good ideas go nowhere all the time. I don't want to shit on your Save the Environment with a Single Internship parade, but if this internship doesn't happen, you'll probably do some pretty kick-ass shit when you get into college and get a job. Honestly, this is our last summer before things are going to change, big-time. I get not wanting to give that up."

"That's actually really helpful advice." I can't keep the wonder out of my voice. "Thank you. Seriously, I feel…" What do I feel? Not exactly better—there's still too much to wrestle with and think through—but maybe like every little tiny decision isn't on my shoulders all the time.

"Hungry?" Lex's stomach growls loud enough to make us both laugh. "Ugh, I think they're serving some tofu travesty down there."

A very un-AJ-like thought curls into my head and leaps out of my throat before I can second-guess it. "Huang thinks I'm going to be with Peter for the rest of the day. Peter thinks I'm with the class. We could call a Lyft…"

"There's a killer taco place ten minutes away from here." Lex's eyes light up with a semievil gleam. He loves breaking the rules, and I think I just made the thrill all the sweeter by initiating this adventure.

I take his hand and a deep breath. "Let's do it."

Lex pulls me close and kisses me on the lips right in the middle of the lobby. "Well, it's not exactly sex, drugs, and rock and roll, but forbidden tacos are a pretty good start for teenage rebellion. My corrupting influence is actually starting to pay off."

7

Good Sister, Bad Sister

Late June
Work Crew: Belo's Bait and Tackle

FLORIDA

"I'm not saying working a grunt job is without merit." Mom's voice, on speakerphone in my Jeep, is interrupting my carefully curated drive-to-work mix. I'm giving up precious time with Lizzo to hear another lecture about how I'm wasting the opportunities of my youth. "It's great to see how hard so many people in this country have to work. But you did this work for the last four summers. You need to spread your wings a little."

"Is that Lilli?" It's a dodge, but a necessary one. If I don't get off the line with my mother and get a chance to mellow out with John Legend, this workday is going to be super stressful. Once I'm in Belo's, it's old-school country music, picked by my father, and it plays nonstop whether he's in the building or not. I love him, but our music preferences definitely do not align, and there are only so many steel-guitar solos I can grit my teeth through during a shift. "How is she doing?"

Mom's voice drops. "You know your baby sister. She's a

workhorse, and she never lets her smile slip. But I think the stress might be getting to her. I got up to get some water at three, and she was still wide-awake, writing music by moonlight on the hotel balcony. I know it sounds romantic, but she's going to be a walking zombie. She needs to get her sleep."

Lilli and I have three years between us. Mom said I told my day care teachers all about my baby every single morning in the months leading up to Lilli's birth. Apparently I cried like my heart would break when Mom told me there was *definitely* no way I could bring her in for show-and-tell.

Maybe I was too young to grasp the whole *You're going to be a big sister* thing when Mom was pregnant with Marnie, or maybe Marnie and I have been so different since our infancies that we just never developed a particularly sweet sister relationship—but I completely *adored* Lilli from the second they brought her home, wrapped in a pink flannel blanket with gray swans on it. She still keeps that blanket—named Swanny—tucked under her pillow every night. Lilli is strong and smart and crazy talented—but she's still just a little kid in so many ways.

"Poor Lilli. I know she loves music, and I know this is a big opportunity for her, but I wish she could relax a little. This whole year was kind of a huge deal. Going from middle school to high school is no joke. On top of her singing, she was on honor roll every marking period, and she helps out so much at church. I wish we could have had more downtime this summer." Basically, I wish there was some way Lilli could be here with me, enjoying dips in the ocean and pool, family game nights, and long drives in the Jeep...but Mom focuses on the opportunity section, and steers the conversation right back to where we started.

"I'd pull the plug if I didn't truly believe she'd wake up one day and regret not taking this opportunity. All the hard work and loss of sleep now could pay off in a huge way for her very soon."

I wait for details, but Mom doesn't elaborate, which is unusually cryptic for her. Mom usually loves to dish in micro-detail when it comes to Lilli's career. Come to think of it, Mom hasn't even mentioned anything about what Lilli told me Ronnie said, which just makes me even more sure the information Ronnie passed to Lilli is way more than just a rumor—I think it's so serious, it must have Mom overwhelmed. Her blog posts have been short and sweet, mostly little paragraphs about trendy coffee shops or music stores she and Lilli find on their travels around Nashville...nothing that would give any hint about how stressful and up in the air things are.

I pull into the tackle shop and am ready to disconnect, but the Good Sister on my shoulder whispers for me to ask about Marnie. (The Bad Sister hisses *She's fine! Run before you get caught listening to another rant*—)

My carefree Della attitude is undone by a combination of being on a call with my mom and Dani's always-perfect Big Sister example, and my inner AJ wins out. "How's Marnie?" I ask, wincing as I wait for the answer. When Mom doesn't immediately launch into a tirade, I casually mention that I haven't seen any social media updates, which is truly bizarre behavior for Marnie.

"The volleyball camp might be a little more...extreme than

Dad and I realized," Mom finally admits, which is basically as close to a full-blown apology for screwing up as she'll ever give. I work hard to keep my gasp under wraps. "It's very regulated, very unbending, which isn't Marnie's style. But the results they get! The percentage of Olympic athletes who went through that camp is unbelievable. Marnie didn't seem too upset until they took the girls' cell phones and made them sign a No Technology pledge."

"Oof." Marnie worked hard to get her phone privileges back after she broke Jepsen House Rule Number 4 last summer: *No phone use after nine on a school night.* Mom caught her texting until two one morning, and Marnie's phone was shut off for six months. My parents *do not* mess around when it comes to house rules. Since she got it back, she's kept to the letter of the law, but that phone might as well be attached to her by an umbilical cord…and it got her into some serious hot water that Mom and Dad still don't know anything about. "Well, that makes me feel better. I thought something was up when I didn't see her updating her posts every two hours."

Mom makes a tight, panicked sound in the back of her throat. "When we dropped her off, she seemed so miserable. She *cried*, right in front of the other girls. That's just not like her. We almost took her with us, but what was the alternative? She wasn't going to be able to come with me and Lilli, and your dad is working overtime all summer while we're out of his hair, trying to get that bedrock test cycle done. There's no way Marnie could have been unsupervised for that many hours every day. I know she's been in a funk this year…"

She lets the sentence trail off, waiting for me to give her a crumb. I'm not usually good at lying to my parents, but Marnie's screwups this past year were so epic and complicated, and the web I wove to get her out of them is so delicate, I can't risk spilling now and shredding it all apart. Not when everything has been so carefully swept under the rug and, I hope, forgotten for good.

She cried, right in front of the other girls. My mom's words echo in my head, and I feel a tight squeeze on my heart, but I push it away.

"Yeah, she has been a little down, but she loves sports, and maybe this whole intense approach will be good for her. She's been posting some really mopey crap lately. Marnie is going to meet cool girls and play volleyball all day… It should literally be, like, her personal heaven."

"That's what I was thinking!" Mom sounds so instantly relieved, I know she was hoping I'd calm her down with my usual AJ levelheadedness. Too bad I can't shake the feeling that maybe I shouldn't be blowing this off. "Oh, and I was going to post about what you girls are up to this summer on my blog. Should I mention the internship? There are a few environmentalist influencers who might offer endorsements if they catch wind."

Mom posts about us regularly all school year, but she usually pulls back in the summer since we're all so busy running in different directions. I'm pretty sure she's not going to include anything about me being in Key West, wasting my potential, if she can brag about an internship instead.

"Mom, the last time some hippies gave you an endorsement deal, we all smelled like pot for weeks."

"It was *organic hemp* detergent, and it was very good for the environment." She pauses. "But, yeah, we did smell like we lived inside a bong."

I laugh so hard, I start to choke. I'm not even sure my mom realizes she's being funny, but sometimes she kills me.

"Besides, the internship projects haven't even been announced on BioLive's site. It's probably a breach of some rule to talk about it online without permission." I hold my breath hopefully, letting out a silent sigh of relief when she agrees.

"You're probably right. I have to keep a lid on the details around Lilli's competition, anyway. Oh, well, I'll figure out a way to talk about it all without spilling the beans. Oh, God! I just realized it's nearly one. I have to go before Lilli's late! Love you, sweetie."

"Love you, t—" And she's already clicked off. "Okay. Kind of rude, Mom," I grumble to myself as I head into the shop.

I push the heavy wooden door open and listen to the sweet chime of the old brass bell. I inhale the smell of rubber, fish, dust, and wood that always mixes pleasantly with lemon wood polish and something else I can't identify—something that's just *home*. I run my fingers along the intricate welcome sign my great-grandfather whittled and enjoy a rare quiet moment alone in the store.

Belo's is like an old-fashioned shop that took one step into modern times, got tired, and sank back into the past. The concrete floors are always polished to a high shine, smoothed from years of people walking up and down the aisles, buying and selling whatever a person could need for any fishing experience, whether it's a deep-sea sport-fishing expedition or a trip down the dirt road to your grandparents' pond. The walls are graying shiplap in desperate need of a fresh coat of paint. There are dozens of photos of my great-grandfather, grandfather, and dad posing with locals and celebrities who have frequented the store, giant fish prominent in basically every one. The cash register on the gleaming teak counter is the original my great-grandfather ordered from Switzerland when the store was brand-new. We use a modern one now, of course, but the old one is too beautiful to get rid of.

I pull my Belo's T-shirt over my tank top and tuck it into my frayed jean shorts, stick a marker behind one ear, a hand scanner in one back pocket, and a retractable box cutter in the other. I grab a rag and bottle of cleaner and try not to panic at how many cobwebs have built up on the first shelf of fishing lures I come to. Dusting isn't exactly exciting work, but it's essential to keep things sparkling clean. A dirty store looks sad and uninviting. Speaking of sad and uninviting, I notice it's very dark in here. A few bulbs have blown out in the big metal bell lamps hanging high above my head.

I make my way to the back to find some bulbs and a ladder. We'd usually have a few trucks backing into the loading bay about this time, and there would also usually be four or five floor workers unloading as fast as they could. Today there's only Dad and Jude, grunting as they heft a single truck's worth of boxes into the receiving area.

"You need help, Dad?" I yell over the croon of Hank Williams blaring out of the speakers.

"All good here, Dell!" he yells back, pulling off the bandanna tied around his forehead to mop up the sweat running down his face. Jude stands up straight and adjusts his cap, fixing his intense gaze on me. I hate that I notice how his sweat-soaked T-shirt clings to the very nice muscles of his shoulders. He's probably thinking about how my tattered shorts violate the company dress code my great-grandpa wrote in the 1950s. My dad still keeps a copy tacked up in his office to chuckle at, but Jude has definitely used them to technically cite an employee who irritated him. "Can you keep an eye out front, sweetheart?"

"Sure. I'll head out in one minute!" I beeline to the back, where we usually keep the light bulbs, but it takes me a while to finally locate a dusty box. "Huh. We need to order more of these." I make a mental note to remind Dad, then grab a ladder under one arm and drag it out front.

I've just finished changing light bulb number three when the bell over the door jingles. "Welcome to Belo's!" I call down.

I can't see who's come in yet, but I want to make sure they feel like they're getting a personal welcome. This isn't some big-box sporting-goods store: this is a family business, and I want people to *feel* like family when they walk in.

"Belo around?" It's a man's voice, thick and a little slurred, like he has a cheek full of chewing tobacco.

"He's out back. Can I help you with something?" I finish twisting the bulb into place, smiling when the warm burst of light shines down on the shelves. I turn to come down the ladder, but the man is standing right at the foot of it, his arms braced on either side.

"Well, now, I think this is a catch-22. If you come down to help me, I get the pleasure of your company, but I'd lose out on a real nice view." His smile makes me think of a cartoon fox's when it has its prey cornered.

My heart thuds, and my palms slick with sweat. I grab onto

the top of the ladder. "Excuse me, but I need to get down." I try to inject authority into my voice, but the Big Bossy Sister is feeling pretty exposed and unsure of her next move. I've asked him to move, and maybe he will. But do I really want to be on the floor with this guy?

"Maybe you can just reach up and get me something off that high shelf." He points to the expanded inventory, his grin oily.

I know for a fact there's nothing in these boxes that isn't on the shelves, because everything is immaculately faced. That's thanks to Jude Zeigler's unrelenting nagging... When I was on the floor last summer, I spent hours facing under his watchful eyes. Some people would have given the boss's daughter a break, but Jude said the fact that I was Belo's daughter meant I should have "higher expectations than the other floor scrubs."

Yeah, he's *amazing* at giving inspiring speeches.

For the first time ever, I realize I'd really appreciate his annoying, buzzkill presence.

"I'll come down and help you find whatever you need." I don't smile, I don't flirt, I don't pretend this is a fun game we're both playing. I feel trapped, and it's making me panic a little. "I need to come down *now*."

"I tell you what. You reach on up and get me one of those boxes of dragonfly lures, and then you can come on down and sell me enough of those rods for me to give to all the guys in my bachelor party next weekend." He crosses his arms smugly.

Down on the shelf, I see half a dozen boxes of the bright green dragonfly lures so close to this guy's hand he could touch them if he stretched his fingers. I look where he's motioning with his chin—Orvis Helios, Daiwa, Combo Bent Butt, and Crowder rods gleam in the display, more trophies than equipment. These are our high-end rods, and even a small bachelor party's worth would be big money for the store. My heart hammers so hard, I grip the rough top of the ladder to keep from tipping off and falling onto the cement—or, worse, into this creep's arms.

It's the voice of my daddy that cuts through my vertigo and lets me breathe a sigh of relief.

"What exactly is going on out here?" My father's voice isn't loud or brash. It's quiet, and that quiet fury raises goose bumps on my arms and causes the creep's head to whip around.

"You Belo? Name's Matt Cantor. Richard Teller sent me to see you. He says he won't go to anyone else in the Keys." He sticks his hand out to shake, and Dad just stares at it until he lets it drop limply at his side.

"Funny. I thought Teller was a buddy of mine," Dad says darkly.

Now that my dad is here, my breathing and heartbeat regulate, and I immediately wonder if I was maybe making too big a deal out of a loser's inappropriate jokes. This is the first customer we've had since we opened, and he's willing to buy a good amount of expensive equipment. It would be so dumb to turn him away. I scurry down the ladder, fake laughing the whole way.

"Dad, are you still mad that Mr. Teller caught that gigantic black grouper and you didn't have a single bite on your last trip out?" My voice is too high and breathy from nerves, which makes me sound like an airhead. I see that Matt Cantor's color drained from his smug face the second he heard me say *Dad*. "Mr. Cantor was asking about rods for his *entire bachelor party*." *Hint, hint, Dad. We can't afford to blow this sale.*

"Mr. Cantor, I'm going to be frank here," Dad says, and I cringe. "I don't much like the way you were addressing my daughter when I came out. I know Teller's no angel, but I don't abide that kind of disrespect to women."

"I apologize. I was out of line." I see Matt eyeing my father's six-foot-four frame. My dad is an avid sportsman who's in great physical shape. Matt Cantor would be no match for him physically. "I had no idea this young lady was your daughter."

Dad still looks pretty murderous, so I step in. "I accept your apology. Now, let's talk rods. Are you looking for something specific to saltwater deep-sea fish, or are you hoping for a more all-terrain rod?" I give my best customer-service smile and gesture for him to follow me to the display counter. I feel safer since Dad came out and Matt Cantor apologized, but something about his apology didn't quite ring true. I have the distinct feeling he's overdoing the gentlemanly act because he's afraid of getting my father riled up.

There have been new products and lines in the past year, so I'm not up to speed on everything, but I can answer almost every question, and I encourage him to handle at least three or four rods to get an idea of what he'd really like.

Dad hovers nearby, and it's like there's a thundercloud over his head. Jude appears to be doing regular store maintenance, but it's obvious his decision to repair some damaged shelving was calculated to give the customer a headache from all the hammering and drilling.

I drive the sale relentlessly, and by the time Matt Cantor

rushes out of the store, his bank account is several thousand dollars lighter. I expect Dad and Jude to give me a grudging congratulations for my awesome salesmanship, but Dad's first words are, "Cancel that sale."

"*What?*" My mouth falls open. "Are you serious? I just spent an hour and a half upselling him on every rod he bought! Dad, that's ludicrous!"

Dad grabs me in a tight bear hug. "What's *ludicrous* is that I let that asshole stay in my store after the way he talked to you. I'm sorry, Dell. That was shitty judgment on my part. I should have kicked him out as soon as I heard him harassing you, period. Don't worry about the sale. You'll still get a bump in your check for the commission."

Jude clears his throat loudly, and when Dad looks over, he shrugs and shakes his head.

"You'll still get a little bonus from your old man. Jude here is trying to help me with the finances, and I just don't have a head for it." Dad chuckles like not being good with finances is a silly quirk instead of a death knell for a small-business owner.

"Dad, I don't care about the commission. I care about the sale! That was thousands of dollars for the store."

"I don't want that shithead's business," Dad says with an easy shrug. "Jude, from now on, if Dell's on the floor, you or I are out here somewhere, too. No exceptions."

I expect Jude to make a reasonable argument about how there's no way in hell that will work, especially with our lack of summer help, but he just says, "Yes, sir," with a finality that reveals he agrees wholeheartedly with Dad's overzealous plan.

"I'm perfectly capable of being on the floor alone. This is

a total overreaction. And it makes no sense. Who's going to handle deliveries?"

I want to grab my father by the shoulders and shake some sense into him, but he rolls his eyes. "I'm not insulting your independence, Dell. Hell, you're one of the most capable teenagers I know. It isn't safe for *anyone* to be alone on the floor. Who knows what kind of nuts will walk in here?"

"But it's safe to be alone unloading a truck full of heavy inventory?" I challenge.

"I won't be alone, smarty-pants," Dad crows. "There's always *the driver.*"

Even though I know he'll be no help, I glance over at Jude, who suddenly doesn't need to run the drill and pound the hammer nonstop. Imagine that. "And you're fine with this, Jude?"

"Belo knows what he's doing," Jude says, like the obedient little officer he is.

We lock eyes for a long few seconds. I glare as hard as I can, but he's infuriatingly impassive. "Brownnoser," I hiss like a middle schooler.

Jude raises his eyebrows but keeps his mouth shut.

"Dell," Dad sighs. "Trust me on this one, okay? Every once in a while, your dad knows what's best." He nods to Jude. "Get that order out of our system, pronto. I'll be in my office trying to plow through this week's accounts."

Jude nods, Dad heads to the back, and Jude and I don't talk again for several long minutes.

"We have a new cleaner for the glass cases. It doesn't leave streaks," Jude finally says as I throw my shoulders into rubbing circles on the glass cases until the glass squeaks clean.

"I know how to clean glass. I've been doing this since I was in elementary school. I don't need the process mansplained, thank you very much." I step back to survey my work and quickly dart forward to rub out the streak that did, in fact, form in one corner.

A few seconds later, Jude puts a bottle with a microfiber draped over it at my feet. The magic glass cleaner.

"I said I don't need it, thank you."

"You're doing double the work, and you don't have to. Come on, don't cut off your nose to spite your face."

I rock back on my heels and glare at him. "I said I'm *fine*. You know what? Maybe instead of micromanaging the streaks I'm supposedly leaving on the glass, you should be figuring out how to save the sale I made so we can—oh, I don't know—pay the electric bill this month."

"Sorry, I don't care how much that douche spent. Belo's right. His money's trash here."

"Really?" I singsong. "And how are we going to afford fancy glass cleaner and maybe another box of light bulbs and a few more people to keep this place from being covered in cobwebs like some crypt? Is self-righteousness paying well these days?" I tilt my head to the side like I'd honestly love to hear the answer.

Jude grits his teeth. "Yeah, things are a little slow, but we don't have to just take any asshole's money."

"Yes, in fact, we do!" I bang my forehead against the glass case, not caring that I leave a smudge on the nearly spotless surface. "That's actually *exactly* how business works. We have things to sell, and people—some nice people, some assholes—want to buy the things we sell. So we *take their money* and use it to pay the bills. I mean, I've only taken AP Econ, but even I know that much about business."

"That's not how Belo's does things," Jude says stubbornly.

I channel all my fury into making the glass gleam, but I'm incapable of staying silent for long because I'm too irritated. "Maybe that's why my dad is in so much trouble with money right now. And maybe he doesn't need anyone encouraging decisions that will lose him money."

Jude stalks over to me so fast, I sit back almost on my butt, eyes wide with shock. He screeches to a halt a few inches from me, crouches down, stares right into my *soul*, and says between his gritted teeth, "Belo *loves* you. He won't take money from a guy who sexually harassed you, and that's a *good* thing. He's a great father. Be glad all he's doing is asking me to cancel the goddamn sale, Dell, because I offered to help by taking out a boat and chumming the waters with that scumbag."

"That's a little extreme, don't you think?" I manage to squeak out around my heart, which is firmly lodged in the middle of my throat.

He swallows so hard, I see the tendons in his neck work. "You couldn't see your own face, trapped up on the ladder. I've never seen you look scared like that. I hope no one ever makes you feel that way again, but if they ever do? They better pray I'm not around."

I feel like I finally understand what people mean when they say their jaw hit the floor, since mine is badly in need of scooping up. Jude Zeigler is always calm, always rule-following, always levelheaded and maybe even a little boring. He doesn't get emotional and issue hardened threats like my middle-school literary crush, Dallas Winston from *The Out-*

siders. And Jude Zeigler *definitely* doesn't care what happens to me, as long as I'm cleaning and straightening the aisles at Belo's according to his meticulous specifications.

Speaking of cleaning, Jude follows up his growled threat to murder the guy who sexually harassed me by grabbing the magic glass cleaner, spraying twice, swiping, and leaving a gleaming case front. He doesn't look my way as he sprays and swipes all the way down the row, leaving a perfect line of sparkling glass in a quarter of the time it took me to do one display.

For the rest of my shift, Jude broods silently, directly across the store from me no matter where I am. I don't know what to say about his heated confession, so I don't say anything at all.

But I do wash every single smeared window in the front of the store with the cleaner he brought out for me. When my shift is over, I head back to say good-bye to Dad and notice Jude's locker is open. I tug a Post-it off Dad's desk and scrawl a note on bright yellow paper. *Stay gold, Jude.* I slap it on the lunch bag inside his locker before I lose my nerve, then drive home, talking myself out of going back and throwing it in the trash the whole way.

8

Ice Storm

Last November
St. Matthew's High School

MICHIGAN

The forecast initially said clear skies, but the winter had taken a freakishly cold turn, even for Michigan. It's the day before Thanksgiving break, and the charcoal-gray clouds rolled in fast and steady just after first bell, releasing torrents of gun-metal sleet that are slicking the roads so fast, administration is left with two equally shitty options: release us into the mess as soon as possible, or lock us down for the duration of the day in what might be worsening conditions.

Harper is sketching on top of the massive radiator box in the art room. She pauses to huff a shaky circle of condensation onto the windowpane and clear it with the flat of her palm. "Holy shit, it's coming down like mad. I'm texting my mom. Do you think she'll be able to drive over in this to get me?"

"Your mom will steal a snowplow to come here if you ask," Tessa says, zero doubt in her voice. "You're seriously so lucky. My mom would be like, 'You'll survive. Logan never needed me to pick him up.'" Tessa's mom is way more of a free-range parent than mine or Harper's, and Harper and I definitely envy her sometimes…but in the middle of a snowstorm, with freedom a treacherous drive away, a tiger mom is where it's at.

"Well, when you pay what my parents paid for a baby, you're protective of your investment," Harper snickers.

Tessa and I shake our heads, used to Harper's cavalier jokes about her adoptive status. I'm sure every adoptee has a unique view of adoption based on their particular circumstances; Harper adores her parents and loves discussing the random details of her adoption…like how much it cost.

"I was more expensive than a Lexus F series, bitches," she whispers as her mom picks up the phone. "Mommy? They haven't announced yet. I know. I *know*…okay! Thank you, love you so much!" Harper makes a kissy noise into the phone and jumps off the radiator box. She calls out to Mr. Owens, our art teacher, "Mr. O, I'm out!" He waves at her over his newspaper. Mr. Owens knows Harper's mom's reputation— every teacher at St. Matthew's does. He's too smart to get between a mama bear and her beloved cub during a Michigan ice storm.

"You guys need a ride home?" Harper offers. Tessa is already packing up her bag, but I shake my head.

"Thanks, but I have to grab Lilli and Marnie. I'm sure Lex will give us a ride if my mom can't make it out."

"Okay. If they call a snow day tomorrow, I'll take the snowmobile out, and we can have a sleepover," Harper says, kissing me on the cheek as she grabs Tessa's hand and starts out. I follow them because I know Mr. O won't question me if I leave with my usual clutch, but I break away from them in the gym hallway, wave, and head off to search for Lilli and Marnie. They have to be somewhere in the connections hallway, since all underclassmen are in their first elective block right now.

The halls buzz with the kind of frantic excitement a fast storm brings out in all of us, regardless of the fact that we've all endured years of treacherous winters. Some kids are milling in the hallways, coats hanging off their elbows, scarves loosely slung around their necks, hats tugged low over a single ear. Parents are already skidding into the circular drive to get their kids home before the worst of the storm blows through. I know the only reason my own mother hasn't buzzed through with a text is because this is her technology-free meditation time. She's in her insulated room, all devices docked on the kitchen counter, for at least a half hour. I don't know if the calm she gets from meditating is worth the panic that always ensues when she comes out and tries to catch up with the thirty minutes of time she lost during her om state.

"Did you see either of my sisters?" I ask an assembly of Lilli's unsupervised drama friends. I pray they don't break into some heartfelt song rendition of their answer, but, thankfully, they just tell me she's rehearsing her solo for the Christmas pageant in the chorus room, too preoccupied with the delicious blur of chaos to try to rap the information my way.

Two puppy-dog-eager underclassmen offer to help me look for Marnie, but I've got it handled. I assume she's in her happy place, practicing her volleying skills in the emptying gym. I elbow through the chaos of too many sweaty, pinned bodies and squeaking rubber soles in the gym, but I don't see Marnie.

She's not in the locker room either, so I head to the old

gym, which is now mostly used for storage. Dusty mats are folded and leaned against the walls, nets full of footballs and soccer balls with crumbling dirt and grass still clinging to them droop on the floor, and taped field hockey sticks tangle in a giant pile. I look past the flotsam of abandoned gym equipment and see a light from a locker room that's never used anymore.

"Marnie?" My commanding echo bounces off the empty walls. "Marnie, are you there?"

I don't worry about poking around in places that might be off-limits to less established students. I relish my VIP status at St. Matthew's, and I go where I want, when I want, for the most part. Sometimes these gleaming, saint-adorned halls feel more like home than my actual house. "Marnie, answer me!"

My voice is drowned out by a high-pitched bout of screaming that spurs me to sprint in my heeled Mary Janes, plaid kilt flying up behind me as I race to stop what sounds like a prison riot but winds up being my sister and her best friend, Jaylen Roberts, in a shrieking match, their hands fisted in each other's hair.

"You fucking slut!" Jaylen screams, yanking a few red-gold strands from Marnie's beet red scalp.

"Hey, let go of her!" I might as well be screaming into a blizzard. The two girls grunt and slap, claw and twist until they thud to the floor in an idiot tangle, their splotchy faces streaked with tears and running makeup.

I rush over and try to find a place to wedge my hands so I can separate the two of them without taking a fist to the face. I finally manage to pry them apart, mainly by knocking my sister into a set of lockers with my shoulder. We're all gasping by the time I finally dislodge them, and I look from one furious, sniveling face to the other and demand, "What the hell is going on with you two?"

Both of them answer at the same time, a flow of high-pitched gibberish so loud and garbled, I have to scream again to be heard over it.

"Shut up!" They both clamp their mouths shut, and I point at my sister's more levelheaded sidekick. "Jaylen. Calm down. Tell me what's going on at a *normal volume.*"

"Oh, nothing much. Your sister is just being a backstabbing *bitch!*" she shrieks, lunging for Marnie. I catch her around the waist with my arm before she makes contact and glare at Marnie.

"What is she talking about?" I demand.

Marnie's chin wobble means she's two seconds away from crying, so I know this is a serious screwup. "I don't know." She shifts her eyes to the side, looking anywhere other than at either of us. *She's lying.* "I have no idea what she's talking about. You'd think being friends since we were four would, like, mean something, but I guess it doesn't. I guess my best friend is just going to spread some stupid rumors like everyone else."

I ignore the dramatics and get to the meat. "Rumors? What rumors?" I demand.

The two screeching maniacs are suddenly silent, jaws tightened in identically obstinate positions. Exasperation and fury make my spine stiffen, and my voice is a low snarl. "One of you better answer me *now,* or I'll drag you both to Deaconess Alicia's office, and we can have it out there."

The mention of our tyrannical principal gets them both

blabbing almost instantly, but Jaylen's word vomit wins out, and I cobble together a story that makes an instant migraine knife me behind the eyes.

"So, correct me if I'm wrong," I say slowly, once Jaylen's narration trickles to silence. I turn to Marnie and squint at her, hoping something in her face will give me some hope, but she's pale and tight-lipped. "Marnie, you sent pictures of the St. Matthew's volleyball playbook to a player on the Queen of Mercy team before the playoff games?" I close my eyes and hope Jaylen has it all wrong, but Marnie can't look up at me. Tears streak her sunken cheeks. "That makes no sense, Marnie. You *live* to play volleyball. Why the hell would you sabotage everything you worked so hard for?"

Even as I utter the words *that makes no sense*, I annotate with a mental asterisk. Marnie's sense of judgment isn't particularly logical at the best of times, and when there are strong emotions involved...

"It was for that bitch! I know it was! She's *using you*, Marnie. God, wake up!" Jaylen yells, tears pouring down her face, spit flying out of her mouth as she yells and points at my little sister. "How can you not see that? Like, do you really think she cares if you get kicked off the team? No! She doesn't care about you or us or anything but herself!"

Ah, so this is about a girl. Not a shock there. If I had to take bets, I'd say she's probably a little bit of a badass, cocky, maybe with crazy dyed hair, a few piercings, a few tattoos—my sister is such a sucker for a bad-girl jock, and she's been off-kilter since she broke up with Katrina, her girlfriend since eighth grade.

"Marnie?" I glare, and she presses her lips together, silent.

I pull out the big guns. "Jaylen's wrong." The second any re-lief glows on Marnie's face, I chop it short at the knees. "You won't just be kicked off the team. What you did is a major school-ethics violation. Students have been expelled for less. And it will be a black mark on your permanent record. Trust me on this… I'm on the student ethics board."

Marnie is a St. Matthew's lion to her core. It would gut her to be expelled in disgrace, and I don't even want to imagine what ripple effects an expulsion could continue to have on her and my whole family down the road. I have to fix this mess she made, but first I need to know every detail, and I'm willing to be ruthless to get the unvarnished truth. I turn to Jaylen, one eyebrow cocked. "What do you know? Don't leave *anything* out."

Marnie suddenly decides to pipe up, but I silence her with a hairy eyeball. I'm sure Jaylen knows too much of this sor-did tale already, and she doesn't need a single crumb more. No one does. If we're going to pull this off, I need to know what fires to put out when, and I need to make sure I stop up any leaks.

Jaylen tells me three important things that will help my sister. The first is that the girl—McKenzie Fisher—is a trou-bled transfer to Queen of Mercy who was already on proba-tion earlier this year. That's good. It means she's most likely expendable enough to serve as a sacrificial lamb if we need her to be.

The second is that Marnie shared the photos through an app that's just had a rash of bad press from hackings and run-ins with privacy violations. It's the kind of app adults don't use and don't really understand. Another major bonus for us.

Blame the Evils of Technology... It's basically admin's favorite lecture topic other than Abstinence Only and Say No to Vaping.

The third important piece of this puzzle is just dumb luck for Marnie. The volleyball team's star setter, Angela Wells, fell ice-skating the week before and sprained her wrist. The team was already on a tenuous path, but Angela's injury pretty much sealed their fate and guaranteed their chances at states had been torpedoed. Making Marnie's screwup disappear when a state championship was in the cards would have been nearly impossible.

"Thank you, Jaylen. We can work with this." I nod, clicking into efficient-fixer mode. I begin to think of all I need to do as soon as I get home to make things right. I have to let my dreams of hot chocolate and fun with my squad die a quick death. "Jaylen, Marnie is *so sorry*. Marnie, *tell Jaylen how sorry you are*." I elbow my sister in the ribs. Not gently.

"Jay, you know I'd never do anything to hurt you guys. She had... There were reasons..." Marnie's ears burn hot pink at the tips, and I know there's more to the story that I probably don't want to hear about but will eventually need to.

"Don't make excuses," I interrupt before Marnie can spill details that will further incriminate her to her still pissed-off buddy. "Make apologies to the person you hurt like a woman, not a sniveling brat."

After Marnie makes her snot-and-hug-filled apologies, I make sure Jaylen feels like the conquering hero, the person who saved her friend's ass. I tell her I'm going to make sure McKenzie stays far away from Marnie, even though I know damn well my sister probably invited that girl and all her subsequent trouble into her life with wide-open arms. And then I attempt to seal a lid on everything. I send my puffy-eyed sister off to find Lilli and turn to Jaylen with my most saccharine, oiliest smile.

"Jaylen, sweetie, you know if this gets out, it will not only destroy the team, it will get Marnie kicked out of St. Matthew's permanently. As much of an ass as my sister can be, you know she hasn't been herself lately. We're trying to help her, but since she broke up with Katrina—"

"What was that even about?" Jaylen scrunches her eyebrows low and twists the hem of her meticulously ironed kilt, leaving a web of wrinkles. "I know she didn't want everyone in their business because of the whole assembly Deaconess Alicia had at Homecoming—which, by the way, we totally *do not* agree with. Like the team was so pissed having to even listen to that crap. But Marnie knew we all always had her back, even if we had to sit through that disgusting speech without saying anything."

Ah, Deaconess Alicia's rousing autumnal hate speech disguised as religious devotion! It was so shocking, the bishop had to drag her from the podium after cutting her mic, and it left more than a few progressive donors at the Homecoming rally slack-jawed. Not that it surprised the student body. We were all used to her outspoken cruelty. Deaconess Alicia is hands down one of the most hateful, intolerant humans I've ever encountered, which makes me wonder why the ministry didn't find some vocation other than high-school principal for her. Wasn't there any position that didn't put her hate-spewing self in direct contact with young, vulnerable teens on a daily basis? Like maybe she could have been the deaconess of some semiabandoned lighthouse? Or deaconess of a slaughterhouse? Whatever. Rumor has it that she'll be giving up her position at the end of the year and moving on to do whatever it is bitter demons do when they're done tormenting high schoolers, I guess.

"Marnie's in a dark place." I say it for dramatic effect, but once the words are out, it occurs to me just how true they really are. Marnie's always been the most mercurial of the three of us, but lately she's been way more off than usual. Like manic highs and lows that are hard to keep up with. "You have no idea how much she needs your *friendship* right now." I take Jaylen's hand in mine, relieved when I see her nod solemnly.

I say *friendship*. I mean *silence*. I pray Jaylen reads my subtext.

I make sure to ask how Jaylen is getting home and give my opinion on the three options for a Winter Formal gown she has saved on her phone. I tell her she has to come to our house to get ready before the dance. My mother has already promised an up-and-coming makeup artist, a stylist, and a photographer publicity on her social media sites and an article in her friend's local magazine, *Washtenaw Now*, in exchange for their help getting us ready for Winter Formal. When I first heard, I was a little bummed—I would have loved to experiment with some techniques Dani taught me over the summer, and it would have been a nice, low-key night getting ready with Tessa and Harper. Now I realize I'm lucky I have this chip to barter with. I can tell Jaylen's already calculating how this will catapult her social media presence to dangerously addictive new heights.

Lex finds me outside the locker room.

"Where have you been? Your barnacles have already headed out in Mama Bear's tank," he snickers.

"Lex, why can't you ever be nice to my friends?" I ask, though I know it's pointless to nag him about it. I'm long past trying to make inroads between my best friends and boyfriend. It's a lost cause.

"Because they're too ridiculous to take seriously. What's up, buttercup?" He slides his hands to my hips and squeezes. "Hey, this old locker room is a good place to disappear for a few minutes. Wanna tell me why you're the only person in the entire school upset about getting cut free? And maybe we can make out after? For good measure."

I debate telling Lex about Marnie's mess because my gut says the less people who know, the better. But if anyone will know how to make this all go away, it's Lex. "Marnie did something…" I frown at Lex's delighted smile.

"What did our resident badass do now? Jesus, this girl must've picked up all the rebellious genes you left behind." Lex worships Marnie. They have the same wicked sense of humor, the same penchant for trouble, and the same ability to get under my skin and into my heart all at the same time. "Let me guess! A knife fight? Arson? Grand theft auto?"

"Lex, be serious for once in your life. I have a plan in mind, but I need your help with one aspect…" I grab his collar in my fist and tug him close, so I can murmur in his ear. "She sent her latest hookup the SMHS volleyball playbook over that shitty Playered app, and big-mouth Jaylen found out."

"Ah, some stealth insider trading. Very white-collar of her." Lex narrows his eyes, and it's like I can hear the gears grinding in his skull. "What's-her-name jacked her ankle up last week, right?"

"Angela Wells," I supply. "And it was her wrist."

"Yeah, without that Amazon, the Lady Lions have a snow-ball's chance in hell of going to states. So, what do you want my help with?" Before I can get a word out, Lex holds up his hand. "Wait. Terms."

I snort. "Why am I not surprised you won't just do this out of the goodness of your heart? Oh, wait, you'd actually have to *have* a heart for that to work."

"I'm always willing to help mastermind a cover-up out of the goodness of my heart—which I do actually have. Sorry if I don't let it bleed out over every loser's problem. But for Marnie? I'd do anything for you or your sisters. You know that. All I want is to see a picture of this girl. She must be a total smokeshow if Marnie was willing to throw her Olympic volleyball dreams away on her." His wink makes me grimace.

"Sometimes you're a real scumbag, Lex, you know that?" Marnie and Lilli make their way into the gym at that second, arms threaded around each other's waists, heads bent close, plaid kilts swishing in unison. "Here comes my hot mess of a sister now." I'm so irritated with Marnie, I can't look at her without rolling my eyes. She's hangdog and miserable. Tears streak Lilli's angelic face. She breaks away from Marnie and throws herself at me like a penitent at the feet of the Holy Mother.

"Marnie isn't getting expelled, right, AJ? You'll fix this." Lilli doesn't ask. When she says those words, she looks at me like I'm some all-powerful knight who can slay any dragon. She believes in me completely. It's a huge responsibility to have someone look up to you the way Lilli looks up to me, and I take it seriously. "What should I do to help?" she asks.

Lex has already hustled Marnie to the side and is making her laugh wetly by wolf-whistling at the picture on her phone. It takes all my willpower not to walk over and slap it out of her hand. The evil desire to hear the crack of the screen is visceral.

"I actually have an assignment for you, Lil. You can convince our jackass of a sister to scrub her social media accounts. Or, better yet, shut them all down." I cock an eyebrow. "Use your influence. Make it something she won't be able to refuse. Maybe some kind of challenge? A social media blackout? Appeal to her competitive nature."

"Hmm, maybe we can set it up as an Advent challenge? Remember how much Marnie loved giving up sugar for Lent?"

"I remember what a grumpy ass she was right up until Easter." I sigh. "Marnie is too dramatic to be a Lutheran. She should just convert to Catholicism and be done with it. But whatever you think, Lil."

Lilli pulls out her phone and taps open her favorite graphics app. Her golden head bends over the screen, and in about thirty seconds, she has a gorgeous visual of a flickering flame set against the swirling midnight sky flecked with stars, emblazoned with the simple message *Go Dark for the Light*.

"I posted it on, like, eight different sites already. It's getting, like, so many hits. Probably because everyone is home." She looks up at me and flashes me the biggest smile. For one heart-squeezing second she's that chipmunk-cheeked cutie whose hair I used to French-braid with ribbons every morning during her first-grade year—then her face clears, and her eyes go hazy, and I see what a gorgeous, passionate teenager she is. "Look, AJ!" She holds her slim arm up, and I see the white down standing straight up on her goose-bumped flesh.

"I have a song idea…a really good one! I need to get to my guitar and get it down!"

Lex is already headed back over. "I need to take a look at Dopey's laptop." He crooks an elbow around Marnie's neck and gives her a hard noogie. She jerks her head away and taps his balls with a tight fist, making him double over and howl in pain. I ignore them as they tussle like lion cubs.

"We need to head out, anyway. Lilli needs to get to her guitar." I check my phone and realize Mom will be done meditating in eight minutes. I give her another three beyond that to leave her room, walk past a window, see the storm, and explode into full-blown panic. "If we get on the road in the next few minutes, we'll probably make it home before it gets too crappy."

"I think that ship has sailed," Lex says between whimpers. "But the Beast has snow tires. We'll be okay."

Lilli and Marnie race ahead, and we button up and prepare to face the arctic blast outside when my phone buzzes. I wonder why Mom's meditation session got cut short. Her usual anxiety along with the fact that her Whole30 diet isn't ending until three days *after* Thanksgiving (she didn't realize how early the third Thursday of November would fall this year, and Mom is no quitter) should blow together to form the perfect storm (pun intended) of irritation when she finds out we'll all be iced-in for the night at least.

I don't pay attention to the numbers on the screen when I pick up the call.

"Mom, don't panic. Lex's parents just put snow tires on the Range Rover—"

"Dell?"

I nearly drop the phone. It isn't my mother calling.

"Dad?"

His voice crackles across the line as the storm winds whip cold slush into my hair and face. I picture him on our porch, rocking in his favorite chair, dressed in a light flannel—I check Key West's weather every morning, and I know it was supposed to be in the midsixties today, which is basically frigid conditions for them.

"You gettin' some ice up there? It's all over the news. Y'all aren't driving, are you?" There's worry in his voice, and it's weird to hear the worry I expected from the parent I didn't.

Lex mouths, *Who is it?* I just shake my head and wave him on urgently, so I can answer my father in private. Lex points a finger up toward the wintry mix that's sluicing down my collar and matting in clumps against my scalp. A barrage of goose bumps screams awake on my skin as ice melts into glacial water and runs down my neck, but I choose discomfort over lack of privacy. If I don't wave Lex on, he'll eavesdrop like it's his right.

Go! I mouth as my father says, "Dell? Sweetheart, I can't hear you."

Lex taps the expensive Swiss watch perched on his wrist, rips his long cashmere scarf from around his neck, tosses it in the general direction of my head, and stalks to the parking lot.

"Dad?" I pull Lex's scarf tighter over my soaked hair and blink away the droplets that cling to the ends of my eyelashes. "Sorry, the weather is crazy today. How are you?"

We have standing Sunday-night calls, but it's so nice to hear his voice out of the blue like this. I close my eyes, and I'm on the porch, too, swinging back and forth in the porch swing with the creaky hinges, inhaling the cool salt air sailing in from the ocean.

"I'm looking at tickets for tomorrow right now. They jumped a bit in price, but I don't want that to worry you. Duke and Dani can't even wait to see you. Have you been able to talk to your boss?" Dad blows a little breath between his teeth. "Hell, I can't quite believe I'm asking my baby if she can ask her *boss* about getting off work. Where's the time gone?"

The wind and ice scream around me, and I feel sick that the white lie I told Dad has blown so completely out of proportion. I actually *did* apply to the local ice rink, and I made the mistake of telling Dad in my excitement. It never occurred to him that I wouldn't get hired. In fact, I did get offered the job. But when I finally told Mom about it, she sat me down with the family planner and pointed out how a job would cut too severely into my extracurriculars for school as well as family and church time, and then she stood over me while I called the rink back to turn the job down, sad at having to disappoint the sweet older lady who'd interviewed me and seemed genuinely excited to work with me.

I should have known better than to try to buck the life that's been so carefully ordered and plotted for my maximum potential. I never got around to telling Dad the whole embarrassing story, but when he mentioned me coming down for Thanksgiving, he said I might want to ask my boss. I didn't correct him because—thrilled as I was at the prospect of seeing him, Duke, and Dani for Thanksgiving for the first time *ever*—part of me feared getting to Florida outside of my pre-arranged summer schedule would be as impossible as trying to get a job on my own had been.

Plus, I might not have a work boss, but I had to get permission from Mom, the boss of every aspect of my life here.

"Dell? Can you hear me? I think the line might be cutting out?"

Dad's voice shakes me out of my silence just as a blast of wind sends me skittering to the side. Another few minutes, and this will go way beyond a fun joyride in the slush for Lex. We'll be putting my little sisters in real danger, and I can't do that.

"I—" I take a deep breath and rush another tiny lie out, peppering it with as much truth as I can. Like that matters. "I was supposed to this afternoon, but it looks like things will be canceled at least until tomorrow. Let me get home and dig out my supervisor's number. I'll call you as soon as I text him, okay?" Inside my Mary Janes, my toes are painfully crossed.

I wish, I wish, I wish I were…braver.

"No problem. I don't want to rush you. I just want to make sure we can still get you on a plane in time. Let me know as soon as you can. Love you, Dell."

"I love you, too." I hang up and hurry—*carefully*—over to the Range Rover, where Lilli is already blasting the Christian a cappella album of carols that's been on endless replay at our house since All Saints' Day.

Lex pulls out without looking over. I unknot his scarf and put it on the console between us. He uses his elbow to nudge it off, so it pools on the floor mats covered with melting ice and grime. I'm not sure why he thinks ruining his own things is some kind of punishment for me, but I'm used to his passive-aggressive nature rearing its ugly head when he can't get a grip on how he feels about something.

"Who's the mystery caller?" Lex asks, jaw tight as a bow-string.

I try to figure out how I can answer, if I should maybe just be honest.

I wish, I wish, I wish I were braver.

"No one."

"Really?"

Lilli's ruby voice belts out a verse from "O Little Town of Bethlehem" I've never heard before. I drop my voice low.

"It's not a guy."

"Just someone you say *I love you* to before you hang up?"

My limbs are already stiff from the cold, but they go completely rigid. "What?" I try a little laugh, like what he said is ridiculous.

"Even an idiot could have read your lips. You looked happy. Like, really happy."

"It's not…what you think." I finish with a shrug. If I was ever going to confess more, it wouldn't be under these circumstances, with Lex feeling hurt and uncertain. He's always extra mean when he's not sure where he stands.

"Look, if you were being honest, it wouldn't even matter. I'm not some uptight asshole. But all this mystery… What the hell is with all the secret calls lately?"

Some of the wetness rolling down my temple is from the melting ice, and some is from my fried nerves. If I tell him the truth, I've handed him the ability to weigh in, to judge, maybe even to mock. I don't trust him to understand my life or family in Florida. I don't feel like exposing this safe, sacrosanct part of myself to him.

"Lex, just because I don't go advertising every aspect of my life doesn't mean there's something tawdry going on."

"Tawdry?" he mocks. "Is this Downton fucking Abbey, AJ? Whatever, don't tell me if you need to keep it some big secret." He whips around in my driveway a little too fast and screeches to a halt as my mother explodes out, her long, camel hair sweater wrapped around her body like a rich lady's bathrobe.

"I was just about to call you!" Mom cries, tugging each of us girls close for a kiss and a hug. She also gives Lex a hug and sighs. "Lex, thank you so much. What would we do without you?"

Lex flicks a hard look my way, then turns the charm up a thousand watts for my mother. "It's seriously no problem Mrs. J. Hey, is it cool if I help Marnie with her presentation for Esposito? She showed me her rough-draft slides…" He shudders theatrically.

We pile into the mudroom and hang our soaking coats and hats and scarves on our personalized hooks, then line our muddy boots on the slate floor.

"Are you kidding?" Mom heads to the kitchen, opens the fridge and starts pulling out eggs, milk, butter. "Honestly, this family would fall apart without you, Lex. While you guys work on that, I'll whip up some warm cookies. How does that sound?"

"Sounds like I hope this ice storm never lets up. You're the best, Mrs. J." Lex winks at my mom, and she laughs.

It's mystifying how Lex talks to adults like he got mailed the secret decoder ring for communication with grown-ups, while the rest of us are still fumbling with the kiddie version. He herds Marnie and Lilli upstairs so they can get started putting out the fire Marnie stoked. He throws me one more dark look and shakes his head before the three of them are gone.

I should be going with them. There's a ton I still have to do before this whole situation is anywhere near under control. But I look at the ice on the windows and imagine escaping the unrelenting gray of this long Michigan winter and the stresses of all I have to fix and figure out in this life—I imagine flying to the warmth and peace of my other home like a migrating bird, and my heart is a slush ball in the spring sun.

"Mom, Dad called me." I watch her shoulders stiffen as the words register. "He asked—"

"I know," she cuts me off quietly. "And I really hate to say no," she says, but I'm not sure I believe her. I think she doesn't want to come off as a complete ogre, but Vanessa Jepsen adores saying *no*. She's the boss, the captain, the queen. It's her prerogative to use her veto power as she sees fit. "There are honestly a few things that make this complicated, AJ. You know I have the opportunity for a spread in a national-lifestyle magazine, and the feature could be a huge jumping-off point for me. The exposure alone is amazing."

I nod. "Okay," I weigh my words carefully. "But Marnie and Lilli will be here."

She twirls around and grabs a copper measuring cup, packing brown sugar a little more aggressively than seems strictly necessary. "Sweetie." She braces her hands on the counter and drops her head. "I don't have many more Thanksgivings with you girls all under one roof. This is really important to me. For the magazine spread, obviously, but also…for me."

I bite down on the side of my tongue. Mom gets so easily hurt, especially when it comes to me. Peter always says micromanagement is her love language, and I know it's hard for her to share me as much as she does.

"And it's important for Dad," I say, hoping a new angle will elicit some sympathy. "I've never spent a Thanksgiving in the Keys—"

She smacks the maple-wood spoon on the granite, and the bang grinds my argument to a standstill. "And you've never *missed* a Thanksgiving here. It's two days before the holiday. Marnie and Lilli will be so upset. I just don't understand why it has to be this year. I mean, you'll see your dad for nearly three *months* this summer."

"But the internship is this summer." It's risky to bring it up, since Mom is still hounding me about making a decision, but I decide to lay my chips out.

"Fine." She cracks the eggs hard enough to show me she's irritated, but not so hard that she'd risk getting shell in the batter. "Fair enough. We'll make sure you can get down there *next* Thanksgiving." She tosses the empty shells and creams the golden yolks into the soft butter. "Maybe you can even spend half of your winter break there. Next year, obviously," she amends, bursting my bubble before it even had a real chance to inflate.

There's flour on her cuffs and a smear of butter glistens on her hand, right above the enormous (but tasteful) diamond ring Peter gave her for their tenth anniversary. I've hardly been out with her without someone—a cashier, a server, another bougie mom—complimenting her on it. It's classy and gorgeous, tasteful and understated, but mostly it's *on-brand*, which has become the most important thing to my mother. I mean, I do honestly believe she'd miss me this Thanksgiving, but I *also* believe she wants that glossy magazine spread to look right according to her definition of *family*…even if her definition forces me to break my heart in two.

The warm, buttery-sweet smell of the cookies is undercut by the sharp whip of frozen wind that snakes in from the front door. Mom and I look up to see Peter, covered in snow.

"Peter!" Mom's face lights up in a way that makes me kind of jealous. Isn't that the way I'm supposed to look at Lex when he comes through the door? "I'm so glad you're home! I was thinking you were going to get stuck at the lab overnight." She hurries over and helps him peel off his layers, kissing him on the lips, first quickly, then a little more slowly. He ducks down and whispers something in Mom's ear, and she shrieks and kisses him again, laughing hard. "Stop it, AJ will hear," she whispers.

"AJ!" Peter hangs his coat on the hook crookedly, and Mom stops to fix it as he rushes over to me. "Sweetie, I have some good news about the internship. They're willing to let you do some of the training on-site. Which means we'd need to coordinate with the BioLive lab down near Orlando, I think? Miami maybe…" He trails off when he sees my face. "What's up, peanut? I haven't seen you this down since your hamster died."

"Poor Aslan the Hamster," I sniffle and laugh in one weird, wet sound, wiping my eyes as I stand up from the counter and try to slip out. "I miss that guy. He really did look like a lion, didn't he?"

"Hey." Peter adjusts his glasses, which are fogging up from the warm oven air, and takes my hand. His hand isn't like Dad's—it's thinner, longer, and only calloused around the fingertips, where he holds pens and pencils and other precision instruments too long and too tight all day long. But it's a good, comforting hand, and it makes me choke out some of those tears I'm trying to hold back. "What is it, sweetie?"

"She wanted to see Belo and the kids this Thanksgiving." Mom crosses and uncrosses her arms like she doesn't know what to do with her hands. She finally settles on scooping cookie dough onto the baking sheets.

"Oh, AJ." Peter's face crinkles in sympathy. "Sweetie, I'm so sorry. I heard about it on the way home."

"Heard about what?" I ask, confused.

"The whole Midwest, the north Atlantic, down to Charlotte, North Carolina, is calling for massive ice storms and hurricane-force winds. They're forecasting one of the biggest holiday shutdowns in a decade."

I go to my coat and reach into my pocket, where I left my phone. I have three missed calls from Dad. Peter comes to stand near me. "I'm sure your father understands. Maybe we can get you down there for Christmas?"

Mom makes a tight sound in the back of her throat, but I throw my arms around Peter. "I'd even take New Year's."

"Let's hope this wild weather calms down a little. Why don't you give your dad a call? Please tell him Happy Thanksgiving from all of us." Peter's eyes are kind, but I can see from the way he glances at Mom with relief that he's thanking God a snopocalypse kept me home and Mom happy this holiday.

It doesn't change the fact that he's a really, really good guy and an awesome stepdad.

"Maybe we can talk more about the internship later?" I smile at him, and he kisses my cheek.

"You got it. Looks like we're going to have a cozy Thanksgiving weekend. How about I whip up some of my famous Philly cheesesteaks and we meet down here for dinner and Monopoly in an hour? Lex, too. I saw his gas guzzler in the driveway."

"Thanks, Dad." I hug him tight and head up to my room. On the landing, I sink to the floor and call Dad in Florida.

"Hey, baby girl. So I'm sure you've heard the bad news. My travel agent called about ten minutes after we hung up."

"Dad—" I can't get another word out, I'm crying so hard.

"Oh, honey, don't cry. We can't control the weather, right? We'll get it one of these years." The way he tries to sound upbeat for me makes me cry even harder.

We talk for a few minutes, and Dad won't get off the phone until I'm laughing at his cornball jokes. When I hang up and walk into my room, Marnie and Lilli are sprawled on the bed. Lex sits on the floor, legs out, feet crossed at the ankles, glaring at the laptop screen.

"And *that* is how you con your father's lawyer's intern into sending over one scary-ass Cease and Desist letter that will have those sites and that hot—but totally outmatched—girl crapping their pants. No worries. You're going to be okay, Marnie."

Marnie lifts her head an inch off the bed and looks at me. Her face scrunches up, and the tears start. She reaches her hand out, and I go over, get in the middle of my sisters, and sigh as they lay their heads on my shoulders. "It's going to be okay. Lex and I have this. Don't worry."

"Mom and Dad would, like, lose it if they found out,"

Marnie says through a sob. "I'm, like, so, so ashamed. I feel like a piece of crap."

I run a hand over her hair, untangling the knotted strands as I go. "Shh, stop that," I tell Marnie, my stomach clenching at the wild way she's talking. "You made a mistake. Everyone screws up."

Lilli takes Marnie's hand, and their interlaced hands rest on my stomach. I place my hand on top of theirs. "Marnie, don't cry," Lilli says, her voice small and scared. "AJ will take care of everything."

"You guys never mess up." Marnie burrows her head into my side, her words raw and harsh. "You never screw up like I do. Why am I always screwing everything up?"

"Marnie, calm down." I look over at Lex, who just shakes his head and shrugs. My tone is a combination of comforting and stern. "C'mon, stop crying. Everyone messes up. It's okay, it's under control. It's going to be like this never even happened, all right? So let's cheer up and put on our happy faces. We don't need Mom and Dad worried and asking a million questions. We've got an hour before Dad serves up his famous Philly cheesesteaks and after we eat, I'm kicking all your asses in Monopoly."

Marnie sits up a little. "Is Lex staying?" she asks hopefully.

"Unless you're booting me out," Lex answers, eyes glued to the laptop screen.

"I want you to stay," I say to Lex. He looks over his shoulder and gives me a quick smile, and I'm thankful he's here, helping me fix the mistakes Marnie made before they ruin her life. I'm thankful for my two sweet, sometimes irritating little sisters. I'm thankful for Peter, cooking and getting games ready, and for Mom's love, even when it's so intense it's suffocating.

And I'm thankful for a dad who makes me laugh when I know his heart is breaking. I'm thankful for a big brother and sister I know I can call when I'm in the dumps this holiday and missing them so much it's a physical pain.

I wish I could crack myself in two and be with everyone I love at the same time.

Or that I could somehow combine these two precious and completely different lives.

9

~~~~~~

Isn't It Poetic?

Late June
Belo's Bait and Tackle

FLORIDA

When you only have two workers on the floor, it's logical to *not* eat lunch at the same time. For the first week of work, Jude and I managed to stick to that rule. He'd tell me I should get something to eat, and I would run out and enjoy a juicy sandwich or savory taco at the beach, my feet in the sand for the entire hour. When I got back, I'd signal for Jude to take his lunch. If it was slow—and it was always really slow this summer—I'd peek in on him, eating his sad little sack lunch at the table in the back, a battered copy of *The Outsiders* open in front of him.

Seeing the cover—my favorite, with the black background and the torso of a guy in a white T-shirt with a black leather jacket, who I always imagined was Dallas—gave me a shivery thrill. Was Jude Zeigler reading one of my favorite books of all time because of the note I'd left him? I loved trying to guess. We barely spoke during our shifts, but there were so many other ways to communicate. Figuring out how to spot his messages and send messages of my own became like a game that eased the boredom and helped distract me from my worry about the fact that the bell above Belo's door rarely chimed. Where were all the customers?

I found a note on my windshield early in the week in Jude's dark scrawl. *"Get smart and nothing can touch you."* —*S. E. Hinton. Take the internship, Dell.*

"I liked my books and clouds and sunsets." —*S. E. Hinton. Get off my back and let me enjoy my summer. I have 3 parents and 2 older siblings if I need anyone bossing me around, thank you very much.* I left my reply in the register drawer when I knew he was opening.

Jude became less annoying in other ways. For example, he backed my idea to repaint the store walls after hours and helped me get Duke and Dad onboard. It's a huge improvement now that the walls are a fresh, bright white. He also helped me set up social media accounts for Belo's, which he promises to keep updated when I head back to Michigan in the fall. We don't attract a ton of followers right off the bat, but I know we'll be able to lure them in soon, and once we get that initial momentum going, we'll be unstoppable.

Jude is also just…nice. He encourages me to go to lunch first, always. He also convinces me to take breaks when I don't feel like it. Whenever he grabs himself a bottle of water, he always gets one for me, too. One shift when Dad is out meeting with his CPA, Jude switches the station from traditional country to general pop.

"What's this?" I shimmy toward him to the sound of Oasis, one of Peter's favorite bands.

"We can't go too wild, or we'll scare the old-timers who

come in. But there's only so much country I can handle." He doesn't look up from filing the special orders, but I catch his lips quirking up in a smile.

"Wait. You don't like country?" I ask, genuinely puzzled. I thought he and Dad were on the same page about the music in this place.

Jude finishes filing and clips the folder onto the board for Dad to check. "Nope. But I like working for Belo, and I respect that he's the boss. And everyone knows the boss picks the music."

"Um, you should definitely tell him. I mean, you practically live here in the summer." I lean on the counter and take a long look at Jude like I'm seeing him for the first time. What else haven't I noticed? What else do I have all wrong when it comes to him?

"I don't *hate* country." He hesitates. "But old alternative? New alternative? Hard rock, metal? That's what I really like."

Later, when I'm sitting in the break room, I notice Jude's backpack is covered in pins: Tool, Foo Fighters, Alice in Chains, Thrice, Black Rebel Motorcycle Club. I look them over like an archaeologist at a fresh dig. There's so much about Jude that I never would have guessed, and I kind of love being proven wrong.

When I get to work this morning, I find a worn copy of Robert Frost's poems next to the magic glass cleaner. Smiling so hard it makes my cheeks hurt, I sit with my back to the gleaming glass and thumb through to the bookmarked poem. Of course. "The Road Not Taken."

I roll my eyes and decide to risk a conversation. Maybe

some miracle will occur, and Jude and I won't end up bickering.

"Are you trying to tell me something?" Not the best intro if I want a nonargumentative conversation, but I always find it awkward trying to figure out how to talk to Jude. He's sitting in the small break room Dani and I painted a pale blue years ago to make up for the fact that it doesn't have any windows or doors. The paint is scuffed and peeling off the walls in long ribbons now—this room holds a ton of humidity, and even with the air set to a chilly sixty-eight, it always feels as muggy as a swamp for some reason.

"Yes." Jude puts down his sandwich—it looks like ham and swiss, maybe, and definitely brown-bagged from home. It's very skimpy, nothing like the double-bacon egg sandwich I got at 5 Brothers before I came in.

I should be out front, working the counter with my dad, and I wait for Jude to point that out. Just to goad him, I settle into the seat across from him and put my feet up on the other empty chair. Instead of reminding me that my break is in an hour, he opens a small bag of Zapp's chips, takes a few out, and turns the bag my way.

"Thank you," I blurt out, shocked. "For sharing your chips," I clarify, biting down and relishing the crispy, salty deliciousness. "Not for lecturing me in poem form." I wave the book at him.

"It's not a lecture." He leans back, and I try not to notice how broad his shoulders are, but they take up a lot of space in this tiny room. Even if I am annoyed that he's trying to bully me with poetry, I can't just ignore perfectly gorgeous shoulders. "Frost is Ponyboy's poet."

I bite into another chip. "Touché, but the poem Ponyboy quotes is 'Nothing Gold Can Stay.'" I tap the spine of the book on the table between us. "*You* marked off 'The Road Not Taken.'"

"I did?" He looks so honestly confused, I flip the book around, open to the page marked with a bright blue sticky arrow tab. He takes it from my hands and reads it slowly, then looks up at me. "It's a great poem, but I didn't mark it. I bought this at Second Stories, downtown. Whoever owned it before must have left that bookmark in."

"Oh." I clear my throat and feel the color rise up in my cheeks. I snatch the book back with a mumbled "Sorry."

He shrugs, those wide shoulders bobbing up and down with a steady rise and fall, like the waves deep out in the ocean. "Don't apologize. I kind of wish I'd marked it for you. It's a great poem."

"I just thought..." I bite my lip, and he finally cracks a sly smile.

"You thought I was trying to push you to do that internship?" He nods when I blush harder. "I still think you should. Belo said you could maybe work on it down here?"

"Maybe. But it's a lot of work. I'd be there all the time, not here. It would be like..." It would be like my achievement-oriented Michigan life trailed me to Florida. "Like school during summer. I take enough credits all year long." To distract from yet another complication I don't feel like thinking about, I reach out and point to the page. "Anyway, maybe the poem means I already picked the right road. Maybe being here *is* my road 'less traveled by.'"

His dark eyes meet mine for a few long seconds, then he

tugs the book back and looks down at the page again, mouthing the words like he's untangling knotted fishing line. "Only there is no right road."

"Yes, there is. The road he chose wound up being the *right* one. It says he chose the one less traveled and that 'made all the difference.'" When he shakes his head slightly, I sigh. "Trust me, I had to dissect this thing for AP Lit last year. I know it like the back of my hand."

"It's just…" He flips the poem back to me and points, his fingertip making a rough rasp against the paper. "He keeps saying both paths are equal." He moves his finger over the places where—right there in black-and-white—Frost very obviously made a case for how the paths were *equally appealing*. "I don't think he's saying he made the *right* choice. I think he's saying that there were good things about both paths, but he'll never know what good stuff he's missed out on or what kind of trouble he avoided because *choosing* is what makes all the difference."

"Let me see that." I take the book with shaking fingers and stare with fresh eyes at the words I studied so hard for so long, I wound up with a perfect 5 on the AP test. How is it possible that I apparently know the poem so well, but missed so much? "'…I could not travel both / and be one traveler…'" I read, the words like an arrow thunking into a target I never even noticed was there. *"One traveler."*

"Dell?" Jude leans forward, so close I could reach my hand up and rub the sandpapery stubble on his jaw. I don't, of course. But I *could*. "Are you okay?"

I could not travel both and be one traveler.

"So basically this poem is saying that making *any* choice

means giving up all other possibilities forever. Whatever you choose, no matter how carefully you decide, you lose. And there's no way to ever know what you lost." I close the book and drum my fingers on the cover. "That sucks. That's seriously so depressing."

"I don't think so." Jude slumps back in his chair and frowns. "What's depressing is never even having a choice."

"What do you mean?" I eye Jude Zeigler with a fair amount of suspicion. Sure, we've come to a kind of truce recently—maybe we even have a coworker-ish type of friendship. And I misread his gift, so he's not as much of a bossy jerk as I thought. But he's still the Jude I've always known and been irritated by. He loves a good lecture. He's an uptight, boring, rule-following pain in the ass.

Right?

So why do I find myself leaning closer when he leans toward me? Why am I focusing on how beautiful his mouth is? What would it be like to kiss that mouth?

What am I thinking?

"Sometimes…" He scrubs his palm over his face and scowls, looking exactly the way I imagined a tortured Dallas Winston would look when I was a tween. "Do you ever feel stuck? Like you're not going anywhere? Like no matter how hard you work, you're going to be in the same place, doing the same thing for the rest of your life?" He balls up the empty chip bag and tosses it into the trash can with a vicious snap, snorting. "Never mind. You obviously don't have to worry about that kind of crap."

Maybe I *don't* want to kiss that infuriating mouth.

"You think you know everything about me?"

"I know you had to choose between a pretty amazing internship and working for your dad, who worships the ground you walk on. And there's a chance you could do both. Look, I'm not saying it's a bad thing. Just...you're really lucky." He flicks at the side of the book like this is all Robert Frost's fault.

"You have no clue what my life's like. Maybe you feel like you're stuck in this one place with your one family, working the same job and hanging out with the same friends, going to the same school...but I'd give anything to not have to divide up everything I love all the time. I always have two roads in front of me, and I love them *both*. So much! But I'm only one person." I smack the table with the book so hard, Jude half jumps out of his seat. "The poem is about someone who can't go back and choose, but I *have to* do that. I have to choose over and over, I have to say no to people I love all the time, and it sucks. I *wish* I didn't have to choose. I wish I had one path like you."

He sweeps the last of his sandwich into the paper bag, crumples it into a hard ball, and thwacks it into the garbage can, then stands up. "I need to get back on the floor. You can take your break now if you want." He pushes his chair in.

"I don't want to take my break." I follow him to the door, and in our rush to get out, we wind up crammed in the doorway together. We're rarely standing so close, but right now we're eye to eye, noses almost brushing. He's breathing fast. "What's wrong?"

"Nothing's wrong, Dell. I just need to get back to—"

"Dusting the shelves we've already dusted a hundred times? Waiting for the customers who never come in?" I move a little closer, definitely too close to be considered polite, too close for work acquaintances. "No one in Michigan knows about my dad or Duke or Dani. It's like they don't exist."

Jude keeps his mouth closed, but his eyes widen.

"I go by my stepdad's last name there—it's Jepsen. Actually I go by my first and middle initials, so I'm AJ Jepsen when I'm in Michigan. Della Beloise doesn't even *exist*. I have two younger sisters, Marnie and Lilli. People call us the Triple Threat Jepsens, and I never correct them because that would be weird. But I feel like a liar, basically all the time, every minute of the day." I'm shaking, from my lips down to my knees, but it's not a bad shake. It's like getting out of the ocean after a really long swim, when you've pushed yourself a little too far and feel a little more exhausted and a little more alive than you've ever felt before. "So maybe not that lucky after all."

He puts his hand out and touches my arm, gently, just for a few seconds, then pulls back. I think that's it, that he'll walk out on the floor, and we'll keep our peace for the rest of the shift, but he suddenly says, "I work here so many hours because I really appreciate everything your dad's done for me, and I love this place. But I also just hate going home. When I'm not here, I'm out on the water, or on the beach, or I just park in random parking lots. I go anywhere that keeps me away from my parents. They basically live to party, and I know that sounds fun or cool or whatever, but, trust me, it's not. It blows. I'm not sure if I've ever seen them both sober at the same time. I'm not sure if I've ever talked to either one of them when they weren't at least buzzed. I worry about them all the time, and I'm pretty pissed at them. I also feel like if I ever leave this place, they'll drink themselves to death. Even though I know they'll probably do that anyway, I feel stuck." His smile is tight. "So not that lucky either."

"Shit." Impulsively, I take his hand and squeeze it tight. "That's rough, Jude. I admit, I always imagined you having this really boring TV-sitcom family."

"Maybe like *Shameless*, but sadder and less entertaining. And with less hooking up."

We both laugh, and he says, "You want some help with that window display?"

He's been stalling on helping me with the display all week. I think it would be eye-catching to anyone driving by and maybe bring in some business. Jude keeps insisting no one would ever see it from the road anyway, but it feels like we have to do *something* else to combat the great, silent nothing as Belo's seems to fade away.

"Sure. Thanks." I let go of his hand, but slowly. Holding it felt really good.

We work side by side, in near silence for the rest of our shift, and when it's time to close up, Jude walks me to my Jeep. The sun is setting, turning the sky into a neon explosion. I have the urge to ask him if he wants to stop by and share some of the fish stew my dad prepared in the Crock-Pot this morning, but I don't feel like watching Dad wink and smirk all night long.

"Hey, Dad is throwing this huge welcome-back party for me Friday night. Seriously, it's no big deal if you don't want to come, but—"

"Are you inviting me to your party, Della?" Jude leans against the hood of his truck and seems to enjoy watching me squirm.

"You don't have to feel obligated. My dad always throws an awesome party, though."

He reaches into his pocket and drags out his rolled-up copy of *The Outsiders*. "Do you think a Greaser would be welcome at a Soc party?"

"Okay, smart-ass, you could joke that *I'm* a Soc, and maybe I am…at least, AJ Jepsen might be. But Belo would fight you—with his switchblade—if you called *him* a Soc!" I raise my eyebrow. "This will pretty much be a Greaser party."

"Does Belo like this book?" Jude tries to hide his shock, but it's probably hard to imagine my overactive father reading anything.

"It's one of the only books he's ever read cover to cover. I think this one, *Of Mice and Men*, and maybe *The Giver*?" I laugh, and add, "Plus whatever I forced him to read to me at bedtime when I came here to visit." I tug my Belo's shirt off and fold it neatly. Jude looks away like a gentleman, but I swear I hear him suck in a quick breath. "My dad used to say he was like Dally and my mom was Cherry, and that's why things never worked out."

"Your dad is *not* Dallas Winston. Maybe Darry? Or maybe Sodapop."

I shrug. "He said he was different back then." I feel my phone buzz in my pocket. I figure it's Dad, letting me know he went straight home after the CPA meeting, but it's just a text from Marnie. Weird. I thought she didn't have phone access. I'll text her later, when I'm home. "I better head out. So maybe I'll see you Friday at the party. I'm off, so Duke will be on shift." I hold back a laugh at how Jude's face falls. He and Duke do *not* get along.

"You know what? That sounds great. I'll see you Friday."

"Come at seven, and you'll be fashionably late." I get into my Jeep and tug the door shut, roll down my window, and wave at Jude. Before I chicken out, I add, "It's a date."

As I'm pulling out, I hear him whistling the Queen song we belted out together while we worked on the display, and my heart flips over unexpectedly.

10

Winter Formal

Last December

MICHIGAN

Jaylen has demanded her pound of flesh plus interest in return for her silence.

She's kept tight-lipped about Marnie's low-level espionage, and she wants to be rewarded for it. At first it was easy enough. I was so grateful that she lied to the administration on behalf of Marnie by backing up our story that we had no idea who took the pictures, that posting them to Marnie's account had been accidental, that it was all a huge misunderstanding. Jaylen was the one who pointed out that the locker rooms had been left unattended the night of the last big game, that there were plenty of people who could have come in and framed Marnie for what went down.

Maybe if it had just been me and Marnie, the administration would have smelled a rat and called foul. But Jaylen mustered the support of the entire volleyball team. And the wholesome, school-wide social media blackout Lilli had organized softened the administration to the Jepsen girls in general. They didn't even involve our parents—Lex pointed out that was probably because they really had no solid evidence, and they didn't want to risk pissing them off with baseless accusations. So Marnie slid by, unscathed, case closed.

Or so it seemed.

As if I'm not stressed enough dealing with Marnie's mess on top of my intense academic and extracurricular obligations, Marnie starts sleepwalking every night, and it's cutting into my already-slim sleep schedule.

Despite a healthy dose of melatonin, a white-noise machine, two rounds of yoga for sleep and a deep meditation exercise, I'm wide-awake under my weighted, lavender-scented blanket, anxious about how tired I'll be for school tomorrow. We're headed for Christmas break, so I have three tests, an intense lab, final rehearsal for the Christmas concert, and a killer in-class essay on my plate, and that's just tomorrow. The day after is equally as stressful. What I need right now is to get more than four hours of sleep.

I'm just about to drift off when I hear a creak outside my bedroom door and sit straight up, my fingers already wrapped around the handle of the field hockey stick I keep next to my bed for protection. I tiptoe out, and Marnie is standing at the top of the stairs, ghostly pale in the silver moonlight that pours from the floor-to-ceiling windows on the landing. Her eyes are creepily wide-open, and they stare ahead, blank. Goose bumps break out from my neck to the back of my knees and make me shiver.

"Marnie," I hiss. She takes a step closer to the winding staircase that descends to a hard marble foyer. I dart out of my room and wrap an arm around her shoulders. She's gotten so thin the last few weeks. I notice she just pushes her food around on her plate at dinner, too mopey to enjoy the dishes Mom is cooking specially for her.

Mom has asked a few times if I know what's wrong with Marnie, but I always manage to dodge her questions. What would be the point of telling her now? Marnie came out of questioning by the principal and the ethics committee unscathed. Since she was never formally considered a primary suspect, they didn't even notify Mom and Peter. We can breathe easy.

If Marnie can just start eating and sleeping again.

"Marnie." I shake her back and forth, and she blinks a few times, then looks around, confused.

"AJ. Why are you on the stairs?" she rasps in a sleep-scratchy voice.

"You're sleepwalking again. C'mon, I'll bring you back to bed." I accidentally drop the field hockey stick with a clatter I half hope wakes our parents. *Please, can someone else come deal with this, with Marnie and her ceaseless sleepwalking?*

I just finished *Macbeth* in AP British Literature, and writing a paper on Lady Macbeth's guilty sleepwalking had been a piece of cake. I used Marnie's guilt-induced nocturnal prowling as the basis.

"No." Tears spill out of her eyes silently, streaking down her cheeks and neck, and soaking the collar of her thermal. It's eerie to watch her cry like this. "I can't sleep."

"I can't either." She's shivering *and* crying now. I rub my hands up and down her arms, fast, to try to make enough friction to heat her up. It doesn't help. "You have to get to bed. You're going to get hypothermia standing out here."

"Can I sleep with you?"

"Sure." As kids, I always hated when Marnie would climb in bed with me after a nightmare or get assigned to sleep next to me on vacation. She kicks and thrashes in her sleep, and she's a total cover hog. She also snuggles, which makes it hard to get comfortable when you're trying to fall asleep. But I'll deal with all of it if it means Marnie might actually get a good night's sleep; then maybe I actually can, too.

We head into my room, and I hold the blankets back so she can climb under. She curls on her side, and I spoon her, only wincing a little when she presses the frigid soles of her feet to my shins.

"I was dreaming about Jaylen," she whispers over the sound of the crashing waves on my white-noise machine. "She was a vampire, and she was sucking all my blood out. I was dying, and she kept laughing and saying, 'Smile! This will look so cute in my stories!' while she took all these selfies."

I curl closer to her. "That sounds like the plot from a really bad teen-vampire movie."

"Do you ever feel like everyone in our whole school is just a bunch of phonies?"

The moonlight spills silver and bright in the room. I should have pulled the shade down. Maybe that would have helped me sleep better. But I'm not sure *anything* can help the nerve-deep insomnia I'm wrestling with lately. I'd be more annoyed with Marnie if I didn't know exactly what she's going through.

"Has Morgenstern started his *Catcher in the Rye* unit? I mean…isn't that what high school is kind of known for?" I swallow hard, thinking about how I've never been able to tell Tessa or Harper about my family in Florida. More and more I wonder *why? Why* does it feel so risky to lay it all out for the people who are supposed to be my best friends?

Why are we so biting and cruel to the people we're supposed to care about the most? And can I change it?

"But why?" Marnie's question echoes the thoughts running through my brain. "Why are we all like this?" Her voice thickens, and I know it's because tears are running down her face again, fast and furious.

"What do you mean?" I ask because I want to see how closely her theory matches mine.

In the dark, I wiggle closer, so close I can smell the flowery hint of shampoo in her newly shorn hair. She's been doing more obviously rebellious stuff—shaving half her head, getting a nose ring that sent Mom through the roof, and attempting a tattoo. The wife of the guy who runs the shop works with Peter, so one phone call had Marnie back home and safe, tattoo-free. Mom long ago showed Marnie, Lilli, and me the blurry moth she'd gotten tattooed on her lower back as a teenager. She told us she wanted us to picture it anytime we felt like a tattoo might be a great idea. It winds up that smudged moth hadn't been enough of a deterrent in the face of this wild, swirling mix of sadness and anxiety Marnie can't seem to pop out of.

"It's like everything is a competition. The only reason anyone likes anyone is to get something—popularity, volleyball plays, sex—"

"Marnie!" I cut in, shocked that my sister is being so blunt about a topic we definitely do *not* talk about so openly in the Jepsen household.

"What?" She rolls over so she's facing me, her features all

pixie-sharp in the silver light. "You can't seriously tell me you and Lex haven't had sex."

"I can very seriously tell you it's none of your business," I shoot back, glad she probably can't see what a deep red I'm blushing. "But no."

One more reason Lex can't seem to quit me is that he has good reason to keep up the endless chase. I haven't yet done the one thing that every other girl he's dated was more than happy to do within a few dates. Lex took great pride in being so irresistible. He liked to brag that before he met me, every girl he'd been with had been more than eager to hop into bed with him, and I demolished his record. But Lex loves a challenge.

I have a suspicion that's all he loves about me.

Marnie curls an arm under her head and scoots closer. "Really? Don't you think he's, like, super hot?" She sounds like a fangirl at some boy-band concert.

"Marnie, you like girls," I remind her, and she rolls her eyes.

"Just being objective, Lex is super hot. Also I like girls *and* I like guys. I like a lot of people." She snaps her mouth shut and purses her lips when I gasp a little. "Don't be such a prude. God, it would be amazing if anyone in this family actually talked to each other about *real shit* once in a while."

"Real shit?" I repeat, laughing at the swagger in Marnie's language. "I have zero interest in talking to *anyone* in this family about who they do or don't want to have sex with." It sounds completely Puritan even as it's coming out of my mouth, but I can't wrap my head around a more cringeworthy topic. Sharing intimate stuff is *not* the way we operate.

"I mean, I love you no matter who you want to be with, no question. But, literally, *no question*. I don't need to know that much information about your sex life or anyone else's, thanks."

"Maybe that's why we're all stressed-out psychos," Marnie huffs.

"Speak for yourself." For a few long seconds, the only sound is the rushing waves repeating in a canned rhythm on my white-noise machine. I clear my throat. "Lex is too…intense. I can never get comfortable with him, you know?" I realize that it's not just sex I'm talking about. I don't feel comfortable telling Lex about so many things—what I really feel and fear and hope for. I don't feel all that comfortable with Tessa or Harper either. That can't be normal. Can it?

Marnie's head bobs back and forth on the pillow as she nods. "I know." She takes a deep breath. "And that's how I feel with Jaylen. And with Mom and Dad. Sometimes I even feel that way with you," she adds quietly.

I think about how I can talk to Dani about anything, anytime. If Lex were someone I brought up in any detail when I'm in Florida, I'd be able to talk about him to Dani. Or I could just say I wanted to talk about a guy, and she'd be there to listen, without judging.

Without giving me the kind of shit I'm currently giving Marnie.

I reach my hand out and grab hers. It feels weird, and as soon as we're holding hands, I'm filled with all kinds of anxious questions; *How long should I hold her hand? Does she mind that my palms are sweating? What if I get a cramp? Shouldn't this be easier? We're sisters. We're sisters…*

But Marnie doesn't seem to feel remotely awkward. She

grabs on and squeezes back, tight, like she's been waiting for me to reach out.

"Tell me," I say suddenly, and I mean it with all my pounding heart. "Anything you want. I won't be an asshole."

"You don't need to fix it," she assures me in a rush, like she's afraid I'll take my offer back if she burdens me with solving her problems.

"I won't try to, for once." We laugh a little, then she goes quiet.

"McKenzie… I know what you think, and you're right. She wound up…using me. But nobody ever felt so real. Nothing ever… She made me feel like she just liked me for who I was. I mean, until she asked me to steal the playbook and kind of ruined my life." Her laugh is a rusty, aching sound. "Also… she convinced me to, um, send her…"

She lags off, and the silence stretches into a tiny eternity.

"Nudes?" I offer gently. *Of course.* Of course that was the flaming sword over my sister's head all along. And in this prude family, in this judgmental community, what would Marnie have done to protect her reputation?

She nods and hiccups around a sob. I tug her closer and rub a hand over her shoulders. "Don't cry, don't cry," I croon, the same way our mom always did to comfort us when we were sick or hurt as little girls.

When I think about it, it's not particularly comforting to tell someone *not* to cry. I know firsthand how good it can feel to let it all out, but I still keep telling my sister to stop anyway. Mostly because I don't know what to do with her tears, and they're shredding my heart.

I know how to be strong. I know how to fix things. But

I'm not really sure how to be sad, how to let things break. I have no experience with that, and it occurs to me that that's a huge problem.

"It's just, like... I was so...kind of embarrassed, I guess? And she talked me into it, like it was just going to be for her and me, like this really secret thing. And I honestly felt like I could trust her, you know? So it's really sick because, first, I feel really embarrassed and really kind of pissed at myself. But I also feel, I guess...betrayed. Like, I put myself out there for her, and she just used me. She just screwed me over, and now she has them, she has *my* pictures for good, and I'm scared she'll use them against me again—" Marnie cuts off because she's sobbing too hard to keep talking.

I've pulled her into my arms, and I'm holding her tight. "It's okay, it's okay," I keep saying, even though I don't know if it is.

What can I do to get those pictures back? Maybe nothing. Will Marnie get into trouble for sending them in the first place? Even if I figure out a way to threaten McKenzie, what's to stop her from using them in the future, when I'm not around to step in on Marnie's behalf? What if she's been contacting Marnie privately? I assumed they were through, but maybe this explains Marnie's behavior and how upset she's been.

Before it was just insomnia keeping me awake, but now a fresh wash of anxiety crests over me. *I don't know how to fix this.* I can't tell our parents—they would definitely not be open-minded about something like this, and anyway, what happened earlier in the year will come rushing out. There's too much tangled up in this now.

"What should I do?" Marnie asks, crying softly. "I can't tell my friends. Everyone hates me because of Katrina, but she was such a jerk to me. I never told anyone, but she's not as sweet as she seems, okay? She made me feel terrible about myself…"

Marnie keeps going, telling me the nasty remarks Katrina would make about her looks and her failure to excel in school, how she was nothing but a dumb jock, how she was so annoying because of her ADHD. I spoon as close as I can and press the tear-sticky hair out of her face, off her cheeks, furious at Katrina for being such an asshole and for tricking us all into imagining *she* was the wronged one after the breakup.

"I can't go to Winter Formal," Marnie says in a choked voice. "Seriously. I just can't spend the whole night faking I like all these people who don't care about me. They all think I'm some kind of Judas. I can't do it."

"Okay," I whisper. "Just calm down now, okay? Calm down and try to sleep. We'll figure this out."

The next morning, while Marnie snores in my bed, arms and legs flung at every angle, I tiptoe down the stairs and find my mother doing her morning yoga stretches.

"Mom?" My voice grates over the soothing intonations of the yoga instructor on the screen.

"AJ." Mom sinks into Child's Pose and speaks to the gleaming hardwood. "I wanted to talk to you about Winter Formal. I have an influencer who reached out to me about custom dresses. I know we already bought yours, but I think one of her designs would look amazing on you. Would you be willing to switch? You don't care, do you?"

I press my lips together, trying to think how I could say no now even if I wanted to. In all honesty, my Winter Formal dress is the least of my worries, but I'm also pissed that my mother so cavalierly positions and repositions us for the benefit of her personal mom-blogger empire. She didn't get the Tide backing, but she did get an organic laundry detergent to endorse her, so now all our clothes smell kind of like hemp all the time, and she's hungry to keep the deals snowballing. According to the vision board in her meditation room, she'd love to reach Goop levels of lifestyle-branding success.

"Sure." It's not just the path of least resistance; it also makes for a nice bargaining chip if I'm going to get Marnie out of all of this. "Mom, you know how Marnie has been having some, uh, stress?"

Mom stands up and stretches deep into Warrior One, shaking her hair out of her face with an elegant toss of her head. "Marnie is *always* having some kind of meltdown lately. What's going on now?"

Mom's annoyed tone doesn't bode well.

"She's not really feeling up to the dance this weekend, and—"

"No," Mom says, shaking her head. "She made a commitment to her date and to the school, and *I* made a commitment to several people for a spread on my blog. This is important. I want you girls as a united front. Plus, it will make her feel better to get out of her pajamas and stop moping. This is *exactly* what Marnie needs, even if she doesn't think so."

"But maybe we could have one of her friends take her place for hair and makeup and stuff?" I try again, knowing before the words leave my mouth it's futile to even try.

Mom stops and stands straight, naturally rigid for someone

who does so much stretching as part of her everyday routine. "AJ, look at me. What is this really about? The truth."

"She's just feeling down," I mutter.

"This isn't like Marnie." She balls her fists on her hips. "What's up?"

Cornered, I feel the panic rise up in the back of my throat. "Nothing. Nothing's up."

Mom narrows her eyes at me.

"She's just bummed about volleyball, I think. The season ended so early," I say, my words limp.

Mom's face softens, and she nods, relieved. "I didn't really think about that. Poor Angela Wells really took the wind out of their sails. I know how much your sister wanted to go all the way to states. Don't tell her, but your father and I are signing her up for that camp, the one where the Olympic athletes rotate through and do the leadership summits with all the…" Mom waves her hands around vaguely "…volleyball skills. It's costing us a small fortune, but Marnie's worked so damn hard. She deserves this."

I swallow around the lump in my throat. "Yep. She does."

"And, trust me, I'm not being the Wicked Witch here. Going to Winter Formal will be fun for Marnie. It will take her out of her funk for the night. When she looks back on this, she's going to be glad she had her mom around to kick her out of bed and get her motivated. Marnie and I are very alike, which is why we're always butting heads. I know exactly what she needs. Okay?"

"Mmm-hmm." I nod, edging back to the winding staircase that leads to my room. I'll have to tell Marnie when she wakes up that she'll need to go on being a phony, faking a smile, keeping whatever hurts shut up tight because that's how we do things in this house.

We barrel through and keep going until all the bad feelings are just a distant memory.

Marnie is pretty resigned to the news. The night of Winter Formal comes. Mom surprises Marnie by having the fashion influencer bring a few velvet tuxes for her to try, which is awesome and proves that Mom *is* trying. When we had gone shopping earlier, Marnie basically agreed to the first dress Mom suggested so she could be done as quickly as possible, but she actually seems kind of excited about the tuxes.

I'm laced into a dreamy, poofy champagne dress that's definitely gorgeous but also kind of boring and adult. I really liked my silky orange mermaid dress, and it would have stood out in a sea of darker tones, but maybe I can bust it out for Junior Prom in the spring.

Lilli has been asked to perform the song she composed for the social media blackout in November, so she's outfitted in a beautiful deep purple dress that makes her soft golden hair look like it's glowing. Marnie wears a burgundy velvet tux, ultrafitted and super sexy. Her half-shaved head and glinting nose ring complete the whole badass ensemble, but the misery behind her eyes as she watches Jaylen shriek and laugh and pose without giving her a second glance tempers some of the rebellion.

"You look amazing," Lex whispers when he gets to the house and pulls me aside to look me over. He nuzzles my neck and holds out the red-rose corsage. "A little basic, right? But your mom said sometimes basic is classic, so…" He pins it on, and I let out a long sigh. "Want to ditch?" It's Lex's most common refrain.

"We can't." My response is also pretty automatic at this point. "Lex, can I ask you something?"

"Sure." He puts some distance between us and studies me, like he smells the unrest boiling over under my skin.

"Are we…friends?" I ask.

"Are you breaking up with me?" he bounces back.

"No." I shake my head, though a tiny piece of me wonders if I should pounce on the opportunity he just tossed my way. Why do I even think that? Things between us have been… *fine*. "You tell me what's bothering you, right? What worries you? What you're excited about?" I ask.

"AJ, I bitch to you all the time, about everything. Are you seriously proposing I whine to you *more* than I already do?" He cracks a wide smile. "Because my complaint list can be long—"

"If you're upset or sad, am I the person you turn to?" I grab him by the elbow and squeeze his arm, willing him to take this seriously.

Lex squirms at the question. Sincerity isn't something he's ever very comfortable with. "I don't get sad. And you're the one who gets upset. It's *my* job to calm *you* down." He comes closer and kisses my bare shoulder, his face so handsome, we probably look like we should be in a cologne ad or something.

"I care about you," I tell him. It's not love. We don't say *that* to each other, and that's fine. I barely say it to my family, so it's not that weird.

"I care about you," he says, squinting at me like he's not sure where this is going. "You feel okay?"

No, I don't. I feel nervous. I feel helpless. I feel like a fake. I feel like I'm on a carnival ride that's malfunctioning, and there's no way for me to get off. I feel sad, all the time, buried alive in hopeless, dark sadness. And I can't make anyone understand how I feel no matter how hard I try because I can never tell anyone the truth. Not the whole truth, anyway.

"Yeah, of course." I lean in and kiss his cheek. The photographer snaps a picture, then flips her camera to show us.

"You two look amazing. That was *the perfect* picture," she gushes.

I look, and it is the perfect illusion, the ultimate example of why you can't trust everything you see on social media. When that picture posts, it'll get more likes than anything I've ever posted before. People will think it's evidence of an incredibly romantic moment, when, in fact, it's the instant I realized I'm basically witty acquaintances with the guy who's supposed to be one of the closest people in my life.

"Okay, let's get your beautiful daughters set up for some shots," the photographer chirps to my mother, who corrals the three of us to the stairs, fussing over our hair and picking invisible threads off our outfits. My sisters and I ascend the stairs and everyone we care about—friends, parents, boyfriends—gazes up adoringly, gushing over the gorgeous picture we make. I'm surrounded by people who love me, and I've never felt so panicked and alone.

Marnie, Lilli, and I hold the bannister, smiles plastered on our faces, as the photographer snaps picture after picture. Lilli leans back into me, an angelic smile on her face that could be real, though I don't know if I'd be able to tell if it wasn't. She's practiced that perfect smile for so long, so regularly, I'm not sure I know the difference anymore. Marnie holds my hand in a death grip, her fingers cold and clammy. She looks tough, but I feel her shaking with nerves. I wish with everything in me that I could either make it all better or make it all go away.

Unfortunately, the only option I really have is to disappear and forget it all for another healing summer, and that option won't be possible for months. Until then, we just have to keep our smiles up and push through the pain.

11

Block Party

Early July

FLORIDA

Being back in my room after a whole year away is a pretty bizarre form of time travel—and a cause for brutal self-reflection.

For example, did I seriously think those oversize white hipster sunglasses were cool, or was I just trying to embrace some random trend? I shake my head at the matte teal nail polish I was obsessed with, the sequin pillow with *I love you to the moon and back* embroidered on it, and the jean vest covered in pins from a local country band Dani loves and I convinced myself I was into, too.

Mom is a total disciple of Marie Kondo and the whole minimalism movement, so things get tossed and donated mercilessly in my Michigan house. Back north, my room is an oasis of neutral tones and a few tastefully eclectic accessories. I have a single bottom shelf reserved for my most precious personal keepsakes. Everything else is constantly on the chopping block, and if deemed less than essential, culled. *Ruthlessly.*

Here I have the luxury to let memories explode around me, collect dust, even—*gasp!*—inspire regret.

"Hey, bugbite." Duke leans against the door frame of my room, thick-framed glasses sliding down his nose. "I have a few good ones for you." He holds out a stack of books—history, manga, essays, fiction. Duke and I inhale them all.

"Thank you. You can put them—" I look around and shrug at the mess.

He pushes aside the refillable popcorn bucket we got when we were going to weekly Friday night drive-in movies last summer and drops the books in the small cleared space. "You need to clean this room, Dell, or you're going to have to add roaches to the list of bugs eating you alive."

I scratch at one of my dozen or so mosquito bites absentmindedly and say, "Dad says the bugs love me because my blood is so sweet."

"And where did he pick up that scientific tidbit? A vampire movie?" Duke snorts as he falls next to me on the bed. "Holy shit, I'm *not* looking forward to my shift today."

"I can go in for you," I offer. I don't admit—even to myself—that I kind of miss seeing Jude on my days off.

"No, you seriously need to clean in here. This room should be condemned." He rubs a hand over his face. "Did *any* customers come in the whole week?"

"A few. I was thinking Dad could do, like, a contest? Maybe have people post photos of their biggest catch or use hashtags for a giveaway—"

"Dell." Duke gives me the same condescending look Jude's been giving me whenever I bring up ways to improve Belo's, and I feel the same burst of rage. "C'mon. You know the only thing that would really help business?"

"What?" I ask, knowing I won't like his answer.

"If, by some miracle, the big-box sports places popping up everywhere *all* declared bankruptcy and went under in the next few months. And, even if that actually happened, Dad would still need to make all the updates and changes he's been dragging his feet about for the last five years."

"Could we help him make those changes?" I ask, tangling one arm in the strand of twinkle lights behind my bed when I sit up too fast, excited at the prospect of being able to help with something, *anything*.

"No." Duke lets that one blunt word hang in the air until it sinks in. "Can I be honest with you, or are you going to pretend like I'm some asshole for speaking the truth?"

I untangle my arm from the lights, twisting some of the burned-out bulbs to see if they'll relight. "Probably gonna call you an asshole, but go ahead."

Duke takes my hands, which is very unassholelike of him and says, "Dell, Dad's heart isn't in Belo's anymore. It hasn't been for years."

I shake my head. "No. You're wrong. He's *so* proud of Belo's. It's been in our family forever. He loves it. He's always happy there."

"It's a burden for him. Listen to me on this one, bugbite." My brother's voice is soft, but his words slam down like a sledgehammer on my heart. "When he needed that place so he could provide for us, he worked really hard. And those few years when you and me and Dani all worked there? Those were his glory years. He didn't love being there…he loved being there *with us*. And then I got the job with the university. Dani opened her salon. And you're just hanging on because you're a good kid, but this is the end of the road, and he knows that. You'll be going to college next year, and then what? It's just him and Zeigler staring at each other until the place tanks? It's time to face facts. We need to take the bait shop off life support and let it go."

It feels like I swallowed a hive of bees. My throat is itchy and swollen and even the *thought* of swallowing hurts. "You're just saying that because you hate Belo's. You've always hated it," I accuse him.

"For sure," he agrees, zero percent hurt by my accusation. "I dread every shift there, and I always have. Sport fishing? Being stuck in a store full of crap I'll never use and couldn't care less about? Helping people find things they need for a sport I have no interest in? It's my definition of hell on earth, and I let Dad know that from the beginning. I was honest with him because I never wanted him to hang on for my sake."

"Maybe *I* want to run Belo's." I sound like a petulant toddler, and I know it.

"Dad showed me your internship project, bugbite," Duke says, rubbing my head so all my hair is pushed in front of my eyes. I knock his hand away, and he grins at me. My big brother can be so serious and so annoying at the same time. "I don't know what you're going to do when you get older, but I'll bet my ass you won't be running some two-bit bait shop in Nowhere, Florida." He squints at me from under his messy, dark curls, which are already outgrowing Dani's cut. "You and me? We aren't made to stay put like Dani and Dad. I love this place because you guys are here, but I want to go see the world. You can't tell me you don't feel the same way. It's time for all of us to move on." He bumps my shoulder.

"I love it here," I sniffle defiantly, curling onto my side. I grab the stuffed Roo toy Dani and Duke gave me for Christmas when I was five and hug him tight. Roo used to travel between this house and my Michigan house, but he's been a permanent resident here since the summer I turned thirteen. "What would even happen if Dad lost Belo's?"

"It would suck if he *lost* it," Duke says. "No one wants that to happen, but that's exactly what *will* happen if he doesn't act soon. He needs to stop dragging his feet and just admit he wants out. Find a real-estate agent, get a buyer *now*, while he still has savings and investments. That's prime property, and he could make a killing off it. If he doesn't, he's going to chew through everything he has saved to hold on to it, and he'll probably lose it in the end anyway. This is our busy season, Dell. We should be overrun with tourists and game fishers, but we barely have enough business to afford the electric bill. Face it—this is Belo's death rattle."

"But what would Dad *do* without Belo's?" I try to imagine my father doing anything other than manning the incredible little store he's always owned and run, and I pull up a blank.

Duke shrugs and stands up. "Maybe finally figure out what it is he *really* wants to do. He inherited Belo's from his dad, so it's not like he had much choice." He sticks his hands in his pockets. "I respect the hell out of Dad for taking such good care of us. I know he did what he had to do after my mom died." Subconsciouly, Duke takes hold of the beautiful gold cross that was his mother's. I've never seen him without it, even though he announced he was an atheist when he was twelve. "But I don't want to get stuck like he's stuck. Dad's had serious obligations since he was just out of high school. I can't even imagine that."

"We aren't obligations," I protest.

Duke gives me a pitying look. "I'm not saying he doesn't love us. But we're *definitely* obligations, bugbite. And now he might have a chance to do something he's always wanted to do. I, for one, am *not* going to blow smoke up his ass about Belo's." He holds out his arms and, with an exaggerated eye roll for good measure, I hop off the bed and hug him until he wheezes. "There's some Lysol under the sink. Disinfect this place. I bet there are plague spores lurking in here."

"Go to work already!" I yell, hurling Roo at him as he laughs his way out the door.

"See you tonight!" he calls from down the hall.

"I want you to sing karaoke with me at the party!" I yell louder.

"There isn't enough beer in the world to get me that drunk!" he screams back.

I fall back on my bed and think about what Duke said. Duke has always loved logic and puzzles. He's not a dreamer or a storyteller. But just because he loves facts doesn't mean he's right about this. Does it?

I think about it as I spend the next few hours deep cleaning my room, which is an exhausting task. It's so grueling, I'm glad for the interruption when I see my mom is calling.

"Just checking in," she says, the edge to her voice letting me know she's definitely going to ask: "Have you accepted the internship spot? Time is running out."

"I've been working a lot, and tonight is my welcome-home party, so…"

"Jesus, it takes two seconds, AJ!" Mom snaps, then takes a deep breath. "I'm sorry. Lilli was up all night last night again. She thinks she may be losing her voice, and she's really worried."

"Oh no!" Every time I get an update from Mom, I feel panic on Lilli's behalf. How is my baby sister juggling all of this?

"I think it's just stress. And humidity! I've talked to housekeeping so many times, but no one can seem to find us a proper humidifier for the room size, and the one I ordered won't be in for another week. Anyway, it's just so much."

"That sucks. I hate hearing that Lilli's not feeling well. I hope they get you that humidifier." I pause. "Um, Mom, can I ask you something?"

"Sure." She sounds too distracted for how serious this question is, but I go ahead anyway.

"Did my dad seem happy to own Belo's? Like, do you think it was something he always wanted?"

Mom pauses. "Sweetie, I was married to your dad so long ago, when he was incredibly young and immature. He was a different person then, honestly. Back when I knew him, he was looking to escape a lot of pain. He'd just lost his wife, he was partying too hard and working even harder. So I think Belo's was something he could focus on when other things were falling apart. But I'm sure things have changed." She makes a soft hum in the back of her throat. "Why do you ask?"

"No reason. Just something Duke said got me thinking."

"How are he and Dani doing?"

It's weird for Mom to ask so casually because for a short time long ago, Mom was Duke and Dani's full-time step-mom. She knew everything about them, could fill out their medical paperwork at the doctor's office and tucked them into bed at night with their favorite books and blankets. There's even physical evidence of Mom around the house—a few pages of their baby books are filled in by their mom, Allie, a few pages are filled in by my mom, and the rest are filled in by Nan Sunny. Pictures of Mom and the three of us at Easter, my baptism, and Christmas are on the walls alongside faded pictures of beautiful Allie, Nan Sunny, various Beloise cousins, grandparents, aunts, and uncles. A picture of me and Duke shoveling sand into a bright green pail at the beach while Mom sits next to us in a cute red bikini hangs on the wall under a picture of Dani from a year or two ago, cradling a curly-haired baby cousin I don't recognize at St. Monica's for what looks like his baptism.

Now Mom just asks for the CliffsNotes on their lives, always keeping a careful distance. I don't know the details of the divorce, but I always wonder how Mom could go from being a surrogate mother to Dani and Duke to a virtual stranger.

"They're doing great," I say. "Dani's salon is always booked. Duke is applying for a semester abroad in Cairo. They're fixing up this really cute bungalow down the street from Dad's place. They'll either flip it, or Dani and Bennie will buy Duke out and move in."

"That's wonderful." Mom still sounds distracted but also sincere. "Listen, Lilli just got up from her nap, and I want to make sure she gets in the shower to give her vocal chords some moisture. I love you, sweetie."

"I love you, t—" I sigh as the phone disconnects. "Almost made it that time, Mom," I mutter.

Dad pokes his head in about an hour later, just as I'm running the vacuum. "Hey, baby! We're getting all set up outside." He rubs his hands together. "You ready to party?"

"I just have to change, and I'll be right out!"

Dad shoots finger guns my way as he dances back down the hall. God, I've missed my goofy, extroverted father.

I notice another text from Marnie on my phone screen. SOS CALL ME NOW it reads. I unplug the vacuum and sigh. She asked me to call her the other day but I just texted with her for a few minutes before bed. She told me she was feeling upset but, no matter how much I asked, she wouldn't say what, exactly, was wrong. I finally reassured her things would get better, texted I loved her, and went to sleep. I wonder what she needs now, but I'm pretty confident it's not an emergency. She's probably hiding out somewhere with her contraband phone, bored out of her mind and looking to whine about it. I'm not about to put off getting ready for my party to deal with Marnie's made-up drama. It's summer, and *I'm officially off duty*. Busy. Call Dad, I text back, then toss my phone on the bed and start getting ready for the party. If it's serious enough, Marnie needs to reach out to Peter, anyway. I try my best to put my sister's problems out of my head and enjoy my night.

I open my closet, which, if I'm being honest with myself, could use a healthy dose of minimalism. Then again, there's something exciting about not having each coordinated, tailored outfit hanging on its designated hanger. I tug out off-the-shoulder tunics in stretchy blends and wildly patterned dresses that would make my mother poke her eyeballs out after she declared them *cheap and hideous*. Some of the things I unearth make me feel like an imposter in my own closet— I have no memory of wanting these things, let alone buying them. But I guess it's no better or worse than flipping through clothes that are chic, gorgeous, and chosen under someone else's watchful eye.

Another two texts pop up from Marnie. CALL ME.

I text back, Can't right now. Talk later.

THIS IS IMPORTANT, she responds almost immediately.

I clench the phone in my hand, wondering if I should just call, but I know she'll break down crying if she hears my voice, and the conversation will drag on and on while I try to talk her off the ledge. She's probably afraid of getting in trouble for lifting her phone from contraband. The thing is, she's probably upset, but she's safe. She's at an expensive, chaperoned camp. She's surrounded by adults who are there to take care of her. I *need* this time off. I do my best to be an awesome sister to Marnie all year long, to look after her and help her with whatever she needs, but today is *my* day. Dad has been planning this for weeks. Not only did I let him down for Thanksgiving, Christmas wound up being a no go, too. I deserve this. He deserves this.

Marnie can wait.

I hesitate, then type You'll be okay. Love you and turn my phone to silent.

I take a few deep breaths to quiet my guilt and flip through more items in my closet. There's a bright white A-line dress covered in ruby cherries with thin straps and a sweetheart neckline that's a little rockabilly and nothing AJ would be caught dead in…but it's perfect for Della. I slip it on but forgo the merciless red heels that accent it perfectly for a pair of sparkly white flip-flops and bounce out of my room, breathing deep the salt-and-coconut-sunscreen smell of our beachy cottage. Out the wide, screened windows I can hear the caw of the seagulls and the hum and drone of a prehistoric multitude of bugs. The sky is darkening to a dusky lavender, and I can already see the stars smattering across the purple arch of sky as I fling open the front door.

Dad's country-music party mix is blaring, there are tiki torches everywhere and so many citronella candles we might actually keep a few dozen of the five billion mosquitoes away. I walk up to the head of several picnic tables pushed together, white tablecloths fluttering over their wooden edges, brightly colored paper plates and cups stacked alongside plastic cutlery. There are huge bunches of bright balloons bobbing on the back of every chair and twinkling lights strung in the branches of every dogwood in the yard.

My dad stands in the middle of all our neighbors, my family and friends, and half our church congregation. He's wearing a *Keep Calm: Dad Is Cooking* apron I've never seen before. Is it a gift Dani and Duke had to pick without me, considering I'm barely ever around to do those things with them? Weird that in Michigan *I'm* the one who coordinates every Mother's and Father's Day gift. A sharp wave of nausea rolls through me when I realize I always send my dad a thoughtful card, but do a whole gift/dinner/activity with my stepdad. How is that fair?

Dad flips a spatula in one hand like a gunslinger tossing his pistol, catching it by the handle to the sound of thunderous applause. His eyes are twinkling when he spots me and yells, "There's my baby girl! Let's hear it for the girl of the hour! Welcome home, Delly!"

"Toast!" Duke yells, lifting a Pabst over his head.

Dani rushes over and hands me a cut-open pineapple filled to the brim with a frothy (virgin) piña colada. I cup its rough base in both my hands, and the sticky-sweet fragrance wafts into my nostrils as I hold it up like a pagan sacrifice, which is fitting. I feel like I'm sacrificing my neat, organized, compartmentalized self to the freer, messier, more chaotic version of myself, who can only peek out in the summer.

"Thank you so much, everyone, for coming out to see me. I know it's a cliché, but I don't say it nearly enough, and I should." I choke up, don't even try to bite at the sides of my tongue or roll my eyes up to dam the tears. I let them spill down my cheeks, unembarrassed by how they ruin my mascara and reveal my tender heart; this is the way Della cries. "I truly love y'all. I do. Every single one of you."

I catch sight of Jude Zeigler in a thin white T-shirt and tattered board shorts, leaned comfortably against a white gatepost twined with cascades of scarlet passion flowers. Peace and goodwill mix with some heavy hormones, and suddenly my gushiness even includes my frenemy, Jude Zeigler. "And it means the world to me to have y'all here tonight. Now let's dance!"

I'd never make a speech that simple and sweet as AJ. I'd be expected to come up with something way wittier, a little barbed, a little self-deprecating. It would take so much more of my brain and only a sliver of my heart—only enough for authenticity. Keeping my brain in overdrive as often as possible allows me to balance on a knife-edge, competitive and ready. But there's something to be said for bald honesty and the ordinary kind of fearlessness that comes from laying your heart bare.

Everyone cheers for my silly speech, and then the music swells and we shake our hips and wave our hands to the beat. Dad throws on quick-tempoed country, some zydeco, some classic rock, and the night shakes with highly danceable tunes for a good two hours. I twirl with Dani, get dipped by Bennie and swung around by Duke until I'm out of breath from laughing. Dad pulls me over, and Dani runs to join our lineup as we do the hustle the way Dad taught us on the rough jute rug in the living room when we were little girls. The crowd joins in, and it's a blur of laughter and questions I have to answer in a shout over the too-loud music.

Yes, school is going great!

No, no decision on college yet.

A boyfriend? I don't have the time for boys, ha ha!

Everyone back home is fine. Fine, thank you. Yep, fine.

Grandma passes me a piece of her divine lemon meringue pie with a wink and two sticky, crimson kisses on my cheeks. Bennie sneaks me a piña colada that isn't virgin (bless his heart), and the warm rum mixed with the icy pineapple slides down my throat in such a quick, delicious rush, I get bold enough to grab a second when Dad's back is turned. I dance over to the food, my fingers trailing the white cloths that cover the length of the tables. They're weighed down with every kind of seafood cooked every way you can imagine. I grab bites of blush-colored shrimp and briny, buttery clam and flaky fish as I run back and forth from the food to the dance floor until my feet ache so badly, I finally chuck my flip-flops.

The moon crests in the sky, and I'm belly-full and slick with sweat, surrounded by the people I love, and finally, *finally* I feel the easy, happy weight of Della slide over my shoulders and hug me tight.

Dad drags out Dani's old karaoke machine, and Duke agrees to do a duet with me—we sing a song called "Love Shack" by the B-52s, which was one of his mom's favorites. We cracked up watching the video of her and Dad singing it at their wedding a million times when we were kids. Duke's definitely a little drunker than I've ever seen him, and amid the laughter and cheers when we finish, Dad comes up and walks him to the nearest table, taking his Pabst and handing him a bottled water instead.

"That's enough, bud," Dad says gently as he helps Duke sit down. "Dell, sweetie, get me a few of those butter biscuits for your brother, will you?"

"Sure." A little of the buzz from our song and the rum wears off when I see how worried Dad looks. When I come back with the plate of biscuits, Duke, who *never* cries, is sobbing. I slide the plate over and stand back, giving them space. Not enough space that I can't hear, and what I hear breaks my heart.

"I miss her, you know?" Duke sticks his fingers up under his glasses and swipes away his tears, then pushes his hair back off his face. "It's not fair. We were so little when Mom died, and then Nan Sunny? She was so young. It's just not fucking fair."

Dad rubs slow circles on Duke's back and encourages him

to sip his water and eat a few bites of biscuit. "I know it, buddy. It really isn't fair at all. It breaks my heart you kids had to lose them both so young."

"I didn't mean what I said at the shop, Dad," Duke says, his head hanging. "I was just being an asshole. I'll work there as much as you need me to. I promise that."

"Hey, you've got plans, and that shop isn't more important than they are, all right? You're going to get into that program, and you're going off to Cairo. Hang out with the mummies like Indiana Jones."

This makes Duke laugh hard. "Okay."

"Look, you and I need to have a little talk about why booze and our genetics don't mix. Tomorrow, we'll go for a drive, okay? We'll go see Hemingway's house, pretend we're intellectuals while we check out the six-toed cats."

Duke hugs Dad tight, stands up, and says, "Sounds good. I think I need some fresh air right now. I'm gonna walk on the beach."

"You sure you're up for it?" Dad's voice is tight with worry, but Duke is already heading along the sand path.

"I'm good!" Duke waves his hand and bows his head, staring at the ground as he trudges in a lopsided path to the water.

"Should we go after him?" Dani asks, Bennie at her side.

"I'll go," Jude says as he heads in Duke's direction.

"Um…" Dani doesn't want to say why she thinks that's a bad idea, but it's common knowledge.

"I know I'm not his favorite person." Jude gives us a half smile and shrugs. "But I'll stay a little behind and just keep an eye on him. I won't bother him."

"I'll go, too," I offer.

"Okay," Dani agrees a little too quickly. I notice she raises her eyebrows at Bennie, and they exchange a *look* that, no doubt, means they've discussed her theory about me and Jude.

I ignore my older sister and jog to Jude's side. We don't say anything until we're on the beach, staying about fifty feet behind Duke as he wobbles along the water's edge, oblivious to our presence.

"Thanks for helping with Duke." I stick my hands in the pockets of my dress and watch the skirt swish in the breeze.

"No problem. He had a rough day at work, and I'm not sure I made it any easier on him. I owe him one." The sharp points of Jude's profile are edged in moonlight, his shoulders are hunched forward, and his head is bowed in thought.

"He apologized to my dad about something…" I fish.

"He wants Belo to think about selling." Jude's mouth pulls to the side, and he kicks little sprays of sand up in front of him.

"I thought you agreed with that?"

"I agree with what he thinks. I don't agree with how he said it." He shrugs. "But that's not really my business. I'm not family, and Duke pointed that out. He's not wrong. I should've stayed out of it. Your dad got pretty mad at him, and it all snowballed fast."

"Oh." We walk together, watching as Duke splashes a few feet into the water, stops, then wades back onto dry land, pants soaked to the knees, and keeps stumbling on. Jude tenses, tracking my brother's trajectory, and relaxes when Duke's back on dry land. "My dad's taking Duke out tomorrow, so I'm sure all will be okay."

"I know Belo's been worried about Duke. He's been a little all over the place lately."

My stomach sinks. "Yeah? What's up?"

"I don't really know. I think he's been talking about leaving for such a long time, but now that it's actually going to happen…it's scary, I guess." Jude looks over at me. "Belo's pretty nervous about the way Duke's been drinking."

"Yeah, I've never seen Duke drunk before tonight. I hope it's just a phase." I reach out, almost on instinct, and graze Jude's hand with mine, then pull back. "It really was sweet of you to come after Duke. I know it has to be hard for you."

"Because of my parents?" He shakes his head. "Nah, this is normal."

"But it's really *not*."

"Not for everyone. What about Johnny? Dally?"

"They're fictional, Jude."

"I don't usually get into books, but I really liked *The Outsiders*. I think it was the first time I read a book that felt like the characters were people I'd know." He nods to my dress. "Look, you dressed like a Soc." With one finger, he traces one of the cherries on my full skirt. "Cherry."

I laugh. "It wasn't on purpose." I tug on his T-shirt sleeve. "You didn't dress like a Greaser, though. Shouldn't this be rolled up? With a pack of cigarettes tucked into it?"

"Yeah. And I need a comb in my back pocket. Just for show, though. I don't have enough hair to be a true Greaser." He runs his hand over his short, dark hair, and my fingers itch to do the same. "You look nice, by the way. I mean, pretty. You look really pretty."

It comes out of nowhere, and I can hear how nervous he is when he says it. He's not fishing, not trying to score points.

He's just doing what he always does, saying exactly what he feels, honestly.

"Thank you." I bite my bottom lip, then say what I'm thinking, even if it makes me nervous. "I know I've given you a hard time for the last few summers. I think I just felt like you thought I was some ditz. And you're bossy."

"Fair enough," he laughs. "The truth is, I have a serious problem thinking I have to micromanage everything. I don't want to play the drunk-parent card, but it's a pretty typical thing for children of alcoholics." He swallows hard and says, "But I never thought you were a ditz. And I always kind of loved getting ribbed by you. I think it's cool that you're not afraid to say what you think. I've always admired that about you."

I throw my head back and inhale the salty air, laughing under the stars with Jude Zeigler. I would never have imagined my party ending like this. "Look at the two of us, finally getting along. My dad would be so proud."

"It's only because there was *literally* no one else at Belo's for you to hang out with this summer." He raises his eyebrows when I balk at his harsh declaration. "Admit it. If anyone else worked there—it could've been the most annoying person on earth—you would've chosen to hang with them over me. It could've been, like, one of those guys who's really into CrossFit and never stops talking about it, and you would've wanted to talk to him instead of me."

I burst out laughing. "Duke said you were probably one of those guys! And a vegan."

Jude blows out a long breath. "Wow. I think I underestimated how much your brother hates me. A CrossFit guy? Really?" He looks at me sidelong. "I mean, I'm not *that* ripped."

"Jude Zeigler, are you fishing for a compliment right now?" I ask, poking his arm—which is actually very nicely muscled, and I decide to tell him so. "Your muscles are very nice." I look up at him and pat his arm, nearly falling over when I step into a dip in the sand. He wraps his arm through mine to steady me, and that one second where I should pull away ticks by. I don't, and just like that, I'm walking arm in arm with Jude in the moonlight, on the beach, and things feel almost maybe *romantic*. "Jude?"

"Yeah?" He pulls my arm in a little closer. It's like he wants me to know he realizes what we're doing and he's good with it.

"You're right. I probably would have hung out with anyone else this summer because I'm kind of an ass sometimes. But I'm really, *really* glad you were my only choice."

He stops suddenly and turns to face me. "Dell—"

I put a hand up to shush him. "Do you hear something?"

It's my name, loud and urgent. My father is bellowing for me, running down the beach, arms waving over his head.

"Oh, shit." Jude pulls back and checks on Duke, who's doing just fine, wobbling down the beach. "I'll go get your brother. You see what your dad needs."

The romantic spell broken, I race down the beach and reach Dad out of breath. Dani is with him, and they both look panicked.

"What's wrong? What's the matter?" I ask, searching from face to face for a clue.

"Dell, I just got off the phone with your mother. She called me in a damn panic. Your sister's been missing all day. Did you get a call from a hospital?"

My throat goes dry.

"A hospital? No… I mean, no I don't *think* so." This cute little cherry dress has pockets—deep ones where a phone can shake and vibrate all night long, unnoticed. I slide it out, and the neon green of dozens of missed calls and texts lights up my face. "It was… I got some texts from Marnie, but I never thought…" I look up at Dani, wanting to apologize, but she doesn't look hurt. She looks furious.

I feel the low-gut kick of panic when the reality of what they're saying finally registers. What the hell happened to Marnie? Why is she in the hospital? And why wasn't I there for her when she needed me most?

The answer to that question is simple. *Because I'm a selfish asshole, that's why.*

"Dell, she tried to reach out today?" Dani asks. Her look is a knife, cleaving my heart in two, in four, in eight, and then chopping it into ground meat. "Why didn't you call her?"

There's no answer I can give her that doesn't expose me for the self-centered monster I am.

I try to imagine calling or texting Dani's phone anytime, *ever*, and not getting an answer or a call back immediately. I've called her in the middle of packed workdays, at the end of long hours of dredging through classes, during romantic dates and quiet beach days, and I can't think of a single time when I didn't get a call from her within the hour on the long side. Marnie's first text to me was nearly twelve *hours* ago now.

I scroll through my notifications and see that, since the

party started, I've had dozens of calls from area codes I don't know. My phone guessed they might be New York numbers.

"I'm so sorry. I really am. I…I just assumed she was being dramatic," I say numbly, unable to meet their eyes. And once I'm done feeling sorry for myself, I realize another way I've failed as a sister—I didn't even ask *why the hospital would be calling me* before I tried to squirm my way out of trouble. Part of me doesn't have the stomach to hear the answer. "I don't understand what happened. Marnie's coaches didn't know where she was? Her team didn't? I thought they were taking care of her," I stutter out, my teeth clacking as my nerves unfurl and fray.

"She ran away," Dad says, and I can tell he's working hard to keep his voice even. "Some mix-up with another girl, some pictures that went viral… I'm not real sure of the details. Your mama was jabbering a mile a minute. Anyway, your little sister took off, hooked up with some friends she met at some other camp the year before. Older kids. I guess they got to drinking, and she packed away more than she should've. Those so-called friends dropped her in front of the hospital, nearly dead from alcohol poisoning, no contact info, nothing. The only emergency contact in her cell was you, Dell. They tried reaching you for hours while she recovered from having her stomach pumped."

"Oh my God." My dad grabs onto my arm and pulls me into a tight hug before my knees give out.

What have I done?

12

Vacation MASH-up

Last New Year's Eve

MICHIGAN

"Play with me. Please. Please. Please." Lilli and I are laid up on the couch, unable to escape Marnie, who's trying to cajole us into playing one of the ten different card games Peter and Mom got her for Christmas.

"Not now, Marnie," I beg. "I'm too weak."

"You're too weak to hold up seven cards?" Marnie pouts.

I sink back into the couch cushions, exhausted from illness and lingering disappointment. Peter surprised me with tickets to Key West as an early Christmas present—I heard him and Mom get into a pretty emotional argument about it, but he stuck to his guns, and I was *so* psyched about it. I was packed, pumped, and ready to go when Lilli and I both came down with a demonic stomach flu from hell. Lilli missed her huge solo in the Christmas Eve midnight service, I missed my flight out to gorgeous Key West, and we were both basically sweat-soaked dishrags of misery, strewn over the couch Christmas morning. So not only am I trying to recover from whatever viral near-death experience I just endured, I'm so upset I missed out on seeing my family in the Keys, I tear up every time I think about it.

I'm really, *really* not in the mood to try to grasp another game about goats or apples or explosive kittens with complicated rules my fuzzy brain can't manage to keep straight.

"Marnie, leave them be." Mom shoos my annoying sister away and sets out a tray with her amazing chicken noodle soup. She tucks the blankets around us more snugly, adds a few logs to the crackling fire, and hands us our steaming bowls of soup. "I'm so sorry you girls have had such a miserable holiday. It's nice to see you out of bed, though."

"I'm at, like, a solid sixty-four percent right now," I joke weakly, sipping the soup.

"Zero out of ten, would *not* recommend being sick over Christmas," Lilli croaks. She swallows some of her broth, and the effort of lifting the bowl practically knocks her out again.

"I can't believe I didn't get even a little bit of flu," Marnie says cheerfully while Lilli and I shoot silent eye daggers her way.

Since we've been so sick, my entire family has been on quarantine. The Jepsens are usually involved in a blitz of holiday functions, parties, church services, volunteer projects, and other assorted social events, but it's been nothing but hanging on the couch under thick blankets, watching the snowstorms outside, listening to Christmas music, and dozing by the fire, waiting for the Tamiflu to kick in.

Marnie's immune system isn't betraying her body, but she's taken advantage of all the unstructured downtime, sleeping in, and social peace and quiet. Honestly, I haven't seen her look this good in months. Her skin has a rosy glow, and she looks so strong and full of energy…or maybe I'm just mentally comparing her normal, healthy look to my haggard, corpselike appearance.

"Marnie, if you're so desperate for someone to play a game with you, why don't you invite a few of your friends over?" Mom asks as she curls up in the big armchair by the fireplace and takes out the beautiful shawl she's knitting. It's based on the one the lady from the show *Outlander* wears—Mom is so obsessed we joked we'd get Peter a kilt for Christmas, and she actually looked kind of excited. *Gross.*

"No, that's okay." Marnie tosses the card deck back under the tree.

We haven't left our Christmas tree up this long since we were little kids. Mom usually has it down in time for the huge New Year's Eve party she and Peter throw every year. We basically need to empty the room to accommodate the giant crowd of people who always show up. Last year she rigged a huge net of balloons across the cathedral ceiling, and when the ball fell, she pulled a string and the balloons drifted down. I kissed Lex amid the cascade of gold and black balloons—very romantic—wondering if we'd kiss again the next New Year. From the looks of it, that will be a hard no… Lex is a total germaphobe. He promised we'd do our own private gift exchange and Happy New Year kisses when he could be near me without needing a hazmat suit.

"I know Lilli and AJ don't look too hot, but they aren't contagious anymore." Mom studies the pattern spread on her lap and carefully loops a few more strands of soft purple yarn. "I could make that giant pizza you love."

"Definitely yes to the pizza," Marnie says. "I just don't

feel like seeing anyone right now. I like it being just us." She sighs and looks longingly at the TV. Mom has strict No Technology stretches during vacation days, and Marnie is always edgiest during those blocks. "Do *you* want to play cards?" she asks Mom.

"Marnie, I need to concentrate," Mom says, her forehead wrinkling as she stares at the knitting needles, then the paper, then back again. "Can't you girls do something unstructured?"

"What does that even *mean*?" Marnie asks.

Mom sighs and folds the partial shawl in her lap. "You don't always have to be playing a game or doing an activity," says our mother, the unofficial queen of the recreational timetable. "When I was your age, my friends and I could sit for hours just listening to music, talking, maybe playing MASH."

"Ha!" Marnie crows. "So you *did* play a game!"

Mom tucks her shiny red-gold hair behind her ear, and her face softens dreamily. "I mean, *technically* MASH is a game, but it's mostly just silly fun." She looks at each of our faces. "Do you three honestly not know how to play this game?" We shake our heads, and she throws her hands up. "What do kids even *do* for fun anymore? Probably send nudes on their phones like idiots and make those ridiculous little videos… tic tacs or whatever," she grumbles.

For the first time in weeks, Marnie's face is a mask of terror.

"Let's play. Let's mash or whatever it's called." My voice is too loud. I sit up so fast, I nearly soak my lap with hot soup. "What do we need, Mom?"

"That soup really does give you energy, doesn't it?" Mom smiles smugly. "I'll do a blog post with the recipe tonight.

I took some pictures of you girls when you were resting. I won't post them unless you okay them, of course."

As Mom rambles, Marnie shrinks into herself.

"Sure, that's fine. So, how do you play MASH again?" I'm so determined to get Marnie out of her state of terror, I'll blindly agree to have a terrible picture of me mouth-breathing through the flu online for all eternity. Mom has perfect aesthetic appreciation, except when it comes to us. I guess mothers really are loveblind when it comes to their children. Mom is unable to look at a revolting picture of one of us and admit it's pure garbage. I'm not saying I don't look good in some pictures; I'm saying my mother has no ability to determine when I do and when I definitely don't.

"We need notebooks or paper or something…and pens," Mom says.

"Marnie, we have our new planners under the tree." Lilli pokes her angelic little face out from her quilt cocoon, mustering some happy energy. "And we got new pens in our stockings!"

Marnie snaps into action, gathering and distributing supplies. Mom moves to the huge driftwood coffee table and turns to one of the blank pages in the back of her planner. We each get to special-order our own planner every December from this organization guru Mom befriended at some influencers' getaway. The planners are freaking amazing, and this is practically my bible for the year. I'll fill every inch of every page with all the things I do and need. I carry it with me everywhere I go, every day. Lex has joked that if I was being mugged, I'd throw my wallet at the mugger's head and beg for them to leave my planner alone. He's not wrong.

I run my hands over the cover, which has a beautiful motif of delicately drawn seashells painted in watercolors, then flip through the months, heart-happy when I hit mid-June. I always ask for an extra week or two of organized box grids after the proposed last day of school in case we have intense snowstorms and wind up in school for an extralong amount of time, but July and August are free of any boxes. They're journal-entry pages, with inspiring quotes at the bottom. It's a tiny reminder that summer is when I can let go of my grueling schedule and thousands of responsibilities and dial down my chronic need to overachieve. Summer is when I can just *be*.

"So you need to write the letters like this." Mom flips her planner to show us the word *MASH* written in her calligraphic writing along the top of the page. "The letters stand for *mansion*, *apartment*, *shack*, and *house*. Then you have three categories. One is love interests. Pick two people who are your dream partners, two people you'd rather claw your eyes out than end up with, and one person you're meh about," Mom instructs.

"*Meh?*" Lilli asks, scrunching up her face. Lilli is serious when it comes to her Christianity, and she really does try to see the good in everyone, which makes it hard for her to be catty. (Unless it's about someone's singing…she's Old Testament–judgmental when it comes to singing.)

"Like, someone who's the human equivalent of a warm egg-salad sandwich," Marnie suggests.

"Hey, I love warm egg salad!" Mom says. When we all groan, she argues, "I mean, when it's warm from the eggs being fresh out of the water. Not, like, left in a lunchbox in the sun all day."

"I'm going to puke again," Lilli moans. "Okay, I picked my meh person. Can we stop talking about rotten egg salad?"

"Yes, no more puking, please. I'm running out of detergent."

"Thank God, maybe we won't smell like the Eastlake Ultimate Frisbee team anymore," Marnie mutters. I snicker, and Mom glares her into silence.

"Okay, next you pick five cars, and you use the same formula. So two dream cars, two ridiculous cars—"

"Do scooters count?" Marnie asks.

"Yes," Mom says regally, like she's the reigning queen of this bizarre game. "And then you pick a number of children. Two options should be your ideal, two can be out there, one is just okay."

We all work quietly, glancing up every now and then to check on each other's progress. For my five guys I list super young Matt Dillon as Dallas Winston from *The Outsiders*; Lex (of course); this guy from my geometry class who's been at St. Matthew's with me since freshman year but is so personalityless I can never remember his name; Mr. Willoughby from *Sense and Sensibility*; and Jude Zeigler.

"How do we decide?" Marnie asks as she fills out her lists.

"We make a spiral," Mom says. "Is everyone ready?" When we're all paying attention, she tells us to start drawing a spiral. After a few seconds she tells us to stop. "Now count the whorls."

I have seven. Lilli has four. Marnie has twelve.

"Twelve!" Mom is laughing. "Marnie, how did you get twelve? I only had you draw for a few seconds."

"I thought the point was to draw as many spirals as possible." Marnie keeps her competitive edge razor-sharp. We all laugh, and it feels good, sitting in the warm living room, cracking jokes and playing silly games with my mom and my sisters.

"So what you do is start with the *M* at the top of the page and count like this," Mom says. "Here, I had five, so that's *M*, *A*, *S*, *H*, and *Brad Pitt*." She sighs. "So I cross off Brad. Good-bye, beautiful." She draws a line through *Brad Pitt*, then goes through her lists, crossing off the next fifth item, which is a *Tesla*.

"You want a Tesla?" Marnie asks, peeking at Mom's list but keeping her own covered.

"Of course!" Mom says. "But I have to give up the Tesla with Brad. So you keep counting by your number and crossing off items until you only have one item left in each list. You circle that item, and, at the end, you read your results. Like this." Mom counts, crosses, and circles. "Oh no!"

"What's wrong?" Lilli asks from her blanket cocoon.

"Apparently I'm doomed to live in a shack, I have to marry our boring CPA who always smells a little like he just farted, I'm driving a very sensible Corolla, and I have *nine* kids!"

We all howl with laughter.

"Dad would totally fight Mr. Capella for you, Mom," Lilli says, wrinkling her nose. "Why *does* he always stink?"

"Because he's a warm egg-salad sandwich of a person!" Marnie crows. "Mine is better than Mom's. I live in an apartment with Megan Rapinoe, and we have three kids. But we drive a garbage moped."

"What's a garbage moped?" Lilli asks.

"Like a garbage truck, only you have to pick up all the trash and carry it around on your moped," Marnie explains as if it's the most reasonable thing in the world. We're all laughing so hard, we're almost crying. "Lilli, you next."

Lilli frowns. "I live in a mansion. I'm married to Jordan Tormei, the cute alto from St. Barnabas's choir. I drive a Chevy...is that a boring car?" We crack up at her question, and she finishes with, "And I have *two sets* of twins!"

"That sounds like a nightmare." Marnie pokes me with her foot. "What about you, AJ?"

"I had to marry Mr. Willoughby from *Sense and Sensibility*—"

"The one who dumped Rose from *Titanic*?" Marnie asks.

"Yes...you do know it's a book, too, right?" I shake my head when Marnie shrugs. "Anyway, we have no kids, which is probably a good thing because we live in a shack and drive a Mazda."

"Lilli and I definitely made out the best," Marnie says. "It was probably all my whorls. Thanks, Mom. That was fun."

"You know what? We should do a girls' movie. How about buttered popcorn and hot cocoa?" Mom asks. She's definitely feeling glowy and happy from playing and laughing with us, because she's breaking her no-screen rule an entire hour early.

We all cheer, and she orders us to find a good movie while she's getting the snacks. We're in a fierce debate between a few romantic comedies—Mom keeps urging us from the kitchen to put on *You've Got Mail*, but Marnie is complaining that she doesn't think she can enjoy a movie when the main love interest is played by the guy who was the star of the Mr. Rogers movie.

"Marnie, come help me finish getting this ready, will you?" Mom asks.

"Sure!" Marnie runs out of the room, tossing the remote to Lilli. She knocks her planner on the floor, crinkling the pages. Marnie doesn't care about that kind of thing, but it drives me wild to see the brand-new, pristine planner page crumpled like that. While Lilli flips through movies, I go to smooth the page out and look down at Marnie's MASH list.

For a second it feels like the fevers and chills from my flu are back.

I read through Marnie's Love list.

1. Megan Rapinoe
2. McKenzie Fisher
3. Candace Howler
4. Angela from *The Office*
5. Meg from *Supernatural* (second version)

The second name on the list is extra scribbled out and crossed over, but I can definitely make it out. I try to rationalize. Maybe Marnie mixed up the order? But I know loudmouthed Candace Howler from the debate team. She's like if a warm egg-salad sandwich became sentient and was given a megaphone to express its mundane thoughts. Obviously Angela from *The Office* and demon Meg in her second form from *Supernatural* are horrible fictional people, and Marnie has a habit of talking to the TV when she finds things annoying or funny, so I know she can't stand them.

So, what's going on? I thought everything with McKenzie was over. And if it's not...what the hell kind of trouble is Marnie in that she thinks she's keeping a secret?

13

Welcome Home(?), Marnie

July

FLORIDA

I left my melatonin, white-noise machine, valerian root supplement, lavender-oil eye mask, and weighted blanket in Michigan because, though I'm rattled with insomnia when I'm in the north, I have no issues sleeping in my Key West house.

"It's that clean ocean air. It'll make you sleep like a baby," my dad always says, and I always do.

At least I used to.

The night of the party, I stayed up late getting filled in by my frantic mother. After she went over the details of Marnie's recovery and what the doctors recommended for her continued healing, she moved on to logistics; as in, where would Marnie go now that camp had wound up such a disaster? Lilli's recordings had made it into the earbuds of a few really big producers in Nashville who'd dropped everything to meet with her and Mom. It was even better than they'd been hoping for, and Mom wasn't about to chance derailing their progress.

"There's no way we can bring Marnie. It will be meetings

and roundtables with lawyers and executives, rehearsals and fittings, all kinds of shoptalk—Marnie needs total rest, and Lilli is running the most exhausting schedule imaginable. Peter has been staying with her, but he needs to get back to work. As soon as she's released, he'll take her to the airport and get her on a direct flight. Your father told me it would be fine if Marnie comes to stay."

"Mom, is it really fair to dump this on Dad? Marnie doesn't even know him. What if she feels weird? Could she maybe stay with Grandma?" I ask, desperate for any other solution. I know—I *know*—I'm being an asshole, but I can't help it. I've spent all year dealing with Marnie's yo-yoing mood swings and problems, and I really just need some breathing room.

"Your grandmother is on that river cruise down the Danube and she won't be back for three weeks. I had a long talk with Marnie. She told me she's really looking forward to spending the summer with you."

I know I could bring out every debate-winning argument in my arsenal and it wouldn't change Mom's mind, so I stop trying and accept the fact that my summer of freedom is over. I have no idea how this will work out, but every scenario I imagine makes me feel petrified.

Dad, Duke, and Dani are in the guest room, getting it ready for Marnie, and they're doing it in that overly quiet way that lets me know they're really eavesdropping on my call. Instead of saying, *What about me? What about what I've been looking forward to all year?* I take a deep breath and say, "Fine. But there's no way I can do the internship now."

"Dad spoke with them, and they said they were willing to

work with you remotely," Mom says, her voice strained with desperate hope.

"How will I work on it with Marnie here? Dad's at Belo's all day, Dani has the shop, Duke is at school. I have to be here for her." Again. Like I am all school year. Which is okay because that's when I have to do it, that's when it's important for me to be there for her. The summer is supposed to be my little sliver of selfish time.

"Shit," Mom mutters under her breath. "I know how much it meant to you—"

"It's fine." My voice is as close to a snap as I dare with my mother. I should be thrilled about the unexpected silver lining of Marnie's off-the-rails bullshit, but I wanted to be able to put my foot down and *decide* not to go. Maybe Jude was right. Maybe the worst thing is not having a choice.

I ask Mom to put Lilli on the phone.

"Hey, Lil. I just wanted to tell you to knock 'em dead."

"AJ! They're, like, really, really excited to see me. Mom wants me to do two French braids, but I think that's babyish, right?" Lilli's voice sounds small and worried, and I remember what she told me about being worried that she'd be pushed into something she wasn't ready for.

"What about a French braid crown?" I suggest. "Pretty and sweet, but not babyish at all."

"Ohmigod, that's perfect! I love you. I wish you guys could come here and see me and the recording studio and everything. It's like, so amazing. You can't even believe the people who've recorded here, right in the same place I get to record. It's *amazing*."

"I would love to take a tour sometime. Make sure you remember your big sister when you're singing a sold-out show at Madison Square Garden."

"Of course I'll remember you. You'll be front row. Mom says I have to go to another meeting. I love you!"

"Love you so much, Lil." We disconnect, and I feel this fluttering excitement for Lilli, tangled with some jealousy. What would it be like to have a passion and talent that enormous? My sister handles it all gracefully, but I'm amazed by her ambition. I understand now what people mean when they say they always knew someone famous would make it—Lilli's going places, and I'm so proud to watch her get there.

Meanwhile I'm stuck babysitting Marnie, and I'm not about to leave my family to do all the dirty work. I march into the guest room, clicking into automatic AJ mode. I clean and spruce, rearranging the perfectly empty space across the hall from my room until it's ready to hold all the trouble and anxiety Marnie always drags with her like Marley's chains. I can't wait.

"Wow, Dell, you have a real eye for design," Dani says when we're done. I used knickknacks and decorations from my room, leftover odds and ends from the linen closet, and a whole lot of fresh flowers in vases to make the room feel homey and welcoming—Marnie's a pain in the ass, but I'd never want her to feel unwelcome. "I wish you could have helped me when I was opening the salon. It took me forever to pick every little thing." She gives me a small, tight smile that's still a little strained since my shitty behavior came to light last night.

"Thanks. I wish I could have been there, too." I wish she could understand how much I mean that.

I realize Dani's surprise about the guest room is partially due to the fact that my own room usually looks like a tornado took a casual crawl through it. I can't even imagine how shocked she'd be to learn that in Michigan, Ella, our housekeeper, always compliments me on how neat I keep my space compared to my sisters.

Dad puts a wide hand on my shoulder and squeezes. "We're all pretty tuckered. Why don't you get some rest, kiddo?" He kisses my temple, and my brother and sister hug me tight.

It's weird being the family baby—forgiveness comes fast and without too much effort on my part. I wonder if this is what it feels like to be Lilli. Maybe my baby sister isn't as perfect as I think she is. Maybe that's just my protective big-sister perspective. I wonder what it would be like to be unhinged, always-feeling-too-much Marnie. A few seconds of trying to imagine it leaves me exhausted. I sit alone in the guest room with the sweet perfume of too many cut passion flowers in full bloom, my thoughts heavy and tangled.

That night I sleep like crap. The next day Dad tells me not to come in to work, that I need to rest up for the next few days, but I can't stop pacing the house, chewing on my nails (a habit I can only indulge for a few weeks every summer— Mom would have cut my fingertips off if she saw my ragged edges). Sleep continues to be a fickle bastard, just out of my reach, and before dawn on the third day—the day Marnie is supposed to arrive—I'm still wide-awake and feeling slightly delirious at five in the morning, wondering how long it takes for sleep deprivation to warp a person's brain.

I've mostly avoided Dad, Dani, or Duke since we finished setting up Marnie's room. Even though they made it clear they love me and aren't pissed anymore, they all keep throwing looks my way like I'm some sullen stranger instead of their much-loved Della. I can't call Harper or Tessa because we really don't talk during the summer as a rule, and this is too big and way too complex to text about. I mean, of course I *could* call and tell them I'm dealing with an emergency…but then I'd also have to tell them that *surprise* I've been living a secret double life for seventeen years. I have no interest in dealing with the emotional free-for-all that will unleash.

I don't even think about reaching out to Lex. He's too… complicated. As always. Plus we're on a break, of course. Rock camp will be packed with so many angsty, tempting girls for him to fawn over, I didn't even pretend I wanted us to try to be committed this summer.

A few days of total isolation leaves me at the fuzzy outer edges of stir-crazy, which explains why I'm positive I'm hallucinating Jude Zeigler sleeping in the hammock on the back porch the morning of Marnie's flight.

But do hallucinations snore?

I go to the kitchen and brew myself a cup of strong coffee, pretty sure the caffeine will drop-kick my brain into functioning and dissolve the mirage of my slumbering maybe frenemy/maybe summer crush in my backyard. I'm into my second cup when hallucination-Jude sits up in the hammock, stretches, and walks to the thick hedges at the far edge of the yard. I turn away with a start when I realize Jude is definitely peeing out in the open, not remotely worried about who might be sitting in the kitchen watching—and I decide for sure that this Jude is definitely *not* a figment of my imagination. I take a quick peek and see he's finished up his business with a peppy zip of his shorts, and he walks across the yard, opens the sliding door into the house, and full-on yawning, heads to the sink.

"Jude?"

"Della!" He nearly topples over one of the counter stools. "Why didn't you say something?" I can see him trying to figure out if I saw him take a piss in the backyard, and a devilish part of my heart loves how panicked he is.

But I roll my eyes for effect. If the incident of the piss in the morning hadn't clinched it for me, there's no way I'd still have any doubt that it wasn't my mind playing tricks on me—only flesh-and-blood Jude could be this obnoxious and this adorable right when he wakes up…

"I *did* say something. I said, 'Jude,'" I remind him. "I think it's hilarious you're acting like it's so weird I'm standing here *in my own kitchen* when I just caught you sleeping in a hammock on my porch." I don't mention the urination portion of the morning as I put my mug down and cross my arms over my skimpy sleep tank.

"You saw me sleeping?" I can practically hear the gears whirring in his brain as he pieces the events together. "Uh, so I guess you also—"

"Forget it," I reassure him with a magnanimous wave of my hand. "I've been camping with Dad and Duke a thousand times. I don't know what it is about peeing outside that men find so irresistible."

When Jude smiles, the angles of his face rearrange, and I'm suddenly aware of just how wildly attractive I find him. "I'm sorry I surprised you. I thought you were going to be on the beach or hanging with Dani at the salon." He pauses, then throws me a quick half smile. "Honestly? I was really kind of *hoping* you'd be coming in to work soon. I'm not gonna lie. It's been super boring without you there to argue with me all day."

"I've kind of missed you micromanaging my life," I tell him.

"So…about the night of your party…" He trails off, and I catch myself holding my breath, wondering if he's going to ask about the almost…what? Was it an almost kiss? An almost confession? "Is everything okay? Belo told me it was something with your sister up in Michigan?"

Of course. Duh. I'm obviously reading a lot more into that night on the beach than Jude is.

"Yeah, so my little sister kind of went off the deep end and wound up getting so drunk she had to get her stomach pumped. The elite volleyball camp she was attending wasn't a big fan of her whole run-away-and-get-blitzed act, so she's kicked out. And there was nowhere else for her to go, so…" I shrug. "Looks like there's only one road for me now."

"Shit." Jude blows out a long breath. "I'm so sorry, Dell. I know—*trust me*—I know how frustrating it can be to have to watch someone you love deal with this shit." He rubs a hand over his head. "Is she going to be okay?"

I press a hand over my heart, which is beating super fast. "I honestly don't know. My sister…she's gone through a lot this year. She never really wanted to go to this camp in the first place, and it wound up being intense in a really shitty way. I guess she just hit a breaking point."

"She's lucky she has you to lean on. Things were definitely easier at home for me when my brother was around." Jude pulls his mouth to the side. "Not that I blame him for getting out. Our parents definitely don't have any plans to change, so staying around means you have to accept a certain level of chaos on a daily basis. I don't like it, but my brother? He told me it felt like he was slowly suffocating."

"Yep," I whisper, trying to catch my own breath. "I get that."

"It's bad enough watching your parents go through it. I can't imagine watching a sibling go through it, let alone two." He shakes his head as I try to imagine how alone and out of control Marnie must have felt, surrounded by people who didn't care about her at all during a totally vulnerable time. "By the way, how is Duke? Was he all right? I dropped him off on your porch. He seemed to be sobering up pretty fast."

"Yeah, he was okay, and he and Dad went on a drive and had some man-to-man time, you know." I attempt a laugh, and Jude joins in a beat too late, his face dark. I remember he told me he couldn't remember the last time he had a sober conversation with his father. So maybe he *doesn't* know.

"Anyway, I've got to pick Marnie—my little sister—up from the airport later, so Dad told me not to come in." For the millionth time, I start to think about how weird things will be when Marnie actually gets here, then push those thoughts away before my brain overloads. Better to focus on the predictable present…like Jude's rigid work policies. "So, how'd you get the day off?" I ask, afraid of the answer.

"Uh, Belo closed the store for the day. He has some meetings to go to." Jude meets my eyes for one brief second, and I read how serious things must be in his look. I decide I can't handle any more shitty news today, so I just hope it's not as bad as I'm imagining. Jude nods to my cup. "You didn't happen to make a pot, did you?"

I point, and he raises his eyebrows, asking silent permission.

"Help yourself." I watch as he adds way too much sugar and no milk to his mug of coffee. "So, what were you doing in the hammock?"

"My parents are…going through some shit. It's been worse than usual at home, and Belo told me anytime I needed to crash, I should come here. I usually take the guest room, but I thought that would be rude with you being here now. I wouldn't want to make you feel awkward in your own house. I mean, what if you walked in the bathroom while I was taking a whiz?" he says, looking at me with a half grin before he sips his coffee.

Jude Zeigler and I are just joking around like two old pals in my kitchen. I know I've been existing on desert-island levels of isolation these past few days, but this is *Black Mirror*–level weird.

"I'm sorry your parents have been off the rails. Seriously, don't feel like you have to crash on the hammock for me. The guest room across from mine will be occupied soon, but the one down the hall used to be Duke's. It's always empty and clean."

"Thanks." He looks genuinely grateful. "I try to just shut my door and ignore the worst of it, but Dad had his poker buddies over, and they were being assholes. They annihilated a keg in an hour and ended up punching holes in the drywall for fun. I wasn't in the mood to be around them or their bullshit, and last week a neighbor called the cops. Which, good for her, but I'm not about to wind up in a cell because my father has shithead friends, you know?" Jude talks a mile a minute while he tells the story, but once it's all out, he stops short and laughs at himself. "I guess this is a pretty weird level of TMI for seven in the morning."

"Hey, no judgment here. My family life clearly has so much drama Lifetime would take a pass at making a movie about us."

"If you need someone to vent to, I owe you. I didn't mean to barge in on your morning and drink all your coffee. By the way, you make really good coffee." He picks his mug up and takes a sip. "I also accidentally took a piss in front of you, so I guess I owe you for that indecent exposure, too." I roll my eyes, but Jude is insistently chivalrous. "Honestly, I really do feel like a dirtbag for that. I'm happy to make amends. Maybe I could grab your sister from the airport? If she'd be cool with that." When my jaw drops, he says, "The truth? I really love the drive out to the airport, and it's not like I'm going home anytime soon."

"Jude, *no one* loves picking anyone up at the airport."

"I mean, my other option is to suck it up, head home, and clean up a thousand empty Miller bottles and probably at least two puddles of vomit. Oh, and then patch some drywall." Jude's mouth pulls into a tight line of disgust. "Please. You'd be doing *me* a favor. I need to keep myself busy."

"This proves it. You actually are a droid, aren't you? I mean, I've always suspected." He ducks his head and cracks a smile at my accusation. *"My name is Jude. I enjoy creating spreadsheets, driving to the airport, and reprimanding employees at work,"* I say in my best robot monotone.

He laughs. "You know, I can't really argue with that. Damn, am I that boring?"

"You're, like, the definition of *boring*. Literally, if I open the dictionary and look up *boring*…" I open a pretend dictionary and fake surprise at the pretend picture I see of him. "Boom! Jude Zeigler, that's your picture right there, illustrating *boring*."

"Bringing out the middle-school burns, I see." Jude toasts me with his coffee mug. "You'd be surprised to hear that *some people* happen to think I'm a pretty interesting guy."

"Really? Like your girlfriend? The one who lives in Canada, though, so we can't meet her." I grin when he whistles between his teeth.

"Wow, you are really going straight for the eighth-grade digs. What makes you think I don't have a girl?" he asks. When I open my mouth to make a crack about his pretend girlfriend's Ontario postal code, he clarifies, "A flesh-and-blood girl who lives in the lower forty-eight."

"Maybe you do," I say, a little surprised at how growly the thought makes me. "But why hasn't she ever dropped you lunch at work? Or come to pick you up so you don't have to ride your bike in every day?"

"I ride my bike in because I want to. My truck is fine. I drove it over here, actually." He leans against the counter, close to where I'm sitting, and I like the way it feels to have him hanging in my kitchen like we're two old pals who maybe almost kissed on a moonlit beach a few nights ago. "And maybe she *has* come by when you weren't around."

"I doubt it. My dad would have updated me."

"Aw, you ask about me when you're not around?" His grin

is wide and very excellent. I don't know if I've ever seen Jude in this good a mood.

"No, but my dad loves to gossip…and he always assumes I want updates about your life." I feel an unfamiliar heat spiral up my spine and fan out over my neck, curling out at my cheeks—am I blushing? "If you had a girl, you'd crash on *her* porch when your family got to be too much," I declare, sure I'm right.

Or maybe just *hoping* I'm right…

"Maybe her stepdad thinks I'm a loser. Maybe he's got a pickup truck and a big gun collection he likes to polish while he glares at me."

I roll my eyes. "The nonstop country music at Belo's has clearly had a bad influence on you."

He's still sporting that big, goofy smile that fits his face so well, I wonder how this is the first I'm seeing of it. "You know, for someone who claims not to care about who I'm with, you sure seem to be hoping I don't have a girl. What's up with that?"

Joking Jude is pretty cute. Flirting Jude? This is uncharted territory, and I'm feeling scarily rudderless.

"Don't flatter yourself, Zeigler. I'm just bored."

I don't let him know I savor being bored. It's something I never get to experience in my Michigan life. You need to have a certain amount of freedom from responsibility and an excess of free time to be bored. You also need a certain level of comfort to be bored with someone, and I'm kind of pleasantly surprised I'm feeling it with Jude.

"Yeah. I know I'm asking for it by admitting this, but I

don't really know what to do with myself when I don't have work."

He's leaving himself wide-open, and I know he'd be game for more of my hilarious barbs, but, at the last second, I swerve and choose to go all earnest.

"Hey, about your offer to drive out to the airport? How about you ride with me?" I say it casually, around a sip of cooling coffee, eyes lowered so I don't have to face an ego-bruising if he shoots me down. "If Mary Sue, your Ontario girlfriend, is cool with it, obviously. I hear her father is super strict."

"Yeah." He says it too quickly, which I love. "That would be cool."

"Cool." I hop down off the counter. "Um, I need to get ready first…"

"Oh, yeah, cool." He starts to walk backward. "I'll chill on the deck?"

"You can hang in the kitchen." I raise my eyebrows. "Or are you afraid of how your Canadian girlfriend would react to you being in the house while a lady showers?"

Jude looks left and right. "What lady?"

I toss a pot holder, a dish towel, and two paper cups at Jude, all of which he dodges with a laugh.

"I'll be ready in fifteen," I promise.

"Don't rush." He folds the dish towel neatly and lays it over the lip of the sink. "I'll be here."

What he says and does is nothing out of the ordinary—he's just straightening up my kitchen and telling me he'll hang around. But it feels intimate, like in the space of one folded

dish towel and five monosyllabic words he's tossed our relationship into a whole new territory.

After a quick shower and change, I peek around the corner.
Jude isn't in my kitchen, so I head out back, and he's sitting
on the porch, two insulated coffee mugs on the side table. Lex
would roll his eyes and say it was *so basic*…and maybe that's
part of the reason my heart swells like the Grinch's when
he unbungled Christmas. I'm not used to basic kindness, no
strings attached, no angle, from a guy I care about.

"I took a guess…light and sweet?" Jude nods to the mug
as I take it from his outstretched hand, enjoying the tingle of
our fingers brushing.

One long sip later, and I want to curl into his lap and kiss
his neck as a thank-you. Or maybe I want to curl into his lap
and kiss his neck because this whole morning is showing me
a new side of Jude that I like. I really, *really* like it.

"Perfect."

"Good. I didn't take you for a hot bean-water martyr. So
I know it's early, but it's probably better to get there with
time to spare—"

"We're not rolling up at the airport *five hours early* to pick
my sister up. God, you're such a dad," I tease, but his smile
tightens.

"Maybe *your* dad. Mine would definitely leave me stranded."

"Ah." I tilt my head and examine this guy I've known forever but really don't know at all. "That explains it, then, I
guess. We either become our parents or become their opposite, right?" I study the way his face falls again, like I deliv-
ered a load of bad news.

"Then I'm doomed to fulfill my dad's prophecy and become an uptight, boring little prick," he says with an easy shrug of one shoulder. That little motion doesn't distract me from the tight sideways pull of his mouth. He's not making an observation into his own complicated character; he's parroting word for word what someone else has told him a million times.

To very loosely paraphrase Tolstoy, every family is so uniquely fucked up, it's unbelievable. And maybe a little comforting. We really are all in this together, even me and Jude Zeigler.

"Hey, let's grab a bite or something. We've got time to kill," I suggest because I have a sudden urge to throw out a life preserver before he drowns in his worries.

"Sounds great. Do you want me to drive?" he asks.

"Nah, let's take the Jeep."

Jude climbs in the passenger seat and nods to the radio. "Requests?"

"You choose." I never usually let anyone choose the music in my Jeep, but today feels like a day to break old rules. I don't recognize what he puts on, but the lyrics are smart, and the music is beautiful and comforting. I sit back and let it play while we buzz by the flat, bright landscape that never fails to thaw the tiny pip at the center of my usually frozen heart.

We drive the extra-long way, no shortcuts. I look over and see Jude squinting painfully out the window. My father details my Jeep for me every summer, so I know there aren't any spare hats or sunglasses. I pull into a five-dollar tourist trap.

"What's this place?"

"You need shades," I say, tilting mine down. "Or a hat."

"I have so many at home. I'm cool."

"I can't watch you squint all day. My treat." When he hesitates, I snort. "Do you see the sign? *Nothing over $5.* C'mon. Consider it payback for all the times you covered my ass when I slacked off at work."

He follows me into the shop, holding the door and hovering his hand a few inches from the small of my back, leaned close but keeping a safe distance. Polite but…maybe wanting something more? The thought of it warms me to the tips of my gorgeously manicured toes.

The place is a kaleidoscope of ornaments, baubles, and tchotchkes advertised with bold slashed-price signs. I beeline for the sunglass rack and study the cheap but cool aviators Jude would look really good in. When I glance up, Jude is wearing a beanie with a spinner, his face dead serious under the ridiculous thing.

I snort. "You look like an ass."

"It's this or nothing."

"It doesn't have a bill. You'll still be squinting."

"Pain is beauty."

"You're an idiot." But I love it. Lex is serious about his image. He'd never fool around unless there was a layer of poignant irony to his joke…and he'd probably want to explain it to me if I didn't laugh enough *or* if I laughed too much.

He ducks his head down and comes back up with a straw cowboy hat. "I take offense to that, li'l lady."

I hold out the sunglasses, and he slides them on. He makes the cheap accessories look cool. "I think you need both," I say.

"And this?" He holds up a pocketknife in a leather sheath with The Sunshine State tooled into the side. "How is there so much cool crap in here for so cheap? How have I never been here?"

"Because you're not a tourist," I say as I drag him past seashells with names and pictures carved into them, neon bikinis, and photo albums made of braided palm leaves.

"So, how do *you* know about this place?" He puts the knife and hat on a random shelf, and I stop short and scoop them back up.

"Because I *am* a tourist." A prickle of irritation scratches at the back of my throat when I admit that. I dump the three items on the counter, smile at the sloth-slow elderly woman cashiering, and put down a twenty. "I'm always a tourist."

"A tourist?" Jude throws up an eyebrow. "You're like Little Miss Keys. Wait, seriously, weren't you Little Miss Keys at the fair when you were a kid? Belo still has that picture of you wearing that big crown hanging in his office."

I haven't thought about that day—the sash, the big, glittery crown spattered with bedazzled jewels—in years, but as soon as Jude mentions it, I'm right back on the float, my cheeks sticky with blue cotton-candy sugar, Dani holding my right hand as I waved at my adoring crowds with my cupped left, like a mini, sugared-up queen.

"That was only because my father donated a crazy haul of shrimp to their low-country boil. Nepotism at its finest." I watch as the cashier bags our goods with delicate hands. She smiles—the most beautiful, sweet smile—like I'm an out-of-towner she needs to charm back for more half-price seashell anklets.

"Okay, that just proves you're no tourist. Nepotism wouldn't apply to someone who wasn't born and raised here." He shoots a finger gun at me, like, *Bam, point proven*, and—if that wasn't ridiculous enough—he puts on the hat, winks at our friendly cashier, and takes my hand to kiss it. "Thank you for the gifts, Little Miss Keys."

"You two make a lovely couple," the cashier says warmly, that come-back-soon smile turning into a genuine one right in front of my eyes.

Instead of denying it or explaining, Jude thanks her, and tugs me by the hand out of the store and back into the Jeep. We drive for a few miles in total silence before I pull in at Kim's, the best little Cuban stand ever, and order breakfast sandwiches to go. The guy behind the counter smiles and offers to refill the mugs Jude and I came in holding on the house.

"See, you're no tourist. They only do that for locals," Jude says, the tickle of his voice on my neck sending goose bumps over the bare skin of my shoulders.

"You did a great job on my sister's hair for her quinceañera. We've been telling everyone about you," the guy says as he hands us our bag and rings us up.

I thank him warmly but roll my eyes at Jude when we turn around. "He thinks I'm Dani. It's just a case of mistaken identity."

Jude shrugs. "Maybe. I don't know, Dell. I think you just aren't seeing what's obvious to everyone else. You belong here."

I don't reply to his comment as we head to a little stretch of beach that's owned by one of my dad's very rich fishing buddies. The guard at the community gate waves us through when he sees the Belo's custom plates. Jude and I park down a cul-de-sac and head to the beach, plop side by side in the sand, and eat our perfect sandwiches quietly—I don't think either of us has any internal peace, though.

"You know how people talk about the calm before the storm?" I look sideways and check to make sure Jude is listening to this strange confession I feel compelled to make. He nods, head tilted. "I think about that a lot. Like, how people are always looking up, looking for wind, looking for the obvious signs of disaster." I pause.

"Makes sense."

The tiny waves break over and over, hypnotic unless you have a warped sense of thinking like I do.

"But I look out where the water is calm and flat and think about the pandemonium that goes on right under the surface all the time." I close my eyes, and I can see it, like some mashup of an episode of *The Blue Planet* and a Hieronymus Bosch painting. "Sharks slaughtering fish and whales in a frenzied bloodbath. Packs of dolphins chasing down panicking schools of fish, screaming with their sonar language, all adrenalined up. Animals mating and devouring each other and dying with shipwrecks underneath them. Grunion fish orgies—"

"*What?*" Jude chokes on his coffee.

"We learned about it in AP Bio. I mean, we were learning about mating habits and a bunch of us googled *animal orgies*—"

"What the hell kind of school do you go to?"

"It's one of the top-rated Christian high schools in the country," I inform him.

"It's a Christian school? Damn, people need to stop knocking the US public-education system. I mean, it's not all sunshine and rainbows at Coral Shore High, but at least we're not reading fish porn."

"We're encouraged to follow our curiosity," I say, just a little primly.

"Fish pervs," he laughs, knocking my shoulder with his. "Hey, aquatic erotica aside, weren't you about to get to some kind of deep philosophical point about the ocean and life before I interrupted?"

"No," I protest, embarrassed now that I was willing to take a chance and get all vulnerable in front of Jude. "It was nothing."

"C'mon, I have the attention span of a guppy sometimes—a nonperverted guppy." When I laugh, he nudges me again, a little harder. "Spill, Dell. The calm before the storm doesn't apply to the ocean...?"

I like the way he can switch from joking to earnest. But more than that, I like the way he's always kind. Yes, he can be boring and rule-abiding and insufferably self-righteous, but he's actually an incredibly thoughtful guy, and he makes me feel listened to. Jude has many attractive qualities, but the way he listens is definitely the one that makes my heart race.

"So all that chaos is going on below the waves, right now. Right out there, where the ocean looks so peaceful, it's probably a clusterfuck. And farther down? We don't have a clue. You know that statistic about space and the oceans?"

"That we know more about Mars than we do about the bottom of the ocean on our own planet?" Jude nods. "It's wild."

"Sometimes I feel like... Don't laugh..."

"I can't make any promises." He shrugs when I pull a face.

"You did introduce me to the idea of fish orgies five minutes ago, so…"

"I feel like all my life *I'm* the ocean on a still day. And people are so impressed that I'm so calm and chill, that there are never any hurricanes or tsunamis with me. They have this idea that I just handle things. But underneath? Where no one can see?" I press a hard knuckle into my sternum, pushing down until I almost can't stand it. "There's some terrifying shit going on, all the time."

Jude sucks a breath in through his teeth. "Holy shit, Dell. That's deep. I never thought—"

"What?" I pick up a handful of sand and let it sift out of my fist in a sharp stream. "That the spoiled daddy's girl who's been annoying you for years might have something on her mind other than working on her tan and flirting with the summer workers?"

He gives me a long, sharp look. "Is that what you think I think?"

I want to stare him down the way I stare Lex down, but something about the honesty in his gaze makes me squirm.

"I'm not right?" I hear how guarded the question comes out, like I'm hoping I'm wrong.

"You're dead wrong."

I get exactly what I hoped for, but it's a sucker punch. I don't know what to do with this wished-for information.

"What *do* you think of me?" Each word drops from my lips cautiously.

"I think the more I get to know you, the more sure I am that you're one of the strongest, coolest people I've ever met." He's staring out at the green-blue expanse of ocean, but he gives me a sly half smile. "Don't let it go to your head, though. I'm still technically your boss. Just because I think you're pretty badass doesn't mean I'm going to let you get away with slacking off at work."

This makes me snort—no, this *allows me* to snort. I can't believe I ever thought Jude didn't know how to have fun. He strikes the perfect balance of sincere and goofy.

"Well, I'm still the boss's daughter. Be careful, or I might cash in on some of that nepotism to get you canned." We both laugh and then slip into a quiet that I let play out for a few long beats. "Jude, can I tell you something I've been worrying about for days now?"

"Of course."

I suck in a lungful of ocean air. I can see he's trying to will his face into a mask of nonjudgmental calm, but he's obviously wondering what I'm about to spill. I'm sure he's running possible scenarios, possibly worrying it's going to be some kind of *Making a Murderer*–level confession.

"It's not exactly a secret." I try to think of how to tell him without bungling it all. "I mean, everyone knows I have sisters back home. And a life back home. It's just… I'm not exactly me." Ugh, I'm screwing this up big-time. "I mean, when I'm here, I'm one person. One kind of person. And back home, that's not me. If you came to Michigan and went to school with me, you'd be really shocked."

"You think so?" Jude raises both dark eyebrows like he's not so sure.

"Definitely." I'm still flailing for a way to express how different Florida me and Michigan me are. I start with the basics. "I don't even go by Della in Michigan," I tell him. He waits. "Everyone back home calls me AJ."

"AJ?" He tests it out a few times and looks at me. "You know, that fits. I can see you as an AJ."

"Not as a Della?"

"You can't look like both?"

It's the simplest observation, but it tilts my reality.

"What's your full name? Adelaide, right?"

"Adelaide Josephine Jepsen Beloise. Try bubbling that onto your SAT forms. It's weird."

"It's not that weird, Dell. Or do you like AJ better?"

Ding, ding, ding. There's the problem.

"It's not a better or worse thing. I'm both. One traveler, two roads." I shrug my shoulders, at a loss for how exactly to explain. "I'm the oldest sister in Michigan."

"Whoa. That *is* weird to think about. I mean, I think of you as being the baby of your family." He studies me for a few long seconds. "Is it weird?"

"Only when I compare myself to Dani. She's, like, amazing and caring and has her shit together. I'm so lucky to have her. My sisters?" I roll my eyes. "I'm a hot mess. I mean, I try to keep my shit together for them, but it's just different."

"What's your mom like?" He shifts nearer and leans his head closer as the wind picks up and whips sand our way. He holds an arm up and blocks the grains from spraying me, which is super sweet of him to do.

"She's incredibly organized," I begin, realizing I've never talked to anyone who doesn't know my mother about my mother. "She's kind of vain, but, like, it's fair because of how beautiful she is. And we live in this enormous house that looks

234 • LIZ REINHARDT

like it's out of a magazine. Actually, it's *been* in a magazine. She does all this social media lifestyle blogging, mostly about being a mother. And, yeah, it's kind of embarrassing to read about myself online. Thank God no one our age would actually follow her, so it's a pretty manageable level of embarrassment." I laugh, a hollow sound that just fills the space. "She's super strict, but we have fun. We get a lot of stuff—we're in clubs, and if there's a hobby we want to pursue or a sport, my parents are both really supportive for the most part. They come to our games and performances. My mom loves us so much. I know that. She also demands a lot from us. And she expects us to do what's expected with a smile… Disrespect is *not* tolerated. She doesn't leave a lot of room for individualism."

He sucks his teeth. "Wow. That sounds intense. I can't really picture you not doing your own thing. Are you the family rebel?"

I snort. "Not at all. That's Marnie, my middle sister, and, honestly, she causes a lot of chaos for me by doing her own thing. But I definitely don't rebel. I toe the line, follow the rules, never make my parents worry. I'm an excellent student. I have to use this special planner to keep track of all the activities I do, and I'm pretty much constantly sleep-deprived because I don't have another choice. I have every single thing scheduled, even my social activities."

"So when you come down to Florida, you can cut loose a little," he says, using the funny old expression for chilling out my dad uses all the time. I bet that's exactly where Jude picked it up.

"That's kind of a major understatement." I push the hair back from my eyes. "I get to be the baby sister here. I get to be a daddy's girl. I can work a job that doesn't need to look good on my college applications. I go to the beach and lie around for hours with no agenda. I don't watch everything I do or say, and I definitely don't need a planner."

"So this is like your safe haven. And that's why you didn't want to worry about a super-serious, amazing internship. You need this to decompress after going full throttle all year." We both stare out at the curling waves, the sparkling sky, the expanse of beauty and calm with all its hidden, chaotic depths. Me, metaphorically.

"Back home, I take care of Marnie. I get her out of trouble, I'm her shoulder to cry on, I'm her sounding board. I *love* her." I look him right in the eye and repeat it, just so there's no doubt. "I love her just as much as I love Dani and Duke and my little sister, Lilli. But...fuck, Jude, she's *exhausting*." I take a shaky breath. "She needs a ton of attention. She's *always* spiraling out of control. Everyone falls in love with her instantly. Back home, I don't mind always being behind the scenes. I don't mind being her cleanup crew. But here? This is *my* time." I push my hands through my hair and let my head fall forward. "I want to be there for Marnie, but I don't know how much more I can help her before I just...buckle under the weight of everything."

I feel the sand shift as Jude moves closer, and I lean into him, hard.

"I'm sorry. That's rough. Damn, I had no idea. Have you talked to your mom about this? Maybe she doesn't realize how much you need a break." His look is so hopeful, I feel a huge surge of affection for him.

Lex would have told me to quit whining, no question.

Then again, Lex knows and idolizes Marnie, so he wouldn't see the problem. And maybe that will be Jude's viewpoint when he meets her—it wouldn't be surprising. Marnie has the Midas touch when it comes to meeting new people. No one can resist her.

"My mom is locked in with all kinds of big-deal stuff for my other little sister's music career. Like, game-changing stuff. Lilli is amazing, and she's focused on following her passion, so I get it. I don't want to mess things up for her so I can have more downtime, you know? And, trust me, my mom knows full well that Marnie has a reputation for drama, which is why she's pushing her on me." I wince. "That's harsh. I mean, Marnie is going through a tough time—"

"It sounds like you give Marnie tons of sympathy and help all year long." Jude moves his pinkie finger toward mine and links the two together. I look at the infinity chain of our joined fingers and feel an unfamiliar rush, the kind of swoony blood-pumping I only felt with Lex when we were doing a whole lot more than brushing pinkies. "It's okay to be selfish sometimes, you know. It's not a bad thing to put yourself first."

"It's okay for *Della* to put herself first." I tug at his finger. "That's why I love her. Della is kind of obnoxious and totally knows what she wants. But my mom asked *AJ*. My mom *needs* AJ."

"I don't want to point out the obvious…" Jude's left eyebrow quirks high "…but you *do* know you're both people, right?"

I shake my head. "You wouldn't recognize AJ."

"Really?" He snorts. "Take charge? Kind of type A? Worrying about her family? Says *pop* instead of *soda*?"

"That's AJ," I whisper.

He taps a finger on my head. "C'mon, brainiac. You can't tell me you don't realize that's Della, too. You think because you dye your hair and fool around at work and run to the beach, people can't see all the other amazing things?"

I lasso his pinkie tighter, pulling him closer to me with one tiny loop of our fingers. "You see all that?"

"Everybody does," he assures me. "Hey, I have a Della/AJ question."

"Okay." My stomach clenches, waiting for Jude to ask something I'm not prepared to answer.

"How does dating work?"

I blink a few times. "What?"

"Does AJ leave her all-American boyfriend back in Michigan waiting with her picture next to his bed so she can hook up with lazy beach bums in Florida all summer?"

Just because it's clearly a joke doesn't mean my feelings aren't bruised.

"What do *you* think?"

"I don't know. That's why I'm asking." He studies my face, we lock eyes, and I silently will him to reverse that statement, but it's no good. He waits for me to answer the question I wish he'd never asked.

"Then you don't know me at all." I shrug like it doesn't matter to me either way and jump up, slapping sand off my legs and feet aggressively enough that I hope a few grains lodge right in his eye.

"Dell!" he calls to my back.

"C'mon, Jude." I wave my hand without so much as looking over my shoulder. "We need to get back on the road."

14

July

FLORIDA

"Marnie! Marnie!" I wave my arms over my head like the people who help guide the planes on the runway.

Marnie whips around and stares at me, her head tilted over to one side, like a ruffled cardinal surveying something new and bewildering. She lets go of her bag and pulls her mouth into a tight line, knits her eyebrows, squints. It's like she's using all of her deductive skills to make sense of what's right in front of her eyes.

Jude steps forward to help out. "Marnie? Marnie Jepsen?"

His voice is the trigger that breaks the spell. Marnie blinks at him, waking up. "I'm Marnie." She holds a hand out and Jude shakes it.

"Jude. I'm a friend of Dell—a friend of AJ's," he corrects.

If I was stripped completely naked in the middle of this busy airport, I'd feel less exposed than I do right now, standing in front of my speechless sister like an imposter.

"AJ." She reaches her hand out and touches the end of my bob. "You cut your hair." Her fingers glide along the blunt edges and close over the back pieces, the bright pink ones. She rubs my hair between her fingers gently. "Your hair… it's *pink*."

"Just some of it," I say.

"Did you contour? You know how to contour?" She presses her face too close to mine. "Are those fake lashes? Are you wearing leggings in public? Mom would disown you! Leggings Are Not Pants would be, like, the motto on our family crest. If we had one." She rocks back on her heels and stares at me. "Who the hell *are* you?"

Jude clears his throat. "It's, uh, just some makeup—"

Marnie throws up a warning hand. "Shut your trap, hottie. This is sister business," she says, never looking at him. Marnie just *stares. Straight. At. Me.* "Mom will be pissed. So pissed. And disappointed."

"I never let her see me like this," I tell her.

I watch it dawn on her that this isn't a new rebellion. "You're really tan."

I nod.

"Sun or self-tanner?"

"A little bit of both." She raises her blond eyebrows. "Maybe more than just a little sun," I amend. "And a lot of bronzer."

"I didn't think you even *liked* the sun." She stares at my leggings. "Those are neon. I've never seen you wear neon. You look kind of tacky. You look…*slutty*."

"Hey," Jude says lowly, but Marnie lets out a growl that informs him she's the alpha in this exchange.

"I know," I say, and I get what Jude doesn't: Marnie isn't seeing clothes and hair, she's seeing choices. Expression. She's seeing me defying our mother's sacred rules about how we present ourselves and what we value. I'm flaunting them.

So is my sister.

The difference is that Marnie did it bravely, to our mother's face. She stares down the disapproval and weathers the judgment and fights like the badass she is. I play dress-up like a little kid and wash it all off before anyone can scold me for it.

I was wrong to tell Jude I was a liar like that was the worst thing about me. The worst thing about me is that I'm a coward.

"What does your dad think?" Marnie asks, rolling the word *dad* around on her tongue. It's an old word that suddenly has no familiar context for us.

"He thinks I look nice. My sister Dani taught me."

She studies the tops of her bright athletic sneakers, usually meticulous, now crusted with mud. "Weird. That's the kind of thing *you're* supposed to teach *us*."

Us. Them. Marnie is using her pronouns to draw some clear lines in the sand. I just hope meeting *them* helps her dissolve that division. My years of secrets and lies definitely haven't helped make things more inclusive.

"I would have taught you. I didn't know you wanted to learn."

"I didn't know you could teach us." Marnie looks shell-shocked. "You're *so different*…"

"I just look different," I lie, but she sees through it.

"No. You're even standing different. You talk different." She nods at Jude. "You have better taste in guys."

Jude dips his head and rubs the back of his reddening neck, making a low hum that's definitely not unhappy.

That comment snaps me out of my stupor. "Are you kidding me? You love Lex!" I exclaim.

"I love *sparring* with Lex. He's fun, in a mean way," Marnie clarifies. "He's never been good enough for you as a boyfriend, though. This guy—what's your name again?"

"Jude." He sticks his hand out for a second time, and Marnie shakes again, smiling with smug approval.

"Jude," she repeats. "This guy already stuck up for you more in the last five minutes than Lex has in the whole time you guys have been dating." She tosses Jude an adorable smile. "Hey, all of this is kind of weirding me out, and when I get stressed, I need food. Greasy food. And a lot of it. Plus, I can't seem to get full since they pumped my stomach. Any good places to eat around here?"

15

Marnie in the Keys

Later the Same Day

FLORIDA

At first my guilt is so intense it's a physical pain. I'd say it feels like a boot to the gut, but I imagine how Marnie feels and close down my self-pity. Now that she's here in front of me, I realize that I have the potential to connect with Marnie in a different way than we have before in this place that's always been so healing for me. It's easy to get so caught up in the worry and frustration that I forget how much I really love my free-spirited little sister, and I'm excited to have her here, seeing my other home and meeting people I love so much and really don't want to hide anymore.

Jude offers to drive when we leave the airport, and I offer Marnie shotgun. I'm trying to think of places that have delicate food—soup maybe? Simple sandwiches?—but Marnie wants a burger, the greasier the better.

"A big one, medium-rare, with fried onions. And raw onions. And pickles. And mustard," she adds, rattling off a new condiment or topping every few seconds.

"By the time they pile all that on, your burger will be, like, two percent beef," Jude says, and Marnie cackles like she's at the edgiest stand-up show of the century.

"You're funny." My unhinged middle sister is in Florida and has anointed annoying, rule-abiding Jude the king of comedy. My worlds are colliding, and it's nothing like I imagined it would be.

"You wanna go to the place where my friends and I always go when we ditch?" Jude asks. "Cheap and extra greasy, but so good."

"Hell yeah." Marnie hangs her head out the window and takes a deep breath. "It smells so good here!"

"Ocean life." Jude smiles. "Anytime I think about moving somewhere else, I think about how much it would suck to live without that smell every day."

"I know this is a ridiculous question, but I paid a nerd to do my geography homework in ninth grade, so I'm just gonna ask. We're, like, *right* by the ocean, right?"

Lex would have howled his arrogant ass off. Jude laughs, but there's nothing mean about it.

"It's weird you ask that, because I've probably taken the only route that doesn't drive basically right along the shoreline." He flips on the blinker and pulls a quick U-turn, drives about three minutes in the opposite direction, and laughs again when Marnie gasps. "Sorry. I should've guessed you'd want the scenic view. This is a pretty nice beach. Not too touristy, not too built-up."

"That's the ocean." I haven't heard Marnie's voice so full of giggly wonder since we were little kids running through sprinklers and spending twelve hours a day in the pool and the other twelve hours wishing ourselves back in the water. "I've never seen it."

We all lurch forward when Jude taps the brakes too hard.

"What?" He pulls into the small parking area by the shore and repeats his question, louder this time. *"What?"*

"Marnie, you've totally seen the ocean," I lecture, then stop short, rifling through our shared childhood vacation memories. I come up with ponds, lakes, rivers, creeks, pools (a million crystal-blue pools), but no ocean.

No ocean?

My ocean memories crowd my brain: shaking sand off an ice-cream wrapper that whips away from our blanket in a strong gust of wind; throwing a handful of chips into the air and not feeling a single one rain back down as the seagulls devour them in midair; my blocked ears and thumping heart as I force myself to keep calm and float through the murderous tug of a riptide; my salt-matted hair and sand-exfoliated, sun-warmed skin hitting the cool sheets, where I fall into an instant deep sleep after a full day crabbing. I zoom through them looking for Mom or Peter, Lilli or Marnie, but these are all memories with my Beloise family.

"Disney World, the Grand Canyon, Universal, Washington, D.C., Dollywood, skiing in Colorado, Grandma's house at the lake, Austin, Texas, Disney World again," she lists, counting off the last decade of summer vacations my family has taken. "No ocean."

"I feel like it's my duty as a certified, lifelong beach bum to take you to see the ocean before you melt your guts eating a disgusting burger." Jude opens the door, comes around to the passenger side, and holds his hand out for Marnie's. "C'mon. It's gonna blow your mind."

Marnie giggles when Jude pushes her back into the passenger seat and points to her shoes.

"No shoes. No socks. C'mon, rookie." He watches as she kicks off her sneakers and leaves her balled-up socks on the floorboard, then they both run, screaming, toward the waves.

I shoulder my door open carefully and breathe deep, wiggling my toes in the sand as I walk down to the ocean's edge. The wind is intense today, whipping my hair around my face so hard, I'm forced to bust out the elastic band I always keep around my wrist for this exact reason. Every breath fills me with a sense of serenity that I can't fake anywhere else, no matter how many scented candles, aromatherapy drops, meditation apps, yoga poses, and happiness mantras I try.

Marnie is in up to her calves, the water turning her jeans dark.

"Oh my God! Oh my God!" she screams at the waves, kicking them and leaning over at the waist to splash in them. "This is amazing!"

I hear Jude's laugh. Who would have thought a sound I'd barely ever heard before today would rank as one of my very favorite sounds, possibly ever? As irritated as I am with him for insinuating I could excuse cheating because I deal with this double life, I can't help realizing what a good guy he really is.

He's more cautious than Marnie, wading out slowly and surveying the distant ocean for what, I'm not sure. It's *so* Jude, though, to always be aware of what's going on no matter what. He loves to be prepared, to take care of things. Watching him reach out and grab Marnie's arm before she topples into the water, I wonder how I could have ever been annoyed by these qualities, which now strike me as excellent.

"Come in, AJ!" Marnie screams, windmilling her arms.

I walk to the waves and wade out to her. She's in up to her knees, and the shove and tug of the sand and shells under our feet creates a soothing rhythm. We walk up and down the shore, with Marnie occasionally breaking into squeals and running, full force, against the current.

She looks happy, relaxed. That makes me feel hopeful that her time here can be a balm for all the stress and anxiety of the last few months. This might be a chance for us to re-connect, maybe come up with a new game plan for tackling problems once we head back home. Marnie and I have both fallen into patterns that aren't healthy for us, but I'm ready to make changes if my sister is.

I'm not paying much attention to what Marnie is doing when Jude swivels his head. "Your sister!" He points franti-cally. "She's getting naked!"

I'm about to yell at her about indecent-exposure laws, but Marnie has already stripped down to her sports bra and boy shorts. She runs back to the water.

"She's not naked," I assure him, and he looks up, relieved.

"Marnie is really cool." Jude watches as Marnie leaps up and slams her body and limbs full force into the salt water. She sputters to the surface and dives again.

"She's really…energetic." I try not to be exasperated by her after the hell she's been through—the hell I played a part in creating—but I feel a little nervous thinking about having to unpack everything Marnie-related, plus deal with my own shit and everything going on with Belo's this summer. I want to tackle it all, but I'm not sure where to start. "I mean, this is Marnie's energy level after having her stomach emergency-pumped a week ago and spending all day traveling by plane. Imagine her on an *ordinary* day."

"I know it feels like your fault, the whole thing with Marnie winding up in the hospital." He focuses on the horizon. "It's *not* your fault."

"It definitely *is* my fault." I nudge his shoulder with mine. "You don't ever have to lie to make me feel better, Jude."

"I'm not. And it isn't a lie or just my opinion. It's a fact. When someone is under the influence, they do wild shit. I know she's still a kid, but alcohol is what was driving the situation that night, and trying to control things when there's drinking involved? Lost cause. Trust me on this one."

I think about what he's told me about his parents and the irresponsible drinking that goes on in his home. It's weird how I had such a specific and detailed picture of Jude—his motivations, his family, his character—based on years of being around him in one context, and it was all totally inaccurate.

"I'm sorry your parents put you through that kind of chaos all the time." I don't know how much he's comfortable talking about. He's gone from a coworker I was reluctantly attracted to to a guy I really like spending time with and have even shared my darkest secrets with in the span of a few weeks. My life is changing so fast and so completely, it's hard to keep up with it.

"My parents are professional alcoholics." Jude's eyes track Marnie as he scans the beach, as vigilant as if he's the lifeguard on duty, the same way he was with Duke the other day. "I have no memory of them being sober for more than a few days at a time, tops. Since I was a little kid, they've been drunk pretty much every single day. Once in a while, one of them will decide they're going to cut back—and let me be clear, that does *not* mean stop drinking. It means trading the harder stuff for beer or wine. They both lost their licenses years ago. They do side hustles down by the pier, fire-eating and acro-performances for money. My mom used to be a really good jewelry maker before her hands got permanently shaky. My dad has some disability claim that brings them in some money, and they live in the place my grandfather willed to my dad before he died. It's falling down around them, but it's paid off, so…" He shrugs. "They have no motivation, internal or external, to stop being fall-down drunks."

"That's terrible," I murmur, trying to imagine how neat, orderly Jude has survived eighteen years in a house built on chaos. "Do you plan to keep living there, with them?"

"I'm moving out after this summer. I have almost enough saved up to get me by for a few months. I didn't want to make a jump without a cushion. I don't think I'll have much luck getting a rental on my own because of my age, though. My older brother went up to Vermont a few years ago. He uses barn wood to make custom tables, and business is good. He needs help, and I'm pretty handy. I might head up there."

"Moving? Vermont? Does my dad know?" My throat squeezes closed. Jude is a part of Belo's, but if there is no Belo's…does that mean my life will be Jude-free? Jude started working for my father the first summer I got regular hours, five years ago. I can barely remember the place without him. And I don't like thinking about not seeing him regularly.

"I'm willing to stay until Belo makes his decision, whatever that is. But honestly?" He clears his throat and unfolds the sunglasses from his collar, sliding them over his eyes as the sun bakes down on us. "I don't think he can afford to keep paying my salary."

I haven't told Jude that I asked Duke to grab Dad's files for me while I was home doing nothing, exiled in preparation for Marnie's appearance. He's been so tight-lipped about his trips to the CPA and his business meetings, but the curiosity was killing me. Plus I needed something to take my mind off Marnie. I've been going through the expenses, the sales, the taxes and rent, looking at everything and reading the QuickBooks manual. I've made some decent headway. I keep meaning to ask Dani to come by and help me, but she's been super busy at the salon, and truth be told, I feel a little weird being around her now that she saw me at a really low point.

Of course I know Dani still loves me. She's my sister, she's obligated to. I'm just not sure how I'll feel when her disappointment is the big, fat elephant squatting in the middle of the room. But I need to get over myself so we can put our heads together and figure out where things are headed.

"Don't make any plans to quit yet, okay?"

"You know leaving Belo is the last thing I want. But I'm not going to watch your dad sink and not try to do whatever I can to help. I, uh, might have mentioned how much an all-family staff would help things along right now. Just until he figures things out."

"*I'll* figure it out. I promise. In my other life, I'm kind of a math prodigy. I'll look through everything and come up with a way to keep you on that won't tank the whole company."

His smile widens, and soon he's full-on laughing.

"What's so funny?" I bristle, pissed that he thinks the idea of me saving my father's livelihood is so hilarious. "I know you think I'm some half-wit—"

"Not at all, not at all." He catches his lower lip between his teeth to stall his laughter, and the gesture winds up causing my heart to skip like crazy. "Just, like, a few weeks ago, you would have celebrated if your dad fired me. Today I offer that option up with a really solid reason, and you're begging me to stay." He leans closer, and I love the way he smells, like mint and salt and clean detergent that's not hemp-based.

"Nothing has worked out the way I thought it was going to this summer." I weave my hand through the sand, until my fingers find his under the hot grains. I hold tight. "The weird thing is, my life falling apart hasn't been the catastrophe I thought it would be."

Jude, the most unsmiling guy I've ever known, smiles wider and wider.

"What now?" I demand.

"Nothing. I'm just thinking about how I don't want to be happy your life's falling apart, but it's been pretty nice for me. Also, I'm thinking about how many fish orgies are going on *right now* out there."

We both look up, laughing at the absurdity of it all, and we both jump to our feet in panic at the same time after a few seconds of searching the water and seeing nothing.

"Marnie! Goddamn it, Marnie!" I scream, running so fast to the shore, I sink to my calves and slow myself down. My heart is racing, thumping out of my chest as I scan the gently lapping water. It looks so calm, but I know just how deceiving looks can be.

"The rip currents were supposed to be bad today. I should have warned her. I should have watched," Jude says as he strips off his shirt and drops his phone, keys, and wallet out of his pockets on the sand. "Stay here. I'll get her."

"Jude, I can't even see her! How will you find her?" My voice chokes as panicked fear tears through me. I picture Marnie under the water, lost, her body limp, her eyes wide-open and seeing nothing, and I double over, terror ripping a sob from my lips.

"Hey." He grabs me by the shoulders and looks at me, his dark eyes locked on mine. "Look at me. I'll find her, Dell. I'll find her for you. Trust me." His hand, warm and rough, cups my cheek for a few seconds before he's off, running so fast he kicks up geysers of sand.

I dig out my own phone, fingers ready to dial 9-1-1 if I don't see my sister bob back to the surface in the next few seconds. Jude dives in and knifes through the water like a torpedo. He swims like a kid who grew up in these waters year-round, and I've never been happier to have a verified local at my side. I cram my fist to my mouth, knuckles hard against my teeth, and try not to think about what I'll do if I let something happen to Marnie the second she pulled herself back from the brink.

I've already dialed the nine when Jude's head bursts out of the waves, a red one bobbing next to his shoulder. It's slow moving back to shore, but he doesn't stop, doesn't give up until he meets me in the churning surf. Marnie is gasping and choking, but she seems okay. I wrap my arms around her and crush her against my body as hard as I can.

"I'm sorry, AJ, I'm so sorry," she sobs between spitting out water.

"Stop apologizing!" I run my hands up and down over her chilly, clammy skin, looking her over frantically. "Are you okay? Does it hurt anywhere? Did you swallow a lot of water?"

When she shakes her head, wet tendrils of red hair stick to her cheeks and neck. "No. I was only under for a minute, I think. I wasn't that far out. It didn't feel like the water was rough or anything…" She glares at the choppy waves like she's offended, like she was tricked by the ocean she was so in love with a few minutes ago.

"Rip currents," Jude gasps. He's on all fours, knees and arms buried in the hot sand, salt water beaded in his hair, gulping air so fast his chest rises and falls like a bellow. "It's really tough to swim out of them. You have to float through. A lot of times that's hard to remember to do. It's easy to panic."

"I didn't know. I'm usually a really good swimmer." Marnie kneels beside Jude and puts one hand on his back, rubbing it in a small circle. "I'm sorry, Jude."

"No worries." Jude spits out a mouthful of salt water and sand. "Swimming in a pool is nothing like swimming in the ocean. There's no way you could have known. And I should have been watching, anyway. I'm supposed to be your ocean chaperone, right?"

"*I* should have been watching." I thump down on the sand next to them, wilting now that the adrenaline that ricocheted through me has run out.

"It's not your fault." Marnie wrings out her limp hair. "You okay, Jude?"

He nods and gives her a weak smile.

"He's okay." She moves toward me, pats my shoulder gingerly. "I'm okay. We're all okay, and it's not your fault, AJ."

"I'm supposed to be taking care of you." This is the thing with Marnie. Even when she has the best intentions, she always finds a way to knot herself into the most impossible situations. And I always seem to be the one who needs to figure out how to unknot her.

Well, it used to be just me. I kneel next to Jude and curl a hand around his shoulder. He rocks back on his heels, his face lined with worry, his brown eyes sweet and so completely understanding.

"Thank you. So much." I move toward him awkwardly, arms open, and suddenly, he falls into my hug.

It's a *fantastic* hug.

His arms tighten around my back, warm and strong. He shifts so I slide lower, and he circles higher on my shoulders, where it feels so good and safe to be squeezed by his arms. My face fits perfectly into the space between his neck and shoulder, which is slightly damp and smells salty from his dive into the ocean to save my sister. Remembering how brave he was, how he didn't hesitate even a second before he went in after Marnie, makes me tighten my hold, and he matches the pressure.

I cling to him like I'll fall off the edge of the world if I let go, nuzzling closer, burrowing deeper into his embrace. In a few seconds he's all I can smell, his warmth is all I can feel, and I swear if I shut my eyes and laid my head against his chest, I'd fall asleep right there on the sand, cradled like a baby in his arms.

Marnie's voice breaks me out of the most indecent hug I've

ever participated in. "So I know disasters spark romance and all that, but you guys really need to get me that hamburger before I faint."

"Of course." He peels me off of his chest carefully, and I swipe sand off his biceps and broad chest. Marnie's whinny of a laugh lets me know I'm tricking absolutely no one with my supposed helpfulness, but I don't care. I've been intoxicated by Jude's good humor, by his kindness and honesty, his bravery and—shallow as it might be—the purely chemical and physical attraction that draws me to him.

Now that I've calmed down, knowing he and my sister are safe, I take a long second to ogle the hero of the hour. When I meet Jude's eyes, they're hot and hungry in a way I've never seen them before, but I definitely like what I see. *A lot.* He nods at me and smiles.

"You were just here, lounging on the beach while Marnie and I did all the heavy lifting. I think you definitely owe us a burger or three."

"C'mon. Let's ease our trauma with some greasy food," I say, ignoring the swirl of emotions about Jude Zeigler fizzing through me.

"Sounds better than years of therapy to me," Marnie singsongs, once again rebounding from a physical blow with a superhuman resistance.

"Funny, but I always want a burger after I leave Al-Anon meetings. It's like burgers and therapy are a perfect match," Jude says.

Marnie gives him a long, curious look. "Huh. Maybe I'll have to try sometime." I suck in a breath and attempt to picture the Jepsens in family therapy. The idea of talking our issues out with a licensed professional instead of burying them until they fester sounds like a huge relief. Maybe we *should* try that. "By the way, that was fun and all, but when can we have a *real* beach day?" Marnie continues, already pinging to the next topic at warp speed.

"A real beach day?" Jude swipes up his shirt and puts it on (much to my embarrassed disappointment). He drops his keys, wallet, and phone into his pockets, and hands Marnie her balled-up pile of damp clothes. "Like a day where we enjoy the water instead of attempting to drown?"

"Yes," Marnie says, swinging her arms. "And we bring a volleyball, maybe? And a cooler full of food, like people do in the movies. That's not just a movie thing, is it?"

"Coolers are real-life beach necessities," Jude affirms, and he winks at me over Marnie's head. "I'm glad the rip currents didn't spook you away from the ocean."

"It was like a rough baptism." Marnie shrugs a muscled shoulder, all swagger. "So when can we head back over?"

"When do you want to come back?" I ask, instantly a little nervous at the prospect of facing the ocean with my mercurial little sister and no backup. I've never been afraid of the ocean before, but then again, I've always been the watched and protected little sister. This is a weird change for me, but I'm trying hard to acclimate to my shifting position now that Marnie's here.

"Do you, like, work?" She directs the question at Jude who nods. "When's your next day off?"

"Sunday I only work until two. The beach is better after the sun goes down anyway, if you wanted to do something late."

"Good?" Marnie checks with me, and I nod like this is

normal, like Jude and I hang out and go on beach dates all the time. "It's a date, then," my little sister crows with just enough of a trill in her voice that I know for sure she's proud of her lame romantic schemes. I'm officially doomed once she and Dani get together.

16

Home (Other Home)

Marnie announces she's tired after stuffing her face with two truly revolting burgers topped with every imaginable condiment on the planet. She climbs into the back seat and, using some balled-up sweatshirts as a pillow, passes out, snoring like a chain saw.

"So," Jude says after fifteen minutes of listening to my little sister's powerful snores.

"So." I'm back in the driver's seat, and I'm glad to have the excuse not to look over and get distracted by Jude's surfer-sexy profile. I was always able to acknowledge his obvious good looks, but, until I found myself cradled in his arms, nursing this intensely possessive thrill, I'd never really let myself fully absorb just how handsome he is.

So handsome, he's more distracting to me than combining carpool karaoke, texting during an argument, and eating a bowl of chili while driving would be. So handsome, he's *literally* a danger to me right now.

"Today was intense." He jiggles his knee up and down

like he's nervous, and I want to reach over and take his hand, squeeze his fingers.

With Lex I would have debated doing it—how would he interpret it? How would our power balance shift if I made a move he could laugh off as corny or vulnerable? But this isn't Lex. This is Jude. I reach my hand over and take his in mine.

He looks at our hands, and I catch his smile from the corner of my eye. "Also, it was a pretty damn nice day." That smile is so wide, it has to hurt his face. Then it fades, and he looks very serious. "Your sister's near-death experience aside. *That* was scary as hell."

"I know I said it before, but thank you. So much. If you weren't there… I'm not that strong a swimmer. And by the time someone came to help…" I shake my head.

"I'm really glad I was there, too. And that I trained for Key West's Ironman this year."

"You did an Ironman?" I don't try to hide my admiration. "I've always wanted to do one!" I pause and tell him, "I came in fourth in my age group in Ann Arbor's marathon this spring."

"No kidding?" He nods his approval. "I don't want to beat a dead horse or whatever, but I never thought you were into stuff like that."

My natural reaction is to stiffen, feel attacked, but I think back to how safe it felt in his arms. That wasn't some romantic figment of my imagination. That was real, and for once, I'm letting my gut take the lead and trusting someone else with my armored heart.

"I actually love waking up before dawn to run in Michigan. It started out as just stress relief, but I'm kind of competitive, so I started timing myself on my runs, then I started entering a few races with friends for charity, and eventually I ran a full marathon." Now that I laid it all out for Jude, it strikes me as telling that I took what started as a simple morning run and turned it into marathon training. Always pushing—hard—is an AJ specialty. "I never do it here, but I bet it's amazing."

He swivels in the seat, gawking with excitement. "So, if I told you I get up at four in the morning to run ten miles, then watch the sun come up on the beach, you'd be down to keep me company?"

"Um, I'd one hundred percent get up to pack us a protein-rich breakfast to eat while we watched the sunrise, like a real running dork."

"I'm in if you are. Tomorrow, dawn?"

This is crazy corny, we know it, and we don't shake it off or make it into a joke. I want to love it, but it's almost too pure for comfort. The cynical part of me that's still kicking holds its breath to see how this will get screwed up.

But the new me—the person who's not all AJ or all Della—decides it's worth at least attempting.

"It's a date."

We don't say another word until we're in my driveway, and I get the feeling it's because we're both trying not to jinx this weird, new nameless *thing* between us. Once the Jeep is in Park, we sit for a few minutes in the relative quiet—Marnie's snores are like white noise by now. Jude rubs his thumb along the edges of my hand, over the bumps of my knuckles, so gently on the inside of my wrist that shivers flutter up and down my spine.

He keeps his eyes down, looking at our hands, and once

in a while, he pulls his bottom lip in and chews on it. It's just hand-holding. This is, like, Puritan-level dating. So why do I feel like I'm running a serious fever?

"I should get Marnie up and let her get settled." I have to get out and get some fresh air because if Jude bites his lip one more time, I'm going to jump on his lap and do indecent things to him while my little sister snores in the back seat. But I'm not quite ready to call it a day. "If stuff is still messed up for you at home, you can come crash in Duke's old room."

"Thanks for the invite, but you guys need alone time together." He glances back at Marnie. "I'm really glad your sister came down."

"I know Marnie seems charming now, but trust me, she's incredibly annoying." I look back at my sister, who has a river of drool leaking out of the side of her mouth, and my heart clenches up with protective love.

"Marnie's cool," Jude says, then pauses. "But I meant I'm glad she came down because I finally got to meet you. The real you." He slides his free hand up and cups my cheek, running his thumb over it in a slow arc. "I really, *really* like the real you."

"How do you know this is really the real me?" I wonder if he can feel how fast my pulse is racing.

"Because," he says with an impish gleam in his eyes, "you finally admitted you have a thing for me. I've been waiting five years for you to come to your senses."

"I *never* said I have a thing for you," I counter. "Maybe you're just another summer fling."

"Well, I'll just ask Belo to put you on shift every single

day with me, so you have no choice. You're gonna be stuck with me."

"What if I go through the books and find out you're actually Belo's biggest expense, so I fire you?"

"I guess I'll reapply, start at minimum wage again, and come in just for the fun of being ordered around by the boss's daughter."

"I hear she's kind of an asshole," I stage-whisper.

Making him laugh is my new addiction.

"Nah." He pulls my hand up to his mouth and kisses my knuckles. "She's just passionate when she cares about something. And misunderstood. And she's got a huge lady-boner for her manager."

"I hear he has a girlfriend in Canada he's super serious about."

"Oh, he dumped her. She smelled like maple syrup, and she kicked his ass at ice hockey. It was too much for him." His smile is slow and sweet. "Plus, he's had this secret crush on the boss's daughter for a while. Like a long while. He just didn't expect it to go anywhere."

"Seriously?"

"Yep." He lowers his eyes, and I admire his gorgeous lashes, his perfect cheekbones, all of this incredibly sweet, hot guy who I somehow overlooked all these years. How did I think he was kind of the worst when summer started, and now I don't ever want him to leave?

I don't have an answer, and I don't want to think about it too much. I'm just grateful things changed. Funny how I was so worried about everything changing, and now I'm scared to think what things would have been like if everything *didn't* change.

We lean close, our foreheads pressed together, and I feel the warmth of his lips so close to mine when my monster of a sister snorts herself awake, half choking on the torrent of drool that's probably rushing down her throat.

"Are you guys making out?" she yelps, rubbing sleep out of her eyes. "Gross. I'm an *innocent child*." She peers out the window. "Is this home? Oh my God. It's *so* beautiful," she says, her voice hushed with awe.

I turn to look out the window and attempt to see my dad's house through Marnie's eyes. Our house back in Michigan is a tasteful colossus of light stone and enormous windows with a beautiful slate roof, very faux-European-palace. Inside it's all gleaming wood and sparkling granite, high ceilings and cool, neutral paints, tons of intricate moldings and high-end fixtures. It has a polished, quiet beauty to it, like a five-star hotel.

My dad's house is a snug and cozy beach cottage with generations of wear, tumbling vines heavy with bright flowers twisted all over the wraparound porch, and lots of nooks and corners to curl up in everywhere you turn. The furniture is a mishmash of wicker and sturdy antiques painted bright colors. The floors are original pine, scuffed from years of sand-covered footwear. There are bright florals and cheerful slipcovers everywhere, and every window faces gardens or the ocean. This house feels like a home because it's been one for so long.

"I want to live here forever," Marnie sighs. "I want to die here."

"You haven't even made it through the front door," I remind her. "And I'd appreciate it if you'd keep the death scares to a minimum. I swear I'm going to have gray hairs after today." I hand her the key. "Jude and I will grab your things. Go take a look."

Marnie hoots as she dashes up the steps.

"When she was little, she always wanted to be the first one in our hotel or rental cabin to check it all out before anyone else." I watch her fling the door open and leave it swinging. "She's kind of a human tornado, but I really do love her."

"I know." Jude gets out and comes around to open my door. He pulls the bags out of the back and brings them up the steps, setting them in the palm-leaf-wallpapered foyer. "I know when you didn't take her calls, you never meant for anything bad to happen."

Unexpected tears sting behind my eyelids at the mention of that terrible night when, despite Jude's valiant attempt to defend me, I acted terribly. I'm committed to figure out how to balance what I need and how to be there for my sister. I wish there was a handbook I could study or an AP class I could take to get the formula just right and ace this test. What's the use of being smart and figuring things out for tests and grades if I can't transfer any of that knowledge to the most important aspects of my life?

"I never want anything bad to happen to Marnie. Ever." I pause and lean close to Jude, shocked again by how the worry seeps out of me when I let myself rest against him. "But sometimes it feels like way too much to be the one who has to stop the bad from happening. I think what I really want is to be able to help Marnie do whatever it is she needs to do to be happy and make choices that don't throw her life into chaos. And maybe I can figure some things out for myself in the meantime. Does that make sense?"

He nods, then wraps his arms around me and kisses my temple. "It makes a lot of sense. Maybe before you head back to Michigan and I jet off to tropical Vermont, we could team up for the rest of the summer? Just look out for each other, help each other out for the next few weeks?"

I slip a hand under the hem of his T-shirt and rest my fingers on the warm skin of his bare back. I try to think of a joke or a super-witty comeback, but nothing comes to mind, so I shock myself and just blurt out what I'm thinking. "That would be amazing."

"Hey," he whispers into my ear. I lean closer. "I can't believe this morning I was apologizing for taking a piss in front of you, and now..." he leans closer, and it's so close I can almost taste it "...now I can't stop thinking about kissing you. Can I kiss you?"

I want this kiss like I've never wanted anything in my life—

"Guys, there's a pool back here! Guys, did you see this?" Marnie's fuzzy head pops out of the door and back in, like a jack-in-the-box in overdrive.

I pull back and press my lips together, then yell, "Yeah, Marnie, this isn't, like, a rental! We live here!"

Jude and I watch her race to the back garden, leaving the sliding door wide-open and probably filling the house with a swarm of mosquitoes. It's weird how my sister can be a totally immature whirlwind of action and make scarily adult mistakes all at the same time.

I look back up at Jude and think about how good it would

feel to just kiss him already, but it seems pointless to rush something so potentially amazing when we've already waited so long. Plus, I have this fear that once I start kissing him, it's not going to be easy to stop. "Rain check?"

His smile is so beautiful, it hurts to look at it.

"For sure. I'll be here tomorrow at four?"

I nod and watch him walk to his truck, slide in, and wave good-bye.

"I like him." Marnie comes to stand next to me on the worn wooden steps of the front porch. "I'm not even just saying that because I owe him *my life*."

"He's cool, right?" I don't usually talk about relationships with Marnie, but now that we're doing it, I realize I care what my kid sister thinks of who I'm dating, maybe because she's made it so clear she has higher expectations for the person I'm with than I ever did myself.

"He's super nice. And funny. Like funny without being a dick. That's kind of rare for a guy. And he's hot." She wiggles her eyebrows at me. "Not my type, obviously, but I'd pick him for *you*."

I bump her shoulder. "Thanks." I look back at the door, gaping open. "Rule Number 1 of living in the tropics, you have to make sure to shut the door, especially if there's no screen. We're going to get eaten alive by mosquitoes tonight."

"Aye aye." Marnie salutes. "Is my room the one that looks like if Joanna Gaines designed a dorm room?"

"You don't like it?" I'm a tiny-smidgen offended my kid sister isn't more appreciative of my design efforts on her behalf, especially since everyone else seemed to like them so much.

"I do." Marnie exaggerates every facial feature when she

lies, and right now she looks like some kind of animated version of herself, all big eyes and overdone expressions. "It's just, the rest of the house pops and has, you know, a lot of character. My room looks like something Mom designed." She wrinkles her nose.

"Mom is good at design." The urge to defend our meticulous, exacting mother swells up in me hard, but Marnie's comment makes me stop and wonder. Do I like the way my mom designs our home in Michigan or do I just admire it? There's a difference, and I'm not sure I know. In Michigan every design decision was made for me; here in Florida, I have no restrictions—I realize I don't love either room. "It's super cute here, but sometimes I get a headache being in my own room. There's too much going on. Decluttering probably isn't a bad idea at all."

Marnie shrugs. "Okay, I guess. If I had to choose one, I'd pick a mess over a museum, though. Can I see your room?"

"You didn't do a tour?" I'm shocked, since that's always been nosy, pushy Marnie's MO—she's like the family's over-exuberant tour guide, forging the path for the rest of us.

"It's *your* room. I'm not five. I respect your privacy."

I watch her face while she says it, notice how she avoids eye contact. My little sister is growing up, getting more mature, and that's awesome, but it's not the reason she didn't bust my door down and do a SWAT search. I realize Marnie is still uncomfortable with who I am here, and barging into my room feels like trespassing into a stranger's territory.

"Let's go." I walk in, and Marnie makes a big show of closing the door, which she thinks is such a hoot until I smack her on the forehead, hard.

"Ow! What the hell?" she yelps.

I hold my palm up so she can see the circle of ruby blood that squished out of the dead mosquito. "The bugs are prehistoric down here. *Shut. The. Doors.*"

Marnie follows close behind me and does a very slow three-sixty turn in the middle of my room. "Whoa."

"What?"

"It's like you have a secret storage unit full of stuff no one else has ever seen."

"Plenty of people have seen this room, Marnie," I remind her. "This has been my room for years."

"But Mom has never seen it. Lilli and Peter have never seen it." She runs her fingers over my mirror, cluttered with taped-up pictures of me, Duke, Dani, Dad, Bennie, and the neighborhood kids I hang out with over the summer. It occurs to me there's no visual evidence of Jude, even though he's been a main player in my Key West summers for years now. I'll have to fix that.

"It looks like a movie bedroom, like out of some John Hughes movie." She goes to my closet and presses her entire body against the bursting explosion of clothing. "Holy crap, there's so much *stuff*." She bounces off of it, pirouettes to the bookshelf and draws her fingers along the spines. "Manga? You read manga?" She pulls a volume off and crows, "The *romantic manga*!"

"It's from, like, five years ago," I mumble. "Lots of people read romantic manga." It was the one subgenre Duke never borrowed from me—at least not that I know of.

"No one back home would even believe AJ Jepsen reads romantic manga." She's already abandoned my bookshelf to inspect the band posters on my wall. "Have you gone to see Billie Eilish? Like, in concert?"

I nod and pick at my bedspread.

"Jepsen House Rule Number 13: no concerts until you're eighteen." She plops on the bed next to me so hard, I nearly get bounced off the mattress.

"That's a weird rule." Jepsen rules aren't questioned back at home. Mom and Peter made it clear our house isn't a democracy. They make the rules, we follow the rules, and I've fallen into line while Marnie fought every rule tooth and nail—or that's what it seemed like, anyway.

"But it's a *rule*. You *love* following the rules."

"Who *loves* following the rules, Marnie?" I chew on my thumbnail. When I was eight, Mom cured that bad habit with nail polish that tastes like earwax. But no one patrols my nails here, so I indulge if I want to. "No one loves rules."

"You come down here every summer and just get to do whatever you want." Marnie says it like it's an accusation. "Why would you ever leave?"

"Because this is one of my homes. I have two." I look at her pointedly. "I have you and Lilli and Mom and Peter. My friends. School. Also, no, maybe I don't *love* following rules, but I understand why there *are* rules. Why we need them."

"Do you miss us when you're here?" She picks at the edge of the tape that holds one corner of one of my movie posters to the wall—two more Michigan design no-nos; no tape, no "tacky movie posters."

"When I'm here, I try to focus on being here because I'm only around for a few months a year." It's the best way I know to answer her question without just coming out and saying *Not exactly.*

"I miss you. Even though you're the golden child, it's better when we can deal with Mom and Dad together."

"I'm not the golden child. That's Lilli."

Marnie snorts. "True. Lilli really *does* love the rules."

"Lilli doesn't follow the rules as closely as you think," I point out to Marnie, who hops onto the bed with her eyes wide and eager. I sigh and say, "How many concerts has Lilli gone to?"

"But that's because she's *in* them. Or auditioning." Marnie's brows press low.

"And do you sometimes see Lilli post things on her phone outside of dictated Jepsen social media access hours?"

"She has to for her contests and auditions sometimes. She needs to be on during peak times." I watch as realization dawns on Marnie's face.

"Lilli doesn't follow all the rules like I do, and she doesn't break them like you do. She manipulates them. Which makes her *look* like the golden child while getting away with doing exactly what she wants."

"That's *diabolical*," Marnie mutters, and I can tell from her concentrated face, she's running scenario after scenario of Lilli—sweet, friendly, pious Lilli—completely disregarding set-in-stone rules to do things her own way. "Lilli is like an evil genius!"

"Yeah, she's kind of scared me since she was little. She's so cute and sweet, but also super calculating and brilliant. Which is why she'll probably be a billionaire by the time she's ready to graduate high school."

I'm incredibly proud of our baby sister. Her level of single-minded drive is something even I can't wrap my head around, and I consider myself pretty damn driven.

"Have you talked to Mom about everything going on in Nashville?" Marnie twists a tassel from one of my throw pillows around her finger.

"Yeah. Lilli seems pretty stressed, but I guess it's all really exciting and mostly good?"

"Lilli played me her new song the other night. She was up, like, at three a.m. She's not sleeping. But, seriously? It sounded *amazing*. Like a real song you'd hear on the radio, just the way it was."

I'm glad Lilli was able to reach out to Marnie, even if I'm a little jealous I didn't get to hear her new song. "She's so talented. I'm not at all surprised this is all happening for her. It's just crazy to think how fast it's going. Like, her whole life could change. *Our* whole life could change."

"What will happen if she signs a deal this summer?" Marnie asks.

"I'm not sure, but you can bet the Jepsen curfew rules won't apply to her."

"Neither will the party rules." Marnie lies back on my bed and props her feet on the headboard. She stares at the glow-in-the-dark stars that constellate my ceiling. "I already took a pretty good crack at those, though."

I turn on my side and look down at Marnie's face. Tears roll out of her eyes, though her features are blank and cool.

"Hey." I squeeze her shoulder. "Hey, don't cry."

"But it feels good to cry. I *want* to cry," she says stubbornly, so many tears pouring from her eyes, it's like she's willing them from sheer defiance. "They just left me. Like I was nothing. Like I was a piece of trash they threw out of the car. I mean, I know we weren't, like, best friends, but what's wrong with people?"

I don't know many details. They were older. They were drunk. Marnie was beyond drunk. Maybe they were scared and didn't know what to do, so they felt like there was no other choice, but I hate them with a level of white-hot rage I don't think I've ever felt for anyone in my life before. And I think it's so intense because I hate myself that much, too. I didn't push a drunk, unconscious Marnie out of the car and onto a hospital doorstep, but I might as well have.

"I don't know why they did what they did, but they have to live with that forever, and I hope it changes them. I hope they realize how much they screwed up. Marnie, saying sorry is so chickenshit. I know saying those words can't fix anything, but I have to say them to you. I have to tell you how sorry I am. How pissed I am at myself. I let you down the day you reached out. Big-time. I let you down when you needed me." My voice trembles and shakes as I confess, and I wait for Marnie to do something, say anything.

I want her crazy Labrador-puppy hugs and her forgiveness. I deserve her anger and accusations. I'd be willing to make amends, strike a bargain, accept a penance of Marnie's choosing. But she doesn't give me any of those options.

She keeps crying until there are two Rorschach-blot tearstains on either side of the pillow.

"Marnie?" Now I'm crying, too, and I *never* cry. Panic envelops me, as suffocating as the brackish ocean water in a rip current, and a fitting pain considering what Marnie's been through. *What I put her through.*

"You were here having a good time the day I texted. There was a party." Like she's a reporter, like this is a detail she's fact-checking.

"Yes." My voice is tiny. "It was my welcome-back party. I didn't realize… I thought you just wanted to talk about camp."

"Mom and Dad spent a fortune on that camp. I told them I didn't want to go, and they were so pissed. They said I had to. I had no choice. Jepsens push through. We're tough. But I was just so tired. I was exhausted from always being tough."

"I know exactly what you mean." They are possibly the truest words I've ever spoken to Marnie.

"I did try. I kept telling myself it would get easier, and some of the girls were nice. Some of the counselors were nice. It wasn't really about them. It was *me*. I didn't want to do it or be there, and I just couldn't understand why that was such a big deal. Like, why can't Mom and Dad ever believe that I might know what I want for myself?"

I think about my long campaign to get to Florida for the holidays and my parents' resistance to my turning down the internship. "I don't know, Marnie. I think they honestly assume they know better and we'll thank them someday for pushing us so hard."

"It will be pretty hard to thank them if we crash and burn before we make it out of adolescence."

"Good point." I clear my throat, nervous to hear the rest of the story, but wanting to give Marnie a safe space to tell it in her own words. "So, did you want to just run away for the day? Or were you planning to leave and not go back?"

"Honestly, it was just, like, an opportunity that I took when I saw it. I was in line to get my blood pressure and weight checked, and I saw the file cabinet with our phones was left open. I pretended I had to go to the bathroom, stole my phone back, and just walked out. Like, it's weird there were a million rules, but no one even blinked when I just walked right past them, out the gates. I guess they didn't think I was leaving for good. I was going to hitchhike, but I remembered some friends from my camp last year lived nearby. When I asked them to meet up, my plan was just to hang out until I could get a hold of you and you could help me figure things out. But it all went out of control so fast."

"I'm glad you didn't hitchhike." I screw my eyes shut and will myself not to imagine a fate worse than alcohol poisoning. "I promise you, I'll never ignore your calls again. I'm so sorry."

She rolls to her side, her eyes red-rimmed. "You didn't want to do the internship?"

I barely shake my head. "I didn't. I don't see my family here enough. I was really interested in the internship, and it was a great opportunity, but not everything is about what looks good on your résumé."

"Would you have gone? Would you have left early and gone back if I didn't screw everything up?"

I shake my head again, with a little more force this time.

"Mom yelled at me for it. So I get the blame for screwing up your internship, and you get to escape again, no consequences." She purses her lips, not mad, just thinking. "You found a way to escape. Lilli found a way to work around it. Why am I the only one banging my head against the wall?"

"You *have* been rocked in the skull by a fair amount of athletic equipment." My joke loses some of its humor because it's true. Marnie's concussion tally is worrisome.

"I wish you'd wanted me to come here. I know I'm a pain in the ass, but I wouldn't have made things hard. I just needed a break. I wish you'd, like, offered to just let me come down."

How many times did she root around, trying to dig up clues about where I went all summer? She wanted in. She knew I did something that helped smooth the jagged edges, helped iron out the pain. I let myself believe some stupid sport camp would do that for her. I didn't listen to her. Mom and Peter didn't listen to her. So Marnie took matters into her own hands and self-destructed.

I could lie to her or fabricate some big excuse, but I don't.

"You're right. I should have. I was tired from this year. I was tired of dealing with all the endless drama."

"Me too." She pulls her sleeve over from her shoulder and wipes her snotty nose on it.

"I was afraid that if you came here, it wouldn't be the same. That things would change."

"I'm sorry. Oh, God. Oh no." Her eyes have flown wide, like she solved a problem that she'd been toying with for a while. "You guys all needed a break from *me*."

"Marnie, don't be ridiculous."

"That's why I have to go to camp. Lilli stays with Mom, you go with your family, Dad works a ton more hours at the lab, I get shipped off. Grandma won't even take me."

"Grandma was on a river cruise. Stop. You're being melodramatic." I don't even realize what I'm saying.

"I'm too melodramatic! I'm too rude. Too weird. Too wild. I'm not smart and perfect like you. I'm not some living angel like

Lilli. I'm the black sheep." She looks at me, and her red-rimmed eyes harden. "I'm sorry you're *stuck with me* this summer."

"I'm *glad* you're here." I reach out to her, shocked at how quickly things unraveled.

It almost makes me want to follow the unspoken Jespen rule about feelings: that there are good reasons to dam up emotions and not let them run wild. Our family honestly invests in the idea that these kinds of situations could be avoided by letting things simmer for a while, then cool. Now we've blown the top off our family's dysfunction, and I have no idea how to set it back to rights, but maybe that's okay. Putting a lid on it is exactly what caused all of this chaos. Dealing with it is ugly and hard and painful, but it can't be worse than the alternative. I know I'm lucky Marnie isn't still in a hospital bed or worse, and I'm not going to waste this opportunity to change the way we deal with things.

The first thing I have to do is accept that Marnie might not be able to forgive me right away. I need to be patient, give her space, and remind her I'm here when she's ready.

Marnie slides off my bed and stalks to the door, turning with her hand at the knob. "I should be pissed at you, but I just feel sad for you. Because it's pathetic, how you're always pretending to be someone you're obviously not. Maybe I *am* the family loser, but at least I'm not pretending. This is me, the real me, like it or not. And I get it… You all *hate it*. But at least I'm honest." She has one foot out the door when she sticks her head back in. "And another thing? If you called me, anytime, anywhere, I'd answer. I'd never, *ever* ignore your calls. Even now I wouldn't. Even though I think I might hate you."

Ouch. Change is definitely going to hurt.

17

Spring Fling

Last Spring
St. Matthew's High School

MICHIGAN

"Orange is your color. You look stunning." Mom reaches a hand out and adjusts the ruffle of my tangerine mermaid dress. "I'm so glad we kept this one for spring. This is the perfect color to complement the green backdrops at the dance."

I don't bring up the fact that I didn't really keep this one for spring so much as get vetoed out of wearing it to the Winter Formal. That's all water under the bridge now, and I'm not going to bring it up and let it ruin what I hope will be a great night.

Lilli is wearing a fluttery teal dress that swishes gently like she's a mermaid underwater. Freshmen aren't technically invited to the Spring Fling, but Lilli is singing with the live band the school hired, so she's going to sneak in a few dances.

"You look beautiful, Lil." I take the enamel-flower bobby pin from her before she jabs herself in the head and slide it into her shiny blond curls, then grab her guitar case while she looks around for her picks. "How pathetic is it that I'm spending my junior Spring Fling experience as my little sister's roadie?"

"It's okay! You don't have to carry my stuff." She's so nervous, she doesn't read that I'm just joking with her. She wrings her hands in front of her body and blows out a few long breaths, stopping abruptly when she catches sight of her reflection in the foyer mirror. "Do I have too much blush on?"

"Sweetie, you're naturally flushed." Mom holds her shoulders and looks her in the eyes. "Deep breath in through your nostrils." She demonstrates and Lilli follows suit. "And out through your mouth, slowly."

While Mom helps Lilli stave off a panic attack with breathing exercises, I race upstairs to check on Marnie. "Hey, are you ready? Harper's mom will be here any minute."

Marnie is staring down at her phone, which she flips over on her mattress just a *little* too quickly. I casually say, "Hey, can you do me a huge favor? I can't get my jewelry box from the top of my closet with these heels on. Will you get it for me? And use the step stool from my bathroom, *not* the chair!" I yell after her, because she's already racing down the hall to my room.

I flip her phone over. Locked.

It's a four digit code.

I try her birthday. Nope.

I try her school ID number. Nope.

I look at her wallpaper picture. It's me and her and Lilli, our faces pressed close and grinning at the school's Valentine's photo booth. February is the month all three of us were born, so we always do a big joint birthday party to celebrate our birthdays on February first, sixth, and eighth.

2-1-6-8

The phone unlocks, and I see there's a chat open on an app

Mom and Peter have specifically asked us not to download because it's had so many issues with bullying and file sharing.

The person—KittyGotUrTongue—wrote: People screw up and make mistakes but it doesn't make them bad people in their hearts. I'm telling you I screwed up.

Marnie—as Ready2NapNapNap—wrote: You did screw up. I can forgive, I won't forget.

KittyGotUrTongue: Thought you went to Catholic school. Aren't you supposed to forgive people?

Ready2NapNapNap: It's Lutheran actually. I said I forgive.

KittyGotUrTongue: But you ignore my friend request?

Ready2NapNapNap: Cause I won't forget.

KittyGotUrTongue: You forget what I have…

Ready2NapNapNap: You can do what you want. Ur choice good or evil.

KittyGotUrTongue: But I wouldn't choose evil. Just want to talk again.

Ready2NapNapNap: Then maybe don't threaten people…

"What are you doing?" Marnie tosses my jewelry box on her unmade bed. Necklaces and bracelets go flying all over her tangled sheets.

"Is this McKenzie?" I hold the phone up over my head when she jumps for it. Luckily the cut of her teal tux jacket—lighter colored than Lilli's dress, a nice complement to mine—is überslim, and my heels are extra tall, so she can't use her monster volleyball reach to grab the phone.

"I was telling her to get lost," she says.

"Marnie, you can't talk to her *at all*. You just need to block her and ignore her. She's clearly morally bankrupt, and this whole conversation is just stoking the fire."

"She won't do anything," Marnie mumbles.

"Really?" I start to read the exchange, and Marnie begs me to stop, looking over her shoulder like she's scared Mom or Peter will materialize at any moment. "Does that sound like a nice, thoughtful person who won't do something extreme, Marnie?"

"No," she admits, plopping on her bed. "I just... I was so lonely after everything happened, and she wouldn't stop messaging me. I ignored her for such a long time, seriously. But I have *no one* to talk to. I feel like a walking ghost at school. It's like people look through me now. The team stood by me when I went up against the administration, but a bunch of them believe I did it. I kind of wish they'd just have it out with me like Jaylen did." Marnie hangs her head. "I don't know how things always get so screwed up."

I mimic Mom's calming breaths to stop myself from screaming, *They get screwed up because you let them get screwed up, Marnie. You make bad decisions. You trust people you shouldn't. You're impulsive, and you just don't think!*

Instead I sit on the bed and brush her hacked-up hair back from her face. "It's okay. It's almost summer. I promise you, everyone will go do their own things, and this will all be a distant memory by the fall. But if you keep reaching out to this girl, it's just going to get stirred up over and over. So, do me a favor?"

Marnie wipes her eyes, getting tear stains on her satin cuffs. "Okay."

"Delete it all. All contacts, apps, conversations. Now. And block her. On *everything*." I cross my arms and wait while Marnie takes the phone. She lets me watch over her shoulder. The minutes tick by, and I bite the inside of my cheek to stop myself from commenting on how many social media sites Marnie has left open for this girl to reach out on. "And change all of your settings to private."

"Most of them are." Marnie swipes and clicks, then nods. "Okay. She's completely blocked, my sites are all private."

I pull her in for a hug, though I still feel like screaming at her. "Now we go to the dance. You stick with me and Harper, Tessa, and Lex—"

Marnie makes a fake retching sound, and I glare at her.

"Lex is the only one who's even nice to me."

"Then stick with him. He can't stand Harper and Tessa either, so you'll have plenty to talk about."

"Why can't we just stay home? Have a movie and popcorn night?" She holds her hands out, prayer-style, and the fact that she doesn't seem to realize Lilli and I might actually be really excited for tonight drives me to the edge of my patience.

I rub my temples. "Marnie, *you* messed up, okay? *You* made some really dumb choices. And I've helped you. I've stuck by you and been there for you. But your decisions alone can't dictate everything everyone else does from now on. I *want* to go to this dance. I want to have fun with my friends and hear Lilli, who's, like, incredibly nervous about going on-stage. I mean, c'mon, Marnie. Think about someone other than yourself once in a while." Sometimes I wish Marnie understood how hard it is being the oldest, keeping everyone's secrets, and being the one everyone comes to when they mess up. I'm so exhausted, and I just want a fun night in a pretty dress with my sisters and friends, no drama.

Marnie's eyes ice over. "Sorry."

"Don't apologize. Just…stop making everything so hard all the time. Why don't you just try to forget everything and have fun?" I suggest. "I already said you can hang out with me and my friends, so just ignore everyone else."

She stands up and buttons her tux jacket, scowling at me. "Sure, I'll just go to this dance at a school where I'm treated like I have the plague and hang out with your two-faced friends all night in a suit that I can barely breathe in, and I'll keep a big, fake smile on my face." She pulls both sides of her mouth up with her index fingers, exaggerating a phony smile. "Sounds *amazing*."

"Maybe you should have thought a little harder about how things would pan out *before* you sold your team down the river for some jackass you barely knew," I hiss.

Marnie sucks in a sharp breath, and I immediately regret being so hard on her, but, Mary, Mother of God, she is so infuriatingly pigheaded. I reach for her, but she's already stomping downstairs. I hear Peter ask where I am. The door opens, and Lex's voice rings out in the foyer, followed by Tessa's and Harper's excited chatter—I'm sure everyone is in a good mood or at least is pretending to be. Except Marnie. Guaranteed she looks like she sucked on a pickled egg, and it's fraying my nerves. I'm doing everything I can to keep everyone happy, but I feel like I'm juggling chain saws. One wrong move on my part and everything will end in catastrophe.

"There you are!" Peter calls out, fancy new camera in hand. "Wow, AJ, you sure do make an entrance. Strike a pose, kid!" He holds the camera up, and I strike a series of poses that leave Tessa and Harper catcalling. "All right, let's do just the sisters, then we'll add my gorgeous wife, then we'll do all the girls, and, Lex, I guess we can squeeze you in for a shot or two at the end."

"Sounds good, Mr. J," Lex says, laughing.

Peter is snapping pictures as we spill into the driveway, and he keeps it up as we're pulling away, waving at him and Mom until they shrink to dots in the distance.

"What's up, glum?" Lex asks Marnie, but she just shrinks into a corner and glowers.

"Are you okay?" Lilli asks Marnie, setting aside her own nerves to try to help her. Classic sweet baby-sister move.

"Fine," Marnie growls. Classic self-consumed middle-sister move.

"That's enough," I snarl. Classic fed-up oldest-sister move. The inside of Harper's mom's Escalade goes silent. "Get your whiny head out of your ass and stop acting like a night out with people who *actually care about you* is some form of medieval torture."

"Sorry I can't put on a big smile and pretend like I'm having a good time like everyone else," Marnie snaps back.

"We *all* have problems, for your information. The only difference is, *you're* the only one who keeps dragging everyone down with yours!"

"Whoa, AJ, calm down," Lex says, and I turn my fury in his direction.

"Don't tell me to calm down!" I'd keep right on going, except Lilli is crying quietly. "Oh, shit, Lilli." My face burns with shame. I'm yelling at Marnie for being a jerk who makes everything about her, and here I am, doing the *exact same thing*. "I'm sorry. I just lost it. I'm sorry, Lilli."

"Me too," Marnie says, putting her hand on Lilli's knee. "I shouldn't have let my bad mood get the better of me."

"It's okay," Lilli sniffles. "I just hate when you guys fight. Let's just make up before we go in, okay? I don't want to get up onstage knowing you guys are pissed at each other." I steel myself for what's coming. Lilli is the most open about her faith in our family, and even though we all pray privately, she's the one who has no issue praying openly. I think she might even prefer it. "Can we do a prayer circle now?"

Marnie and I look at each other, united in our willingness to do whatever it takes to make Lilli happy, no matter how much we'd like to take a hard pass. Lilli takes our hands in her small, cold ones and squeezes our fingers tight. We squeeze back. Lex, Tessa, and Harper go quiet and bow their heads. Harper's mother, who's been ignoring us and jamming to her favorite station, glances in the rearview mirror and turns the volume knob down.

Lilli closes her eyes, and her clear, sweet voice makes her words feel so honest. "Jesus, I know we're all failing in so many ways every day, but we really do try to walk in Your light and model ourselves after You. There's nothing in the whole world more important than loving each other, and we pray that You can guide us to do that even when we don't see eye to eye on everything. Please let us keep Your words and Your love in our minds and hearts tonight and every night. Amen."

"Amen," we murmur in unison. Marnie and I meet eyes over Lilli's bowed head, and we're both a little teary. We nod our truce.

"Amen, Lil," Lex says. "Man, you should consider joining the clergy. I actually feel like a bad person who should try to do better. I never even feel that way in church."

"I could never do that in front of anyone other than you guys," Lilli says, her big, blue eyes wide.

"What?" Lex's eyebrow crooks high. "Seriously? You're about to sing in front of the entire school!"

Lilli goes green as his words hit home, and I kick Lex in the shin. "Shut up, Lex!"

"It's okay." Lilli takes a deep breath. "I can do this. I know you guys will be out there, so I'll just pretend you're the only people I'm singing to."

We all huddle around Lilli when we get out, trying to keep the glow of good energy strong as we get her to the back, where the band's setting up. We leave her with shouts of *Good luck!* and head to the dance floor. Marnie sticks to Lex like his shadow, and they're busy snarking about everyone else's outfits—I guess Lilli's prayer didn't move their hearts all *that* much.

As for me, I was actually really touched by my baby sister's earnest words. Harper, Tessa, and I wander around the gym smiling and making small talk with our friends. I try to notice underclassmen who look nervous or out of place and make an effort to compliment them or give an encouraging smile.

"Holy shit, isn't that, like, Bethany Provos?" Tessa whispers, pulling me and Harper aside. "What is she doing here?"

"Her son just transferred in after the Christmas break. I heard he got kicked out of, like, *nine* private schools, and now he's living with his dad, who's the CEO of some big car company," Harper whispers back. She bounces up and down, making the red fringe on her dress sway from side to side.

"But who *is* she?" I don't keep up with gossip sites the way Harper and Tessa do, but of course I want to know the details!

"She's a huge scout for Visionary Records, the recording studio that signed, like, half the people who took home Grammys this year!" Tessa smooths the lace of her ivory dress and nods to the stage. "Bet me they aren't here for Lilli."

My stomach drops. "Do you think?"

"That Advent song she put out over the holidays? It's not just huge on YouTube. I've seen that video reposted *everywhere*. She even has some pretty up-and-coming musicians doing covers. It's still a *huge* deal," Harper informs me.

"I... Really? I mean, I knew it had a ton of YouTube views. Why didn't you guys tell me?" I demand.

Harper rolls her eyes. "Why aren't you paying attention? Jesus, AJ, you're always micromanaging everything else. Why don't you focus on the shit that matters? Like Lilli getting us into Grammys after-parties and scoring us front-row seats to all the best concerts?" She winks at me. "Spoiler alert—we're totally riding your sister's coattails straight to the top."

We laugh. It's funny. Except...is it? I'm still debating whether Harper's comments were just playful or kind of gross when I notice Danica Gerber giggling and talking to Marnie like they're best friends.

"Ugh," Harper says. "Now, *that's* disgusting coattail-riding. Danica's been a stone bitch to Marnie since elementary school, and now, just because she got the lead in the spring musical, she thinks she's got a chance to elbow in on Lilli's *actual* talent?"

Tessa snorts. "The only reason we had to listen to her squawk her way through *Annie Get Your Gun* is because Lilli had *professional* callbacks and recordings. Like, she shouldn't flatter herself. She sucks."

"I should go break that up," I say, waving at the girls as I hurry over to my sister, indignant fury propelling me. Marnie is so starved for any sign of friendship, she actually looks happy to be talking to that double-decker, warmed-over egg-salad sandwich in human form. "Marnie, we need to go check on Lilli's bags," I say, not even acknowledging Danica as I march Marnie away.

Lex is at our heels. "Jesus, Danica was laying it on thick. I guess she doesn't realize it doesn't really matter who you know in the music biz if you're tone deaf."

"What?" Marnie looks from one of us to the other. "She was talking to me about topspin serves."

"Sure." Lex points. "And while you were explaining, she was making eyes at that music exec who, I bet, is here to scout Lilli."

"Is that Bethany Provos?" Marnie asks, eyes bugged out. "Holy shit. Holy shit! Lilli's going to be famous. I mean, unless she, like, faints onstage or something."

My head spins. I feel so out of the loop. I would have helped comfort Lilli more if I realized just how high the stakes were tonight. As usual, I laser-focused all my energy on Marnie and her issues. I don't have long to brood about it, though. The lights dim, our vice principal makes an announcement about having fun and following the rules, and then Lilli is onstage, looking so small and beautiful framed by the perfect circle of the spotlight.

Then she grabs the mic in both hands, leans forward, and opens her mouth.

I've heard Lilli sing a million times in church or at home, but this is somehow so different. Maybe because it feels the most like a real concert, maybe because she's singing her own song, maybe because she looks so grown-up in her gauzy dress and gorgeous makeup with her golden hair curling down her back, and it's making me more than just a little teary. Marnie, who has been pissing me off nonstop all day, puts her arms around my waist, and I put mine around her shoulders. Our disagreements and fights evaporate with the first note Lilli sings, and I know there's no one else in the world I'd want to be by my side right now. We lean our heads close and listen to our baby sister finish her slow, soulful opening and swing her guitar around. She starts straight jamming, and the entire room is clapping, stomping, and dancing along as her song—her incredible, smart, amazing song—fills the entire gym with this buzz of electric energy. Marnie and I look at each other, mouths open, then join the cheers and screams.

I forget to check on the big-time music executive. I don't think about Danica or Jaylen, or even Tessa, Harper, or Lex. Marnie and I, arms around each other, and Lilli, singing to us, are the Triple Threat Jepsens. When her set is done, Marnie and I rush to meet her backstage.

"How was it?" she asks, her eyes lit up like she has a fever.

"You were *amazing*." I put an arm around her and one around Marnie, and we pull into a tight hug. "You were incredible, Lilli. That was...that was..." I look at Marnie.

"That was fucking *awesome*," Marnie whispers, and we all burst out laughing, hugging and leaning on one another.

My middle sister is unraveling, my baby sister is ascending to stardom, and I'm left with the oldest sister's defining job—holding us together through it all. I hug them tighter and wonder if I'll be able to manage it.

18

July
Marnie's Second Day

FLORIDA

I'm up before the sun, ready to meet Jude and run. But he never shows. I run, hard, for five miles, scouting the beach for him, but he's nowhere to be seen. The old me would have been deeply wounded and gotten super defensive. She would have told herself nothing mattered, that she didn't care about being blown off.

The new me trusts the Jude I've gotten to know over the past few weeks. He wouldn't stand me up without a reason. I head home as quickly as I can and check on Marnie, who's still sleeping, then head to the back porch and find Dad sitting on the swing, the chains squeaking back and forth as he rocks.

"Hey, sweetheart." He pats the seat next to him.

"Are you sure? I smell like a bog monster."

"Honey, you ever smelled a crew full of dirty guys who've spent the day sweating it out tryin' to reel in a swordfish? I'm immune to stink." He pats the seat again, and I sit down. He wrinkles his nose. "Phew. Maybe I underestimated your stench just a little."

"Dad!" I play-shove him, and he chuckles. "Hey, Dad? Jude was supposed to meet me this morning to go running, but he stood me up."

Dad puts his arm around me and frowns as he rocks us back and forth with a slow, steady motion of his foot. "That's not like Jude." He sighs. "Could be he's tangled up in something that went on with his parents. Things have been getting worse for them lately."

"He mentioned it's been bad for a while." I am so relieved to be talking about this big, incredibly scary thing with an adult I can trust.

"I met Jude when he started coming to Al-Anon, years back," Dad says, keeping his eyes on the smudge of gray-blue ocean far in the distance. "His situation was bad then. He's better at handling it since he got support, and that's a good thing—because it's gotten a lot worse for him at home."

I study his profile for a few long seconds. "Al-Anon is for kids whose parents are alcoholics, right?"

"Yep. Al-Anon and Alateen are for people who have loved ones who are alcoholics." Dad keeps the swing moving, and I just wait, not sure where to go with this. It's not long before Dad takes the lead. "Your grandfather died before you were born. It wasn't drinking that killed him, officially. But years of being an alcoholic left his body pretty messed up. I grew up seeing the way alcohol made my dad big and fun and easy to joke with, and I loved all that about him. I also saw how it made him sloppy and selfish and act like a fool, but I thought it was because he drank *too much*. When I got to be around your age, I thought I could get the good from drinking and avoid the bad. It took a long time and a whole lot of meetings for me to put together that it doesn't matter how much or how little an alcoholic drinks—one or twenty, it's always too many for someone who's addicted."

"I'm so sorry, Dad." I think of the pictures all over the walls of Belo's, my larger-than-life grandfather grinning and winning with celebrities and tough sportsmen. I just assumed he was godlike, a perfect provider and patriarch. Once again, my assumptions don't remotely match the reality. "I never knew."

"Back in my daddy's day, it was a secret you kept shut up tight, and once he was gone, it didn't seem right to dredge things up, since it still upset your grandma so much. People's views on addiction have changed a lot since your grandpa's day. Nowadays, people are a lot more understanding about how hard you've got to fight to break an addiction." He drags his ragged ball cap off his head and rubs at his hair. "I wish I'd gotten wise to all the bad parts before I let it tear my life apart."

I silently chew on this, yet another shocking admission from someone I thought I knew inside out. Dad struggled with alcoholism? How could I not know such a huge fact about my own father?

"Are you worried about Duke?"

"I worry about all of you, because my daddy passed those genes to me, and I passed them to you three. But I know lecturing doesn't work, or your grandma would've stopped me from ever drinking a drop when I was young. I know ignoring it won't work, and I know thinking you can make some rules and your kids will be safe is wishful thinking."

"What *can* you do?"

"I just try to be honest with Duke. Talk to him, man-to-man, about how my drinking almost led me to lose everything I love. Give him some hard questions to ask himself, and let him think. Luckily, thinking is something your brother is really good at, so I don't have to press him about that." Dad glances at his phone. "Hold up, I'm getting a call from inside the shop." He furrows his brows. The shop doesn't open for hours. I stay quiet enough to eavesdrop, and whoever's on the other end sounds pretty upset. "Yes. No problem. Stay put. I'm coming." Dad slips his phone into his pocket and stands up, offering me his hand. "I found Jude. Do you want to come by and talk to him? I think he'd appreciate your company."

"Is he okay?" My heart pounds as I run scenarios through my head. What could have happened?

"He's going to be fine, but he needs our support. Maybe wake Marnie? She mentioned she'd like to see the shop anyway." I nod and turn to run to her room, but stop when I hear Dad call, "Dell?"

"Yes?"

"Maybe a few extra swipes of deodorant?"

I roll my eyes as his chuckles bounce around our kitchen. I shake Marnie awake, ignoring the way she glares at me. "Jude needs us. Get up."

She doesn't even ask what it's all about, just rolls over and grabs whatever clothes she finds on the floor. I make quick work of putting my hair in a bun and changing into non-sweat-soaked shorts and a T-shirt…along with deodorant and a few spritzes of perfume. At the last second, I grab the files on the shelf by my bed and stuff them in a backpack. We head to the Jeep a few minutes later and are pulling in at Belo's a few minutes after that.

"Wow." Marnie cranes her neck back and stares at the facade. "This place is so cool. Very old-timey. Oh, take my picture next to the fish!" She runs up to the wooden sign with a fisherman holding a huge catch. There's a hole where you can stick your face, and Marnie squishes hers in, cheesing a big smile our way. "Belo, look at me! I caught a big one!" she says in, inexplicably, a really terrible attempt at an Australian accent.

Dad chuckles and shakes his head. "Man, she's a firecracker. She's your mama reincarnated, for sure." He nods for me to go in. "Why don't I snap the picture, and you can check on Jude."

I squeeze Dad's hand. "Thank you."

The lights are off in the shop, and there's a peaceful stillness, like the whole store is just resting, breathing, waiting for us. I know Duke would laugh if I said it, but the store feels alive, and that's the thing that would hurt the most if we had to sell. It would be like selling a family member.

I head to the back, past the break room, to the loading dock where you can open the overhead door and sit in the fresh air. I've noticed this is where Jude likes to hang out when there's not much going on in the shop, and it's where I find him now, head bowed, crying.

I've definitely never seen Lex cry. I tiptoe over and crouch close, put one hand on Jude's shoulder. His head whips up. "Dell," he croaks. His eyes are red-rimmed, and there are deep circles under them. He reaches his arms out for me, and I tumble into them, holding him tight, smoothing a hand over his hair. "I'm so sorry I stood you up."

"'S'kay," I murmur. "Are *you* okay?"

He pulls back and presses the heels of his hands into his

eyes. "My parents…fucked me over. Fucked everything up." He blows out a long breath. *"Fuck."*

I thread his fingers through mine, loving the feel of our hands pressed tight. "That sounds…fucked up. Care to elaborate?"

"Same old, same old. They got blitzed, I took their keys, like I've done a thousand times. Only they were pissed because I wouldn't make a liquor run for them—"

"You can't even buy liquor!" I exclaim.

Jude gives me a sad smile. "Do you know how much revenue the local liquor store would lose if the Zeiglers sobered up? They've been selling to me since I was thirteen. But I wouldn't do it last night. Just…things were good with you and me, and I didn't want anything to do with my parents' fucking bullshit. So I said no, went to bed, woke up to sirens." He shakes his head, disgusted. "They found my spare key, wrecked the Comanche. It's scrap metal. They're lucky they're only bruised up. They're lucky they didn't kill anyone. Fucking idiots."

"Jude, I'm so sorry." I wrap my arms around him, and he crushes me close. "Do you need a ride to the hospital?"

He shakes his head. "The cops brought me there as a favor last night. They've been to my house enough times to know what's up. My dad is already booked, my mom will be released in a few days to county. I would've called you, but my phone was in the truck, and I didn't memorize your number."

"It's fine. I knew if you didn't show, there had to be a good reason. I'm just glad you're okay." I rub slow circles between his shoulder blades, and he makes a low humming noise in the back of his throat. "What about bail?" I'm not actually exactly sure how bail works in real life—I've watched a few of those reality bounty-hunter shows with Dad, but they never got into the mechanics of it all—but I do know we could definitely figure out a way to scrape something together if I asked Dad, Dani, and Duke.

"Honestly? I wouldn't post even if I could afford to. They'd just get out and start drinking. It's better to leave them in. At least it will force them to sober up." He looks ashamed when he meets my eyes. "You must think I'm a piece of shit for saying that. I know if it was Belo—"

"I didn't even know my dad ever had a problem with alcohol until today," I say, my voice soft. "I have no idea what I'd do if I was in your shoes. Don't you dare beat yourself up. You're one of the most logical people I've ever met. Trust your gut, and don't feel guilty. We're here for you. *I'm* here for you."

He rests his forehead in the crook of my neck. "You don't understand how good that makes me feel. Thank you for saying that." I feel the damp warmth of his tears slide down over my collarbone, and I rub the back of his neck. He burrows closer to me. "I know I should be crying for them, but, trust me, this is all just frustration. I'm so pissed off. I had a stash of money hidden under the seat in my truck. They found it, and they spent a bunch of it last night. That was everything I saved to get to Vermont so I could stay with my brother. There's no way I can make that back now."

"Oh, Jude." I let my lips brush over his hair, down to his temple. He lifts his head, and his face is wet with tears. "We'll figure it out. You and me, we'll come up with a plan," I say, and I feel positive that what I say is true.

The kiss is coming. I can feel it, sparking and magnetic, pulling us into each other. I lean in, close my eyes—

"AJ!" Marnie skids into the back and stops short. "Shit, sorry."

I pull back and let loose a long, frustrated sigh. When I open my eyes, Jude's expression is partially disappointed, partially amused.

"It's okay, Marnie. We were coming out front," Jude says, standing up and offering his hand to help me.

"Duke and Dani and Bennie came by. Belo introduced me, and Dani said she and Duke and Bennie consider me their little sister, which was cool, right? They brought food, and it's, like, super delicious. C'mon!" Marnie takes Jude's hand, then stops short when she sees his face. "Whoa, you look rough. Do you need to hug it out?"

"You know what? A hug would be pretty amazing right now." He opens his arms, and Marnie folds herself into his embrace.

"It's gonna be okay, I promise," my little sister says confidently, rocking Jude back and forth as she bear-hugs him. "Whatever it is, Belo will help you. But right now, you look like you maybe need a sandwich."

A smile tugs at my lips. I can't believe how quickly Marnie's woven herself into the fabric of the Beloise family, but I love it. I also love that we're both getting a chance to see a group of people facing a complicated, emotional situation by staring it down and *dealing with it*. No one's made any attempt to sweep this under the rug or shush anyone's pain or anger, and I'm paying attention. These are the kinds of emotional skills Marnie and I don't have yet, but maybe we can start collecting them right now.

"I'm actually starved." Jude lets Marnie pull him out front, where my brother and sister and Bennie are spreading a buffet of delicious food on the gleaming counter.

"Hey, man." Duke holds out a hand and slaps Jude's, then pushes his glasses up on his nose. "So I know a guy who can hook you up with a really decent truck for a couple hundred bucks. I can front you the cash, and you can just pay me when you've got things together, no rush. It's a beater, and it's ugly as hell, but he's a mechanic, so it runs great."

"I can't ask you to do that," Jude protests, but Duke glares at him.

"Look, I went out on a line asking my buddy for help. You're not seriously going to turn your nose up at it because it's a little shitty-looking, are you?" Duke's words are barbed, but there's no malice in his tone.

Jude finally recognizes my brother's attempt to help him save face, and he accepts the offer graciously. "If you're sure it's okay, that would really help me out. I promise, I'll start repaying right away."

They shake hands, and my heart swells with love for Duke, who might be an ass sometimes but always looks out for people he truly cares about.

"Jude, are your parents okay?" Dani asks, handing him a plate loaded with a piping-hot, mouthwatering breakfast sandwich and perfectly seasoned potatoes. "Dad filled us in. I hope that's okay."

"Yeah, of course. You guys are like family to me," Jude says, and Dani smiles like her heart melted a little at his words.

"Um, they're not great, but they're alive and, honestly, jail keeps them sober and off the roads, so it just might be the best place for them right now."

Bennie puts his arm around Dani's waist and says, "You need a place to stay, don't hesitate to crash at our place. The extra room is a little small, but it's yours if you need it." He passes Jude a bottled water, and Jude fumbles it a little, then wipes his eyes with his wrist.

"I really appreciate everything. I don't even know what to say."

"No need to say anything." Dad walks around the counter and squeezes his shoulder. "You aren't in this alone. We're here for you, Jude."

"Thank you," Jude says, the words thick with emotion. I mimic Bennie and slide my arm around Jude's waist. Duke gives me a startled look, but Dani and Bennie fist-bump, and just like that, Jude and I become official in front of my family.

There's a warm, happy glow as we all eat, and Marnie follows Dad around, poking at things on display, asking him a million questions about fishing and rods and superior bait.

"I think Dad may have finally found someone who's genuinely interested in fishing." Dani watches them, her eyes warm. "Maybe, after all these years, he can finally get one of us to deep-sea fish with him."

Happiness bubbles through me when Dani refers to Marnie as *one of us*.

"Dad will probably throw Marnie overboard if he takes her out. She's pretty annoying on long trips," I say, but the joy keeps cresting when I see how well my father and my little sister get along, like they've known each other forever. I guess they kind of have if Marnie is as much like a younger version of Mom as everyone says. "Hey, Dani?"

"Mmm?" She puts down her sandwich and watches as I unzip my backpack. "I had Duke send over some files, and I worked the numbers through QuickBooks."

"Where did you learn QuickBooks?" Duke asks, leaning over to look at my spreadsheet. "Is that a spreadsheet?"

"I taught myself when I was off work." Everyone stares at me. "Surprise! I love math…and spreadsheets," I admit.

This time Duke's irritation with Jude is genuine. "What the hell did you do to my sister?"

Jude holds his hands up, proclaiming his innocence. "We've never talked about spreadsheets before, I swear to God."

Dani takes the folder and pushes her plate aside. She flips through the pages, then looks back at the original documents, checking and double-checking the numbers. She makes marks on the report with quick, efficient swipes of a pen, and the four of us look up at each other, then back at Dani nervously.

"Is it okay?" I ask, chewing on my thumbnail.

"Your work is dead-on, which means…" Dani looks up at me, her face stricken. "No. Everything is very, very not okay, Dell."

19

Little Sister, Big Sister

July

FLORIDA

We're careful not to say anything in front of Dad as we pack the papers back into my bag and clean up the food and place settings. Duke and Bennie offer to stay and help Dad with some repairs around the shop. Jude insists on staying, too. We try to get him to come with us, but he won't back down. Dad finally ends the argument by saying Jude can help for a few hours, then he can borrow the Jeep and come by the house to relax, and Duke will drop Dad off later. Before we leave, Duke pulls Dani and me aside.

"How bad is it?" He looks over his shoulder at Dad, who's helping Bennie hang a new rack of shelving on the other side of the store.

Dani presses her lips together and shakes her head. "*Bad*, Duke."

"He talked to the CPA, but he won't tell me what's going on." Duke presses down on his thick curls, and they bounce right back up. "I feel like there's no way I can leave the country next semester unless I *know* he's going to be okay."

"We'll figure it out, don't worry. Dell and I are on this," Dani assures him, but her words don't seem to ease Duke's worry.

A few hours later, Dani and I are pressed side by side, paperwork pouring all over the table and floor of the dining room, sketches for two alternative plans scribbled on a notepad. Neither plan is a great one, and the one that's the clear winner breaks my heart. I get up to bring our second full pot of coffee over to the table when Marnie peeks out of the bedroom, where she's been hiding out since we got home and took out all the paperwork.

"I can see your head poking out, you soulless ginger. Come here, and I'll let you guzzle some coffee. We can even go swimming," I singsong.

Marnie is still as excited to go swimming as she used to be when she was a little kid. She slides out of her room on her socks and dances up to the table. I ignore her running man, her sprinkler, and her floss because I'm used to Marnie being a wild showman. Dani, on the other hand, isn't acclimated to Marnie's particular level of constant physical comedy, and she bursts out laughing.

I roll my eyes. "Sorry, Dani. Marnie's got a poorly programmed, android level of social skills."

"It's okay." Dani holds Marnie by the shoulders and shakes her head. "Wow. You look *just like* your mother. So beautiful."

Marnie ducks her head and blushes a little, which shocks me. Marnie is so *not* the duck-and-blush type.

"Thanks." Marnie tucks her hair behind her ear nervously, and Dani takes notice, combing it over with her fingers.

"When did you last have your hair cut?" Dani asks sweetly as she surveys my little sister's hack job.

"I, uh, did it myself," Marnie admits. "My mom would never have let me get something edgy, so I just used my dad's clippers."

Dani glances at me, eyes wide with horror, then shakes it off and smiles at Marnie. "Was she upset? Your mom?"

Marnie's giggles are half-embarrassed, half-pleased-as-hell with herself. "She screamed so much at me, she had to drink this disgusting ginger tea and only talk when it was, like, *absolutely necessary* for two days."

"Yikes." Dani grimaces. "I was going to offer to shape it up for you, but I don't want to get you in trouble—"

"You know I drank myself into a stomach-pumping session this summer, right?" Marnie positively glows when she realizes she's managed to shock Dani. "To be honest, I kind of love getting in trouble. And you don't have to be nice to me. I know I did a hack job on my hair."

Dani can't stop smiling and stroking Marnie's crazy head of fluffy hair. "All right. I shouldn't do this, but if you *promise* not to rat me out to your mother, I'll help you fix this up, okay?"

Marnie hugs Dani, then does a little shiggy over to the mugs, picks the biggest one she can find, and pours herself too much caffeine spooned with too much sugar, and slurps it down loudly as I wince. I know what Marnie's like hyped up on coffee, and it's not a calming picture.

"Okay, Marnie, a *cup* of coffee is fine. Don't drink too much," I caution. One of the last things Marnie said directly to me the other night was that she hated me, and I want to work to fix what's still off between us. But there's this primal sister tic that overrides my rational sense and activates my autoboss feature when Marnie's in the room. It's way too strong to ignore.

"You can't boss me around here, General Buzzkill." Marnie nods to Dani and narrows her eyes at me. She isn't oozing hate, but she's definitely not being floppily affectionate with me. "*She's* the reigning big sister here, not you. Bow down."

Dani bursts out laughing, and I get it. It's a joke. I should laugh, too, and I know that.

"But she's not *your* big sister. She's *my* big sister. *I'm* your big sister, and I know you get obnoxious when you have too much caffeine, so slow it down," I snap.

"Dell!" Dani pulls a carbon copy of the face she gave me when she found out I let twelve hours of Marnie's calls and texts go to voice mail, and Marnie practically throws her mug on the countertop.

"She's right, she's right!" Marnie says, holding her hands up. "I'm going to jump in the pool and swim laps, or else you'll wind up shaving my whole head. I won't be able to sit still. She's *right!*"

Like a little red squirrel, she darts to her room, darts back out with her new neon-green one-piece on, and cannonballs into the pool.

"Oh my God," Dani whisper-laughs. "She's like watching a real life Quicksilver from the Marvel movies."

"Yeah." I twirl my pen nervously. "I'm sorry if I seemed harsh—"

"It's okay, Dell. I know it must be weird for you." Dani puts an arm around my shoulder and rests her cheek on the top of my head. I curl myself into her hug, so relieved I could cry. I've missed having her approval and open love. "So, you're the big sister back home in Michigan. Weird that I know that, but I've never actually put it into perspective before."

"Yep. Unlike you, I'm a shitty big sister, though," I say, gesturing to Marnie's coffee mug. "In a million ways."

"Hey, don't say that. Marnie obviously loves you. And, to be fair, I think you're probably a much more low-key little sister than Marnie is. Plus, I've only ever had you around for the summers. I definitely would have been a way crappier big sister if I didn't only see you when we were both on vacation growing up." She bites her lip. "You always looked up to me, Dell, and I love that. But, trust me, if you'd been around all year, you would have realized I mess up. A lot." Her laugh is rough and a little angry. At who? "A *lot*," she emphasizes.

Herself, I decide. I know self-loathing when I hear it.

"You never left me hanging like I did to Marnie."

Maybe I'm feeling inspired to confess because of the way Jude fearlessly unloaded his pile of problems and emotions today and just *owned* them. Maybe I feel better now that Dani has seen me and Marnie together firsthand, so she has a more accurate feel for what I've had to deal with when it comes to playing the role of big sister. Whatever the reason, the result is that my chest loosens for the first time since my dad, sister, and brother looked at me with total disappointment the night of my party. After years of burying everything I feel, it seems impossible that throwing it all out in the open could feel good, but it's actually really cathartic.

Dani pulls me into a full, tight hug. "I should never have made you feel like shit for that. We all make mistakes. And, trust me, your mistake was minor—*really* minor—compared to the mistakes I've made. That was a jerk move on my part, to judge you like that when you needed me to be there for you."

"No, you guys were right." I'm speaking into her shoulder and wondering what my hug ratio is like in Florida compared to Michigan. "I was ignoring Marnie because I was being selfish, and it was shitty."

"You are *way* too young to be dealing with these kinds of things," Dani says, her voice so gentle and forgiving, it instantly loosens my tears.

"But I'm the big sister. I'm *supposed to* handle these things," I protest.

"Hey." She pulls back, and I'm shocked silent by the sadness on her face. I don't know how to explain it except to say it's not equivalent to the level of pain that we're bringing to the table. I realize I'm missing something, though I have no idea what it could be. "You aren't ready to handle these things, Dell. These are really hard things, and it's better to leave them to the adults to figure out."

It's not a rocket-science concept, but I think back to this past winter and consider how much easier everything would have been if I'd had Dani there to tell me that one simple fact. Or if I'd had Jude there to force me to be honest. Instead, Lex and I got Marnie tangled deeper in a web of lies and cover-ups that eventually led to her being dumped outside a hospital like garbage.

The image of my sister, half-dead on the curb of some random hospital makes coffee-tinged bile lap at the back of my throat. I'm dealing with things now, but I can't do it all at once, so I pivot.

"Good thing we didn't leave *this* to the adults, though,

right?" I gesture to the pile of papers on the dining room table and realize as soon as I uttered the words that Dani's not going to treat this like a joke. And it's also so clear that we're facing a new divide in our relationship: Dani *is* a full-fledged adult now, which is both comforting and a little scary. I'm not that much younger than Dani, which means I'll be putting my big toe into the adult world sooner than later.

"Della, I don't want you to be nervous. I'm so glad you got a head start on the books for me, and, by the way, girl, you're *amazing*. You have a great head for numbers and the logic of this whole program. It took me an entire semester to learn what you taught yourself in a few days. But we don't necessarily have all the pieces we need. I'm going to sit down with Dad and get him some permanent financial help. This isn't something you need to worry about right now. I want you to enjoy your last summer before senior year."

"Everyone says that." I thumb idly through a file folder. "But there's no way I'm going to enjoy anything if I know Dad needs me. Or Marnie. Or you. I want to keep helping. It feels crappy to let the people I care about down. I'm done with that."

Dani kisses my head. "Okay. You can help. But you also need to unwind. This vacation hasn't been very fun so far, and it's kind of my job as your big sister to make sure it is. We've done a really good job going through financials this morning. Let's go lounge by the pool with Marnie before we head over to the salon. You guys need a pedicure." She looks at my chipped toenail polish and clicks her tongue in disapproval.

"I'll never say no to a pedicure." I half hug her. "And I'll get my suit on. But, Dani?"

"Yeah?"

"If you think you're going to be able to lounge by the pool while Marnie is around, you're about to be sorely disappointed."

Half an hour and several ridiculous rounds of Marco Polo (complete with near-hysterical, bloodcurdling screams from Marnie) later, Jude comes onto the back porch in his board shorts with a big smile directed right at me.

I can feel Dani watching my reaction, and I couldn't hide it if my life depended on it. Just seeing him flips on this automatic happiness switch in me that's ten times stronger than the old irritation switch used to be.

"It sounded like someone was being murdered or playing an epic game of Marco Polo." Jude tries to sound cheerful, but his mouth has a tense pull to the side, like he's gnawing away at the inside of his cheek. One of my go-to stress tics, too.

"Jude!" Marnie screams so loud we all wince. My little sister operates at several decibels and octaves beyond her normal range whenever she's in a pool. "There's a net! Get the volleyball! Get it! You're on AJ's team!"

"AJ?" Dani says softly, like she's taste-testing this new name option for me. "I love it." She tucks a strand of wet hair behind my ear. "It suits you."

"I'm pretty crappy at volleyball," Jude says as he scoops the ball up and walks it over. "She may not want me on her team."

"She'll be too busy checking out your ass to notice how crappy you are!" Marnie crows. Jude's eyes go wide, Dani chokes back a laugh, and I glare daggers at my irritating little sister.

"Seriously, no caffeine for you ever again, Marnie. *Ever*," I growl.

Jude tosses the volleyball in, dives into the water, and bobs up next to me as Dani swims to Marnie's side.

"I don't mind if you check out my ass," he murmurs.

"Good, because I was going to do it anyway." I smile at him, and my entire body itches to be close to his. I resist the urge, since my sisters are staring at us across the net. "Are you feeling a little better?" I ask before we start.

"Yeah." He nods. "Your dad made me take a nap on the couch in his office. Crazy how much better sleep makes things."

"So true."

"C'mon, lovebirds!" Marnie squawks. "Enough pillow talk!" I can tell she's not sure she's making any sense, but Dani's laughter definitely won't help detract her from more asinine commentary.

I turn to look at Jude. "I'd really, really love to just knock my little sister's block off with this volleyball, but she's legit semiprofessional. So, just to prepare you, she's going to trash-talk us, and then she's going to trounce us mercilessly. You good with that?"

His smile curls on his lips so deliciously, I want to take a bite.

"Never been more ready for anything in my life."

My first serve is so pathetic, Marnie should have the good grace to *not* rub it in, but the beauty of a little sister hopped up on caffeine is that her already-blurred boundaries pretty much evaporate.

To say Jude and I get pummeled by Marnie (who gallantly intercepts every wonky ball that was about to clock Dani—who also kind of sucks) would have been a massive understatement. But, considering my little sister wasn't even talking to me last night, I willingly accept the trouncing. Jude obviously has no idea what it's like to grow up with an übercompetitive athlete when your own athletic skills are middling at best because he keeps giving me very sincere words of encouragement.

The sheer corniness is so sweet, it almost makes me nervous. But I try not to let my naturally cynical nature grind the goodness out of this new kind of romance.

"Okay, time to head to the salon, ladies," Dani announces after Marnie drags her around the pool—twice—in a very unsportsmanlike victory lap.

Marnie nearly falls on the wet concrete jumping out of the pool and skids into the house, leaving the door wide-open. Dani, Jude, and I stare at the long, wet streaks her feet leave on the concrete.

"She's, like, a force of nature," Jude says, pulling himself out of the pool and holding a hand down to help me out.

"That's how she runs on a few extra hours of sleep and two sips of coffee?" Dani muses. "That's a supernatural energy level."

"Marnie has intense energy levels." I stand in front of Jude, dripping dry in a very cute new bikini, and I try my best not to blush at the way he looks at me, like he wants to do way more than just look. "Once I helped out at our church's day care. Seven three-year-olds having a field day after a cupcake snack—I didn't even break a sweat. Dealing with Marnie's level of energy is like a constant endurance test."

"I'm going to head inside to get ready for work. I'll peek in on Marnie and make sure she's not sneaking another cup of coffee." Dani gives me a not-so-subtle wink before she heads into the house and leaves me alone with Jude.

"So." He can't stop smiling. Every time we make eye contact, he smiles more, which makes me smile, and soon we're both laughing at each other and shrugging because we have no clue what's so funny. I wonder if we'll just keep cycling through this weird laugh phase indefinitely when he finally says, "I want to kiss you. But I can't."

"Oh, you can. You definitely can." I point to my lips. "Bring your lips over here, and I'll show you how. Didn't that Canadian teach you anything?"

"We were always wearing hockey masks." It feels so good to laugh this much with him. "Seriously, though, I don't want to get weird, and this isn't some antifeminist thing about asking your dad permission or whatever. Just, Bennie and Dani's offer was really nice, but they don't actually have a lot of extra space. Or an extra bed. Belo offered to let me crash in Duke's old room until I'm on my feet. And, the thing is, I can't just mack on you right under his nose. It's weird."

"Trust me, he won't mind. He's basically been trying to arrange our future marriage for the last three years." I want to tell Jude that if he's serious about wanting to delay kissing me, he shouldn't gnaw on his lower lip like he's doing right now. "I actually hope my kissing you makes him squirm a little. It would be fitting payback for all the teasing I've put up with from him."

"Dell, this can't be, like, a joke." He swallows hard and pulls back from me. "That sounds really douchey. It's cool, like, *to* joke. I just mean…it hasn't been that long since you decided I'm not the scum between your toes—"

"Unfair," I interject. "I was never *that* mean to you."

"You were pretty irritated with me, basically all the time," he says with a grin that lets me know he's forgiven my immaturity. And poor judgment. "I don't want to get too weird on you, but I've been waiting a while for you to figure out we might be good together. I had, like, a thirty-step plan to get you to go on a date with me. Yesterday started at *maybe* step five? Five and a half? It's barely been twenty-four hours, and I'm already staring down step thirty-five, easy."

"What was step thirty-one?" I ask.

"Getting food with you."

"Thirty-two?"

"Some sexy hand-holding."

"Thirty-three?"

"Warm hugs."

"Are you a magical snowman?"

He ducks his head and shrugs. Oh, and chews on that lip. I'm going to kiss him, his plans be damned.

"Thirty-four?"

"Getting you to the beach so I could ogle you in a bikini."

"You went from friendly snowman to lecher in one quick jump." I shift closer to him, bracing my hand against his chest, and he pushes my palm tight over his heart. Which is thumping, hard.

"I'm not a saint, Dell." The hungry way he looks at me makes it entirely clear that there's nothing saintly going through his brain right now.

"Even saints probably kiss sometimes." I stand on my toes, rubbing my nose back and forth against his. His heart thrums under my palm. "If you're not a saint, are you part of one of those cults where you don't kiss until you're at the altar?"

He nuzzles my neck. "No. But if you and I start with a kiss, it won't end there." His voice is low and husky. I press closer. "I like you."

"Mmm. I like you, too," I whisper, watching the goose bumps break out on his neck where my breath warms his skin.

"I *really* like you, Dell. But I'm not interested in being your summer fling." He straightens his back and raises his eyebrows.

I push past the foggy stupor in my brain and consider what he's asking. "You want to date me?"

"Yeah."

"But also move to Vermont?"

"Well, my parents might have screwed that up for me, so…"

"But if you could? If you had the money, would you want to go?"

"Maybe. Long distance doesn't bother me. I know you're going back to Michigan in a few weeks anyway. I'm not saying we need to be in the same spot physically. But I want to know that what we have means something." He pauses and looks me right in the eyes, his pupils huge and dark with need. "I can't be something else you hide."

"Oh." I furrow my brow and take a step back just as he leans forward. He sees my frustrated sigh and raises it an irritated grunt.

"Just think about it, okay?" He backs away, hands up. "Let's hang out, and you can decide if you really like me."

"I like you." I've never liked anyone more than I like Jude Zeigler. "I really like you, Jude."

"Let's see if you still like me in a few weeks."

"You're sure you don't want to see if making out would help me make up my mind?" I pop out my bottom lip and am rewarded with another husky laugh.

"Don't get me wrong. I *want* to make out with you. I just don't want to get my heart broken." He grabs my hand and kisses my palm before walking backward into the house, the vulnerable truth of his words a cold slap to the face.

I try to imagine Lex spilling his guts like Jude just did, but my imagination can't even conjure that. Then I try to imagine what it would be like to show Jude's picture to Tessa and Harper and answer their questions about what he's like and why I fell for him. To take his calls in front of my mom and Peter. To actually make good on my vows to fly down to Key West during the school year so I could see my family and *my boyfriend, Jude Zeigler.*

My imagination isn't very good, and it's painting a fairly awkward picture of my future, but I think I can see a glimmer of a whole new committed me.

20

JZ + AJJB

Mid-July

FLORIDA

By the time a week has gone by, I can barely remember what life in Key West was like before Marnie crashed into it. An even weirder development? Marnie isn't just some ward I'm blood-bound to watch out for. She's becoming a real friend.

I tried to sit her down and ask for her forgiveness again a few days after she declared her hatred for me, and she rolled her eyes. "You're my sister. I'm allowed to love you. I'm allowed to hate you. I'm allowed to love you *and* hate you. And I *have to* forgive you. It's the rule, dummy."

That was good enough for me.

Dani is head over heels in love with Marnie. Marnie let her practice shaving and barbering her hair in etched patterns. My always-moving little sister sat still for *hours* while Dani styled her hair in patterns of intricate Viking braids and took a thousand pictures for her portfolio.

"Badass," Dani breathed as she looked at image after image of Marnie, decked out in her gray tank and shorts, biceps curled, hair braided and carved, nails painted black, cocky smile on her face. "She's amazing, Dell. I'm *so* glad she came down this summer, and I finally got a chance to meet her."

Duke thinks Marnie is hilarious and adorable, and Duke doesn't usually find *anyone* hilarious or adorable, so it's a testament to Marnie's intense charisma.

My dad instantly took her under his wing like she was another one of his daughters. To his delight, his adopted daughter actually loves fishing and crabbing, so he doesn't have to guilt Dani, Duke, or me into going out with him anymore. Jude still goes, of course, because he loves the ocean just like my dad does, and spending time with my dad is still one of his favorite things.

Jude.

Jude Zeigler.

Another weird development? Jude and I—frenemies to friends to much more—live under the same roof. We cook and eat meals together, clean up and work together, hang by the pool, watch TV, climb up to the roof and stargaze together. We hold hands. Brush by each other. Hug. Snuggle. But we *don't* kiss. And, actually, Jude's even pulled back on hugs, after the last one started innocently and ended with the two of us grinding against each other in a totally unromantic, intensely satisfying fifteen minutes of hormonal heaven.

"The second I'm in my own place," he rasped in my ear, "I'm taking you on an actual date. And I'm kissing you. And…"

"Hmm." I breathe in the scent of his neck, salt and lime and clean, delicious Jude. "I have this suspicion you don't actually *know* how to kiss, and you're scared I'll dump you when I find out."

"Excuse me?" he huffs. "I've been making out with a pillow for forty minutes a night, *every night*. Get ready, Dell. I'll have my own place in a week, tops, and you're going to be so jealous of my pillow."

I snicker but face the grim reality that I actually *am* a little jealous of his damn pillow right now.

"So, you got a place?" I ask to double-check.

"Your dad hooked me up, again. He knows a guy who was renting the studio above his fish market. Not many takers because it stinks like fish. But that doesn't bother me."

"You probably don't even like me. You just know the only girl who'll put up with your stinky apartment is the bait-shop owner's daughter. Are you excited?"

I wonder what it would feel like, not living in a place your parents set up and decorated and made the rules in. I've determined so much of who I am and what defines me based on my parents' choices. What would it be like to be free of all that?

Terrifying.

Intoxicating.

"I am," he says slowly. "I guess I just wish it was more this thing I was doing because I wanted to be more independent, and not because I had my hand forced."

"Hey, if you don't mind my asking…" Jude is totally blunt when it comes to talking about anything that breaks his heart or makes him sad, but I still feel anxious bringing up his parents. "How are…they?"

"They're not twin Voldemorts." He laughs to reassure me, but the sound is grating. "You can ask about them by name if you want. It doesn't freak me out. But there's no exciting update. They're just two drunk clowns who were forced to sober up in jail, and that's what they did."

"My dad would have bailed them out." I study Jude's face as a whole parade of emotions flicker past. Sadness, anger, disappointment, and then, finally, resignation. Which is probably the saddest one of all.

"I know it." Jude wraps his arms around me and buries his nose in my hair. He told me the smell of my shampoo is deeply calming to him, which I thought was incredibly sweet. "I'm still not sure I made the right call. But Belo doesn't have money to burn, and it hasn't historically been a smart move to invest in my parents' law-abidingness. Plus, there's no way to convince an alcoholic to get help until they're ready. But a stint in jail might nudge them closer to being ready. And being sober for a few weeks might help, too."

"Where is your fish palace again?" I ask. It's hard for me to imagine this mystical place. There's something so much more permanent about getting your own apartment—even a tiny one that reeks of snapper—versus moving into a college dorm or student housing.

"It's off Hyacinth Ave., behind 5 Brothers, by the pier. Close to Belo's and close to downtown."

"Good." I splay my fingers over his ribs, loving the way his breath catches. "So, we have an ugly, old make-out pad all set up?"

"Hell yeah, girl. Get ready to hop into my beater and collapse on a futon I bought used from a woman who doesn't smoke and only had it in her guest room for one year before deciding to upgrade to a bed for her great-aunt who visits twice a year. It's going to be a true evening of romance." His smile, usually super bright, is a little strained. "Damn, that would be so much funnier if it were *actually* a joke and not a description."

"It's funny either way." I poke him in the chest. "Don't get weird. You know I don't care."

"You only *think* you don't care. It's a pretty ugly futon, even if it's in good shape." His game face goes sour before his next admission. "I'm sure Lex would have been able to buy a hilltop palace for you guys to make out in."

"Ah, but I don't *want* to make out with Lex, and I could if I wanted, so…don't be a jealous fool. I *only* want to make out with you. Even if I have to make out on a lumpy futon."

He locks my hips against his and sways us back and forth softly, like we're dancing to music only he can hear. "I never would have pegged you for a romantic."

"Trust me, no one's more surprised by all these changes than I am."

That's maybe the truest thing about this summer. For the first time in seventeen rigid years of keeping up two personalities and two existences because I was afraid of… What *was* I so afraid of? I can't figure out an answer to that, which is weird because worrying about it was basically a constant stressor in my life. This summer I've figured out there's a complete me that's made up of bits and pieces of the two people I was pretending to be before, and I'm kind of falling in love with her.

The changes I've made this summer are big and small, surprising and not that surprising at all.

For example, I discover that I hate putting on fake lashes and contouring every day. It's fine for special nights out, but I think I confused my pride in mastering the art of makeup with actually *liking* it. The first time Jude sees me made up to the level I'm truly comfortable with, his wolf whistle lets me know I should have listened to my own instincts from go.

Dad nearly has a heart attack when he comes home early on one of my days off and finds the living room full of boxes and bags of *stuff* from my room.

"Baby, are you really cleaning that pigsty?" he asks, eyes wide.

"You should see her room in Michigan." Marnie looks up. She's wearing three different pairs of ridiculous sunglasses from my donation box, one on top of the other. "Elsa's ice castle has more decoration."

Dad laughs and rumples her hair. "You have no room to talk, miss. You've only been here a few weeks, but your room already gives your sister's a run for its money."

"I've embraced my slovenly ways. There's no hope for me." It's crazy what her impish smile lets her get away with down here. Dad is wrapped securely around Marnie's little finger. "And I want those posters if you don't." She points to a roll of posters with frayed corners I'm about to trash.

"They're yours if you want them. I've decided I don't like clutter," I announce. "Or maybe I like a *little* clutter. Not too much." Once Duke and I are done hauling the donation boxes next to the mud-crusted excavating tools in his truck, I'm exhausted, and my room is nearly bare.

Duke looks around and shakes his head. "Wow. Is this you turning over a new leaf, bugbite?"

"Believe it or not, it's an old leaf." I toss him a Twizzler from my cleaning-snack stash. "You look beat."

"Dani's been working with the financial guy, but Dad's gonna need some big overhauls, whether he wants to sell the place for top dollar or attempt to keep it. We don't have money for paid labor, so familial servitude it is." He shoves his glasses up into his curls and rubs his eyes. "Why couldn't he have chosen to operate some seedy business that's open all night?"

"Like a strip club?"

Duke laughs. "Maybe not *that* seedy. Selling bait without a paycheck is bad enough. I wouldn't want to dance in a thong for no money. But I can't keep the hours and hold on to this internship. They've been really understanding, but that only goes so far."

Marnie pokes her head in. "Twizzle me!" she demands.

I toss her a Twizzler, which she catches in her mouth. She flops on the bed, forcing me and Duke to roll to the side before she smashes into us. "What's up?"

If we were back home, I'd keep Marnie out of the loop because I'd assume she was too immature or that it just wouldn't interest her. But this summer has taught me that putting things out there generally works better than sealing things up.

"Duke got an amazing internship this summer. It was super competitive."

"Go, nerd-bro!" Marnie says, fist-bumping Duke. "Why do you look depressed? Do you wish you never got it?" I know Marnie is thinking about her place in the expensive, prestigious volleyball camp. There are girls in competitive volleyball who would have scratched each other's eyes out for a chance to go to that camp, and I think my sister still has residual guilt.

"No, I love it, dork." He bops her on the nose with a Twizzler. "But my dad needs me to fix up the decrepit family business, so I kind of have to be a reluctant hero." He shrugs. "Oh well. With global warming, there are going to be so many unearthed specimens to investigate before the planet's inevitable collapse, anyway. What's a few more years of indentured servitude to my dad?"

"You're just, like, spackling and painting, nothing that's even *remotely* hard," Marnie says.

"Sick burn, sprout." Duke gives Marnie a wry smile. "I know it's not that impressive, but I never had those big bait-and-tackle dreams like your buddy Jude."

"I'm not actually being rude," Marnie informs us.

"Debatable," Duke says, eyebrow cocked.

"Seriously. I'm saying any idiot can do your job!"

Duke turns to me with a quizzical look. "Do you think she knows the meaning of the word *rude*?"

"I'm your idiot!" Marnie declares. When Duke shakes his head, she explains, "Belo has been letting me hang out and work a teeny-*tiny* bit, but he said I'm not allowed to do more because this is my vacation and I'm supposed to be resting or whatever. But I don't want to rest. I want to spackle and paint!"

"You *want to spackle and paint* on your summer off?" Duke asks. "I need you to think long and hard about what you're saying. Also, unrelated, but have you recently sustained a head injury? Could you currently be suffering from a concussion?"

Marnie squishes Duke's cheeks between her hands. "Go find all the fossils, nerd. I'll be covering your shifts."

"I appreciate the offer, but even if I was enough of a loser to stick a kid with my responsibilities, Belo will never go for it. He already hates you working the few hours you do now."

"Let me handle that," Marnie says with admirable confidence.

Later that night, my little sister—wearing swimming goggles and an oversize bathrobe—presents such an ironclad argument on the character-building nature of summer jobs *and* the essential need for fossil research that my father actually okays her scheme. Immediately after he gives his blessing, he and I stand at the screen door, watching Marnie scream and run victory laps around the pool.

"This was a bad idea, wasn't it?" A wry smile tugs at his mouth.

"Nah. You can trust Marnie. All goofiness aside, she's a hard worker and a great kid."

Dad wraps an arm around me. "Yeah, your mom did a damn incredible job with you girls. Seriously, she should be so proud." He kisses my temple, and I close my eyes, thinking of my weekly chats with my mother.

I love her. She infuriates me. Life is all about Lilli right now, and though she asks lots of questions and is definitely listening, I can't help feeling like she's a little checked-out when it comes to me and Marnie. Part of me also wonders if the changes from this summer will hold up when I go back home and enter my mother's territory again. My life in Michigan taught me how to compete, how to excel—but I don't know how to balance that part of my life with my newfound determination to take it easy and be a little more honest and vulnerable.

Because I've changed, and I want the changes to stick. Plus I want to make more changes, keep evolving and growing.

For example, I love my morning runs and maybe even want to move on from running marathons to training for an Ironman—but I need eight solid hours of sleep to be a less stressed, kinder human. And, as much as I enjoy extracurriculars and appreciate the idea of an internship, I want a *job*, even a crappy, entry-level service job, so I can have my own money and take responsibility for some of my own expenses. I like to dress up and look good, but I also love a buttery pair of leggings in a bright pattern—and I want to wear them out. I want my hair dyed and to wear big jewelry. And I want a boyfriend who isn't résumé-perfect and effortlessly charming, with a pedigree to die for. I want honest, hardworking Jude, who doesn't know if his future will ever take him out of his tiny hometown, but who I know will always be the kindest, funniest, most honorable guy I've ever met.

I want to deepen the friendship I'm forming with Marnie and link Lilli in. And I don't want to be a fixer anymore. I want to be an ear to listen, a shoulder to cry on, a spine to support, but no more digging holes to dump secrets into, no more webs of lies. I want to be the big sister my little sisters deserve, and I'm ready to fight for that change.

I want less snark. I want to cry in front of my family and have them ask me what's wrong. No more hiding, no more making everything look perfect.

I want it all. But I'm afraid when the summer ends and I get back on that plane, *all* will be impossible, and even half will be a joke.

I have lived my entire life scared of what would happen if my two carefully separated worlds ever crossed over, and now I'm petrified what will happen if I have to go back to pretending to live a seemingly perfect life. Now that I've seen the flip side of perfect, I don't think I could ever go back.

21

First Date

On date day, I head to Dani's with Marnie in tow. "Will you leave me there?" she asks.

It's Marnie's day off from Belo's, where, I hear, she's not only helped organize and straighten but has kept Dad in good spirits as he tries to decide what to do with the bait shop. The fact that Marnie has my dad rapping in the kitchen and howling over TikTok videos in the midst of one of the most stressful moments in his life makes me love her and her boundless energy even more.

"Sure."

"So, what are you guys doing tonight?"

"I'm not sure."

I don't want to admit that Jude insisted he foot the bill for this date, even though I know money has been a real struggle for him since he moved out of his parents' place. He was able to recover some of the money he thought they stole when he was cleaning out the house before he left, so that helped, but he doesn't have much extra. I lectured him how I'm not interested in accepting tired tropes about the man as a provider, and he told me I could pay for every single other date if I just let him handle the first one without giving him any more shit.

"Probably just, like, hard-core making out for hours. Just like—" And Marnie rubs both her hands up and down her face, moaning and sticking her tongue out.

I roll my eyes. "How old are you? Seriously?"

She drops her hands and pops a bright smile my way. "Kidding! You've waited pretty much as long as Bella Swan waited for Edward Cullen to kiss her. Did you remind Jude he's not immortal? The clock is ticking." She taps her wrist.

"Stop comparing us to those weird vampires you're obsessed with," I say, but my guts twist at the realization that we really *don't* have many weeks left together.

My time with Jude is just one more thing I'm about to lose, and it makes my head spin thinking about it. How will I stay true to myself without Jude there to lean on?

"Seriously, I hope you guys have fun. I've shipped you two *hard* from day one."

I can't hold back a smile. "Not to change the subject…" Marnie snorts her disdain for that obvious lie "…but we have a call coming through from Mom." I nod to my phone, buzzing on the seat, and pull over. It's been a few days now, and I've missed our updates.

"Lilli!" Marnie and I both scream when our little sister gets on.

I was afraid the next time I saw her, she'd be wilted and stressed out, but she's glowing the way she was the night of the Spring Fling.

"AJ! Marnie!" She bounces up and down, her eyes wild

and bright. "I *just* got out of a recording studio. Like a *real* studio with, like, super-talented musicians, and we were recording one of my songs, and then this lady, Maude—she's a super, super famous guitar player—she was like, 'Lilli, let's just jam and see what happens,' and *we came up with a song and it's amazing*!"

On the seat next to me, Marnie takes my hand and squeezes hard.

"You have to play it for us, Lil," I say.

"Yeah, like, *right now*," Marnie adds.

"Mom! Did you see my pi—thank you!" Lilli holds up her pick, and Mom, in the background, waves and yells that she loves us and she'll call at dinnertime. "Okay, okay, ready? Guys, it's *so* good. I'm, like, I'm shaking. Look." Lilli holds up her hand, which is shaking so hard, she drops her pick twice. When she finally settles down, she says, *"Listen."*

We do. Marnie and I listen, hands held so tight my fingers ache, as Lilli plays the most haunting, beautiful, powerful song I've ever heard. I know my emotions are looser down in the Keys, but I start to cry and can't stop. The song is about unbreakable love, love that lasts across time and space, and, sung in Lilli's pure voice, it *wrecks* me.

When the last chord quiets, Lilli peers into the screen. "AJ? Are you…crying?"

"It's…it's amazing, Lilli. It's *so* beautiful." I wave a hand in front of my face and laugh as tears spill down my cheeks.

"I'm actually, like, covered in goose bumps." Marnie pushes her arm to the phone, and I verify.

"She looks like a raw Thanksgiving turkey. I don't know what to say. That was incredible. What did everyone think?"

"Everyone in the studio was, like, cheering and wanting to break out champagne. Not that I could drink it, of course." She giggles, and it's a little unnerving how her incredible talent sometimes makes me forget she's a fourteen-year-old kid. "We send the track out tomorrow…and then we wait." Lilli holds up both hands, fingers crossed. "I have to go to my guitar lesson now, but I love you both, and I miss you so much. I wish we were together."

"We love you," Marnie and I croon into the screen, and then Lilli is gone, and the Jeep feels incredibly empty.

I start the engine, and Marnie stares out the window at the ocean, which she's now visited several times with no repeated near-death experiences and a growing addiction to the saltwater life. She's declared herself a long-lost mermaid and announced that she'll probably wither and die if she gets too far from the ocean for too long.

"How weird is it that we're here without Lilli, experiencing all of this, and she's there without us about to become super famous? I miss her so much." Marnie looks over at me, her face pinched with terror. "That song? It was *amazing.*"

"Yeah." I laugh around the word, still stunned by what I heard. "I mean, Lilli has always been so talented, but that was other level."

"She's going to be so famous. Will we ever even see her if she signs some big deal? What if they want her to tour and they just, like, homeschool her on the road or something?"

All this time I've been so worried about what life will be like when I make my big move to college at the end of next year, I never even considered all the other ways our lives could change.

"We'll figure it out," I tell Marnie, though I'm not sure how exactly we'll manage that.

"It's depressing," Marnie says. "It's also depressing to think about moving away from the ocean. I *need* to see it every day."

"You've lived your entire life without seeing the ocean every day. You'll get used to it." I don't want to be gruff, but her sudden descent into melodrama scares me a little. When Marnie spirals, she can get low very quickly. I don't want that for either one of us.

"Hey, AJ?"

"Yeah?"

"What's going to happen when we go home?" Marnie's voice is small.

"What do you mean?"

"Like…how will it…how will *we* be?"

"We'll be tight. This isn't just a summer change, okay? This is real." I look over at her and smile. Her return smile isn't as confident as I hoped it would be.

"But how will we be us, the way we are now—how will we do that *there*?"

"Some things will change." I grip the steering wheel too tight. "That's the way it has to be. But change isn't bad. It's nothing to be scared of. I *definitely* learned that this summer. Change is actually a really good thing."

"*Some* change is good. Not all of it." Marnie sighs. "Like, who will I hang out with at school if I stop being friends with my old crew? I'm not a new kid. Everyone has their cliques already, and lots of them wouldn't touch me with a ten-foot pole. Should I, maybe, join the drama club or something? I don't think I've offended any of them."

"We'll figure it out," I promise Marnie again, knowing I have to do what it takes to keep my word.

I know if I stay on top of the social stratum, I can negotiate terms for Marnie's protection. Jaylen is a social climber, so proximity to the top means a lot to her. But girls at the top don't date guys who work in bait shops, and they don't give up their after-school leadership roles for menial labor jobs. They dress meticulously, makeup and hair perfect every day. They're clever and sharp and smart and tough even when it hurts other people. Even when it hurts them.

I'm not sure I'd be able to reclaim my former life even if I knew it would save my sister from social annihilation.

I try not to think about it as we walk into the salon and Dani straightens and blows out my hair, shapes my eyebrows, and takes out the latest makeup samples she got so I can experiment.

"I love your new routine, Dell." She turns my face gently with her fingers under my chin. "You're so gorgeous, it's better to go understated." She tucks a loose piece of hair back into place. "You'll have to show me what your techniques are sometime."

"Me too." Marnie isn't remotely embarrassed to have been caught eavesdropping.

She turns and looks at us, a blue lightning bolt drawn over one eye, à la David Bowie. I fail to restrain my chuckle, and Dani full-on bursts out laughing. I throw my arms around their shoulders and hug both of them close, shocked that I ever thought the two of them together in one place would be anything other than pretty damn amazing. I bet adding Lilli would only make things better.

I don't want phony friends or precarious social pyramids. I want my sisters and a loyalty I know will last through thick and thin, through love and hate.

By the time I leave the salon—with Dani and Marnie shouting good-luck wishes at my back—it's time for my big date with Jude. I drive to the isolated beach where I'm meeting him and think about how I feel comfortable in my own skin for the first time in my life, and how I know this is just the beginning as long as I'm brave enough to keep fighting for what really matters.

Which brings me to what really matters.

Jude stands on the beach in gray board shorts and a slightly wrinkled button-down, cuffed to his elbows, the sunglasses I bought him from the junk shop protecting his eyes from the unrelenting Florida sun. He's tan and relaxed, and his smile communicates genuine happiness.

He told me not to dress up too fancy, so I opted for a soft, light blue sundress that's a little romantic and a little sexy. The way his eyes light up when he sees me lets me know I made an excellent fashion choice, though I'm sure I could have worn my pajamas and Jude's face would have lit up when he saw me.

That's romance.

He pulls off his sunglasses and opens his mouth to say something. I'm sure it would have been funny or sweet or some combination of the two, but for now, I've said and heard every single thing I want to say and hear. There are some moments where words aren't necessary, and this is definitely one of them.

I run down the powdery sand so fast, my flip-flops kick off behind me. I head straight to him and, before he can list a single reason why we should wait or slow down or *whatever*, I launch myself into his arms, wrap my legs around his waist, and kiss him.

He tightens his arms around my waist, pulling me up close to his chest, and then he makes this noise, low in the back of his throat, like a deep hum of satisfaction and happiness. His lips are soft and eager, and I kiss him with all the hunger that's built up from weeks of being together without this release. I lick at his mouth, loving the taste and the warmth of him. My fingers work through his hair, down his strong neck, pull forward to hold him under his jaw and tilt his head to deepen the kiss.

I could kiss him all day. I could put down permanent roots in this spot, in his arms, close and safe and totally, mind-blowingly happy. Finally, he pulls back, just enough so he can look at my face. He puts one hand on my cheek and rubs his thumb along my lips.

"Dell, you know you're never getting rid of me, right? Because there's no way in hell I could ever go back to regular kissing after getting kissed like that."

"So, we had a good first kiss?" My lips are sore from kissing him for so long and with so much pressure.

"It was all right." He smiles when I glare at him. "I don't think it's gonna hold a candle to our second kiss, though."

22

Kissing... A Lot of Kissing

Late July

FLORIDA

We kiss on the beach, for a long time, not caring what crevices get caked with sand—and they all do, in a chaffingly unromantic twist to our otherwise sexy first make-out session.

"You ever make out on a boat?" Jude asks breathlessly, his lips smudged around the edges with the pink tint of MAC's Amorous.

I wipe his lips down with my thumbs, but touching his face just makes him pull me tight to his body again. He runs his hands up and down my back, his fingers digging into my hips, then riding up my spine, all the way up to tangle in my hair. That makes me moan, which makes him growl into my mouth, and the kisses go from excited to wild.

"So, this is a boat date?" I ask the next time we peel away from each other, panting.

"Partially. A beach date. A boat date. Maybe a lumpy-futon date? Maybe a rooftop-deck date? Maybe a beachside-campfire date?"

"I love it. Let's do it all. What are you waiting for, Zeigler? Let's make out on a boat!"

I grab his hand, and we race to the pier, laughing as we clamber into a very old but seaworthy fishing boat. It's big enough for the two of us plus a large cooler to fit comfortably, but we might be in danger of capsizing if we attempt to get too frisky. Jude starts the motor, and the resulting roar is so thunderous, we can't talk, so we just glance at each other and laugh as the wind whips our clothes and my hair. We get so damp from the ocean spray, our clothes stick to our skin and become see-through and slightly crunchy with salt when they dry out again in the sun.

When Jude finally stops the boat, we're bobbing in the turquoise water over the man-made reefs, one of my dad's favorite fishing locations. Jude pulls out his rod and nods to the cooler.

"I brought you cherry Dr Pepper. In the cooler."

I dig one out of the ice, crack it open, and take a long, satisfying swallow. "Thank you. How did you know?"

He pins me with a long *seriously?* look. "You've been drinking that on your lunch break for the last five years."

"Why didn't you ever take your lunch break with me before this summer?" I demand.

"I know being lovesick over me and my sexy body is warping your memory...but you were pretty much the president of the I Hate Jude Zeigler fan club since we hit puberty." He casts his line and makes adjustments, squinting into the water. "Last year I decided to shoot my shot when I heard you broke up with that townie you were kind of dating who was an asshole to you. I got you a bouquet and everything, but he came in—without flowers, 'cause he's a loser—and you took him back. So that plan was a wash."

I clench the can of Dr Pepper so hard the metal crackles under my fingers. "Tiger lilies," I say.

He looks at me with furrowed brows. "Yeah. I bought them from this farm stand down the road from my parents' house. They were really bright and beautiful... They just made me think of you."

I remember seeing them tossed in a clean mayonnaise jar on the table in the break room—fresh flowers are beyond rare in the bait shop, so they stuck out in my memory. They were orange, the same brilliant color as my rejected Winter Formal dress, the one I wore to Spring Fling. After Lilli's amazing song, Lex and his friends got tipsy from a flask of whiskey one of them snuck in, and he tried to talk me into having sex. When I turned him down, he said I looked like a traffic cone anyway.

I lean over. Even though he's not facing me, Jude notices and leans to meet me halfway, his arm stretched to keep a firm hold on his fishing rod. I kiss him softly on the lips, transferring some of the Dr Pepper sweetness to his mouth with a quick flick of my tongue.

"Thank you. I was an idiot." I sit back. "That guy? He really *was* an asshole. A major one."

"Yeah, I noticed there was kind of a pattern to the guys you dated every summer." He pauses, and I can tell he's debating whether or not he should say something else. Before I can press him, the line goes taut and he reels in a very nice snapper.

"That's a big one!" I yell, helping him wrangle it off the line and tuck it into the cooler.

"I hope you like snapper," he says. "That's all I ever manage to catch."

"I love snapper." I watch as he baits the line and casts it again. "You were going to ask me about Lex, weren't you?"

His shoulders stiffen. "How did you know that?"

"Because a sweet guy like you is probably curious about why Lex didn't bother to keep up a long-distance relationship over the summer."

There's only the sound of the slapping waves against the side of the boat and the whir of the wind as it picks up and dies back down. The sun glints off the ocean water, and I can occasionally see the gleaming, rounded back of a dolphin or maybe just a big fish arch and roll near the boat.

"So?" he finally says.

"So, what?" I tilt my head back and let the sun warm my face and neck, under my chin and even my armpits—all the sun-deprived places I like to give a little extra vitamin D when I get the chance.

"Did he ask to do the long-distance thing? Or was it, like, a mutual decision? To break up for the summer?"

"Mutual," I say automatically. "Mutual-ish," I amend. "Lex was always happy to keep everything really shallow and distant. And that worked for both of us. It's not like that with you."

Jude snorts.

"What?" I demand.

"That's not a real relationship." Jude's line goes taut again, and he reels in another gorgeous snapper. I scramble to help him with it, and he meets my eyes over the body of the flapping fish. "How could he be cool with not even *talking* to you all summer?"

It's too obvious a question for Jude, who doesn't care about hiding his hand or playing a long game, so love seems like a straightforward equation—a give-and-take between two people who care equally. Anything else wouldn't be enough.

"Lex liked that there were things about me he didn't know. Nothing made him happier than a chase or a puzzle."

Jude snorts again, puts his fishing rod away, and settles across from me. When he was focused on fishing, it was easy to talk about all this like it was no big thing, just a shallow, meaningless relationship. But now, with his dark eyes trained right on my face, soft and full of the kind of love I never even considered with Lex, it's hard to keep up the whole devil-may-care bullshit facade.

"You're not a toy. You're not a party trick." Jude's voice is ice-cold, and I get a secret thrill knowing he's so pissed off on my behalf. "If Lex couldn't see that you were worth more than his half-assed attention, he didn't deserve to be with you." He shrugs. "Which is good, because it means I finally had a chance to get you to notice me."

It's on the tip of my tongue to make fun of last year's wispy mustache, but we're in the middle of the ocean and—even in the middle of a room full of the people I care about most—I don't have to do that shit anymore. I don't have to show off or use witty barbs to blunt the uncomfortable, vulnerable feelings.

I put my fish-smelly hands on his face and pull it close to mine, until we're eyeball to eyeball. "I notice you now."

"Took you long enough." He kisses me. It does rock the boat. We don't care.

"Hey." I push him away with my hand. "You must have had a girlfriend. Other than the Canadian. There's no way I believe you're this good-looking and this awesome at romantic stuff but you never had a girlfriend. Spill."

His smile is all sly, half-cocked smugness. "There were girls. Just none that mattered." He cups my face with one hand. "No one ever felt…right. I've been nursing a pretty long crush on you, Dell."

"Why didn't you just ask me out?" I shake my head.

"I was waiting for a sign that the odds would be in my favor." He closes his eyes for a long second. "To be honest, this still feels kind of unreal."

I nod, taking both his hands in mine and crushing them tight, like I want to prove to both of us that this *is* real, we *are* real. This is the most real I've ever felt in my life.

The question I can't shake is, how can I go back to a life built on lies, now that I've finally started living my incredible, unbelievable truth?

23

The Trouble with Perfection

Late July
Still Date Night

FLORIDA

Jude drives the boat back slowly, and I drink in the way the sky changes colors over the water as the sun slides into the ocean like a giant piece of butterscotch candy.

He docks, and we head to shore, where he has a premade woodpile ready. He motions for me to sit as he lights the tinder. Flames flick and dance, purple and green from the salted driftwood. Jude takes two tightly sealed tinfoil bags out of the cooler and unwraps them gently so he doesn't tear the foil. They're filled with fresh vegetables, and it looks like olive oil. He cleaned the fish back on the boat with the precision of a boy who grew up on the water, and now he drops them into the bags, then puts them on the hot coals, turning them every few minutes.

"Marnie asked me if I was looking for a roommate," he says suddenly.

I shake my head. "She's got a few screws loose."

He pokes at the fire. "I think she was at least a little serious, though." He moves closer to me, kisses my temple, and drops his voice low. "Obviously she wasn't serious about living with me, but I think maybe she wants to stay here."

"Here?" The idea is so far removed from reality, I'm not even sure how to process it. "She doesn't have any family here, except for me." When he shoots me a disappointed look, I mutter, "You know what I mean."

"We all love her. Belo totally adores Marnie," Jude says.

"*Peter*, her father, adores Marnie," I say, my voice edged with warning. "So does her mother and her little sister. The people who live in her home, back in Michigan."

"So, what's got her so scared to go back?" He flips the foil packs again.

I sigh. "Probably just our whole life. She's made some mistakes that cost her a lot of social currency. In our school, it's a pretty ruthless scene—once you're out, it's hard to fit back in. And our parents love us, but they're not like Belo. It's not a democracy in the Jepsen house. Their expectations are so high, it can create a lot of pressure. I know Marnie is nervous about going back. I have a rough adjustment every year, and I don't have to face the kind of crap she's going through with her friends."

Though, honestly, what will it be like for me when I get home? I won't be dating Lex, that's for sure. Will I bother to try to reconnect with Tessa and Harper? I feel like they're distant memories already, relegated to acquaintances in my mind.

"That all sounds...miserable." Jude shakes his head sadly, and I rush to explain myself.

"I mean, I think I made it sound worse than it is. We have a great life. We're crazy privileged, and we know that. We have everything we could want or need, and our parents support whatever we're interested in. We go to an elite school, we rank high, and when we graduate, we'll have every opportunity we could want. Our pick of colleges, a ton of internships or campus jobs."

"That's…amazing," Jude says flatly.

"You don't sound amazed." I don't mean for my voice to lash out as sharply as it does, but his pious act is making me remember exactly why I would never, ever have imagined anything happening between me and Jude before this summer.

I try to keep the memories of how he kisses me and supports me, cheers me on and makes me laugh in the forefront of my mind, for perspective. Also so I'm not tempted to kick sand in his irritatingly gorgeous face.

"No doubt, opportunity like that is awesome. You just both seem so totally stressed and unhappy. Not now," he corrects, "but when you talk about home. Or think about home. That can't be good. That's not normal."

I sigh. "C'mon, don't be so self-righteous. You're going to tell me you're perfectly happy here?"

"No." He pulls the packets out of the flames. "But I think I can face why I don't want anything my parents planned for me. I know what I want, and I'm not afraid to turn down shit that doesn't make me happy. It's not being unhappy that's the problem. It's pretending things are so good."

"You really think you know what you want?" Überdefensive AJ suddenly rears her ugly head, trampling over all the memories of kissing on the beach and long, soulful confessions over cans of cherry Dr Pepper out on the ocean. "So, what's *your* heart's desire? Running a bait-and-tackle shop? Or following your brother to some random outpost in Vermont?" I wave my arms around like I'm going full debate-team-captain on him. "The thing is, maybe you don't have many goals because you never had anyone push you hard enough."

The second the words leave my mouth, I wish I could suck them back in, erase them from existence. But I can't. Once they're out in the open, words have a way of sticking around in the deep, sticky corners of memory.

Jude doesn't get pissed. He doesn't attack or go low. He doesn't so much as sniff at my bait. He drags the cooler over, takes a sealed plastic packet from under the lid and scoops two pops out from the ice. He spreads out a little red and white checked tablecloth, puts down two tin camping plates and a fork and knife for each of us, and sets a tinfoil packet on my plate, then his. He hands me one of the pops, cracks his, and cuts open the foil packet.

My stomach is drumming a mile a minute, making me feel fluttery and faint. This isn't like when Lex gets passive-aggressive and gives me the silent treatment. This feels more like a parent waiting out a toddler's tantrum.

He nods to my packet. "Try it."

I slice it open and the smell of herbs, sweet butter, and fish wafts out. The snapper is delicate and flaky-white. The vegetables taste like summer warmed over garlic and fattened with a little salty butter. I can only moan happily around a hot mouthful.

"Good?" He grins at my combination moan/nod.

The fire crackles and flares in front of us, popping with the occasional burst of bright orange sparks that shoots into the navy sky. The sun has slipped so far down, there's only a tiny crescent of neon tangerine over the purple waves. Soon the ocean will swallow it whole, and we'll be left in the cooling darkness. I'll be alone with Jude and this fire he built for us, the ocean, the moon, and the thick spread of stars. My words from before still buzz in the air like a cruel cloud of biting gnats. Now that I've tossed them out there so carelessly, I have no choice but to wait and see what harm they'll cause.

It sucks.

"I have goals." Jude finally says. He's not mad, but I can see he's hurt by what I said. "And, crappy as my parents can be, even they had goals for me. The addiction blurs things, but they don't *want* to do a shitty job parenting. They don't *want* to screw up. It's a disease."

He turns to a backpack he brought with him from the boat and tugs out a thick wool blanket, scented with bug spray and the smoke of previous campfires. He puts it around my shoulders gently, and it's only then that I look down and notice I'm shivering. I'm not sure if it was the chill of the deepening night or my slink back into my old mean ways that left me with goose bumps. The fire hisses, and thick plumes of smoke curl up into the sky.

"I think it's better to be driven, like you are, and to have parents who are supportive. And part of me is probably kind of jealous that you do have so many options and so many opportunities." He rubs a hand over his bristly five-o'clock shadow. "But the last couple of weeks, I've listened to you and Marnie talk about the price you pay for all of it. I don't think I'd ever want that kind of pressure. I think I'd rather figure things out for myself. I'm okay with accepting my screwups. I think that's a better option than going down a path someone else chose for me. If I'm going to ruin things, I'll own it—my mistakes *and* my wins."

I watch the flames lick higher and higher and think about the first day of senior year. How I can drop back from things, stop doing what I did before. I try to imagine myself letting go a little, backing off. And it works, mostly, in my mind. Lex loses interest in me. Tessa and Harper maybe get it more, maybe understand what I'm going through and are there for me. Mom and Peter will probably insist I still do some of my activities, but they'll say I pulled back so I could focus on getting ready for college next year.

College. If I don't know where I want to go, they'll press me to go wherever they think is best. That's four vital years that I have to fight for or settle for.

"I think I can change things for myself. The problem is Marnie," I tell him.

"Marnie is really smart and so strong." He wraps his arm around my shoulder and squeezes tight. "She needs your help, but she can do things on her own."

"Look what happened to her at that volleyball camp. That was *after* she spent months begging my parents to let her pull back and give her some breathing room. Her friend group basically crumbled this past year, and she's got this secret that only her former best friend knows. If this girl decides to unleash it for any reason, Marnie's social life, her athletic life, her whole world at school will collapse. She'll be a total outcast." I release a shaky breath I didn't even realize I was holding. "If I keep up appearances, my social status can make things so much easier for her."

"Keep up appearances?" He pulls back, and the concern

on his face looks even more pronounced with the fire's shadows flicking over his features. "Like…not changing things?"

I nod. "I'm popular. I'm connected—"

"I bet dating Lex helps that." He only moves an inch or two away, but it feels like he sprinted to the other side of the beach.

"Lex would be happy to pretend if I didn't want things to be serious," I assure him, and the face he makes shows me he's anything but assured. "What's wrong?"

"Just so I'm clear… Lex would be your pretend boyfriend at home, and I'd be your dirty little secret?" Before I can protest, he rushes on. "And this would all be so some two-faced bullies, who poor Marnie has to suck up to, don't destroy her social life and make her a pariah?"

"It's complicated," I admit flatly. "But this school, we've all gone there, and it's actually really incredible. We love it, Marnie loves it—"

"Yeah, it sounds *really incredible*." His sarcasm is edged with mockery. "C'mon, Dell, *listen to yourself*. This is not normal! You shouldn't have to plot like Machiavelli to get through fucking high school!"

"What other choices do I have?" I cry, throwing the blanket off my shoulders. My indignation has warmed me up nicely. "*This*, my life here, this is a *vacation* from reality. This is too perfect to be real! Real life is hard and screwed up. There are no easy ways to fix things." I'm horrified to find my chin wobbling like mad. Am I about to cry? "I know it's not a good answer, and it's not what you want to hear, but you're acting like I have all these great options I'm just rejecting, and that's not true!"

Jude puts both hands on my shoulders and suddenly kisses

me, long and hard. "It's not easy," he says, his forehead pressed to mine. "I know that, but I can't stand by and say nothing. Dell, you deserve better. Marnie deserves better. I don't know the answer, but I promise, I'll help you figure it out. We can come up with something else. We have to." He cups my face in his hands. "Because knowing you're thinking about pretending to be someone you're not to make a bunch of assholes happy? That breaks my heart."

I wrap my arms around his neck and press my face into his shoulder, loosening big, gulping sobs onto his shirt. My whole body shakes so hard, it feels like it might crack open, but I just ball my fists harder in the cloth of his shirt, weeping like a banshee for as long as it takes until every last bit of terror or sadness is gone.

My eyes burn, and my throat feels like I swallowed a grater. I go limp against Jude, and he holds me tight, close to him. "Do you feel a little better?" he whispers into my hair.

"Having emotions is tiring." I yawn, loud and wide.

"We need to get you home." He tightens his hold on me, and I cling to him and shake my head. "You're tired. You're about to pass out."

"I need a lumpy futon."

"No way. Belo would *murder* me."

"I'll tell him I'm spending the night at Dani's," I say.

He pauses. "You'll get caught."

I tilt my head back. "I won't get caught because no one will want to catch me," I whisper. "C'mon, I need to practice a little rebellion."

He nods, suddenly looking nervous. "Okay. I'll put out the

fire." He kisses me one more time. "I'm only agreeing to this to strengthen your resistance to unfair parental authority."

"Huh." I laugh.

"What?" Jude asks.

"Lex always said *he'd* be the one to corrupt me into rebelling against my parents." I smile at Jude and raise my eyebrows. "He'd be super irritated to know you managed to talk me into this." It's not much, but I need to make amends for being such an asshole before, and this is a pretty good peace offering.

I see the way Jude's eyes glow and know my confession at least helped.

"Just because I know you're totally susceptible to my charms doesn't mean I'd ever try to make you do anything you didn't want to do," he says. "I'm just a good boyfriend supporting his woman…and her rebellion." He turns to the fire. "But your ex better get used to disappointment."

I realize it's not very noble to feel a rush of giddiness over my usually calm and rational boyfriend—who just officially called himself my *boyfriend* for the very first time—showing his jealous side, but this whole character-growth thing is a work in progress for me. And corrupting Jude a little along the way is just a nice, unexpected bonus.

24

Long Night of Rebellion

Late July

FLORIDA

I text Dad, I text Dani, I text Marnie, and I power my phone off because I know they have each other, and Jude and I are running out of time. I drive to his place once we've cleaned up and taken proper care of the fire. The ride over is quiet, I think because we're both chewing on everything that happened, good and bad, today.

When we pull in, I tell him, "I'm sorry I was a jerk to you. That was shitty of me, and I'm pretty ashamed of myself for punching low. I'm going to try to stop doing crap like that. But I'm not sorry, like, that we talked about things in general. Hard things. Weird, emotional things."

His smile is so big, it's positively dopey.

"So emotions are, like, uncharted territory for you?" He shoulders his door open before I can answer and walks around to my side, opening my door and helping me down. "You *did* hurt my feelings a little, but remember, I have *a lot* of feelings."

"A surprising amount," I add, and he rings his arms around my waist.

"The upside of all these *weird, emotional* feelings is that being sad about getting my feelings trampled only makes up about two percent of my overall feelings." He shrugs. "But wanting to make out with my girlfriend on a lumpy futon is more like seventy-six percent."

"I thought for sure you'd go for *sixty-nine percent*," I cackle.

"Excuse me? I'll have you know *maturity* makes up a solid eleven percent."

"What's the rest?" I lean close to him and look at the way his eyes crinkle at the sides when he laughs at his own dumb jokes. I like being with someone who doesn't take himself seriously, and who gives me the benefit of the doubt, even when I probably don't deserve it. It still weirds me out that I was so completely wrong about this amazing guy for so many years.

"Thirteen percent hungry, twenty-six percent really tired, four percent excited to see your face when you see my six-pack again, but also three percent afraid you'll drool on me."

I'm laughing into his shirt and poking his—undeniably impressive—six-pack with a jab of my finger. "That's one hundred thirty-five percent."

"Oh, I forgot. Eighteen percent sucky at math." He takes my hand and walks backward. "Question. Are you ready to enjoy the lingering aroma of fish for the last part of our date?"

"You're so lucky I grew up with an avid fisherman for a father."

I feel him tense up at the mention of my dad, so I decide to keep parental talk off the table for the next little while. I wish I could rebel without putting Jude in an awkward spot with my dad, but that isn't possible.

We walk up a set of rickety metal stairs to a chipped door.

Jude fishes a key on an old Belo's key ring out of his pocket and slides it in the lock. We both watch the key turn smoothly, like we've never seen a door unlocked before, and then Jude turns the doorknob, and we're inside.

It *definitely* smells a little like fish. And dirt? I look around and notice a few sad potted plants. The decor is rummage-heap chic, but it's neat and totally clean. I can see traces of Jude everywhere; the carefully folded dish towels, the neatly stacked, mismatched cups and plates, the saggy throw pillows on the futon arranged perfectly. It's all one big room, so the one-wall kitchen is in the living room, which also functions as a bedroom.

There are no blinds on the windows, no rugs on the floor, none of the plush trappings of security you'd find in a family home. But there are also no draconian parental rules. No melt-downs or screaming matches around fraying constraints, no hiding things that your mother or father wouldn't approve of.

It smells like fish…and freedom.

"I know it kind of sucks." Jude's words come out like an apology. I know exactly what he's doing; he's looking at this room through my eyes, and he's panicking. "I'm lucky to even have this shithole. And I really appreciate that Belo put in a good word for me. Honestly, I don't mind the fish smell. Most of the stuff in here I got for free—people give away all kinds of perfectly good stuff—"

I kiss him quiet. When I pull away, his mouth is hanging open ever so slightly, and his eyes are bugged wide. "It's weird… Every time you throw yourself at me and kiss me like that, it just gets better."

I laugh and tug at his shirt. "Throw myself at *you*? *You're* the one who admits to crushing on me for years." I look him over and just feel *happy*. And proud. I'm proud to be with this guy who works hard and does what he thinks is right even when it's scary. And who gives excellent compliments, sandwiched in the middle of dumb jokes. "So, you like my kissing style?" He nods. "Cool. I'll give you some pointers sometime, help you up your game."

"Harsh." He takes my hand. "I know you're on eggshells waiting for the grand tour to begin." We walk six steps. "Here you'll find the four and a half upper cabinets and two lower cabinets, tiny sink, single burner, and weirdly small fridge that make up my kitchen, a space so limited, I'd rather build a fire on the beach to cook my dinner."

"Is the linoleum on the floor vintage?" I tap my toe on the brown and white tiles, and he nods.

"If you loved the decor on *That '70s Show*, this is the place for you!" He leads me two steps farther. "Can you believe someone was going to throw this table and these chairs in the garbage?" He shakes his head and points under the table, where two paperbacks are wedged under one leg. "The woman was even kind enough to throw in a free copy of *David Copperfield* and *Middlemarch*, which happen to be the exact size of the chunk of leg she had to saw off when her dog chewed it too badly."

"Bonus, you have something classic to read if you can't afford cable!" I grin at him as he takes me by the waist and whirls me around, so I'm looking at his futon, which appears to be four wooden crates pushed together, and a dresser that has Lego Batman stickers all over the drawers.

"Seriously, though, who needs cable when you have this

view from my combination living room/bedroom." He leads me over to the futon—which is as lumpy as he said it would be—and we plop down together like two puppies, legs and arms twined. The futon faces three large windows that show the twinkling lights of downtown and the dark spill of the ocean.

"It's seriously beautiful," I whisper, though there's no reason to whisper.

"It sort of makes up for the fact that this place is a total dumpster fire, right?" He shifts so he's lying down, head on my lap, trading the view outside for the view of my chin.

I look down at him, pushing my hair behind my ears when it swings into my face. "Don't do that."

"What?"

"You'd tell me to stop selling myself short. You know how many guys your age have their own place and live off their own money and work full-time? You're, like, *adulting*. Hardcore adulting! And that's amazing." I run my fingers through his short hair. It was nearly buzzed when I first got here, but it's longer now—one more tiny, unavoidable reminder that the sand is running through the hourglass too fast.

"Can I tell you the truth?" His eyes are closed tight, and his lashes are super long, lying against his cheeks.

"Mmm-hmm." I brush my fingertips through his hair, touch the edges of his ear, trace his jaw and his full lips.

"It doesn't feel amazing at all." He swallows hard. "I'm already worried about how much I have saved and how far it will get me. And I'm so pissed at my parents for screwing things up so badly and making shit so unlivable. I promised myself I'd just keep my head down and deal with their bad days, because they actually did have some pretty good days. But I couldn't do it anymore."

"That really sucks, Jude." I bite my lip hard.

"It's cool to be out of the chaos, but it's lonely as hell. I know Belo is going to lose his shit over you being here tonight, but sometimes it's so creepy and quiet, I'd actually rather face your dad's full-on fury than spend another night here alone."

"Jude," I sigh, and I have to blink super hard to avoid more tears.

I don't care what Jude says, radical honesty about emotional crap is hard and draining and terrifying. I'm impressed by his willingness to embrace it, but man, a good, old-fashioned stiff upper lip can help you soldier through some shit.

"Here, get up for a second." I nudge him up and pull the futon flat. He brings over a stack of clean sheets and a light blanket. We make up the futon, and when the lumps have been disguised by hospital corners, we both stare.

"So…could I borrow something to sleep in?" I ask, and Jude rushes to the dresser. I watch him rifle through the drawers. "I like the stickers."

"Yeah, I was going to peel them off, but the kid who used to own it told me they're collector's editions. He said no one else in the second grade had any like them, and I honestly think he was pretty salty at his mother for getting him a new dresser. He was shooting eye daggers at me the whole time I was moving this one out." Jude slaps the top and holds a Belo's Bait T-shirt and a pair of boxers out to me.

"I know I got the grand tour, but this place *does* have a bathroom. Right?"

Jude jumps and leads me to a tiny bathroom, so clean it still smells like bleach. I use my finger to rub some toothpaste on my teeth and wash my face with a hunk of nondescript soap that sits on the sink. His towels are all Belo's beach towels, the kind we give away during sales. It's cool to think about how connected Jude and I have been for so long. It feels like our roots set at the same time, like we have the same grounding.

Back in the living room, Jude has lit two candles that smell faintly like cinnamon. He uses the bathroom and comes out wearing just boxers, which is technically the exact amount of clothing I see him in every time he's at the beach, but it feels different for some reason. The flickering light is romantic because we're both here, snuggled on the futon, but I imagine it would be a little creepy if you were the only one in the apartment.

I kiss Jude softly and wonder if things will go further, but I'm not nervous or worried. Right now, kissing feels really good. Being held by Jude feels even better, and when I realize I've turned into a wet noodle and am about to drift off but he's still completely tense, I nudge him to roll over.

"Are you uncomfortable?"

"No." I only partially lie. I can feel every lump and bump in this unevenly stuffed mattress, but I've never felt safer or more secure in my life. "I just want to big-spoon you."

"Really?" I like the way Jude's chest shakes when he laughs. I wrap my arms around him and hitch one leg over his hip, nestling the other between his legs. I drag my fingertips from his shoulder to his elbow over and over until his muscles start to loosen.

"Everything is changing so fast," he says sleepily. "This is the last summer—" A long, noisy yawn cuts him off mid-sentence.

"The last summer for what?" I prod when he seems to be drowsing off.

"Can't be a kid anymore," he mumbles. "Time to grow up… Don't know if I'm ready."

I run my fingers over the hair on his forearms and down to his long, calloused fingers. My palm presses to his palm, and I weave my fingers through his, holding hands as tightly as I can.

"We'll figure it out," I promise. "We'll fix it."

"I don't think…" His voice drifts out on a snore. I poke him in the ribs so he can complete his thought. "I don't think there's anything to fix, Dell. It's just…growing up. We just have to do it."

This time when he rattles out another snore, I don't wake him. I sit up on an elbow to blow out the candles so we don't die in a fire, then lie back down, the acrid burn of smoke coating the back of my throat.

This date wasn't what I was expecting, was nothing like the predictable dates I'd gone on with Lex in Michigan—the ones where we were careful not to say anything too honest and made sure all the jokes had a nice, sharp razor's edge to keep either one of us from getting too close. Being with Jude isn't some perfect romance or some untouchable ideal. It's real, it's sometimes super uncomfortable, and it hurts as much as it feels amazing.

I watch Jude sleep, his features soft and dreamy. I think about how I was so scared for my life to change in one incredible big bang that I hardly noticed it morphing by way of a thousand tiny stretches and pulls, until it doesn't look anything like it did a few weeks ago.

I guess that's growing up. I curl next to Jude and realize that he's the person who gave me the courage to start growing up, and he's also the person I want to keep growing up with.

I kiss his neck and whisper, "I love you, Jude Zeigler," smiling when he gives a little moan and nestles closer to me in the dark.

25

Comeuppance

The next morning Jude and I eat oranges his neighbor left in a basket on his doorstep, picked fresh from her tree.

"These are amazing." I tuck my knees up to my chest and watch the distant ocean out his window. "Should I be worried you're going to leave me for Orange Lady?"

"These *are* pretty amazing oranges," he muses as he takes the peel off one in a single, long curl. "But—and I don't want to come off as ageist or anything—she's probably around seventy and has a husband who's an ex-Marine. He could definitely beat me to a pulp." While I laugh, he throws an arm over my shoulder as we readjust on the lumpy futon. "Oh, yeah, and I love you, so there's that."

My entire body goes light and then flutters, like there are winged creatures exploding from their cocoons under my skin, searching for a way out. Yes, I said those exact words to him last night. Was he just pretending to sleep? I don't think so. Even if he was, there it is, his declaration of love, in the bright morning light, slightly sticky with orange juice and absolutely honest.

I have a chance to reciprocate in a brave way, but I don't. Jude doesn't even seem to mind, but I know it has to hurt to put it out there and get nothing back, because it hurts me to hold it in. I try to force it out, but I don't want the first time to be like that.

When my stomach lining is sizzling from an overabundance of citric acid and I can't face the awkward silence my nonreply leaves in the air, I grab my dress and head to the bathroom. Jude owns nothing in the way of products that might make me decently presentable. No mousse or hair spray, no gel or antifrizz cream. There is no makeup, just a single solid stick of deodorant, the soap, and the toothpaste, so I do the best I can.

When my rumpled, wrinkled, unkempt self remembers to turn on my phone, I have sixteen missed calls from my father and forty-eight messages from him and my sisters. I listen to messages one through six, and then I stop listening. This is nothing any amount of hair serum could ever fix.

I make my way out on shaky legs, and Jude stops tidying up the second he sees my face.

"What's wrong?"

"I'm in trouble," I say, my head light. "Big trouble." I wring my hands. "Um, I've never been in trouble with my dad before. He's really, really, *really* pissed off."

Jude's face goes pale, but he nods. "It's my fault. I'm going with you."

I hold up a hand. "First of all, it's not your fault. I made a decision, and I can deal with the fallout. Second, if he's this mad at me, I don't think he's going to be super happy to see you. I've got to go alone."

"You're sure?"

"Absolutely. You can't be near my dad until I have a chance to talk to him."

He grimaces. "I have work in an hour, but you can call me. Maybe Belo went in, and he can direct his fury at me. Make me clean out the back freezers that blitzed during a thunderstorm last week." Jude looks a little green just thinking about it.

I pull him close and kiss him hard. "Thank you for offering. And thanks for last night." I blush, even though we barely did more than hug.

Well, *physically* we barely did more. Strange how we kept things so innocent, but it feels like he surgically extracted my secret feelings and forced me to perform a spoken-word dissertation on each one. I guess it's a good thing I got some practice dealing with feelings before I head to see my dad and deal with what promises to be an entire typhoon of emotions.

"No problem," he says, kissing me one last time. "Sorry if you got a crappy night's sleep."

"It was so good, I might trade my mattress in for a futon, extra lumpy." I pull him close and whisper, "Or maybe it was just the hot guy who made me spoon him all night."

He can't bite back the huge smile. "Probably the futon."

I keep that smile in my mind's eye as I drive back to my house. I realize I'm going to need a talisman when I see my father on the porch, coffee mug in one hand, cigar in the other. He never smokes unless he's *really* stressed. He puts both down when I pull to a stop. He stands, arms crossed, and watches as I do my walk of shame down the driveway.

"Um, hey, Dad," I say, wincing as I wait for him to start screaming. I've seen my dad lose his temper very few times in my life, but it's always a little scary.

Instead of yelling, he grabs me to him and pulls me into a rough bear hug.

"You are in big trouble, Dell. I'm serious. But I'm so glad you're okay. You're okay, aren't you?" He pulls me away and looks me up and down like he's checking for shark bites or hickeys.

"I'm fine. I just… I was with Jude," I admit.

"Jude." I've never heard my father say Jude's name with anything other than absolute affection, but now he grinds it out between his teeth. "I thought I'd be able to count on him to keep his head, do the right thing."

"We didn't…um…"

Dad holds his hand up. "Please," he begs, his eyes wide with panic. "I want you to talk to Dani. And if you were… not…careful, we're going to make sure you have whatever you need—"

"*Dad!*" The blush that crawls up the back of my scalp is definitely going to incinerate my ears. "I just told you we *didn't* do anything!"

"Yeah, well, I know it seems impossible to imagine, but I was seventeen once, too, so sorry if I'm not swallowing that load of malarkey." Now that he knows I'm safe, Dad starts revving up. "What the hell were you thinking, anyway? I knew being the fun dad would bite me in the ass at some point. Your mother tried to warn me, years ago and even a few weeks back—"

"It's not your fault," I tell him. "This is all my fault."

"Damn straight, missy!" Dad bellows, blowing my hair back just a little. "How does such a bright kid like you go off, half-cocked, out on the ocean all day, no phone? You don't even check in? I spent all night promising God I wouldn't yell at you if you came back in one piece, so now I'm pissed you kept me up all night *and* you have me breaking vows to the Lord!"

"It was just a date… I should have come home, but we don't have that long together, and Jude just moved into his new place, so we were trying to—"

Dad waves his hand at me. "I don't need to know, Dell!"

"Dad, stop!" I cry, dropping my voice. "I'm really sorry I worried you, but, listen, *please*. It's really not a big deal, I swear. It was one night. Next summer I'll probably be moving into a dorm. I could be out every single night, and nobody would be checking in on me."

"Well, how 'bout we make it to college, okay? You don't realize how quick one night can change things! And I *know* your mom runs a tight ship. I've never had it in me to do that, but I'm not gonna sit by and see you get yourself into trouble because you think you can let your hair down while you're here." He rakes his fingers through his hair and paces back and forth, his bare feet thumping on the floorboards of the porch.

"I swear, it was just going out in the boat and eating on the beach. Jude's new place is kind of weird and lonely, so I just slept—Dad, look at me!—I *just slept* there. That's it," I promise.

"Did you wear your life jackets out on the boat?" he asks, his eyes narrowed.

One major downside of finding my truth and being more honest is I've lost my poker face. I no longer have the ability to lie.

"Damn it, Dell!" Dad closes his eyes and blows a long stream of air out of his mouth. "You know three kids capsized just this spring, and they never found the body of one of them—"

"They were from South Dakota," I object with the finely honed *debate* section of my brain. The much wiser *quit while you're ahead, you idiot* section seems to have gone dormant. "What do they know about the ocean?"

"And you've lived most of your life in Michigan! Quit playing like you wouldn't be in over your head!" Dad snaps.

It's not even a big thing, what he said, and I know it's rooted in his worry about me. The fact is, Jude and I should have been wearing life jackets. We both knew better, and we didn't do what we should have. But Dad framing it like I'm some dumbass out-of-towner?

Ouch.

He shakes his head and squeezes my shoulder. "I didn't mean it to come out like that. You've just always hung tight with Dani and Duke. This is the first summer you've been going off on your own. And it's not about Jude. Trust me, if I could pick a guy for you, there's not one with more sense and grit than that kid." He draws his hand down his face. "But he's eighteen. He's getting his first taste of freedom. He's had a thing for you for a long time, and now you two are finally together. That's a perfect storm and a straight-up recipe for disaster."

"Dad, *please*," I plead, not sure if it's embarrassment or guilt that's making me beg him to stop.

"Love can be intoxicating," he says, hands clamped on the porch rail, eyes trained out to the blur of sand and water.

I go still, afraid to break the spell being woven right in front of me, because all of a sudden my father isn't talking to me like I'm his little girl. He's talking to me like I'm an adult. "You know I was married before your mom. Allie, Dani and Duke's mom, was my high-school sweetheart. Probably my true soul mate on this earth. She was so young when she got sick, and it was lung cancer, which made her so pissed. She never smoked a day in her life. Hated cigarettes." He tosses his cigar a guilty look. "She'd have my head over this. Anyway, everyone said we were crazy to get married so young, but I'm always glad we did because it wound up we only got a few years together."

An enormous lump has set up shop in my throat. There are pictures of Allie around the house, old snapshots of a pretty woman with dark hair and a sweet, heart-shaped face playing flag-football, cradling Duke and Dani, running on the beach, smiling in front of a birthday cake. But they're like looking at the contents of a time capsule. The pictures of Dani and Duke and Dad keep showing them getting older, but she just…stopped. One of those pictures might be the last picture anyone ever took of her, and that's the saddest thing I can imagine for any family.

"I'm sorry, Dad. That sucks for you. And it sucks for Duke

and Dani. I couldn't imagine growing up without a mother. I wish my mom had…" I trail off and shake my head.

"What were you going to say?" Dad asks, turning to look at me, honestly curious.

"She should have stayed," I whisper. "Even if you two didn't get along, she should have stayed for Dani and Duke. What kind of mother leaves kids that young? Even if they aren't hers?"

"Hey." That one word is edged with warning. "You don't have all the facts, Dell. It's not your business to judge. Your mother is a good woman and an excellent mother."

I can't hold back the snort. "Okay, then."

"Hey!" This time the warning isn't implied. "I won't hear your mother disrespected. She gave it her best shot, and it didn't work. I was still half-crazy with sadness over losing Allie, drinking like a fish, two sheets to the wind half the time. I left her here with three little kids and my dead wife's mother. Allie's mom had moved in to care for Allie before she passed, and she stayed on for the kids. That meant two strong women with a whole lot of opinions trying to cohabitate under one roof. Between me drowning in sadness and whiskey and Nan Sunny barking orders—well, you remember how Nan could be."

I nod, recalling Nan Sunny's sweet face, heart-shaped, like Allie's. She always treated me like one of her own grandchildren, which means I got the kisses and hugs as well as the tongue-lashings and lectures. But I loved her fiercely and still miss her so much. "I didn't know she was around when my mom and I lived here."

He grimaces. "She was…and you know it wasn't like Nan

to keep her thoughts to herself. She was still raw from the grief of losing her daughter, and I think…my being with your mother so soon after, I think she saw that as a slap in the face. She should've taken it out on me, but I wasn't around, so she directed a lot of it at your mom. I should've put a stop to that," he mutters, his face drawn.

I pause and clear my throat. "How did…how *exactly* did you and Mom meet?"

Mom never really talks about it, and Dad only shares the funny stories and good times, which—based on what he's telling me today—were few and far between.

His mouth pulls into a tired line, and for the first time maybe ever, my beloved, handsome father looks weary and kind of old.

"I don't know a delicate way to put this for you." He sighs and says, "She was bartending to put herself through college, and I went to have a few beers. We…" he clears his throat "…spent the night. Just once. I heard from her three months later." Dad must see the look of pure shock on my face because he rushes to add, "You were so wanted, sweetie. You may not have been a plan, but both of us were over the damn moon."

"Over the moon?" I repeat, still a little shell-shocked that my mother's "love at first sight, married too young" version of her marriage to my father has morphed into "one-night stand leads to shotgun wedding" right before my eyes.

"Yes, *over the moon*." Dad puts his hand on my shoulder and squeezes. "I lost a lot that year, and I was losing sight of what was really important. Your mom and you, you made it so I had to shake off my sadness and come back to the living. I remember holding you in my arms after they had you cleaned and swaddled." He puts a big hand on my hair and ruffles it. "You had so much hair, fluffy and dark. Like a baby crow. And big ol' blue eyes, just looking right through me, so serious." He laughs. "You were such a pretty baby, but so serious it was kind of spooky."

"Do you ever think about…" I stop because, before this summer, I never let thoughts like this run wild. I have to agree with my lifelong logic: there's no point imagining what could have been.

"What it would've been like if I'd managed to keep us all together?" He sounds haunted.

"It's not all on you, Dad," I remind him. "Mom must have been unhappy. She must have wanted to go, too."

He blows a long breath out. "Your mother was young and gorgeous and smart, and she didn't need to settle for a brokenhearted, drunk fool who couldn't appreciate the second chance he was handed." He runs a hand over his face. "Sometimes I feel like I was given a shot at two good lives. I lost the one I had with Allie. And then I blew it with your mom. Maybe that's fate, though. Maybe no man deserves that kind of love twice in one life."

Two lives? Two loves? Two outcomes full of possibility? My father was given two chances at love and netted zero in the end.

"Dad," I say, throwing my arms around his waist. "That's ridiculous. Of course you deserve love, *all* the love. You're the best man I know. You're the man I compare everyone I date to."

His eyes glisten when he looks at me, but he does his best to crack a big smile. "So, that's how you ended up with a moony fisherman?" Dad laughs, then his expression goes stern. "You two didn't use life vests on the boat."

"I'm so sorry. That was stupid—"

"It's also a metaphor," he cuts in, steeling his gaze. "This conversation is your mother's terrain. I'm no good at this kind of thing, but I should have done better with your sister. I owe it to you to remind you that good people sometimes do real dumb shit in the moment. And one moment can have a lifetime of consequences." He cups my cheek. "One moment can bring you a lifetime of happiness tied up with regret."

I swallow hard. "Ah. I think I see the metaphor." My blush is probably singeing the roots of my hair.

"Don't mistake what I said," Dad warns. "I don't regret that night with your mother. But I do regret missing out on raising you, and that was a consequence of an action I didn't think through. It took me two years to sober up enough to get your mother to trust me seeing you alone. I missed so much, Dell, and there's no getting that time back. Of course, being your dad has been worth every sacrifice I've ever made. But not having that time with you has been one hell of a sacrifice." He kisses my temple and gently pushes me to the house. "Marnie won't admit it, but she's been worried. I think she's scared I was going to ship you two home early."

My heart thuds nervously at the thought of having to leave without figuring everything with Jude out. I hold my dad's hand for a long moment.

"Thank you. For telling me about you and Mom. No one…no one talks about it. To me. It's like that part of me doesn't exist."

"Of course it exists," Dad says with a crooked smile. "It's

just not an easy story to explain. There's a lot of pain and a lot of loss wound up in it, and those feelings have rippled out for years now." He squeezes my hand. "You're growing up, Dell. All your mother and I want for you is happiness, but part of that involves making good choices. That's why we go hard on you when it doesn't seem like it should be such a big deal."

I nod, wishing my mother had told me her version. I attempt to envision my charming, controlling mother butting heads with a dead woman's mom while married to a man in love with a ghost and struggling with his own demons, and it is completely out of the realm of my limited imagination. My mother would never have been happy in that situation. Of course she would have left. She would have been miserable.

She chose to leave to honor her own needs, her own happiness. I think about what Jude said about my life. Am I happy? What should I do?

I stalk to Marnie's room, noting how it's like we flipped bedrooms. Hers is no longer the peaceful oasis of beachy calm. It's an explosion of hand-me-down clothing, stolen posters, random beach finds, ticket stubs, fair prizes, and the manga comics she made fun of me for reading, all strewn over every square inch. I actually have to lift her covers and check her closet to make sure she's not in her room.

I find her doing laps in the pool, her breaststroke so clean and effortless, I'm instantly jealous. Duke always says I look like a worried frog when I do the breaststroke. She even jumps out of the pool smoothly, running over to me on flopping wet feet like a giant penguin.

"AJ!" She jumps at me, hugging me tight. "How was it?" she whispers.

"Kind of romantic." Marnie has become enough of a confidante this summer that I indulge my giddy need to tell her everything. "Like if you wanted to kiss your hilarious best friend who also made you confess all your darkest secrets *and* wouldn't take your crap."

Marnie presses both hands on her chest, over her heart, and says, "Um, swoon. That's, like, true love. Marry him right now."

I roll my eyes. "Enough manga romance for you."

"Belo was pretty mad." Marnie twists her hands like she only does when she's worried. "Is everything okay?"

I nod. "Yeah. He's feeling all kinds of things because of stuff that happened with him and Mom. It's like how adults think you're going to make all of their mistakes."

"Stupid." Marnie squeezes the water out of her hair, which, I notice, is now purple at the ends. "I average more screwups in a week than Mom ever could in her life."

"He was worried about me and Jude...you know." I raise my eyebrows.

"Did you?"

"None of your business, but no," I whisper.

"He knows it's not, like, *abnormal* to do that, right?"

"I think he just wants to make sure we use...life vests." I wiggle my eyebrows, and Marnie cackles.

"Sexual life vests?" she snorts.

"What are you two talking about?" Dani steps onto the back porch with a huge smile on her face and three iced mochas in her hands.

"Your dad is afraid AJ didn't use a sexual life vest with Jude, so he was giving her a lecture," Marnie explains, grabbing a drink, giving Dani a wet hug and a thank-you, and traipsing inside, leaving the door wide-open.

"She's a nut. Dad was just nervous about me sleeping over at Jude's, but we talked it out, and I let him know he has nothing to worry about. Thanks for the coffee," I say as I shut the door, and I'm about to tell her about my date when I notice her sunny smile has slipped. She looks ashen. "Dani. Are you okay?"

She clears her throat. "Um, you're on birth control, right, Dell?"

"I didn't…we didn't, um, do anything. Like that," I say (and don't actually say) for the thousandth time today. I'm definitely missing my Michigan family's buttoned-up attitude toward sex right now. "But, no, I'm not. The pill made me kind of flake out. I would use condoms."

"You know, a backup form of protection is smart." She peels the label off her coffee with jittery fingers. "Like, you might think you'll always be rational and in control, but just one time can really mess everything up, and…" Dani breaks off, turns to go in, almost walks into the glass door, and winds up dropping her cup, sending a wave of coffee over the cement. "Damn it!"

"Dani?" My big sister is always composed, always graceful. "Is everything okay?"

"I know you know this, but *one time* can be all it takes." She presses her knuckles to her lips. "And it can change… everything."

"I know." I touch her arm. "Dad told me everything."

Her face darkens. "He *told you*?"

"Yes." I take a deep breath. "It was shocking."

Dani makes a strangled sound in her throat, like she's about to sob.

"It's okay," I rush. "I mean, I didn't totally buy the whole *love at first sight* thing. But it's kind of weird to know for sure that I'm the product of a one-night stand, you know?"

Dani shakes her head. "What?"

"Dad told me that he and my mom met one night and… you know. I guess they didn't even talk again until a few months later, when she realized she was pregnant. Scandalous, right?" I crack a smile, fully expecting Dani to join me in a laugh, but she doesn't.

She presses her hands over her face and sobs, her shoulders shaking up and down.

"Dani? Dani, what did I say? Are you okay? Dani?" I'm about to tug her hands away when I notice the diamond ring glinting on her left ring finger. "Um, is this ring real?"

She looks at me, mascara smudged under her eyes, and sniffles. "Yeah, it's real."

"You and Bennie?" I squeal. That would explain why she's so emotional. Getting engaged is a huge deal! "You said yes!"

She squeezes her eyes shut and nods.

"You…you look kind of sad?" I say, not sure if I'm right about this.

"I had to tell Bennie something before I could say yes." She takes a deep breath. "And I thought I'd only tell him and Dad and Duke would know, but walking in to you talking about…everything… It's like a sign, I think. I just don't want you to look down on me…"

I nearly roll from laughing so hard. "Look down on you?

You're, like, the perfect sister. And daughter. And girlfriend—no! Fiancée! I could never, ever look down on you."

She drops her head and exhales slowly. "I have to tell you something that I'm really, really sad about. And also really happy about. It's the most complicated thing I've ever done in my life, and I think keeping it a secret from you has made it feel sadder than it should be. You deserve to know, and I want to tell you."

Dani says all this like she's talking herself into telling me something.

"Okay." I nod, wait a few beats. Dani doesn't say a word. "Um, do you want to tell me now?" I ask quietly.

"I'd like to tell you tomorrow. At church," she says, wiping her eyes. "Okay?"

"Sure." I give her a questioning look, but she shakes her head.

"Tomorrow."

"Can Marnie come?" I ask.

She nods. "Yes. Definitely bring Marnie."

"Can Jude come?"

Her nod is more vigorous. "Yes, Jude, too. Okay, I have to go." She pulls me into a quick hug, kisses my cheek, and practically races through the house and out to her car.

I walk back through the house and find Dad, still on the front porch, cigar smoked to a one-inch stub.

"Was Dani pissed?" I ask, nodding at the cigar.

His smile is sad. "Dani knows things have been a little rough for me. She's taking it easy on her old dad."

"Is everything okay?" My voice wobbles on the question.

What the hell happened in the *one night* I slept over at Jude's? It feels like the whole world tilted on its axis.

"I'm not sure, baby." Dad takes another slow pull of the cigar and squints through the blue smoke. "But I think changes might be coming. Big ones. And I'm not sure I'm ready. I'm not sure any of us are ready."

26

Hail Mary, Full of Grace

August

FLORIDA

"Can I wear one of those little veils on my head?" Marnie pulls a vintage silk navy blue dress out of my closet and starts to put it on.

"You're not an extra in a Mafia movie, Marnie. It's just a normal church, like our church back home." I tug the dress out of her hands. "That dress would never fit you."

"Would anyone, like, judge me if I wore a little veil, though?" Marnie has done this very dramatic black winged liner and used a dark berry lipstick, and she kind of has a freckled goth vibe going.

"Only as a fashion victim." I root around and pick out a white T-shirt and blue-and-white-striped skirt "Here. This will fit, and you'll look nice."

"Remind me again, what do I do before I get in the pew?" She's bouncing on the balls of her feet. I'm trying to suppress a migraine.

"You half kneel and cross yourself."

"Spectacles, testicles, wallet, and watch," she intones solemnly.

"Who taught you that? Don't say that in the chapel," I hiss, as if Father Rodriguez were standing right behind us, his jolly face contorted with shock and horror by my sister's sacrilege.

"Jude taught me when you guys went to Mass a few weeks ago, and I thought I maybe wanted to go." She fingers a set of rosary beads my grandmother gave me. "Can I carry these?"

"No." I buckle the ankle strap on my heel and glare at her. "It's not dinner theater. You don't need props."

"Can I carry one of your Bibles at least?" she begs.

"Sure, whatever," I say with a sigh. "They have Bibles in the pews, you know."

"But do they have all this *gold* all over them?" Marnie asks, squeezing the Bible to her chest.

"You're going to love Catholicism." We both jump when we hear the doorbell. "Jude!"

I skid down the hall and fling the front door wide-open, mosquitoes be damned. Jude stands in a white button-down cuffed to the elbows, a thin black tie, dress pants, and polished shoes. He's holding a small paper bag out to me. I open it and see five brown bulbs with bright green shoots pointed out the top.

"I'm sorry if you got in trouble. I should've at least tried to talk you into going home the other night." He nods to the bag. "Tiger lily bulbs. I thought you could show me where you wanted to plant them, then you'd have them all the time."

"Thank you." I kiss him softly, and he keeps his eyes closed for a few seconds after we pull apart. "I love them. I couldn't call last night—"

"It's cool. I got your text."

"There was so much…too much. It was just—it was crazy," I sputter, not sure how to put everything I learned and all the questions I still have into proper perspective. "And Dani wants us to go to church today, so that's kind of weird, too."

"Don't you guys go to Mass every week?" Jude knows my grandmother doesn't play when it comes to our immortal souls.

"Gram was visiting my uncle in North Carolina for two weeks, so we've been playing hooky." I glare at him and he raises his hands, surrender-style.

"Your secret is safe with me. I'm way more scared of your grandmother than you are." Jude looks over my shoulder. "I like your hat, Marnie."

I don't even turn around. "Take it off." Marnie stomps away, and Jude's laugh fades when another set of footsteps comes down the hall.

"Hello. Um, Belo…sir. About the other night, I just want to say I'm sorry. That was irresponsible of me." Jude acts like a cadet addressing his superior officer.

It's strange to watch my father look at Jude with cool eyes. I've never seen them this uncomfortable with each other. An evil piece of me wants to remind my dad he should have been more careful of what he wished for, but that's a little too petty. Plus something is off. With Dad, with Dani…something just isn't sitting right, and I don't think it has anything to do with me and Jude.

"Jude Zeigler, I find out you took my baby into open water without a life vest again, *ever*, and you're chum. I don't mean that metaphorically," he adds.

The tendons in Jude's neck move when he takes a hard swallow. "Yes, sir. Got it."

Marnie waltzes out wearing a pill hat. "I told you to take it off," I bark.

"I took off the other one, with the big veil," she whines. "Lots of people wear hats to church."

"Where did you even find that, Jackie O?"

"Who?" Marnie pats her weird little cylinder hat, and Dad gives this big belly laugh.

"It was Nan Sunny's," Dad says. "And I think Marnie looks very nice."

"Don't encourage her," I moan, but no one is listening to me. I realize I'm officially the older, nagging sister and Marnie has embraced her role as indulged little sister—which is a nice switch for her. And probably why she's relaxed into some obnoxiously childish behaviors.

Like insisting on wearing a stupid hat that no one under ninety will think is cute.

We pile into Dad's truck. Jude makes a big deal about buckling his seat belt and policing all of us to do the same. The drive over is fairly quiet, with just the sound of Dad's favorite old country station humming in the speakers. When we pull into the parking lot, Dad sits for a few long seconds, holding the wheel.

"Dad?" I wonder if he's just zoned out.

"Dani has something to tell you all. I know I can count on you guys to be supportive." Dad swings his head around and gives each of us a long, serious stare.

Jude looks at me for clarification. I shrug and shake my head, wondering if this has something to do with Bennie and their engagement. I'm not sure Dad even knows about that yet, so I just keep my mouth shut and give Dad a solemn nod.

Marnie pops a thumbs-up. "You know you can count on us, Belo."

Dad gives her a half hug and a small smile. It's strange being ousted from my position as family baby. It's also a relief to be the older, responsible one again and to see Marnie looking so healthy and happy. And, secretly? I kind of love that she has the chutzpah to embrace her own bold (and totally odd) fashion choices. It feels like Marnie is also finding a skin she's most comfortable in this summer.

We head into the chapel, where Grandma and Pop sit with Dani, Bennie, and Duke. Marnie takes a dramatic pause so she can genuflect theatrically, then slides in, holding the Bible she borrowed from me up like a shield. Marnie pokes Duke, who gives her a pained smile. Duke hasn't worked up the nerve to confess to Grandma that he's a hard-core atheist, and I doubt he ever will, so he has to grin and bear it through Mass every Sunday.

I try to look around Duke to get a glimpse at Dani's left hand, but her gauzy cardigan is pulled low over her fingers. The smile she gives me is a weak imitation of her usual greeting.

"What do you think's going on?" Jude asks quietly.

"I don't know," I whisper, then lean extra close. "Dani and Bennie got engaged yesterday. I *think*."

Jude's eyebrows raise up. "You think?"

"There was a big ring. But she was crying. And it didn't seem like happy tears," I confess. "Also she didn't tell my dad. I don't think."

Jude drops his eyebrows and knots them together. "Hmm."

Marnie is coughing to get my attention. When I look over, she holds up a fist and shakes a set of rosary beads in triumph. My grandmother smiles beatifically at this new, pious addition to our religiously lukewarm crew. Little does my grandmother know that Marnie is basing all her knowledge of the Catholic church on her role as Friar Lawrence in her AP Literature's original twist on Shakespeare, *We Ship Romeo + Juliet*, and fifty thousand viewings of the movie *Ladybird*.

"You don't even know what to do with those," I hiss down the pew.

Marnie adjusts her goofy hat and flaps a navy pocket guide at me. "Your grandmother gave me the manual." She sits up primly and checks my grandmother, who holds up her beads and smiles encouragingly.

"Marnie is such a ham," I sigh to Jude. His laugh moves the hair near my ear, tickling it. Despite the fact that my glowering father is two feet away, he puts his hand on top of mine and links our fingers together. Nothing has ever felt as good as the warmth of his fingers between mine.

We're smack in the middle of the liturgy when the doors open and a little boy, maybe three years old, runs down the aisle and into our pew, his harried parents apologizing as they race after him. He crawls over all of our feet and legs and sits on Dani's lap. I recognize him from pictures in Dad's house and Dani's salon.

The little boy stays on Dani's lap and shreds the program busily for a few minutes, then climbs down and scuttles over to his mother, curling on her lap and accepting a sippy cup she pulls from a diaper bag. He kicks his chubby legs lazily and looks around with big, brown eyes while his mom strokes his dark curls off of his forehead. His dad leans down to kiss his cheek.

This is the church my father has gone to since he was a little boy. I wonder if he used to bring me here with my mother. Though my mom is a Lutheran now, she only converted because that was Peter's denomination. Did my father and mother sit in a pew—maybe *this* pew—and hold hands, maybe like Jude and I are doing right now, and give baby me a sippy cup and press my curls back and kiss my cheek?

How weird, to think of this whole other life, this whole other family that existed, then ceased to exist before I was even able to form a memory of it. At one point in my dad's life, he drove home from Belo's to his wife and kids, and that meant Allie and Dani and Duke. Later on, he made the same drive home to his wife and kids, but then it meant my mom and me and Dani and Duke. And my mom probably used to make my dad's coffee and get stains out of his clothes and cook him excellent dinners—and now she does all of that for Peter, like that's the way it's always been.

"…as it was in the beginning, is now, and will be forever. Amen."

I've been so focused on this idea of my own split life, it's never really occurred to me that I'm surrounded by splits and divisions. The mathematics of the relationships all around me are complicated, but no less beautiful because of their complexities.

My family stands when it's time to take communion, and Marnie shoots me a panicked look. I nudge around Jude.

"You don't have to," I whisper.

"But *can* I?" she asks, her eyes shining.

"Technically, no—"

"I don't think Jesus would say no," Jude interrupts, and considering he's by far the most peaceful and Christlike of all of us, we go with his lax interpretation of communion law.

Marnie hustles close to Dani, and my two half sisters—two people who are wholly in my heart—open their mouths and accept the communion wafer, drink wine from the same gold chalice. I barely hear Father Rodriguez's *The body of Christ*, my *Amen*, a quiet echo of Jude's, because I'm watching the little boy in our pew tug on Bennie's pants. Bennie doesn't even hesitate to swing him up on one hip and jostle him a little to make him laugh. He's going to be a great dad, and the dreamy way Dani stares at him makes it obvious she thinks so, too.

When the service is over, we're about to head to the hall for socializing and snacks, but Dani pulls me aside.

"I need to talk to you. You can ask Marnie and Jude along, too." She tugs her sweater tighter and hurries over to the altar of the Virgin, votives flickering at the Holy Mother's feet.

"Can I light one?" Marnie asks, in a high flush from all the religious pageantry.

"Sure." Jude leads her to the altar and takes a dollar out of his wallet for the donation box, then leads Marnie through the simple steps.

She settles on the kneeler and bows her head over her lit candle, and I watch her lips move in silent prayer.

When she's done, we all look at Dani, whose head had been bent for a few minutes, her hands pressed together. When she looks up, there are tears in her eyes that she brushes away quickly. Her diamond glints on her ring finger.

"Jude, I'm sure you probably guessed what I'm going to say," she says with a tight smile.

Jude nods and puts a heavy hand on my shoulder, like he's bracing me. I narrow my eyes at him, but he shakes his head and nods to Dani.

"A few years back, my grandma passed. You remember that summer, Dell?"

"Yeah." I swallow hard because seeing Dani cry has put an instant lump in my throat. "I know Nan Sunny meant so much to you. That was really hard, losing her so suddenly."

Dani nods around a wet hiccup. "Yeah. I'd lost my mom when I was so young. I just took it for granted that Nan Sunny would be around for a long time. And all of a sudden, she wasn't." She crosses her arms tight. "I had…a rough time. To put it lightly. I lost my way, and I did some things—some things that I didn't think through. And…" she stalls, licks her lips "…I got pregnant."

The only sound for a long, drawn-out moment is the hiss and pop of the votives as they extinguish or burst into bigger flames.

"What?"

I feel like I hear myself say the word, but the shock is so intense, I'm not really sure I spoke at all. Jude stares intently at the stone floor. Marnie has on her expressionless warrior face.

"Dani?" I gulp. "You…were pregnant?"

"Yes." The word clips out so loud it echoes around the chapel. "I was young. And depressed. It was with someone who I didn't know well at all. Someone I met and didn't have contact with again. It wasn't… There was nothing forced or anything," she vows, and I think she means it. I *hope* she means it, because the Holy Mother is right here, and I'd never want Dani to think she had to lie about something like that in front of the Holy Mother. "I didn't realize for a few months. My period has always been really irregular. Even if I'd wanted…another option, that was not possible by the time I pieced it together."

I nod, my head still spinning. Pregnant? Teenage Dani? *Pregnant?* She graduated top of her class. She was always the most confident, driven person. How did I not notice?

"At first, it was this big secret. Dad was…he was just devastated," she says, her voice shaking. "The doctor got me put on homebound, but the school only knew I had a medical condition. Everyone assumed it was mono." She takes a deep breath. "Grandma came to help me, to talk to me. We talked a lot. And she knew this couple at church who had been praying and trying for a baby for *years*. Nicole, the mother, she'd had twelve miscarriages. *Twelve.* She and David, the father, they ran up huge amounts of debt trying all kinds of treatments. They had *three* failed adoptions." Dani shook her head. "I wasn't ready for a baby. There's no way I could give a child a stable home. I needed to finish school, get a degree, start my business. I wanted to have kids with my husband, raise a family when I was ready. So I met with them. And it was like everything felt immediately *right*. I honestly had this feeling like it all happened exactly the way it was supposed to, like there was no mistake. It was in God's hands, and He took all of this doubt and pain and turned it to pure love. To an answered prayer."

I kneel in front of the votives and watch them flicker and

spit, extinguish and hold steady—prayers from all different sinners at all different stages of hopelessness and hope.

"The little boy in the pew was the baby."

"Isaac." Dani wipes away her tears with the back of her hands. "I am Isaac's birth mother." As soon as she says the words, a shaky smile spreads across her face. "Wow. *Wow*, it feels good to say that, finally. I've wanted to tell you for years, Dell."

I am trying so hard to wrap my brain around what Dani tells me. I look at my gorgeous sister and try to imagine her hugely pregnant. I try to imagine her *giving birth*. Damn, it's so life-altering. It's so adult. Was she scared? What did it feel like? It must have been intense. Tears sting my eyes.

I wasn't there. I wasn't there to meet my nephew for the first time. I wasn't there to give my sister balloons and a bouquet in the hospital.

Dani gave up her baby. She gave him to a family who cradles him and smooths his hair and looks at him like he's the actual baby Jesus in the manger. But still…

"Do you…regret it?" My words are hushed.

"No." There's no question in her voice. "Isaac is *so* loved. Nicole and David are so happy. At first we were going to keep it between us, but as I got older and started talking to a therapist, I realized I'm not ashamed. There's no need to hide anything. I'm proud to be part of this beautiful little family. I'm proud I was strong enough to make that choice for this baby I loved but knew I couldn't take care of."

"Does he… I mean, I know he's still little, but does he know?" I ask.

"He knows he was in my belly," she says, cupping her hand

over her flat abdomen. I try so hard to imagine it, but my mind is a cool, dark blank like the end of an old-fashioned film reel. "But he knows his mama is Nicole. And she and David have been so wonderful, inviting me to holidays and celebrations. I stood with them at Isaac's christening. Bennie knows the truth about everything now, and he loves Isaac as much as I do."

There are a few more beats of silence.

"You were in high school?" Marnie asks.

Dani nods. "I was actually able to finish senior year early and fly through a ton of my online college coursework because I had all this extra time to work from home. Isaac helped make it possible for me to finish college quickly and get myself established at the salon." She twists her hands together. "Dell, I wish I'd known how to tell you before."

"Why now?" I'm shocked by how cool and collected my voice sounds to my own ears.

Dani looks relieved to hear me speaking so calmly, but I can't trick Jude. He sees the way my hands are shaking and takes them in his, squeezing to let me know he's there to lean on.

"This summer you just seem…different," Dani finally says. "Grown-up, I guess. I always felt like I had to protect you, set a good example for you. But this summer I feel like things shifted. You're not just my little sister, Dell. You're my best friend."

Marnie's spine stiffens, and she shies away from Dani's attempt to stroke her shoulder. The fact that I take notice of their interaction is the reason Dani could trust me this summer. She and I are finally able to see each other eye to eye, eldest sister to eldest sister. *That's* what changed everything.

"That's how it is with sisters." I look over at Marnie, who's staring down at the snake twined under the Virgin's bare stone feet. "One second they're annoying the crap out of you, and the next second they're the people you need most in the world." Marnie raises her eyes, and we share a long look. "Dani, I'm so glad you trusted us. Can we meet Isaac and Nicole and David? Would that be okay?"

Dani pinches the bridge of her nose and waves her hand in front of her face. "I'm going to cry. Okay, deep breaths. Whoa. Okay. *Yes*. Of course. I'd love you to meet my other family. I'm so glad I don't have to keep them a secret from you anymore."

Her other family.

A whole set of other people she loves but felt like she had to hide.

Jude gently pushes me toward my sisters, and we three gather in a tight hug while I wonder what the hell is going to blow my mind next. I've spent my entire life thinking I'm some kind of mythical lone wolf, carrying this impossible burden, but it winds up I've been surrounded by people shouldering pain and loss I can't even imagine. This entire summer has rerouted my brain and my heart and blown away all my carefully preconstructed ideas.

Everything Dad and Dani have shared with me and everything Marnie and I have gone through this summer make one thing perfectly clear: there's no way we can ever go back to the way things were before. There's no way I'd ever *want* to. The girl who divided herself, who hid her love across state lines and buried her feelings deep in her heart is long gone. I'm done living a half life. I just have to figure out how to take all the divided parts of my life and make them whole for good.

27

End of Summer

Late August

FLORIDA

Jude zips my suitcase while I sit on top of it, gnawing on my tongue to try to stop the tears.

"Cry if you need to," he tells me. I glare at him, and he topples me on the bed, looking over his shoulder when the springs creak.

"No one's home. Marnie is at the shop with Dad." I tug him down by his collar. "Come and kiss me."

Jude complies happily. His kisses are slow and sweet, punctuated by moments where he pulls away and just *looks* at me, like I'm the most interesting, beautiful thing he's ever seen. I love the way he smells, the feel of his hands on my skin. I love how calm and kind he is, how he's not afraid to show me how he feels.

I'm thawing out, and the pins-and-needles burn is excruciating, but I know it's necessary.

I kiss along his jaw and down his neck, licking his salty skin. We went for a predawn run, then jumped into the ocean for a swim. Floating with our arms wrapped around each other, talking and kissing as the sun came up, is the kind of perfect I don't want to live without.

I stop kissing Jude and lean my forehead against his shoulder, drinking in the perfect *Jude* smell of his skin. Being around him makes me feel like I finished back-to-back yoga and meditation classes, but he's way hotter and calmer than those annoying, overly perky yogis who love to drone on and on about inner peace.

"You okay?" He checks in with me as a habit, and he doesn't back down when I tell him I'm not.

"Nope." I press my cheek against his chest. "I don't want to leave my family. I don't want to leave the ocean. I don't want to leave *you*."

"I don't want you to leave." Jude gathers me tighter to him and kisses me.

"So what do I do?" I know before the words are out of my mouth that he's going to volley that question right back to me.

"What do you want to do?"

Bingo.

I shake my head. "I don't want to stay here just because I'm hiding from my life in Michigan. I looked into the local Catholic high school, and it's good, but what about Marnie? I'm even worried about what will happen with her after I graduate. I'm pretty sure Duke is going to go after that graduate program in Boston when he gets back from Cairo, and Dani and Bennie will be busy with the wedding. And you—?" I let the question hang in the air between us.

Jude sighs. "So it winds up the smell of fish bothers me more than I thought, especially if you're not around to distract me."

"Are you still thinking about Vermont?" When I look into his tanned face and sun-kissed hair, it's hard for me to imagine Jude *not* living near the beach.

He nods. "My brother knows a lot of really talented people. Artisans. I could learn something there. I love it here. And I love Belo. But you were right that day at the beach. I'm not going to stay at a bait-and-tackle store forever. Especially since—"

I nod to stop him from saying more. Yes, I've been able to face things without running scared, but I've also learned not to dwell on the terrifying maybes until they're a sure thing, and the future of Belo's is still very much up in the air.

Dani sat down with Dad and showed him the numbers we worked up and our options for Belo's. They hired a financial adviser, and she had a few solid ideas for different directions Dad could go in with the business. Dani sat in on all the meetings, and she pulled us aside at her engagement party to tell us that the most fiscally responsible path might be selling Belo's. The financial adviser thinks it would bring Dad a ton of money even after he paid off his debts.

But nothing has been decided yet. Dad promised to let us know as soon as he made a decision.

"We don't know for sure if my dad's going to sell." My voice goes thick just saying those words.

No Belo's? It's a concept I'm having a really hard time getting through my brain. That shop is my second home in Florida, my family's legacy, my dad's pride. It's the place where I met Jude. The place where Marnie learned to count change, stock shelves, and had—and I quote—"the best summer ever."

"You're right. We don't know anything for sure."

"Don't patronize me, Jude Zeigler," I growl, nipping at his chin. "Are we going to video chat?"

"I want to. I mean, I love your voice, always bossing me around and putting me in my place, but it's an added bonus to get to see your beautiful face." He rubs his thumb along my bottom lip, and my stomach flips.

"You think I'm beautiful?"

"Gorgeous." He pulls me closer and kisses me slowly.

"You're pretty good-looking yourself." I work my hands under his shirt and feel his warm skin and the tight pull of his muscles. "What if you meet a girl in Vermont? I bet there are so many Canadians there."

"Nah." He kisses down my neck, sending shivers along my spine. "Canadians are too friendly. I have a thing for mean girls."

"You think I'm mean?"

"Mean and perfect." He keeps kissing. "That's what I love about you."

My body goes rigid. He didn't actually come out and say *it*, but that's really close. We haven't said it since I told him in his sleep and he said it to me while we ate oranges together. I never responded, and I know that had to hurt him. He pauses, his lips an inch above my skin, and I can feel his heart pounding like there's a drummer on speed in his chest. I wait for him to backpedal, make a joke to break the tension.

"Dell?"

"Yeah?"

He cradles my face between his hands. "I love you."

An entire summer's worth of emotion rocks through me

when I hear those words, and I bite back a yelp of happiness, kissing him hard instead. "Jude?"

"Yeah?"

"I love you, too."

Our kisses turn into something way more fevered and frantic than the lazy good-bye kisses we shared a few minutes before. I can't touch him enough, can't hold him as tight as I need to. My entire world has shifted, and Jude is my anchor, the one thing keeping me from going adrift and forgetting who I am.

For a few frustrating minutes our clothes are a hindrance, pushed up and to the side, but still in the way. With a few quick pulls, they aren't an issue anymore. Our hands are everywhere, and Jude is talking to me, his low voice against my ear, telling me how much he loves me and how this all scares him, too. The fact that he doesn't feel the need to play this off as no big deal makes me feel totally at peace with the big plunge we're about to take.

There's so much I've been afraid to do all this summer, all my life, so much I've hesitated about—but I know with my whole heart what I want, and I tell him.

"You're positive?" he asks.

I nod and kiss him again. "I am. But if you're not sure, it's okay."

"No, I'm sure. I love you, Della. I should have said it again earlier. Not because of this," he says, gesturing to the tangle of our bodies, the closeness that feels so intoxicating, it pushes all my nervous fears to the side.

"I love you, too. And I should have told you sooner, but I'm still wrestling with being a huge chickenshit on a daily basis." I stroke his cheek, and he turns his head, kissing my palm with his eyes closed, which for some reason makes it even more romantic.

"You're not a chickenshit. You're one of the bravest people I've ever met." He kisses my wrist, down the inside of my forearm, the bend in my elbow. "Not everybody has the courage to change the way you did. I never would have had the guts to leave my parents' house and move into that apartment if you weren't there telling me it was going to be okay. I mean, I'm still scared." He drops his lips to the soft skin of my upper arm, trailing light kisses up along the curve of my shoulder and the sensitive spot at the base of my neck. "I'm still not sure what I'm doing. There's a pretty decent chance I'm going to screw it all up in the end."

I arch my head back, and Jude kisses up my neck and under my jaw.

"Well, *I'm* sure about you. I'm sure you're going to be amazing. You're going to do incredible things." I wait for his lips to meet mine and kiss him deeply and slowly, each second exploding into a rippling sweetness that imprints on my heart. "I believe in you, Jude."

A few months ago, I wouldn't have been able to have this conversation. I would have laughed off the idea of saying all of these vulnerable, kind of cheesy things unironically. I didn't realize how exhausting it was to keep up the tough-as-nails mask until I let it drop permanently.

Suddenly, everything comes into sharp focus. Like the way my boyfriend looks at me, as if I'm the smartest, funniest, most beautiful person in the world. Like the quiet, stolen hours where we let our love spiral out of control because we trust each other completely. We're safe, we're cautious—Dani's real-life warning about throwing caution to the wind has done its job plus some—but we're also brave. And so totally in love.

I know now how rare that is. And I know I want, more than anything, to make our time together count. Because the biggest lesson I've learned this summer is that there's nothing to be gained by doing anything by halves. To make up for my fractured version of loving and living, I'm committed to doing everything with twice the passion, twice the honesty, and twice the love.

And twice enough is only the beginning.

28

Imperfect Decisions

Marnie refuses to come out of her room to say good-bye. My eyes are red-rimmed from crying and making promises I don't know if I can keep. There's a dark cloud hanging over the entire family because my father announced his final decision about the fate of Belo's last night.

We sat together in the backyard, under the same twists of lights that illuminated the flowers and trees at my welcome-home party. It's crazy how these last few months have felt both like an eternity and a blip and how much has changed in one single summer.

"I know you've been waiting to hear this, and I'm not proud to admit I've been avoiding having to say it out loud."

One hand crushed the crab leg I was about to eat into the newspaper, which was spread thick on the table for the low-country boil we were devouring. Marnie put down her corn on the cob, Duke stopped salting his potatoes, Bennie pushed the sausage rounds to the center, Jude grabbed my hand and squeezed too tight, and Dani took Dad's hand and did the same. There were white knuckles and twisted stomachs all around the table.

"Belo's has been in our family for generations," Dad began, and we all knew no good news was coming. The meat of his speech will be forever lost in the rush of my blood, swishing overloud through my body and brain. But I do remember the last thing he said. "In the end, it's just a place. Sticks and stones. We've all had real losses in our lives. This stings, for sure, but it's nothing important in the grand scheme. All of you, being here, being healthy and happy? That's what matters. That's *all* that matters."

Duke looked visibly relieved, Bennie and Dani started to talk to Dad about what he might want to do now that the sale was going through, Jude put an arm around me, and I reached a hand out to Marnie, but she bolted, a sob tearing out of her throat. She dashed to the pool, tore off her dress, and jumped in, wearing the swimsuit she'd interchanged with two others on a permanent rotation for the last several weeks.

"Marnie!" I called, standing to go to her, but Dani stopped me.

"Let her go," she advised. "We've all had Belo's forever. She only had a few weeks. It's got to hurt her more."

We picked at our food while the moon rose and the swell of the bugs' songs exploded in our ears, but Marnie kept doing lap after punishing lap, even though I knew she had to be exhausted.

Dad whistled between his teeth. "Man, I wish we had a stopwatch. I guarantee she's breaking records right now."

No one left until she finally dragged herself out, limp as a dishrag, and stumbled into the house, where she took a hot shower and fell into a deep, snore-filled sleep.

"Marnie, please come out!" I plead the next morning. "We'll miss the plane."

"That's fine with me!" she calls.

"Um, it definitely *won't* be fine with Mom and Dad." I wait a second, and her door finally creaks open. Marnie appears, looking haggard and miserable. "It's just a place. Everything we love is still here."

"It's *not* just a place," she counters darkly. "That's like saying St. Matthew's is *just a place* or our house in Michigan is *just a place*. Places have souls."

I bury my face in my sister's soft hair and let the tears fall for the first time since Dad's announcement. "I know."

I didn't want to say anything to my father because his point had excellent logic—we're all here, healthy, together (at least when we can be). For a man who buried his high-school sweetheart when their kids were just babies, this is just a drop in the sadness bucket. But pain isn't equal for everyone, and we haven't lived the mixed blessing/curse of a heartache that puts everything else into stark perspective. Sure, we've grown up this summer, but the loss of this place where we all worked so hard together represents something much bigger—the loss of a piece of our childhood. It's also the loss of a way of life that made every one of us stronger, smarter, and overall better people.

"It sucks," I say, smoothing her hair. "I'm sorry it all fell apart the summer you finally got to come visit."

Her shoulders rise and dip under my hands. "At least I got this one summer. I'll never forget it."

She stands straighter, wipes the tears off her cheeks, and heads out to the living room, throwing her arms around Dani, Bennie, Duke, and, finally, Dad.

"Belo, thank you for letting me stay here," she cries into his neck.

My father closes his eyes and wraps his arms around Marnie tight. "You're family, Marnie. You come here anytime you need to. Anytime."

This is the first time in my life my father won't drive me to the airport. After dinner the night before, he said he knew I'd like to spend some time with Jude, and anyway, he needed to head to Belo's and work some things out for the shutdown.

"I'll have some free time this year, and I'm going to take a little break. There's no rush to figure out what to do yet. The sale of Belo's will leave me in a good spot," he says. "Let's see each other during a season other than summer." He hugs me hard and kisses the top of my head.

"I want to go to Disney World," I announce. "I have fall break in October. I'll find hotel rooms. Let's go."

"Disney World?" Dad looks surprised. "Like with Magic Kingdom and that new Star Wars park?"

"Yep." I nod. "Do you remember the four of us watching every single Star Wars movie outside on the projector screen? And I was so obsessed? I've wanted us to go together so badly, but Belo's was always too busy in the summer, so I never asked. And so what if I'm almost an adult? I want to drink some disgusting Blue Milk at Oga's Cantina. I want to fly the Millennium Falcon through Smuggler's Run. I want to build my own *lightsaber*."

"Well...that actually sounds pretty damn fun." Dad gives me a quick side-eye. "What color lightsaber were you planning on building?"

I tilt my head and roll my eyes. "Is that a real question, Dad? Are you even my father? Yellow, just like Rey's."

"I'm not sure I'm a cool enough Jedi to hang with you, then," Dad admits.

"Dad, don't tell us yours would be blue," Duke says, wincing.

"Blue is classic, like your old man." Dad winks at me. "Plus, wasn't Luke's lightsaber blue? He's, like, the best Jedi there is."

Duke immediately turns the same shade of purple as Mace Windu's saber, about to bluster into a long, complicated argument about Jedi merits and Luke Skywalker's lightsaber evolution, when Dani cuts in.

"I definitely want purple," Dani says decisively. "And spare me your lecture, Duke. I don't need some Star Wars encyclopedia explanation about what that color means. It's beautiful and Samuel L. Jackson's character had one, so obviously it's awesome."

"Wait, Samuel L. Jackson was in Star Wars?" Jude asks, and I gasp out loud. No single question has ever made me doubt our future together like this one.

"Mine would *definitely* be red," Marnie chimes in. "Can I crash this vacation, or is it a dad/daughter thing?"

"You can *all* crash. Even those of us who don't know who Mace Windu is," I gripe. "Should we plan on it? A big, crazy Disney World adventure this fall?"

"Should I watch all the movies first? Even the super boring ones that came out when we were little kids?" Bennie asks, an adorably bewildered look on his face.

"Dani, get your house in order!" I rub my temples. "I cannot have a brother-in-law who is Star Wars–ignorant!"

It's a good way to leave the cozy little cottage I love so much. Everyone is chattering and laughing, planning and promising. I'm a little shocked at myself for wanting something so childish so badly, but I can picture how much fun it would be, and I'm ready for a new, different adventure.

It's also a good way to force my hand once I get home. Step one of my new life involves taking a stand, and I have to do it immediately. As soon as the plane touches down, I have to make sure I hit the ground running to keep the momentum so I don't fall back on old habits. I know I can't go back to being the person I was before, and I'm not exactly sure how to avoid it, but announcing my nonnegotiable plans for this vacation seems like a good start.

"Are you sure we'll make it on time?" Marnie asks from the back seat. "Jude, we only have *three hours* to get to the airport that's *ten miles* away. You drive like someone's great-*great*-grandpa's great-grandpa."

"Very funny. Look, I'm not going to be shamed into speeding. I'm towing precious cargo." He winks at Marnie, and she blows him a kiss. "So, should we make a beach pit stop? Maybe grab tacos and eat before you guys get to the airport?"

Marnie and I both squeal our affirmatives, and we take off at an only slightly grandfatherish pace. By the time we have a sack full of tacos and bottles of icy Coca-Colas and are sitting on the beach, everything starts to hit me at once.

"I don't want this," I whisper to Jude, shoving my taco away.

"Do you want to try the pork?" He looks worried. I realize he thinks I'm turning down the taco, and that's what's making him anxious. I've never said no to a taco before.

"The tacos are amazing. This is amazing." I spread my arms out and indicate the soft white sand beach that Marnie is cartwheeling down, the lulling rush of the waves, the cloud-dotted sky. I turn to him. "You. *You* are amazing. I can't do this. I can't leave you."

"You have to." He puts his taco down and faces me. "Belo is going to be looking for a job or a hobby or something now that the shop is closing. It's your senior year. You need things to be stable. And me? C'mon, you're too smart to let it all go down the drain for a guy who's going to wait for you no matter where you are." He leans close and stage-whispers, "That guy is me."

"Did I ever mention how much I like you?"

"I wouldn't mind hearing it again."

"I really, *really* like you." I kiss him and pick up the taco. Jude's words calm me down and revive my appetite. "I still don't know what to do when I get back. I still don't know how to be myself back there." I blow out a long breath. "Everything is going to be so different."

"This summer was different, right?" Jude points out. "You thought that meant it would be terrible, and look how everything turned out."

"You're right. But I had *you* this summer."

"You have me forever." He pulls my hand to his chest so I can feel his heart hammering. "No matter where we are or how long we have to go without seeing each other, we'll always be there for each other."

"I wish the summer didn't have to end like this. I wish my dad was still keeping Belo's and we could just keep going the way we've been going. I mean, maybe there's still a way…"

Like he can hear the gears in my brain turning, Jude takes decisive steps to shut that train of thought down completely. "Dell, I can't stay here. My parents are out of jail, back home, and shit isn't going to get better just because I want it to. Belo's is gone, so I have no job. My apartment is month-to-month. I'm going to head out before I run through everything I saved. And you need to go after what you want, whatever that is. We had this summer, and it was awesome, but we have to face the facts. Even though they suck. This chapter is over, Dell, and we've got to move on."

I suck a sharp breath in through my teeth and nod. "You're right." I hate that he's right, but I know everything he said is true. I have to force myself to be grateful for what I gained and let go of what I lost. "Are you going to Vermont soon? How long do you think you'll stay there?" I try my best to sound excited for him, but I fail. I can't pretend to be happy about this, even if I know it will all work out in the end.

I feel like my safe haven—both as a place and a person—is disappearing right in front of my eyes.

"I want to stay here as long as Belo needs help closing down the shop. After that, I'll probably be in Vermont for a while." He rubs my arms when I grimace. "Hey, I have to figure out what I want to do with my life. Y'know, since I already figured out who I want to spend it with."

"I'm *so* glad I never convinced my dad to fire you," I sigh, leaning into a long kiss.

Jude's kiss, the sound of the ocean waves, the smell of tacos, my sister's crazy laughter, and the sand sinking beneath my feet crystallize into this perfect happy moment I promise myself I'll carry with me to help get me through the tough ones that are coming up fast—like our good-bye at the airport terminal, for instance.

I crush myself in Jude's arms one more time and sob like a baby as I walk through security and look back—*of course* I look back—to see him watching me, looking like his heart is breaking, too.

I stuff my feet in my shoes, grab my carry-on, and trudge to the gate with Marnie patting my shoulder and telling me, through her fat, wet tears, that everything will be okay. We head to the restroom to wash our faces, and I pause to look in the mirror.

"This is the first time I've ever left the airport looking like *me*," I tell my sister as I take an appraisal of my reflection.

I'm tan, no foundation to hide my freckles. My hair is loose and still pink, sun-bleached in spots and wild all over. My clothes are best described as yoga chic, perfect travel wear that my mother would dub *gauche*. But, more important than my clothes and hair, my eyes are bagfree from good sleep. The worry lines on my forehead have smoothed out. I've gained some weight and stopped chewing my nails. I look happy. I look loved. And that, it winds up, is the most beautiful look I've tried on yet.

29

The Death Rattle of Summer Vacation
or
Good-bye, Childhood Home

Late August

MICHIGAN

When the plane finally lands, Marnie and I look around for Mom and Lilli, but we only see Peter, his blond hair, wiry frame, and thick glasses visible all the way from the baggage carousel.

Marnie's whole face lights up. "Daddy!" she yells, racing to him. She jumps into his arms, and he hugs her tight, rubbing her hair and clearly asking what she did to it. They're talking animatedly when I come around, dragging the bags like a good older sister.

"Hey, Dad." I look around like Mom and Lilli are hiding, about to jump out and surprise us. "Um, where are Mom and Lilli?"

"Hey, sweetie. You look great! Very relaxed, very beachy." I smile at Peter's reaction—of course my laid-back stepdad would take what I think of as a major transformation totally in stride. He puts his arms around our shoulders. "So…there's news. And it's big. And I have very specific instructions from Lilli on how to present it. Please allow me to escort you to Golden Bamboo—"

"Without Lilli?" Marnie gasps. Golden Bamboo is the traditional Jepsen go-to restaurant for celebrations and birthday parties, and we *always* go as a five-piece.

"Not *without* Lilli," Peter says, waggling his eyebrows and grabbing the suitcases from my hands. "Come on, girls."

We chat on the way over about our summers. "How was Florida, Marnie?" Peter asks, looking in the rearview. She's sprawled across the back seat, head on her balled-up sweatshirt, dozing. But she springs up at Peter's question.

"The *best*!" Marnie exclaims, and she's off, talking a mile a minute about swimming and the tackle shop, Isaac, the beach, our family dinners...

Marnie doesn't stop to take a breath until we arrive at Golden Bamboo and sit in our favorite semicircle corner booth, near a bubbling fountain and a painting of a herd of wild horses running through a field. Fancy, starched white tablecloths, bone china, and silver pots of fragrant tea accent the enormous tables. Marnie and I giggle like little kids as we sugar our tea and scoop up crispy noodles with incredibly delicious duck sauce. Peter smiles at us and says, "I can clearly see you girls had a great summer. You both look so healthy and rested. Maybe I can come along next time."

"Dad, we *have to* go back to the Keys," Marnie says, practically elbowing the fancy jar of soy sauce off the table in her enthusiasm to sell Peter on the best the Sunshine State has to offer. "You'd love it there. Belo can even teach you to fish."

There's a ripple in Peter's usually perfect calm. "The Keys

sounds great. I *do* know how to fish, Marnie. Don't you remember, I got you your first rod, and we fished Grandma's lake when you were in first grade?"

Marnie talks around a mouth crammed full of crispy noodles. "No, like, *real* fishing. On the ocean. You'll see. Belo will show you how it's done."

I bump her knee under the table and mouth *Shut up!*

She gives me a hurt shrug but says, "I just mean you'd probably have a lot of fun fishing out on the ocean. I'd like to go with you."

"I'd love that. The Jepsens are long overdue for a family vacation."

Nice save, Marnie. I wonder if I should bring up Disney, but the server arrives with bowls of steaming wonton soup, and I keep my mouth busy with some seriously tasty noodles instead.

While we eat, I slide my phone out from under the table and text Jude the boring details about my meal and guesses about what Peter's going to announce at this fancy restaurant, then read his return texts about how he's already packing up his fishy apartment and how he decided to order his truck something called *snow tires* while they were on mega summer sale, because apparently he'll need them in Vermont this winter. He asks if I've ever heard of them.

I snort and look up to see Peter and Marnie staring at me.

"It's Jude, isn't it?" Marnie crows.

"Jude?" Peter asks casually.

"Yes." I pause, deep-breathe, and take my first crack at living my more authentic, honest life. "Jude is my boyfriend."

Peter's light eyebrows crunch together. "What about Lex?"

"Lex and I break up every summer so he can date any girls he wants at the camps he goes to just to irritate his dad." Once I say it out loud, the full force of this plan's stupidity hits me. "I went along with the idea. I even dated a few guys because I thought that was the mature thing to do. But I realize now, it wasn't what I wanted. Like, at all. I want someone who cares about me, and that's Jude."

"Oh." Peter gives me a quizzical look. "I didn't realize, the thing with Lex… So, every summer he convinced you to break up?"

I nod.

Peter shakes his head, confused. "Huh. I always thought he was smarter than he apparently is. Well, I don't know this Jude guy, but if he makes you happy, I'm happy."

"Thank you, Dad."

It's a big step—the Jepsens don't usually just splat their feelings and secrets on the white linen tablecloths of fancy restaurants, but I did it, and Peter was as wonderful as ever. That said, his face is completely relieved when the server comes to take our order, breaking the awkward silence that followed my confession… Peter waits until we've eaten our fill and have bowls of green tea ice cream in front of us before he says, "So, the news. Okay. Right."

Marnie licks her spoon and taps it on the table. "It's okay, Dad. Whatever it is, it will be okay."

His eyes soften, and he gives her a grateful smile. "All right." He pulls his iPad out of the laptop carrier he brings everywhere and sets it up on the table. He goes into his email, finds a file, and opens a video.

Lilli's sweet face fills the screen. "Hey, AJ and Marnie!

So, you should be at Golden Bamboo right now, and if Dad followed my instructions, you guys are eating green tea ice cream, and I'm, like, pretty jealous because it's the best. I really, really wanted to be there with you to tell you this in person or even video chat the second you landed, but I had to record a message instead because we got some big news, *aaaaand* it's that I'm basically going to be in the studio all day every day for the rest of the summer so I can get my record finished before school starts."

Marnie and I look at each other and then at Peter.

"Is she serious?" I ask slowly. "Did Lilli—"

"Yep, I got a record deal!" Lilli screams, like she knew exactly what I was going to ask. She jumps up and down on the bed, making her iPad fall over. "Okay, okay, that's the super really good news. But, um, there's a catch." Lilli's face is back on-screen. She sucks in a breath and lets it whoosh out. "I have to stay here, in Nashville. Like, this will be my home base now, and I seriously cried when I thought maybe we wouldn't be together, but then the record company added some extras to the deal to help us move, and we can *all* live here. I think you guys will really, really love Nashville. I know it's, like, insane, and I seriously have been either so excited or crying really hard because I already miss my friends and St. Matt's and church…but I miss you two most of all. And you, Daddy!" Lilli blows a kiss to the screen. "I know maybe you're not as excited as I am, and that's why I made this recording because Mom said, like, maybe you guys would need time to process the news. But I love, love, love you, and I want to play you this one song I wrote for us. It's called 'Triple Threat.'"

Marnie and I hold hands the way we always do when Lilli

plays her music, and by the end of the song—a soulful, soaring, incredibly beautiful song about sisterhood, a song about *us*—my tears are mixed with the pale celadon ice-cream puddle in my bowl.

When the final guitar chord fades to silence, Lilli waves good-bye and tells us she loves us one more time. Peter clicks off the screen and looks at both of us. He bypasses the emotions and gets right down to brass tacks.

"I know you girls support Lilli and are proud of her, but this isn't just about Lilli. Mom and I talked for weeks about this. Really, it's an incredible opportunity for all of us. Mom and Lilli have fallen in love with the city and the people there. My company was able to move me to a lab just outside of Nashville." Peter pulls a few pamphlets out of his bag. "And here are some really great local schools you girls can look into. It's late in the summer to start applying, but the label has been extremely generous to the area schools, so there are ways to make things happen. It's all part of our relocation package."

"We're moving." I can't lie; it's a shock I'm not sure how to deal with in this moment. I was so focused on everything I was about to lose in Florida and everything I needed to change in Michigan, it never occurred to me that more changes—changes totally out of my control—might be edging into my reality. My brain flips to AJ mode. "When will this be?"

"And there's the sticky part." Peter pauses. "Mom wanted you to come home earlier so it wouldn't be such a shock, but I talked her out of that. I know how important your time with your father is, AJ, and I think these last two weeks will be just enough time to get things figured out if we work fast. I'm relying on your top-notch organization skills to keep me and Marnie on schedule while we transition." Peter's smile is stress-tight, but warm and comforting. A dad's smile, and one I truly love. "And I just want you to have time to process now, because this one is a biggie—our house has been sold."

"What?" All the chop suey I just ate churns dangerously in my stomach. "I don't understand. Like, we can't go in it? We can't see it?"

"We can," he says. "The movers will be here in three days, and we don't officially close for three weeks. I'll fly in and out for the closing, since I have obligations at the lab here in Michigan next month, anyway. I'm so sorry, girls. Things had to move quickly, and your mom and I had to make some tough calls. We know this sucks. And whatever you need, whatever you want to do, we're doing it. I'm on leave for work for the next two weeks so I can just be with you girls until we're settled in Nashville."

"Can we go home?" Marnie's voice is so small, I find her hand under the table again and hold on tight.

"Yes, of course. Let me grab the check." Peter springs up, probably glad to have something concrete and useful to do, and I turn to Marnie.

"I love our house," she says, her lip wobbling. "I won't be a Lady Lion anymore. My volleyball team, I'll be gone for real! And no more St. Matt's." Her eyes brim with tears. "I was so scared to come home, and now I'm so scared to not even *have* a home!"

"Hey." I yank a fancy linen napkin off the table and mop up her tears with it. "I know it's been a lot this summer. I know you've gone through some crap. But your home is with us. With your family. That's all you need for a home."

"Okay." She sniffles.

"We'll be back with Lilli and Mom. That's good. And Lilli—" I stop dead in my tracks, still awed by my baby sister's raw talent.

"That song—" Marnie just shakes her head. "AJ, Lilli is going to be, like, crazy famous, isn't she?"

"Yep. It's going to be amazing. And terrifying."

"We need to call her." Marnie pulls her phone out, but I stop her.

"Let's call her when we get to the house, okay? At least we get to say good-bye. She can't even do that."

Marnie sniffles, tears sliding down her cheeks. "I thought Belo selling the shop was hard. Why does everything always happen at once? It's like a pile-on."

"Hey, this whole situation actually has a silver lining." I gnaw on my lip while Marnie looks at me, ready to follow her big sister's lead. She nods for me to continue. "We get a do-over, Marnie. We get a chance to make some changes, and we're going to play a strong hand, okay?"

"What are you thinking?" Her eyes narrow with determination, as the sadness fades and that space left behind refills with something more satisfying and way scarier. But Marnie's always been tough, and I know she's ready to grab this situation by the jugular.

"First thing, we negotiate Disney in the fall." Her eyes light up, and I tick off a few more key points. "We're going to do some heavy research and figure out what we want to do schoolwise. And we're going to change some of the Jepsen House Rules *for good*."

Marnie nods, then a few fresh tears roll down her cheeks. "I'm ready. But I'm super nervous."

"That's okay," I tell her.

"And Lilli? Do you think she's going to turn into a fame monster?"

I shrug. "Maybe. But she's our little sister. If we see her going that direction, it's our job to pull her back down to Earth. Keep her humble."

"Mom is going to be even harder to deal with now, isn't she?" Marnie studies the glossy tabletop, I'm sure wondering what kind of stunts she'll need to pull to keep Mom's attention now that Lilli is a bona fide star.

"Maybe." I'm not going to lie. It's a real possibility. "But maybe not. We don't know what's going to happen. But we need to change the way we operate as a family, and this is our chance to start with a clean slate. I think… I think we might be luckier than we think right now, Marnie. I don't want to be melodramatic, but it's kind of the answer to all of our prayers about what to do this year." I'm super cautious when I say this because I know all these changes have to be harder on Marnie. My sister is probably in need of some consistency right now. She almost lost it over the sale of Belo's, which wasn't remotely as hard-hitting as the sale of our childhood home is going to be.

Her shoulder goes up and dips down in a reluctant shrug. "I did light a votive and pray for a solution to the mess I got myself into. But this isn't what I had in mind." She sighs. "Maybe Catholic Mary is pissed at me."

"Maybe Catholic Mary knows exactly what she's doing."

Marnie and I flip through school brochures while Peter

drives us home, chattering nervously. I look at the glossy pages that show pictures of other students at other schools studying other things, and the dread about going back to St. Matthew's evaporates like a fog in the morning sun. I was so tied to this idea of being the best all the time, I never considered the simplest alternative: maybe I could just *change my goals*.

Even if I stayed here, I could do it. I could be another version of myself. A newer, wiser version. We pull up to the house, and Marnie and I just stand in the circle driveway, looking at it.

"It's really beautiful. Like your church in Florida," she whispers.

We walk in, side by side, and see the house through brand-new eyes. It *is* beautiful. And full of amazing memories. Holidays at the huge dining room table, cookies baking in the warm, clean kitchen. Fancy pictures taken for dances and recitals and graduations on the gleaming staircase, long hours doing homework in the cool quiet of my room. Now that it's almost not ours anymore, I realize how fiercely I've loved this house, how lucky I've been to grow up somewhere so safe and lovely, with a flawed but loving family who made this place our home.

I sit on the steps, Marnie beside me, and we soak in the warm patches of sunlight thrown by the windows, the lemony smell of polishing wax, the cool current of air that always runs up the stairs no matter the season. We soak up the house that's been the body to our family's soul.

We're eventually interrupted by a knock at the door. I get up to answer and am shocked to see Lex standing on the doorstep, hands in his pockets. He's as gorgeous as he ever was, but somehow the idea of ever having dated him seems kind of impossible now that I'm with Jude.

"Lex. How are you?" I open the door and let him in, not remotely uneasy about the obvious way he looks at me—my hair, my outfit, my makeup—up and down with an *are you serious?* eye roll.

"Sorry I didn't call to check in this summer. Rock camp was pretty damn intense, *stick it to the man* and all that shit. Rough plane ride home? What are you even wearing?" So recently those words would have made me shrink into myself, but now it all just rolls off my back. He moves to tussle Marnie's hair, but she dodges his hand with a scowl.

"Stop it," she snaps. We both look at her, shocked. "Stop talking to her like that."

"Whoa, *really* rough plane ride, eh? Did you two skip your complimentary peanuts? I'm seeing the signs of low blood sugar everywhere." When Marnie glares at him with extra fury, Lex shrugs and says, "Sorry if I hurt your feelings, Marnie," without an ounce of actual regret.

"Not *my* feelings." Marnie stands up and gives Lex a look of pure disgust. "How can that be the first thing you want to say to AJ? You haven't seen her *all summer.* Why do you walk in the door and talk to her like she's a piece of crap?" She stomps up the stairs, into her room, and slams the door.

Lex looks from me to Marnie's door and back, shaking his head. "I feel like I just fell into a cheesy sisters' drama or something. Hey, maybe I should come back once all the fun that got sucked out of you builds up again."

"Lex, we're moving."

Lex is already at the door, but the words I blurted out have him turning on his heel. "Have I fallen into some alternative dimension? What the hell is going on with you guys?" He tilts his head and narrows his eyes, like he's not sure if I'm joking with him. "Moving? Are you being serious right now?"

I look him right in the eye, and I'm so earnest he recoils a little at my measured explanation. "Marnie and I went to Florida and stayed with my biological father and my sister and brother. I fell in love with my childhood nemesis, and he's pretty much the most amazing guy I've ever met. And when we got home, our dad told us the house has been sold because Lilli signed a big record deal in Nashville."

"Lilli signed a deal?" He looks around our house. "You had a summer fling? You're selling your house?"

"Yeah, Lilli is super excited. No, it's not just a fling. And it's hard to believe. My dad took us to lunch just after our plane landed and gave us the news. We're leaving in a few days," I tell him. "So… Marnie is feeling a lot right now."

Lex presses his thumb to the center of his forehead, a trick he swears gets rid of an oncoming migraine instantly. "I'm… I don't know what to say. What do you mean? You're *moving*?" He steps closer, like he's trying to read if maybe this really is just a prank after all. "Before our senior year? AJ, what the hell am I hearing?"

"I know." I take his hand. It's a fine hand, the hand of a person I genuinely like but am definitely not in love with. "It's a ton to take in."

"Also, back up. Wait a minute. You have a family in Florida? I thought you were nerding out at, like, space camps or something." He shakes his head. "Why wouldn't you tell me?"

"Lex, I'm not even into space," I laugh, then realize I can't blame him for not knowing me or what I'm into. *I* barely knew me. "I didn't tell you because it was complicated, and you and I were never good at complicated."

"If I didn't stop by…would you have told me all this?" He asks the question slowly.

"Yes," I finally answer. "We were together for a long time. I owe you a proper good-bye."

He pushes his overlong hair out of his eyes, then sinks down on the steps slowly. "Sorry, I'm just having a hard time wrapping my head around all this. You never even told me that Peter's your stepdad." He looks up at me, like he's weighing respect and confusion. "Why would you have kept that a secret?"

"I guess because I cared what you might think. What everyone would think. My family in Florida…they're not as rich or polished as you are. And I didn't want you to know what I was like when I was there because I thought that didn't fit my life here."

"This is seriously fucking with me," Lex says, pinching the bridge of his nose.

"I'm telling you now because I don't give a shit what you think." When his head jerks up to look at me, eyes bulged wide, I explain, "Sorry, that was harsh. Not you *personally*. You *understood*. The general you. I don't really care if anyone likes how I dress or look or talk. And I don't care if anyone wants to judge my family or my new boyfriend. I'm happy with them. I'm happy with myself. And I don't have time for anyone's bullshit anymore."

Lex holds up his hands, surrender-style. "Very *born-again*

feminist of you. So, is this new dude living... Where are you going? LA?"

"Nashville," I say.

"Right. That makes sense." He widens his eyes. "Wow. Nashville. Is he there?"

"No." I realize Lex isn't following the details because I've crammed more truth into the last five minutes than I ever bothered to put into our years of dating. "Jude is from Florida, but he's moving to Vermont. I've never been to Nashville. Mom and Lilli have been staying there this summer, and my parents worked out all the details of the move without really asking us."

"Why not just ask me to do the long-distance thing, if that's what you're doing with this guy anyway?" Lex asks, and I could totally be projecting some of my overabundant emotion onto him, but I think he looks kind of hurt.

"Because I love him." I put a hand out and touch Lex's shoulder. "I care about you. I want the best for you. But I don't love you."

Lex startles, gets to his feet and nods. "Harsh, but okay. I mean, I don't love you either, for the record."

"I know you're probably upset. I'm sure this is...a lot."

"Uh, yeah, you think? We may not have been the perfect couple, but shit...you're my girlfriend. I care about you."

"I care about you, too. And I'll miss you, Lex." I'm not sure this is actually true, but it feels like an appropriate white lie in the moment. "I hope you have the best senior year."

He keeps staring at me. "You're different. Not just..." He gestures to my outfit and pulls a face that makes me clench my fist. "It's like you got brainwashed or something. I kind of feel like I'm in *Invasion of the Body Snatchers*." He peers into my eyes, like he's trying to see through to my soul. "AJ? Are you in there?" he stage-whispers.

I shrug off his theatrics. "I just got comfortable being honest with the people around me and with myself. You're shocked because you're used to me trying to make everyone else happy."

He frowns. "I guess I'm happy for you? What else am I supposed to say? I still don't get why you needed to lie your ass off like you did, but honestly? I always got the feeling something about you was a little off. I mean, you're hot as shit, but there were clearly always a few screws loose and—"

"Get out!" Marnie yells from upstairs, where she's clearly been eavesdropping. "Why did she ever put up with you? No one needs anything mansplained, so see yourself out!"

"So, this is probably the last time we'll talk to each other," I tell Lex, who's casting a wounded look up the stairs. I think Marnie's anger might be hitting him harder than our (official) breakup. He always liked her the most. "Thank you for everything, Lex. I honestly wish you nothing but the best." I hug him, long and hard, the way I rarely did when we actually dated.

He pulls back slowly. "Gotcha. Thanks, I guess." When he looks at me, his eyes shimmer. Lex is a really good actor, so maybe it's for show. But I choose to believe it's evidence of actual human emotion. "Wherever you end up next year, take care of yourself, AJ." He kisses my cheek, and then he's gone.

Marnie pokes her head out when she hears the door slam. "Was I mean?"

"Yes." I wave her down the stairs, and she sits next to me

again. "But he kind of deserved it." I lean my head against my sister's.

"AJ?"

"Yeah?"

"I'm really going to miss this place."

"I know."

"Let's call Lilli."

"Good idea."

I pull out my phone, and our little sister picks up. We shriek and scream and congratulate her with total love and support, now that the shock of her announcement has had time to wear off, which is exactly why Mom got her to send a video message instead of calling in real time.

"Are you guys, like, really sad, though?" Lilli asks as we go around the house, saying our good-byes to the doorway in the pantry where our heights have been recorded since we were tiny kids; the stained-glass window in the upstairs bathroom with the lily pads and frogs we all love; the closet where Marnie locked herself away for three hours during a hide-and-seek session, prompting Mom to call the police in a panic; the fireplace where Peter popped us popcorn for dinner when a blizzard knocked the electricity out for two days.

"We're okay," Marnie says. "It's sad to leave, but it's sadder to be apart. AJ and I really missed you this summer, Lilli."

"I missed you, too! I love you guys so much," Lilli says, wiping her eyes with the backs of her hands. "And, I promise, you'll love Nashville!"

We laugh and sit and talk for a little longer, letting go of the last remnants of a life we're ready to move on from, eager to forge our new chapter together, as sisters…and friends.

EPILOGUE

Perfect Imperfection

June
Graduation Party

NASHVILLE

"Speech, speech!" Marnie yells. She and her drama friends are still rolling like royalty on their high horses since the glowing reviews of their spring musical made it into some of the bigger papers in the area.

Honestly, the play was *fantastic*. Marnie's scenes actually made me tear up.

Of course, I'm not going to tell any of them that. Not yet, anyway. They've got big enough heads as it is.

Before I leave, I'm going to sit down and tell Marnie how proud I am of her, not just about the play, but about how she dealt with everything like a total boss this year. Like when a text came through from McKenzie, demanding more from her, and she told her new friends the whole story because she knew she'd chosen good people who loved her, flaws and all. She told her counselors because she believed them when they said they could help her handle hard things. She told our parents because she knew they'd love and respect her no matter what bonehead things she did. And it winds up, Marnie was right about everyone. She was surrounded by love and acceptance and help. And once it was out in the open, it was uncomfortable and it was shitty, but it no longer held the same power it had when it was a big secret.

Marnie changed in other ways. She's now a recreational jock. Acting and music have replaced sports as Marnie's first, passionate love (though she can still slaughter me and everyone else in any backyard badminton tournament or "fun" game of pickup soccer). She heads up her school's alcohol-and-drug-awareness club and is part of the LGBTQ Alliance. One of her major demands when we had our first Jepsen family meeting was family therapy, and my parents actually agreed. It took three counselors and a lot of nervous throat-clearing and talking over each other and then stalling, but we hit our stride, and things began to slowly change. For one thing, the old Jepsen House Rules were taken down, and we *all* sat together to make a new set that's fair and respectful.

Marnie also asked to go to individual therapy, where—along with incredible emotional breakthroughs—she was prescribed some excellent medicine to manage her ADHD. She and Mom are dream-board obsessed now and forced us all to make our own, one family night. Marnie's big goal is to move to NYC and be on Broadway, and I'm rooting for her. We're *all* rooting for her because, frankly, she's amazing.

But today it's *my* graduation party, so Marnie isn't talking drama and Broadway ambitions. Lilli isn't fretting over her sales numbers—which are phenomenal. Her last album is in contention for so many awards we've lost count, and we're trying to balance how proud we are of her with keeping it real by reminding her that she's still our baby sister and *yes*, she does actually have to ask permission to borrow my new MAC lipstick, and it doesn't matter if she thought I wouldn't mind because Kacey Musgraves complimented her on it at an awards dinner. (There's something very satisfying about lecturing a Grammy contender about how the Jepsen House Rules *still apply to her*.) Mom and Dad aren't worrying about the sexier wardrobe Lilli's publicist thinks she should embrace, the possibility of Lilli going on a European tour and how that will impact Marnie's school year, or the predicament of whether we should bite the bullet and buy our beautiful house in Tennessee or continue renting.

Right now, tonight, we're celebrating my big accomplishment.

Which didn't wind up being as full of pomp and circumstance as I envisioned once upon a time.

I didn't graduate as the valedictorian, though I'm in my class's top ten percent. In the all-girls school where I transferred, there was a heavy emphasis on community service and life skills. So, no, I don't have the highest GPA, but I'm one of the best sous-chefs at the soup kitchen on Montgomery, and I can tie every kind of nautical knot known to humankind *and* set up and take down a tent in under four minutes, which were skills I mastered during an extreme-survival camping weekend. Obviously, I survived and kicked ass.

Even though the BioLive internship I was selected for never panned out in the end, the project proposal I submitted shaped my entire senior thesis statement on ecological reform. Dad was also able to talk to some local Key West ecologists, and they want to work with me to see how we can implement my ideas and make real changes. I also talked about my proj-

ect on my college applications, and I got really exciting offers from a few of my top schools…which made Mom kind
of lose her shit when I decided not to accept any of them, yet.

I walk to the front of the hall Mom, Dad, and Peter rented
for me, and raise my glass (of seltzer) to my school friends,
who cheer me on from their table in the back. They're a great
group of girls who didn't become my friends based on a shared
social status. This time around, I chose people who would
push me to push myself and who sincerely wanted to see me
become a better person. It's not that there are better people
in Tennessee than there were at St. Matt's—it's that Marnie
and I grew up enough to realize our worth and choose the
right friends for the right reasons.

"I want to say thank you to the bad bitches of Elmgrove
Academy. Without you, I would have *never* imagined that
a night in a flooded tent could actually be incredibly fun if
you're with the right people. We're gonna run the world,
girls, and I love every one of you!"

They cheer, and I turn to the table where my parents sit—
all three of them—with my siblings—all four.

Dad and Peter are going over deep-sea fishing plans now
that my father owns his own fishing-excursion company. My
dad's very sweet new girlfriend just happens to be in finance,
and she helps him with the business side of his enterprise.
Being out on the boats all day, sharing his love for the ocean
and sport fishing, is Dad's idea of heaven on Earth, and his
business has taken off. He's happier than he's ever been, and
he's been filling Peter's head with deep-sea fishing adventure
stories. Peter is *definitely* intrigued.

Mom and Dani have been discussing the relative merits of

extensions for Lilli while Lilli is busy playing matchmaker. She's focusing her skills on Duke and the college-age folk singer she's touring with—which just might work if a gospel singer can overlook my scientist brother's atheism. *Or* if my atheist brother becomes born-again for his devout Christian crush.

Weirder things have happened.

For example, our blended family trip to Disney this Christmas. Lilli was doing a show in Orlando and wanted to join the "sibling trip," so Mom and Dad just made it happen. They even made sure Jude came down, and I had the most amazing Christmas with my boyfriend—or the most amazing Christmas that I could have had with my family lurking around every corner and affording us absolutely zero privacy.

"I'd like to thank my incredible family. I could never have finished this amazing year without your love and support. Y'all annoy me, but I love every one of you!"

They cheer for me, and I scan the room one more time before I close it up.

"Thank you so much for coming, everyone! Enjoy!"

The room applauds my fine but not spectacular speech, and I circle tables, thanking family, friends, and the random business people we invited to help Lilli's team rub elbows.

The whole time I'm distracted because I don't see the *one* person I've been waiting for all day. I knew he'd probably be late, but I was hoping he'd make it before the party is over. He needed to drive here so we'd have the truck this summer, and—classic, responsible Jude—he has his phone programmed to not take calls while he's driving, so there have been very few updates all day.

I should be used to this technology dry spell. This year,

Jude decided to do this whole hokey love-letter-a-day thing, where he wrote me a letter every single day we were apart.

At first I thought it was going to be too hard not to text and video chat whenever we wanted, but sending and receiving letters actually wound up giving me this incredible window into his life and forced me to describe what was going on in my world with so much more intentional detail and thought.

Not that I don't love texting—but having to be witty and cute and use the right emojis and send the right gifs sometimes reminds me too much of my pre-Tennessee AJ life. Jude and I still texted and video chatted and called on weekends, but letters were really the primary way we corresponded.

I think the whole letter-writing experiment aged Jude into the old man he's always been in his soul.

Which means it still doesn't occur to him to pop me a text every hundred miles or so.

I slip out of the party once I've talked to everyone in the room and the dancing is in full swing, so I know I won't be missed. I lean on the wooden railing of the wide balcony and look over the stunning mountains that have *called to my soul* since the second Peter drove our U-Haul along their winding roads last summer.

I always loved the harsh but gorgeous frozen winters of Michigan and the sun-soaked beaches of Florida, but Jude and I discovered we were having a weirdly similar love affair with mountains this fall and winter. For as many lines in his letters as there are about how beautiful I am and how much he misses me, there are at least five times as many that described the mountains he and his brother hiked. It was kind of like being romantic pen pals with Lewis (or Clark).

Even if I was jealous of the way Jude waxed poetic about yet another rock formation, I understood completely. I'd always liked walking around in nature, being out in the sun or the snow, but I never realized how much I'd come to truly crave the outdoors on a daily basis until I started filling my schedule with long, regular stretches under the shade of huge pines, dawn and dusk hours watching the sun rise and set over the crests of mountain ranges ringed in fog, and meandering walks over the slippery, spicy pine-needle-carpeted forest floor. Now I'm what Duke lovingly refers to as a *born-again tree hugger*. He said it's worse than a CrossFit vegan who's deep in an essential-oil pyramid scheme, but he loves me anyway.

My peaceful-nature vibes definitely did not translate into general laid-backness. The biggest rebellion of my life had to do with my digging my heels in and committing to a gap year—or maybe two. Mom, Dad, and Peter collectively threw every college catalog they could find at me. Between scholarships, money from the sale of Belo's, and what Mom and Peter put aside for me, I could go anywhere I wanted to go.

"But I don't *want to go anywhere.* Not yet."

"Millennial," my dad snorted.

"Don't use words you don't understand the meaning of, boomer," I snapped back.

The insults were low-key but continual, all deriding my choice to do without a formal education until I had a better idea of who I was and what I really wanted. The AJ/Della from a year before would have been easily talked into reaching out to the impressive schools that came knocking. She would have loved to show off her college of choice on sweatshirts and caps. But that's not who I am now, thanks in part to the fact that I learned to embrace the changes my parents all forced me to deal with last summer.

In other words, I'm too tough to take anyone's crap to heart, and that's been the best gift of my life.

"Dell?"

My thoughts are interrupted by a voice that makes me feel warm all over. My heart pumps faster, my head feels a little dizzy. I spin around, and he's right in front of me, road-weary, purple moons bagged under his eyes, and the biggest smile I've ever seen stretched across his face.

"Della!"

We run at each other, full speed, and he catches me in his arms, spins me around, and kisses me until I'm dizzy.

"Jude, you look like a mountain man!" I laugh, rubbing the dark beard he grew.

"Do you hate it?" He kisses me before I can answer, and it's weird how familiar his lips are even as I adjust to the wiry hair of his beard.

A beard!

"No." I pet it, trying to adjust to his new face. "It's just weird. Like I left you a boy, and you've become a man."

He buries his face in my neck and laughs hard, shoulders shaking. "Letter Della is like this philosophical, romantic poet. Real Life Della is such a dive-bar comedian."

"Sorry I'm not living up to your idealized pen-pal version of me." I tug on his ears, and we look at each other and laugh again. His real-life laugh is the best sound I've heard in a long time.

"I'm not sorry. I mean, you can't make out with a letter.

Not without paper cuts." He gathers me into his arms and squeezes tight. "Hey, have I mentioned I love you?"

"Not yet."

"I love you, Dell. I've missed you like crazy." He touches the ends of my hair gently. "It's long."

"I love you, too. We both got hairy." I kiss him softly. "Do you like it?"

"You'd be beautiful bald. There's nothing about you I don't like."

"Really? Nothing?" I drawl.

"Nope. I even like getting made fun of by you and your really terrible sense of humor." He nods to the hall. "Are you ready to go in and hear stories about the probable death and dismemberment that awaits us as we hike the Appalachian Trail?"

"Trust me, I've gotten every article emailed to me all year long. My mom has a Google Alert set up." I roll my eyes, then wrap my arms around his hips and whisper, "Are we doing something crazy? Like *too* crazy?"

"Yes," he says without hesitating. "Hey, listen, if you don't want to do this, it's okay. Say the word, and you can pick a college. I'll find work nearby. Or I'll leave you alone. Head back to my shack with Jonas and write you letters through a long winter full of Vermont snowstorms." He shivers.

I laugh and kiss him. "You can't even say that without wincing."

"I'm still thawing out. Vermont is *so* beautiful, but I've never been anywhere that cold. All the time! And I really missed you. I made out with my pillow so much it's flat. And Jonas has, like, three jokes he just tells over and over. I mean, I guess his extreme artistic talent and natural affinity for woodworking are *okay* and all, but I'd like to talk to someone with a sense of humor." He puts his forehead against mine. "Don't send me back to Vermont with my humorless brother. Please don't."

"Don't worry. I'm not scared. Not really. We can figure anything out together. I'm ready for an adventure, and you're my only acceptable travel applicant." I lead him into the hall. "Let's go be defiant together."

"Dell." We stop short of the doors. "I know this year has been hard, but I'm so happy you didn't head back to Michigan and wind up with Lex—"

"That was *never* going to happen—"

"And graduate valedictorian and do it all the safe, expected way. I think... I really think *this* is who you were always meant to be."

"I'm not sure I've figured out *exactly* who I'm supposed to be yet. But I do think I'm headed in the right direction." I kiss him again, softly, slowly, excited to keep kissing him as much as I want, now that he's finally here. "And I'm really glad you're along for the ride."

Jude takes my hand, and we walk into the hall together. I think about where I was one year ago exactly—a family split in half, a love life that was tepid at best, friends I couldn't trust, a life so scheduled it gave me migraines—and am proud of the crazily imperfect life full of love and chaos I now embrace.

I used to be a girl split in half, living two lopsided lives. Now I'm a girl who keeps testing the boundaries of her one beautiful life to see how much love and adventure it will hold, and I'm loving every perfectly imperfect second of it.

★ ★ ★ ★ ★

Acknowledgments

When I put aside the draft of a book that just wasn't working and pitched the rough concept of *The Flipside of Perfect* to the lovely Natashya Wilson, I was several months pregnant with my second daughter—who just cut her two-year molars last week. It's been a long journey.

Sometimes you write a book and all these elements of your life get mixed into the pages as you write and rewrite. AJ/Della is dealing with so many changes in *Flipside*, and as the book went through developments and edits, my life was changing in huge ways, too. My family of three grew to a family of four (an awesome, if *very* unexpected, development!). After fifteen years in our first home, we moved in with my parents and then bought our new home all in the span of a single year. I gave up a teaching job I adored with teammates who are still incredible friends to be home with my baby and found new work I've fallen in love with. Friendships I thought would last a lifetime didn't, and friendships I never saw coming bloomed unexpectedly. And that was just my personal life—the world also changed in huge and sometimes overwhelming ways, and it's still changing now. I truly hope that all these changes wind up to be, as Della/AJ found, ultimately good!

I want to thank my husband, Frank, who I love and also really *like*, and who inspires all the really good, funny relationship stuff that ends up in my books…and all the kissing. So much kissing! My kids are truly funny, interesting, awesome people I love, and I'm thankful for the inspiration they lend me for characters, as well as the more practical drinks/snacks/quiet time things they do to occupy themselves while I attempt to get writing done. Amelia and Beatrice, you two are *the best*, and I can still say that honestly in the midst of months of quarantine. I know I'm incredibly lucky to have such funny, sweet girls to hang with (literally) 24/7.

A huge thank-you to the entire Inkyard Press, Harlequin and HarperCollins team! Thank you to my wonderful editor, Natashya Wilson, for fielding all questions/worries/panicked musings at all hours and being so damn kind all the time. Thank you to Bess Braswell, Brittany Mitchell, Laura Gianino, and Linette Kim. Thank you to the Children's Sales team, Heather Foy, and Andrea Pappenheime. The book's gorgeous cover art is all thanks to the exceptional artistic talent of Gigi Lau and Elita Sidiropoulou! Brittany Mitchell does an amazing job putting books out there for social media (which is extra nice because I kind of suck at it!). Thank you to Vanessa Wells for the thorough copy edits and for adding a nice comment when a line made her laugh out loud! Huge thanks to Cam Soto for combing through my shaky draft after I patchworked a thousand bits and pieces of this story for years on end. Thanks to her sharp eye, it all actually makes sense and flows…and she had a sweet, wonderful sense of humor about all the glitches and weirdnesses! A metric ton of thank-yous to Dill Werner for an incredible read-through that illuminated things I would have otherwise glossed over. The very best edits force an author to stretch and grow. I needed to rethink and resee my characters' world through a more open lens of tolerance and love, and that's exactly what Dill's edits helped me do. This book is better, smarter, and has more heart thanks to them! Thank you to Kevan Lyon and Patricia Nelson at Marsal Lyon for their advice, support, and encouragement!

Most of all, I want to thank my siblings, who are so weird and amazing and awesome. Our relationships have changed and developed so much as the years have gone by. For some sibling sets, growing older means growing apart and talking less. We've been really, really lucky that, as we've gotten older and started our own families, we've reconnected in new ways and strengthened our bonds. My goal is to keep on deepening those relationships. My siblings are people I feel lucky to get to grow older with, and I owe the inspiration for this story to them. Love to my brothers and sisters, and here's hoping we can all get together in real life at some point in the near future!